PRAISE FOR THE FIRST BOOK IN THE SERIES

'A gritty and steamy post-apocalyptic novel. Written with an intentionally rough and raw pen, where every scene feels packed with the potential for explosion, this is a bold and gratifying read for action, romance, and dystopian fans of all kinds, especially those drawn to the darker edge of genre-hopping romance.'

Self-Publishing Review

'Harley is an entertaining character with sharp wit, excellent dialogue, and a thirst to prove she doesn't need the protection of others.'

Independent Book Review

BOOKS BY MARGOT DE KLERK

THE VAMPIRES OF OXFORD
Wicked Magic
Wicked Blood

THE IRON FISTS
Rise
Revolution
Redemption

REVOLUTION
THE IRON FISTS

Margot de Klerk

Dedicated to my dad, who bought me books as a child, put me through university as a teen, and boasts to everyone about my books now that I'm an author.
Thanks for the support, Dad!

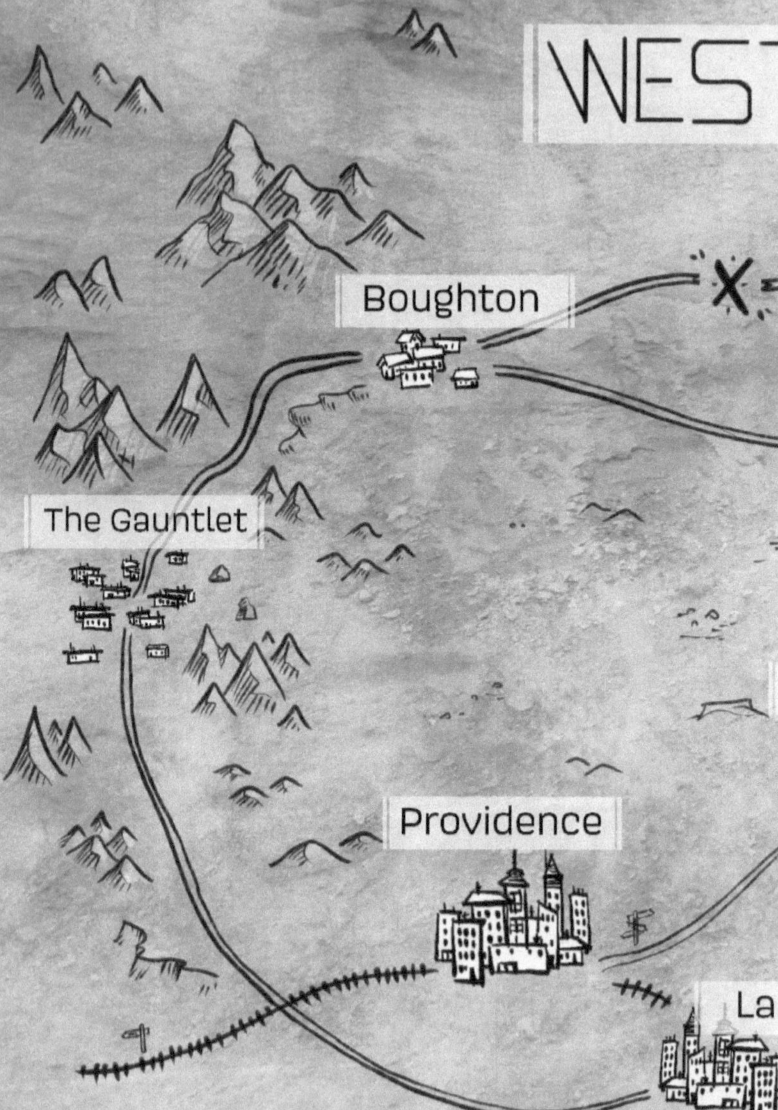

WEST
Boughton
The Gauntlet
Providence
La

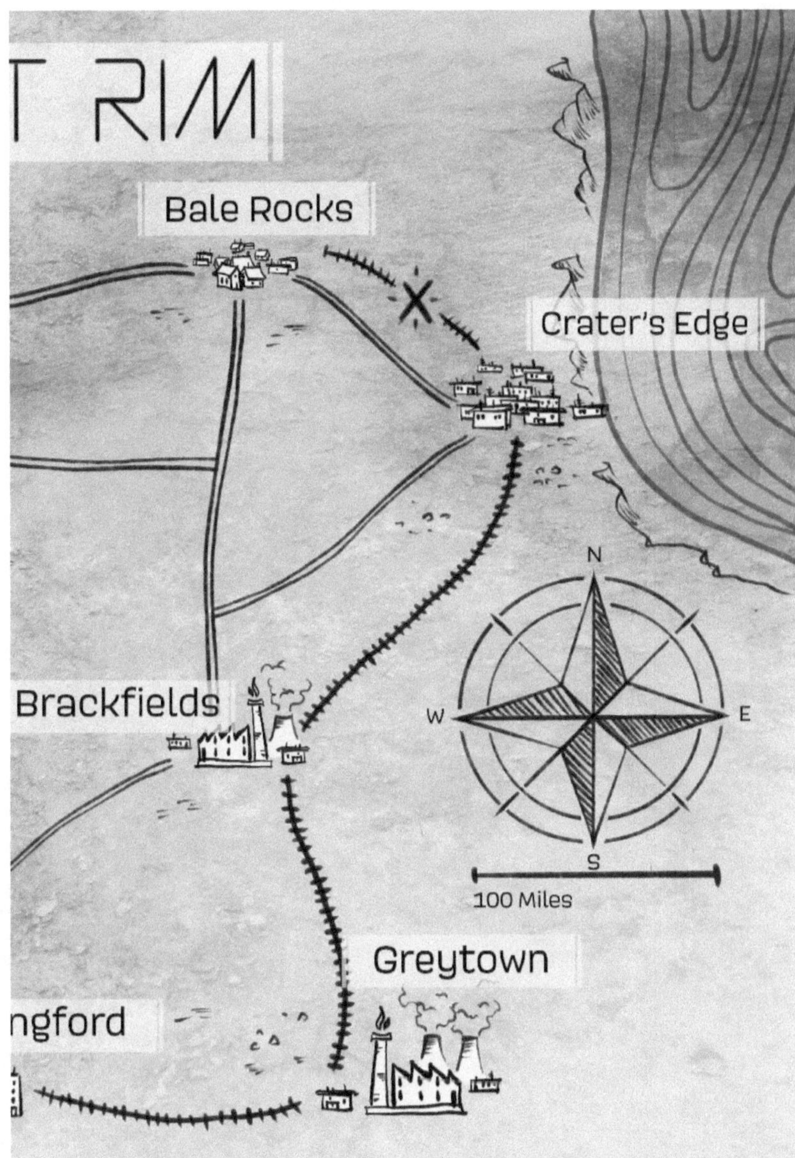
T RIM
Bale Rocks
Crater's Edge
Brackfields
N
W
E
S
100 Miles
Greytown
ngford

AUTHOR'S NOTE

Dear reader,

Welcome to REVOLUTION, the second book in my slow-burn post-apocalyptic romance series, The Iron Fists Series. Please note that this is not a standalone—you will need to read book one first.

As a reminder, here are the content warnings for the series:

- Violence, firearms usage, and gang warfare
- Drugs
- Swearing
- Sexual content, including non-consensual sex, consent under duress, and sexual harassment
- Slavery

If that's not your cup of tea—I totally understand! I have cleaner reads available as well. If you are interested in pursuing this, it's time to turn up the heat! I hope you enjoy Harley and Bas's adventures!

Thank you for sticking with me during this little adventure.

Margot

'I think the devil will not have me damn'd, lest the oil that's in me should set hell on fire'
— The Merry Wives of Windsor, Act V, Scene V (William Shakespeare, 1602)

ONE

THE LIGHTS FLASHED, RENDERING THE club-goers as strange blue, green, and purple-skinned aliens. Behind me, the crowd roared with excitement. I, however, kept myself steady, rotating slowly around the pole. My thighs burnt with the effort of holding myself aloft. My skin was a patchwork of agony from the friction.

I tilted my head, allowing my long brown hair to slide over my shoulder, and released one thigh so I was supported by my left leg only. As I turned, the cage came into view again. Wilder, a burly, boorish specimen, got a grip on Ellery's shoulder and jammed his knee into Ellery's chest.

Fuck.

My grip faltered. My heart lurched in my chest. I wrapped my right leg around the pole again and brought my hands up over my head.

Fortunately, no one was watching me. The cage—and the brutal fight within—occupied the entire room's attention.

Ellery was getting his arse kicked.

The music reached a crescendo, and I found myself with my back to the cage again, facing the crowd. The bunker spread out around me in every direction, the enormous underground room filled to the brim with the Saturday night crowd: dancers and drinkers, fighters and gang enforcers, gamblers and businessmen.

This was the centre of the Iron Fists' empire. No one knew exactly who had built it, but the bunker had been around since before the Crash, when the meteorites had hit Earth over two hundred years ago. Once, it had been used by smugglers, drug dealers, and homeless people. Then Sayle had taken it over, and now the smugglers, drug dealers, and homeless people worked for him.

Business, Bale Rocks style.

Two years ago, I had escaped this place. I'd paid my debts and gone to work as a waitress, where I thought I was safe from the influences of the Iron Fists and the other local gangs.

Now, I was back—once again dancing for the amusement of the gamblers and gunmen of my town.

Except this time I had a secret second job: I was spying on them too.

Another roar blasted through the tense crowd. A deft twist brought me around to face the cage again. Ellery was on the ground, but even as I watched, he managed to get one arm around Wilder's neck and flip the larger man off to the side. Wilder hit the deck, and Ellery landed a series of vicious punches to his solar plexus.

This sucked.

When I had first danced in the bunker, I had never enjoyed the fights, but I also hadn't been personally invested. Now, I seemed to feel every blow that Ellery did, as though Wilder's punches were landing on my chest, reverberating down my spine.

With every hit, I wondered if this was my fault.

I had never seen Ellery being this reckless before. I'd seen him fight hundreds of times, but never like this. Never like he wanted to lose.

Was I the reason he'd changed?

Was it my stupid mistake?

Familiar shame burnt through me. I breathed deeply and pushed myself into a particularly tricky twist, supplanting the shame with the ache of overexertion. I wasn't as fit as I needed to be for the moves I was pulling off—but it didn't matter. I was the only one who'd pay for it in the end, and I needed this job. I needed everyone to want me around—because it was the only way to ensure my security.

Mine and my sister's.

Around me, the cheers and taunts ramped up into screams. My throat tightened, but I forced myself to move unhurriedly until I could see the cage again—and with it, Ellery. As I watched, he pounced like a caged lion finally set free. Wilder crashed to the ground under a flurry of punches, again—again—again—

DING! DING! DING!

And he'd won.

Behind me, someone slapped the stage. I slid off the pole and twisted around.

'Benoit, you're paid to dance, not watch,' Carlos snarled, spittle flying from his mouth. Carlos was the floor manager, a beefy man with a shaved head, who was almost universally hated. I offered him my smarmiest smile.

'Just making sure everyone gets a three-sixty view.'

Carlos scowled so hard he practically went cross-eyed. 'Back to work, or I'll have you warming laps the rest of the night.'

He wouldn't—we both knew my talent was wasted on lap dancing. But Carlos liked to have the last word, so I let him. 'Yes, sir.'

'Good.' He nodded sharply and stomped off to find someone else to harangue. I signalled one of the serving girls for a drink as I stretched my legs out.

Lisette wended her way over and leant across the benches to the stage. 'Water or whiskey?'

'Just water.' I took a glass from her tray. 'Thanks.'

'Welcome. You see that? Ellery's got the devil in him tonight.'

I downed my glass in one go and took another. 'Maybe those punches to the head knocked things straight again.'

'More like they knocked things loose.' Lisette waggled her brows. 'Good for the rest of us—there'll be plenty of wounded egos to soothe.'

'*You've* got the devil in you.'

'Course I have.' She wiggled her butt and tossed me a saucy smirk. 'So have you. We all know you'd kiss Ellery better if you weren't stuck on this stage.'

'I would not!'

She laughed. 'See you later, beautiful.'

Lisette sauntered off, pausing a short distance away to flirt with a few men. She was one of the women who had been here back when I first worked in the bunker, though we'd never really been close. Still, it was nice to see the old faces again.

If only I was here by my own choice.

I finished my water and climbed back onto the pole. Half an hour to go until my break.

Eleven-thirty rolled around, and Callie clambered up onto my stage.

'Break time, babe.'

I slid down and arched my back, grimacing as my abs stretched. 'Fuck, that burns. Am I taking over your stage when I'm done?'

'You're relieving Jules on west.'

'Thanks.'

I slithered off the stage and made my way across the roped-off area around the cage where the fighters and VIPs could hang out, which we called the circle. The common rabble was relegated to the outskirts of the room to watch and gamble away their money. You wouldn't expect there to be many people who wanted to gamble in a town like Bale Rocks—but Sayle was nothing if not a marketing expert. Everyone who rolled through our town stopped at the bunker. Fight nights were the best party in the West Rim.

I reached the rope that barred the way to the back rooms. Posy was waiting for me, her short black hair pulled up in a messy ponytail and a robe wrapped around her lithe form. She lifted the rope so I could duck under it.

'Girl, you were on fire!'

'Thanks!' I bumped my shoulder against hers, and she shot me a grin. Posy had been my closest friend when I used to dance at the bunker, and I'd been surprised to discover how much I missed her.

'Here.' Winking, she produced a bottle from under her dressing gown and handed it to me. 'Leanne gave me it at closing last night. It's the good stuff.'

I turned the bottle, reading the label—it was the high-end whiskey that we reserved for rich guests. 'Nice.'

'There's enough for us to share while we watch.'

'Watch?'

Posy's tanned face split into a big grin. 'You mean you don't know? Girl, you are in for a treat. Come on!'

She snatched my hand and dragged me through the metal halls. Our footsteps echoed loudly and the floor-level emergency lighting cast strange shadows over the walls above us. I stumbled on my heels, and when we reached the ladder we both paused to strip our shoes off.

'You go first,' Posy said.

I shimmied up the ladder and into the control room above. This was where the real work went on: lighting, sound, air circulation, and a heap of other machines that I didn't understand. I gave Posy a hand up, and we meandered past a few techies to the one-way window that looked out over the main bunker.

From above, the place looked like the inside of an anthill—an entire ecosystem of dancers, fighters, and guests, all moving together like a single well-oiled machine. Posy took the bottle of whiskey and settled beside me on an old crate.

'Who's fighting?' I asked.

'Wait and see.'

'You're mean.'

She smirked. 'It'll be worth it. Here.' She swigged the bottle and passed it over to me, sighing in satisfaction. 'Dang, that's good.'

I took the bottle and sipped daintily. 'If you make me fall off the pole later, Carlos will turn my intestines into a flag.'

'Fuck Carlos! You should have seen his face when he heard you were coming back. Damn near shat himself in excitement. That guy has such a crush.'

'On me?' I wrinkled my nose. 'Ewww!'

Posy laughed. Down below, the fight had ended. One of the men was being carried off, the right half of his face covered in blood. The victor pumped his fists, revving up the crowd. To us, it was all silent, rendered in stop-motion by the flashing lights. He vaulted over the side of the cage, and several towel boys rushed in to wipe it down and prepare for the next fight. Beside me, Posy was practically vibrating with excitement.

I raised an eyebrow. 'Is your new woman fighting?'

'What?' Posy turned to me, her voice rising in surprise. 'Nah, Gianna doesn't fight. This is *way* better.'

'Then who—'

'Wait and see,' Posy sang.

Scowling, I peered back into the ring. A man climbed up to the cage, stripping his shirt off as he went. I registered his tattoo first—a pair of dragons twining around his left arm. Then I looked at his face, and my stomach sank at the same time that my heart began beating at a mile a minute.

It was Bas.

If there was one person who I didn't want to see fighting, it was Bas—Ellery's friend, and my other big mistake.

The man who had saved me.

The man I had betrayed.

I swallowed hard. 'Bas is fighting.'

'You know him?' Posy waggled her brows.

'He's on Ellery's team,' I muttered uncomfortably.

'He's hot.'

There was no denying that—tall, slender, with olive skin and chestnut brown hair, Bas was quite the looker. He had the physique of a fighter, the scars of a survivor… and the personality of a block of concrete.

'He's a jerk.'

'They're all jerks.' Posy snatched the bottle of whiskey. 'That doesn't mean we can't… *appreciate* them.'

'No thanks.'

'You've never seen him fight before.'

'I don't like watching the fights.'

'Harley, babe, you are such a liar.'

I scowled. It wasn't a lie, at least not exactly. I desperately wanted to see Bas fight, but at the same time, my chest felt tense with anxiety. What if he got hurt?

His opponent sauntered up the stairs, and my anxiety boiled over into full-on nausea.

Shoulder-length dark hair, tanned skin, and a compact, strong frame. It was Dean Hannover, one of the lieutenants of the rival gang the Black Hands. Except he was more than just that.

The Black Hands were well-known for being the only gang in town that traded slaves. Since Sayle and the Iron Fists had taken over — around twenty years ago now — the slave trade had been banned within the town limits. But that didn't mean Moriarty and his Black Hands were listening. Somehow, someway, Bas had once been Dean Hannover's slave. He'd freed himself — though I had no idea how. But I did know one thing: nothing good could come from putting the two of them in that cage together.

'Bas is fighting Hannover?' I leant forward, my nose almost pressed to the glass as I tried to make out their expressions. Hannover had his back to me, but I could see Bas's face. It was set in fixed, guarded lines.

If I knew one thing about Bas it was that when he was giving away the least, he was feeling the most — but what was he feeling? Anger? Hatred? Fear?

'I know,' Posy cooed. 'Gianna told me he's been begging for it for ages. Apparently Sayle always blocked him before.'

'He's fighting Hannover for the first time?' I gaped at her.

'And they're two of the top fighters here!' Posy sat forwards, taking another sip of whiskey. 'This is going to be awesome. My bet's on Hannover. Guy's a dick, but he's a hell of a fighter. And he has experience on his side.'

I shook my head, as though that could clear the fog of confusion. Why had Bas never fought Hannover before? Why would Sayle prevent him?

It was well-known that the bookies had a hand in arranging who fought whom, and when. The Iron Fists took a cut of the betting money, so obviously they wanted to make the most they could. The best fighters were held in reserve, their fights scattered parsimoniously amidst the regular mediocre and boring fights. Ellery used to complain about it when I first met him. Once the fighters got to a certain point, they got pulled from fights, and their skills tended to plateau.

From what I knew of Bas, he was good. He had to be. He was the most precise, disciplined person I knew. I couldn't imagine him allowing himself to be anything less than perfect.

Which meant that the timing of this fight was no coincidence. This was planned.

But why?

Behind us, the techies called instructions to one another as they prepped for the next fight. It was about to begin. My stomach lurched, anxiety creeping into my blood. I wished I could run down there and stop the fight—but why the hell did I even want to do that?

The lights dimmed, and then the spotlight flared, illuminating the cage. The crowd was jumping and screaming, almost inaudible through the sound-proofed walls. The announcement came through as a tinny murmur.

'Ladies and gentlemen! Next up we have an absolute smasher for you. On my left, a man who fought his way up from nothing through the Iron Fists. And on my right... an old staple, straight from the southside... I give you... BAS AND DEAN!'

I could see, but not hear, the bell ringing. The two men began to circle each other like caged lions. Bas's face gave nothing away. Hannover, when his face came into view, looked smug.

Like he had Bas exactly where he wanted him.

But why? I wouldn't want to be in that cage with a former slave. I could only imagine what awful deeds Bas might want revenge for.

Abruptly, Bas darted forward, jerking his arm in a rapid uppercut. Hannover blocked it, and they were on. Their hands moved in a flurry of punches, and their feet never seemed to be entirely still as they blocked, dodged, or parried.

A glancing blow from Hannover sent Bas stumbling into the side of the cage. He bounced off, using the momentum to attack Hannover's chest—no, he'd feinted. His foot swept out and he kicked Hannover's knee.

Hannover's leg buckled, and he dropped to one knee.

Beside me, Posy gasped loudly. I was frozen, my hands gripping the crate so hard that it dug in, my breath coming in short, sharp pants.

Come on, Bas. End it.

Bas took a step back.

'Is he *prolonging* the fight?' Posy hissed.

'Maybe they told him to?' I suggested hesitantly. Sometimes the fighters were instructed to drag out their fights so the spectators would get all revved up and start raising their bets. Maybe that was it.

Please, let that be it. Do not be doing this just for revenge, Bas. Please.

Why did I care?

Something to consider later, because at that moment Bas darted in for another brutal punch. Hannover blocked him, then arced his leg to take out Bas's knees. Bas dropped to the ground, taking Hannover down with him.

Hannover was fighting harder than ever, his every punch more brutal, his expression wild. His message was clear: *You should have taken me out when you had the chance.* They grappled, and by some miracle, Bas managed to roll Hannover. Instead of landing a blow, he pulled away and stood, his hands up to guard his face as he breathed hard.

'Who's winning?' Posy asked tensely.

Who indeed?

Hannover stood as well. He was facing our window, and for a moment it felt like he was looking directly at us, as though he knew that I was hidden behind the black glass, watching.

Then Bas stepped in again, throwing another punch, and Hannover looked down.

Everything seemed to happen in slow motion. Hannover dodged the punch, and I saw his lips move. Whatever he said, Bas abandoned his form and threw himself at Hannover. Hannover slammed against the railing, then somehow managed to flip Bas—Bas's head hit the ground, but then they were rolling, both of them throwing punches. It looked more like a bar brawl than a fight.

'What the hell?' Posy asked. 'What's he doing?'

I sat forward, the edge of the crate digging into my bum. My heart was in my throat. They rolled again, and suddenly Bas was on top. He slammed a fist into Hannover's neck—an illegal move. Hannover's face went red, his struggles ebbing. The fight was over.

But Bas didn't stop.

He kept on punching Hannover's face, over and over. I lurched to my feet.

'Oh my God,' Posy moaned.

I couldn't speak—my throat and chest ached. My heart was racing.

Bas kept punching—and punching—and punching.

'He's killing him!' Posy gasped.

He was definitely giving it a good shot. There was blood everywhere—the cage was starting to look like a horror scene. My stomach churned with bile. I wanted to look away, but I couldn't— couldn't close my eyes, couldn't avoid the gut-wrenching scene.

Security came sprinting up the stairs and leapt over the railing. The biggest guy grabbed Bas and hauled him backwards. He fought like a wildcat for a moment, writhing to try and break free. One of the security guards clocked him right in the face, and he gave in, his body going slack. They hauled him to his feet.

Two of the other guards had descended on Hannover. Medical arrived at the same time, throwing the gate open and rushing in. I clutched my throat, as I watched in horror. If Bas had killed Hannover, they'd have no choice but to hand him back over to Moriarty. That was the rule.

Between the backs of the meds, I caught movement. A second later, they shifted, and I saw that Hannover was sitting up.

All at once, the tension rushed out of me. I sagged against the glass, limp and panting, feeling as though I'd just been in the fight myself. Posy stood beside me, swearing quietly under her breath.

'What the fuck? What the actual fuck?'

'I... I don't know,' I mumbled. Bas had lost control. I'd never seen him lose control like that before.

Security and medical conferred briefly before Hannover was transferred to a stretcher and carried out of the cage. Bas followed behind, a guard on either side of him. They walked through the VIP circle, directly in our direction, heading for the back rooms, and for a few moments, I had a perfect view of the expression on Bas's face: angry, hateful, afraid. Even though he was surrounded by people, I couldn't help but think he looked terribly alone.

TWO

POSY AND I HURRIED DOWN the ladder to the floor below. By the time we got there, security, medical, and the two fighters had all vanished. In their wake, they'd left a hubbub of panicked dancers and confused techies. Lisette caught sight of us and broke away from the crowd.

'Did you see that?' she hissed. 'Bas just—he just—' She shuddered viscerally. Her eyes were wide with fright. I wondered what the scene had looked like from floor level, whether that had diminished or enhanced the horror.

'We were upstairs.' Posy lifted the whiskey bottle she was still holding and poured the remainder down her throat. 'Holy fuck. What happened?'

'No one knows. It happened so fast!' Lisette scraped her hands through her hair. Tina, the oldest of the dancers, approached us.

'There you are! Did you see what happened?'

I nodded absentmindedly.

'Do you think Bas will get in trouble?' Lisette asked, twisting the hem of her skirt between her fingers. 'I hope he doesn't. He's always so… gentlemanly.'

I choked on a hysterical laugh. That was one way of describing Bas. Posy, apparently thinking the same thing, snorted loudly.

'Yeah, if you ignore the fact that he can't go more than ten seconds without insulting someone.'

'It couldn't have happened to a better person,' Tina said grimly, smoothing down her sparkly leotard. Tina was tiny and lithe, several inches shorter than me, but damn, did she have muscles on her.

'Hannover?' I asked.

'He treats the girls in the circle awfully. Jenna didn't want to suck him off last week? He threatened to cut her tits off with a hunting knife.'

I shuddered. 'He's disgusting.'

Posy nodded emphatically. 'He makes me glad I know how to

dance.'

Lisette had gone quiet. Of all of us, she was the only one who worked in the circle. I caught her gaze. 'Are you alright, Lisette?'

'I just don't want Bas to get in trouble,' she muttered. 'Hannover definitely deserved that.'

'OI!'

We all jumped a mile, spinning around to see Carlos storming into the hall. 'ALL OF YOU, WHAT THE FUCK DO YOU THINK YOU'RE DOING?' Spittle spewed from his mouth, his face reddening as his eyes darted from one of us to the next. 'WELL? GET BACK TO WORK!'

Techies, dancers, and serving girls scattered. Posy grabbed my arm. 'Come on. What stage are you on?'

'Uh… west, I think.'

There was similar disarray out in the main hall. Although the music was playing and the lights were flashing, no one was dancing. The crowd was oddly still, watching the cage.

'Bas sure made a fucking mess,' Posy muttered. 'Well, we better get to work. Try and rev up the crowd or something, alright?'

'Right.' I waved to her, then climbed up onto the west stage. The responsibility always fell on the dancers to keep the crowd happy, but today they weren't playing along. I pulled out my best moves, but the uneasy vibe remained.

My tips suffered for it too. At the end of the day, the amount Carlos handed back to me after taking his split was paltry. He passed me my wage too, and I eyed it.

'That's less than we agreed.'

'Management's call. We gotta cover the loss somehow.'

'Not out of my salary!' I hissed.

'You're new, Benoit. Suck it up.'

Fuming, I spun away from him. Fuck him—and fuck Bas too, for going off the rails. Next time I saw him, I'd take my missing salary out of his fucking ego.

Still spitting nails, I stomped down the hallway to the dressing rooms. As I turned the corner, I slammed into someone and staggered backwards.

Think of the devil, and the devil shall appear.

It was Bas. He was sporting an impressive shiner on his face where security had decked him, and his lip was split, but apart from that, he looked relatively unharmed. His gaze skated over me, and the anger that had been written across his face vanished behind a blank mask.

'Harley.'

I'd never met a man who could make me feel so small—but Bas managed it every time. He didn't notice the way my top pushed my boobs up, or how toned my stomach and legs were. He ignored the tasteful makeup I'd painted across my face and the tall heels that were pinching my toes. No, Bas didn't care about any of that.

Bas didn't care about me at all.

That was entirely my fault. A week ago, I'd finally admitted to Bas how I had cut a deal with his estranged brother to pass intel to him. To my incredible surprise, he'd accepted my explanation and continued to teach me self-defence. He hadn't once acted like he was angry.

I hated it.

Bas now treated me with absolute cordiality and apathy—which honestly ought to have been an improvement over our old relationship, where we'd been at each other's throats most of the time.

So why didn't it feel like it?

Maybe because despite our frequent arguments, we'd had some kind of connection between us—and I hadn't realised until it was gone.

Or maybe just because I was a weirdo who liked arguing with people.

I dropped my gaze to the floor. 'Sorry,' I muttered. 'Didn't see you there.'

'Whatever.' He stepped neatly aside and walked around me. I turned, staring after him as he strode away, a sick feeling in my belly.

A few months ago—a few weeks ago, even—he'd have told me off for not looking where I was going. He'd have probably insulted me. He still wouldn't have cared about my sexy outfit or makeup. But he might, a tiny little bit, have cared about me. The person. Because beneath the stoic exterior he'd built up as a defence, Bas—Sebastian Rochester—was actually a good person.

But I'd gone and ruined our things.

'Sorry,' I repeated softly, though he was too far away to hear me.

In the dressing room, I hurriedly swapped my dancing costume for jeans and a jumper, along with the heavy steel-toed combat boots that I wore year-round. I was wiping my makeup off when Posy came in, swearing bloody murder.

'Bas is such a dick. A hot fucking dick, but such a dick.'

'Did Carlos cut your wage too?'

'No.' She sat down and kicked her heels off. 'But he took two thirds of my tips. Fucking arsehole.'

'He cut my wage.' I tossed the rag I was using into my bag.

'Wanker.' Posy dragged a pair of jeans up her shapely legs. 'If I could get another job… Oooh, that jerk.'

'I saw Bas,' I said, perching on the edge of the bench opposite. We shared the dressing room with about half a dozen other dancers, but they had already left.

'Me too,' Posy said.

'Really? When?' I had to work to keep the curiosity out of my voice. The last thing I wanted was for people to find out that I was interested in Bas. Rumours spread faster than diseases round here.

'Just now. He was entering the office with Jackson.'

Huh, that's interesting. Was Bas in trouble? Almost certainly, yes. I glanced around, a very bad idea occurring to me.

'Harley?'

'What?' I turned to see Posy by the door, bag over her shoulder.

'You coming?'

'Uh… not just yet.'

Posy frowned. 'You don't want a lift with Kade? The taxi-trucks don't come this far out.'

'It's alright. I can get a lift with Ellery.' The lie flowed off my tongue. Ellery probably wouldn't spit on me to put out a fire right now, but that was a problem to worry about later. Right now, I had a prime opportunity to do some spying—except I wasn't motivated by my cruel masters. I was just fucking curious.

I wanted to know what had gone wrong in Bas's fight.

'Okay then. See you next week?'

'Yep.' I nodded. Posy let herself out, the door falling shut behind her. I kicked my boots off and climbed onto one of the dressing tables. It wobbled but held my weight. Above me was the metal ceiling that all of the rooms here had—a false ceiling. When the bunker had been operational, all of the tech systems had run through the crawlspace above that ceiling. Over the years, I'd gleaned a lot about how the bunker worked—and how Sayle had restored it—from listening in to the Iron Fists or the techies talking about it, but this particular tip had come from a dancer who had worked here when I first started, Cindy. She'd used to hide things in the crawlspace, stuff she'd stolen from the customers and the gang members. Unfortunately, she'd gotten too brave, because Carlos had caught her and she'd lost her job.

Fortunately, they hadn't discovered her hiding place or sealed it up.

Stretching my arms, I pushed the ceiling panel up and out of the way. A cloud of dust puffed out of the opening, and I covered my mouth. *Yuck.*

Scrambling down, I grabbed my scarf from the pocket of my thick overcoat and wrapped it around my mouth and nose. Then I clambered back up, jumped to grab the edges of the hole, and walked my feet up the wall until I could get them through and hook them over the edge.

Thank you, dance. Without my years of training, I'd never have had the flexibility and strength to get up there.

My foot hit something, which skittered away. I froze, listening hard. It sounded like a bottle. Hauling myself the rest of the way up, I saw that it was exactly that. And not just one bottle; there were dozens. Packs of cigarettes, baggies of drugs, jewellery, clothes, even a few knives and a gun. It was a treasure trove.

But it was more trouble than it was worth.

I cleared a few things out of the way to make space, then crawled slowly away from the hole in the ceiling. It was light, but not bright up there. Emergency lighting cast eerie shadows between all manner of pipes and cables, which were needed to keep the bunker fully operational. Centuries of dust coated most of it, and in a few moments it began to coat me too.

Ugh.

The rooms up here didn't match the ones below. I paused to orientate myself, before crouching and manoeuvring through the cramped space. Several times, I had to duck to get beneath low-hanging pipes. Occasionally, I heard the skittering of rodents or veered off course to avoid spiders. I could hear people moving about and talking below me.

Finally, I estimated that I was over the hallway I needed. Stiff and silent, I rounded a large metal box and found the office. There was a trapdoor, faintly illuminated by an orange light, but it was screwed shut.

Damn.

I lay on my belly and pressed my ear to the ground, trying to filter out the oppressive hum of machinery around me. At length, I managed to pick out a gruff, raspy voice.

Jackson. He was one of the Iron Fists' most senior members, and from what I knew, he was often the one who kept the ranks under control.

'…send them a message, not send them a body.'

'I know,' Bas said stiffly. 'I apologise. I thought I could handle it.'

'We took a big risk on this.' Jackson's tone was one of warning.

'It won't happen again.'

'It's not going to.' *If only I could see in!* But the only clues I had were the shifts in their voices: Jackson sounded terse. 'Sayle certainly won't let you fight Hannover again.'

'Of course not.' Bas's tone was impassive, the same way he spoke to me. 'I understand that I overstepped.'

'That's one way of putting it.' There was a long moment of silence, and once again I wished desperately that I could see in. 'You're barred from the fights in the interim. I'll try and dissuade the Black Hands from retaliating, but you know as well as I do that we can't risk a war right now.'

'Yes, sir,' Bas said emotionlessly.

'Alright. Here, this was left for you.'

Something rustled. 'Thank you,' Bas said.

'Go,' Jackson finished coolly. 'Get some rest. You look like crap.'

'Sir.' The door opened and shut again. Everything was silent for a while, and then Jackson spoke.

'I hope you're happy.'

Was there someone else there? I held my breath, afraid to miss even the tiniest clue.

'Ecstatic,' an unfamiliar voice said drily.

Jackson snorted. 'Let's go, then.'

The door opened and shut once again. I waited for a few minutes, listening for clues, but the room below was silent.

Who was that? Why hadn't Posy mentioned a third person entering the room? Why hadn't Bas addressed them? Questions whirled through my mind as I manoeuvred my way back to the dressing room. I checked the room was empty, then lowered myself down and closed up the ceiling panel.

I was so confused.

It took a few moments to get the dust off of me, and then I pulled my coat and boots on and slipped out. The hallways were already practically deserted, only a few cleaners and techies around to do clear-up. I hurried through the narrow corridors until I got to the tunnels, wide highways which crisscrossed beneath the wasteland north and east of our town. They were everywhere, many of them caved in—you could be walking above them and not even realise it. Some of them led to storerooms, and others even had tracks that had obviously once been used to move goods. Now, the majority were closed off, except for the ones that the Iron Fists used and guarded. I entered the weapons check and found Hank there, a guy a few years older than me who had a chip on his shoulder a mile wide.

'You're late, Benoit.'

'I got held up changing.'

He scowled but threw open the weapons locker and pulled out my knife. 'Get off, then. I don't get paid enough to hang around waiting for whores who want to get one last client in.'

The dig made me grind my teeth together. I took the knife, shoved it into its sheath, and hid it under my coat. 'See you around.'

Hank rolled his eyes and gestured expansively to the door.

I hurried out, setting a quick pace down the longest of the tunnels, which went south towards the train station. Truth be told, I didn't want to hang around. The long, shadowy corridors and distant rattling of machinery made the place spooky when it was empty.

My footsteps echoed in the empty tunnel. After about ten minutes of walking, I finally reached the exit. A sturdy metal ladder extended into the ceiling. My heavy combat boots clanged loudly against it as I climbed up and jumped out.

'Late,' an amused voice said. 'Who held you up, pretty girl?'

'Eff off, Greene.' I rolled my eyes. 'Why weren't you at the fights?'

Alex Greene was a few years older than me and had grown up on the same street as me. He had voluminous brown hair and an explosion of freckles across his face and neck, and he was almost as short as I was. He grinned and said in a patronising tone, 'Someone has to make sure none of the riffraff get in.'

'You just like fleecing people for money.'

'Abso-fucking-lutely.' He waved me through. 'Get out of here. I wanna close up and go home.'

I flipped him off playfully. 'Tell Ilona hi for me.'

'Will do!'

I hurried off through the depot—from one spooky location to another. The entrance to the tunnels was hidden in a side passage in the train depot. Once upon a time, this had been where we received deliveries from Brackfields and the other cities to the south, where the larger factories and farms were located. That had been before the gangs had started throwing their weight around and blockading the train lines. The mayor of Brackfields had stopped the trains going north after Crater's Edge, the next town on the line.

All of that had happened when I was really little. I barely remembered life before that. Our current reality was all I knew.

Beyond the deserted depot was the trainyard. I climbed over the tracks and rounded the small platform where passenger trains had once pulled in. On the other side was a gravel lot—when I'd arrived, there had been plenty of cars parked there, but now there were only two: Greene's battered four-by-four, and another with matte black paint and scratches down one side.

Bas's car.

I gave it a wide berth, though I couldn't see if he was inside. The further I got from the depot, the darker it got. The station was quite far out from the main town, and after twenty years of neglect, the road leading to it was barely passable anymore. The only people who came out here were the ones trying to get into the bunker because it was the most convenient of the entrances.

But why had Bas used it when he could have come in directly through the Iron Fists' compound?

Weird.

When I reached the road, I paused to pull out the torch I always carried and shine it ahead of me. A narrow track extended mostly dead straight through the wasteland: gravelly dirt speckled with scrubby bushes and lumps of concrete. A chilly breeze made the bushes rustle.

'The only thing that grows here is concrete.'

That had been my dad's favourite joke. I thought of it every time I had to walk through the wasteland… and every time it sent a pang of hurt and nostalgia through me. He'd been dead going on eight years, and it never got easier.

All of a sudden, light flared around me. I squinted, stepping aside as a car approached from behind. It slowed and pulled up beside me, then the driver-side window rolled down.

It was Bas.

Of course.

'What are you doing here?' he growled.

'Walking. Home.' I mimed walking with my fingers. 'It's this thing those of us who can't drive do.'

Bas scowled—which was more reaction than I'd got out of him in weeks. My triumph blossomed, then died instantly as he snapped, 'Stupid.'

'I missed my lift back.' I glowered at him. Not that it was his fault, but it also definitely wasn't his business. 'What do you care anyway? Just move along.'

Bas's expression twisted. For a moment, I thought he might do it, just leave me alone. It would tally with his apathy over the last few weeks. Finally, looking incredibly annoyed, he said, 'Get in.'

'I thought you were done being nice to me.' One day, I'd learn to shut up and just accept favours. That day was not today.

'I'm not being nice. I'd have thought you'd have learnt your lesson by now.'

I glared at him. Reminding me of the time I'd been assaulted? Not cool. 'I'm a grown-up. I can look after myself. Anyway, you're not going to be here to drive me back every time I have a shift.'

'Next time don't miss your ride back.'

'I don't need you to tell me what to do.' I crossed my arms. 'I'm good, thanks.'

Bas groaned loudly. 'Harley, get in.'

'I'd hate to burden you.'

He made growled in the back of his throat. 'Get in the fucking car, you infuriating *child*.'

I tilted my chin up stubbornly. 'No. Fuck off.'

'*Harley!*'

'What? I never asked you to pull up next to me, and I definitely didn't give you permission to talk to me like that. If that's how you do favours for people, go suck a dick.'

I turned on my heel and stalked down the road.

Bas slammed his hand against the horn, the sound cutting through the night air and making me jump. My heart lurched into my throat. Maybe I shouldn't have pushed. After all, he was being nice. Sort of.

But that didn't excuse him from talking that way.

Bas cut the ignition. The car went silent and the lights flicked off. I kept walking, head down. A moment later, I heard his door slam and footsteps slapping the ground as he jogged after me. I whirled around, and he almost ran into me, drawing up just in time.

'It's not safe,' he said. 'You can't really be this reckless.'

'I know I haven't exactly given you the best impression of me,' I said coolly. 'But I'm not getting in the car with a man who swears at me and calls me an infuriating child.'

Bas rolled his shoulders. 'I shouldn't have said that. I was just—'

'Angry.'

He shrugged. 'Not at you. Can I give you a lift?'

Bas was such a confusing man. He was a jerk one minute, caring the next. He talked to me like I was dirt, but protected me from rapists and offered me lifts home. He called me a whore, but never asked me to do sexual favours for him. He taught me how to defend myself, even though I'd betrayed him.

'I don't understand you,' I said, turning and walking past him. 'But seeing as you want it that badly, fine.'

Bas followed me silently and climbed up into the driver's side. The car was warm, a nice break from the wintery air outside. A two-way radio was mounted against the dashboard, and his jacket was discarded on the passenger seat. I moved it carefully to the back and sat, hugging my bag to my chest. Bas turned the ignition and began to drive slowly over the rugged terrain. An awkward silence permeated slowly through the car, emanating from the stiff, unyielding man sitting beside me.

'Thanks. By the way,' I mumbled.

'You're welcome.'

From passionately arguing with me to total apathy in the space of moments. Guilt churned in my stomach. More than anything, I wished I could go back in time and tell Rodney Rochester to fuck off.

Rodney Rochester—Bas's older brother. He'd offered to pay me for information on his brother, and I had caved under the pressure of desperation after my rent had been hiked. At the time, I'd struggled to find another solution, so I'd broken Bas's trust to save my own pride. Now, I could think of dozens of options that would have been better—including what I was doing now: dancing in the bunker.

Hindsight was always twenty-twenty.

Eventually, the silence got too much for me.

'I saw your fight,' I said in a small voice.

'We're not discussing that,' Bas said stonily.

'Uh, okay. Do you mind if I switch the radio on?'

He jerked his hand dismissively towards the centre console. 'If it works, go for it.'

At least that gave me something to do. I switched the radio on and fiddled with the dials, trying to tune it to one of the local stations. I'd just found Crater Tunes when the two-way radio crackled.

'Bas, this is Anton. Over.'

Bas slammed his hand onto the console to kill the music and hit the talk button on his radio.

'Anton, this is Bas. Go ahead. Over.'

There was a moment of static. Anton's voice was unrecognisable over the radio. 'Bas, location. Over.'

Bas pulled the car up. 'Just left the station, turning onto main in five. Over.'

I glanced at Bas's face. Worry tugged at his features, though his voice was impassive.

'Distillery north guard non-responsive. Swing round to check. Over.'

Bas's features shifted to pure irritation. He shot a glance at me. 'Bad timing. Is there anyone else? Over.'

'Negative. You're closest. Over.'

Bas tapped his fingers against the steering wheel.

'On my way. Out.' He slammed the radio back into its cradle and jabbed a finger at me. 'Not a word.'

I mimed zipping my lips.

'And stay down. And do exactly as I say.'

'Sir, yes sir.'

Bas growled. 'Snark falls under the remit of 'not a word,' Harley.'

I suppressed a totally inappropriate giggle. 'Do you want me to curl up in the footwell like a little kid too?'

'If we get shot at, you'll be doing exactly that.'

'Yes, sir,' I muttered, though with considerably less sarcasm this time. I'd been shot at once in my life, and it wasn't an experience I was eager to relive. Especially as that particular incident was directly to blame for my present employment with the Iron Fists.

Bas hit a couple of buttons on the console, then abruptly swung the wheel, sending the car off the road. We bounced between piles of rubble and flattened a scraggly plant. I grabbed the edges of my seat, swearing.

'Holy shit, warn me next time!'

'We're going offroad,' Bas said, deadpan.

Fucker.

Gnashing my teeth, I braced myself against the back of my seat. Bas jerked the wheel to avoid a gigantic lump of concrete, then steered us around the skeleton of the building it had come from.

'How do you know where to go?'

At school, we'd been strictly warned against entering the wasteland. Leave the roads and you'd get lost. Maybe you'd find your way back… maybe not. And it wasn't the sort of place you wanted to spend the night. In twenty-five years, I had wandered into the wasteland maybe a handful of times, but only ever in the company of my best friend, Theo, who was an expert navigator.

'*Do* you even know where we're going?' I added, panic building in my chest.

'Yes.'

Would it kill him to provide a few details? I glanced at Bas's profile. His expression was fixed. *It probably would kill him, actually. He'd spontaneously combust if I forced him to explain himself.*

'Hold on,' he said, and then we were climbing. I grabbed the edge of my seat again, but a moment later we righted ourselves and Bas turned sharply, the wheels bouncing as we crossed the train tracks and began driving along between the north- and southbound tracks.

'Oh,' I mumbled.

Yeah, that made sense. The whiskey distillery was on the train line. So the quickest way there was to follow the tracks towards the north of town.

We set a good pace away from the station and around to the northside, past wasteland on one side and farmland on the other, and finally the large metal warehouses came into view of the headlamps. This time, I was prepared for Bas's next manoeuvre: he jerked the wheel and turned us off the tracks, the car bouncing as we drove down the steep incline until we were hidden from view on the north side of the tracks.

Bas cut the engine and engaged the brake, then leant back and grabbed his jacket.

'Stay here,' he instructed as he clipped the radio to his belt.

I swallowed. 'Yeah, alright.'

'I mean it. Don't get out the car, Harley.'

'I said alright!'

He shot me a stern look. I scowled back. Did he have to treat me like a disobedient child? 'Look, I know I shouldn't have grassed on you, but you can at least talk to me like an adult.'

Bas wrenched his gaze away and pushed open his door. 'If you want that privilege, earn it.'

Dick.

He pulled a torch off his belt and switched it on, then shut the car door and started up the embankment to the train tracks. I watched his little puddle of light get further and further away—and then vanish.

I was alone.

A second later, the in-car light switched off, leaving me in total darkness.

Oh. Oh, no.

Instantly, my throat started to close up. I *wasn't* scared of the dark—I really wasn't—but this was a new level of creepy. The darkness seemed to press in on me—I could barely see a foot out the car. The silence was even worse. I huddled down in my seat, staring fixedly ahead.

Whoo-whoo!

I jumped. My elbow slammed against the door window.

'Fuck!'

Shit, that had hurt. Worse was my heart, beating so fast I felt like it was going to explode out of my chest. *What the hell was that?*

'Whoo-whoo!'

Something fluttered by and I groaned. A bird. A fucking pigeon.

'Harley, you idiot,' I whispered.

Weirdly, talking to myself helped. So I did it again.

'You're fine. Bas will be back in a minute.'

But what if he doesn't come back?

'Don't be silly. It's Bas. He's pretty steady.'

Well, he hadn't been when he was fighting Hannover. What had happened in that fight anyway? I was dying to know what Hannover had said to him. Did it have something to do with when Bas had been a slave? It would be just like Hannover to torment Bas by bringing up the past.

Risky moment to do it, though. He must have known Bas would go off at him like a rabid dog.

Unless that was what Hannover had wanted?

But why?

A strange scuffling noise reached me. A moment later, I pinpointed it. Footsteps, but the person seemed to be limping, their steps heavier on one side than the other. I stilled, swallowing. I wasn't alone.

Who was that?

Was it Bas?

No, Bas had been much lighter on his feet.

I glanced around the car, trying to move only my head. Where were they? Were they friend or foe?

In the distance, maybe thirty yards or more, I saw a pinprick of light. A torch. It was moving slowly across my field of vision from left to right... away from the distillery.

Who was that?

Had Bas seen them?

Don't get out the car, Harley.

What if Bas hadn't seen them? What if they were important, whoever they were?

Swallowing again, I grasped the door handle and inched it open. Every sound seemed magnified in the silence; twice I stopped, afraid that I'd be heard.

The light kept moving steadily into the distance.

I shifted my feet out of the car, then reached down and fished my torch out of the side pocket of my bag. If I switched it on and held my hand over it, I should have just enough light to see by.

I squeezed out of the car and closed the door, then crouched down. The car light was on, illuminating me.

Don't look, don't look, don't look.

The light went off.

I stood. The torchlight had paused in the distance. A moment later, it began to move faster than ever.

They'd noticed me. *Damnit.*

Throwing caution to the wind, I hurried up the embankment to the train tracks. From up there, I could see a fair distance—at least, I could have by day. By night, there was the glow of the town to the south and west, but the north and east were empty and dark. I switched my torch off and squinted after the pinprick of light moving rapidly away from me.

All of a sudden, headlights appeared in the distance. A car. Did it have something to do with the mysterious figure? Yes, he was running towards it, and a moment later the internal light switched on. He'd clambered inside—but they weren't moving.   Something was happening.

Someone climbed out again.

It hit me suddenly: I was standing on top of the embankment, silhouetted against the glow on the horizon. A perfect target.

I dropped to the ground, metal rails and chunks of gravel digging into my chest. A hollow crack rent the air, followed by a strange crackle. Once, twice.

They were shooting!

My heart sprang into my throat as the world seemed to slow down around me. Did they think *I* was a threat? Would they come back for me?

That… that had been close.

I needed to get back in the car.

My pulse still roaring in my ears, I dragged myself on my belly to the edge of the embankment and shuffled down in a crouch. Halfway down, I heard the car engine. I paused, following the lights. It was driving away. Where were they going?

Who was that?

Footsteps crunched softly but urgently behind me. Panicking, I jumped up and threw myself down the slope. I scrambled back into the car and ducked down, my heart pounding. Not a moment later, Bas came into view, sprinted around the car, and hauled the driver's door open, leaning inside.

'I told you to stay in the car!'

'I—There was—I saw—' My words tumbled over each other in my panic. I cleared my throat and dragged in a deep breath. 'There was another car!'

Bas tensed, the fury draining out of his expression. 'What? Where?'

I pointed a shaking hand towards the north. 'That way. I only got out to see what was going on. I thought you'd want to know!'

Bas shook his head. 'And they saw you. You could have been shot!'

'I was trying to help!'

He covered his eyes with his hands, then raked his fingers through his hair. 'You have *no* sense of self-preservation whatsoever.'

'I do!' I insisted. 'I was just trying to help!'

Bas groaned. He climbed into the car and slammed the door. 'How about for once you leave figuring out what's going on to the people who are actually capable?'

Ouch. The accusation hit me like a sledgehammer. 'I am capable!'

Bas made a noise of disbelief. 'You almost got shot and you warned them we were here.'

'If it weren't for me, you wouldn't have known at all!'

'I don't need your help, Harley.' Bas jerked the wheel, turning the car in a loop so he could climb the embankment.

'Some gratitude,' I sneered.

'Why should I be grateful? You're going to get yourself killed over a radio malfunction.'

I ground my teeth together. 'I'm more capable than you give me credit for.'

'You're reckless, impulsive, and careless.' We crested the embankment and bounced over the tracks. 'And you are not a member of the Iron Fists. We can take care of our own problems, without the help of a glorified stripper.'

Ouch. Stung, I pressed my back into the seat and clenched my jaw. I had nothing to say to that. If that was what he thought, then screw him.

We rode the rest of the way back to town in silence.

THREE

BY THE TIME I GOT back to my dingy third-floor flat in the centre of town, I was exhausted, and it was long past four AM. That, however, did not mean the entire building was asleep. I heard the couple in the ground-floor flat arguing as I passed, and one of the first-floor lights was on—James Maddock's light.

What was he doing up so late?

Maddock was the newest resident in town, and I still hadn't figured out whether I could trust him or not. He seemed friendly enough, but he'd been dropping not-so-subtle hints that he was here to stir things up. I had enough trouble in my life already.

My flat, by contrast, was dark and deserted. A plate had been left out for me with a neat, handwritten note beside it.

Made you dinner. Back tomorrow. Sav

I crumpled it up, worry and irritation dancing a pas-de-deux in my chest. Savannah was my twin sister. We were identical twins, and she was the only family I had left. No matter that we got on terribly most days. I hated the idea of losing her. But lately it seemed like she was deliberately flouting every attempt I made to keep her safe. I was the one meant to be making up our financial shortfall. I was the one meant to be dealing with the gangs. Savannah was supposed to do her charity doctor work and help the town and stay out of danger.

Except she didn't much care for that role anymore—even though she was the one who had chosen it in the first place. At any point after our father had died when we were seventeen, she could have changed her course. At least once, she'd been offered a well-paying job at the nearest hospital in Crater's Edge. But she had chosen to stay here and help our town, and so long as she did that, I was stuck here too.

For better or for worse, I would stick with my sister.

If only she'd stop going out late at night.

It was a new habit she'd picked up, and I knew exactly who was to blame: Greg Talbot, a member of the gang that controlled the casinos on the west side of town—the Aces.

I'd left my appetite somewhere in the wasteland, between being shot at and fighting with Bas, so I transferred the food to an airtight jar and leant out the window to put it in the crate we used as a fridge. One of the benefits of it being freezing cold right now: we didn't have to pay for electricity to keep our fridge on. Of course, all our other expenses had gone through the roof, so it didn't help much.

The bedroom was empty, killing my last hope that Savannah might be home. I peeled my clothes off and crawled under the covers. Even if I wanted to shower right now, the hot water wouldn't switch on until six.

I was exhausted the next morning on my way to work. Back-to-back shifts were going to kill me.

The brutal autumn weather was giving way to the unending harshness of winter. A brisk wind whipped up dust and other rubbish and carried with it a frigid chill that made my ears ache. I pulled my collar up to cover my chin and jammed a knitted hat down low over my ears, but no matter what I did, the cold still seemed to find a way in.

It took me twenty minutes of brisk walking to reach the Kranikovska. My day job was as a waitress in the hotel bar—I'd have liked to say it was an improvement on pole dancing in glorified lingerie, but although the clientele was supposed to be classier, they all took just the same liberties.

The hotel was one of the older buildings in town, a five-storey structure with a dirty brick façade. It occupied one side of the square in the centre of town overlooking the daily market.

I rounded the edge of the market and took the side street that led to the back of the hotel, dodging a man who was huddled in a doorway, half-concealed by the bins. The back door was heavy steel, and took all my strength to open.

Inside was a hive of activity, cleaners and kitchen staff bustling around. The seasonal merchants' market, which was held every six months, was coming up in two weeks. Tom, the owner of the Kranikovska, had sent everyone into a preparation frenzy. I ducked around a few people who were standing in the entrance to the laundry room, passed the open kitchen door from which smells and shouts poured, and exited through the swing door into the bar.

The lounge was quiet compared to the back rooms, with soft music tinkling over the aged sound system. A few people were scattered around finishing up their lunch. We did serve food for hotel guests, but it was mostly drinks. The hotel itself was empty at the moment. In two weeks, when the merchants' market arrived, we'd be run off our feet.

'Hey, Harley,' Anna said unenthusiastically. I felt a familiar stirring of guilt when I laid eyes on my pretty blonde coworker. Anna was the owner's niece, and I'd worked with her since I started here. We'd always been friendly... until this last week. Things had been strained between us since our argument the night before Gabriel Tam, Anna's beau, had mysteriously skipped town.

Of course, he hadn't actually skipped town. His body had been abandoned in the wasteland for the scavengers. But Anna didn't know that, nor could she know of my involvement. I offered her a careful smile, though inwardly, the thought of him filled me with a strange coldness that made my fingers tingle.

'Hey, how you doing?'

Anna shrugged and turned back to wiping down the taps. Tom strode over from the doorway, an athletic redhead in tow.

'Harley—right on time. I want you to meet Laura Malone.'

Tom was a short, unassuming man with a balding head and a booming voice. As a boss, he was as fair as he could be, considering that he spent most of his time trying to appease the three gangs who all but ran our town, along with the mayor and his rich cronies. I didn't envy him his position, stuck in the middle, but Tom insisted on keeping the Kranikovska neutral in our local politics.

I shot a glance at the red-haired woman. She had freckly skin and an easy smile, and her clothes were in the same vein as mine: tight jeans and a low-cut top. 'Hi.'

'Laura moved to town from Crater's Edge a few months ago,' Tom explained. 'I'm hiring her on a trial basis during the merchants' market. To help you girls manage the bar.'

'Oh.' I dredged up a bit of enthusiasm from beneath my exhaustion. 'Great.'

Tom turned to Laura. 'This is Harley, and my niece, Anna. They'll show you the ropes.'

'Awesome.' Laura had a soft voice. I had visions of her trying to scold drunk men in that tone—no way would that work. 'It's nice to meet you both.'

'You too,' I lied.

'Alright.' Tom clapped. 'I'll see you all later, then.'

He took his leave, and Anna leaned over the bar, smiling. 'So what brought you out here?'

'I was born here.' Laura shifted her weight, glancing around. 'I went to Crater's Edge with my husband—but he passed last year. Gang violence. You know…' She cast her eyes downwards. I swallowed.

'Yeah, we know.' My voice came out hoarse.

'So I came back to be closer to my family. It's just… easier.'

'Family does make things easier. I don't know where I'd be without Tom,' Anna said. She reached out and laid a hand over Laura's. 'If you need anything, just let us know, okay?'

'Thank you.' Laura smiled. Her eyes flicked to me, and I forced my lips up in what I hoped was a moderately friendly smile.

'So, waitressing, huh? Here, come grab an apron. I'll show you round the back rooms.'

Laura was a quick study, but I worried about how she'd cope on Friday and Saturday nights when the bar was full and you couldn't hear yourself think for the shouting. How would she break up a fight between guys twice her size if she couldn't raise her voice to be heard?

She shadowed me at a safe distance as I cleared tables and served drinks. How would she react if Briggs or one of the other Iron Fists members came in and tried to grope her?

When I'd started, Kayla had taken me aside and warned me: '*The men get handsy. You got two options. You either let 'em, or you fight 'em. Either way, what you do the first time is what you stick with, got it?*'

I didn't know if I could deliver that advice with the same panache she had managed. It would sound hollow coming from me—I'd taken the coward's way out and let them touch. Kayla kept a firm hand on the boys, and they respected her a hell of a lot more than me.

The dinner rush was more of a dinner trickle that evening. It was winding down, a couple of tables against the wall still occupied, when I heard heavy boots on the tile floor of the lobby and two familiar figures strode in.

Ellery and Briggs. *Uh oh.*

I glanced around for support, but there was none to be had—Anna and Laura were in the back so Laura could meet the kitchen and hotel staff before they went home for the evening.

Ellery and Briggs were two more of Bas's four-person enforcer team—and two more mistakes to add to my impressive tally. Briggs was a burly man with brown hair and the demeanour of a poorly socialised pitbull. Ellery, with his golden hair and skin and friendly brown eyes, was the sort of man any woman would want to spend the night with.

Unfortunately, I'd blown that one by pretending I wanted to… and then flaking out halfway through.

Up close, it looked like Ellery wasn't faring too well after his fight the previous night. He had a pattern of bruises around his eyes, and I was sure his arms and torso were the same. A general sense of fatigue hung over him too, visible in the dark circles under his eyes and creases in his clothes.

'Ellery, Briggs,' I greeted in a careful, reserved tone.

'Harley,' Ellery returned in a subdued tone.

'*Kitten.*' Briggs's voice dripped with malice. 'How's it going? You looked mighty fine on the pole last night. That outfit…' He put his fingers to his lips and mimed a kiss.

'Funny,' I said drolly. 'I didn't notice you at all last night.'

Fury flickered across his features. He leant forwards. 'You need to work on your attitude, *kitten*.'

I was coming to hate that nickname. It had originated with Ellery—he'd called me that for years—and now everyone and their dog thought it was just grand and had started using it: to compliment me, to mock me, to insult me, and everything in between.

I was done with it.

'My name is Harley, and I'm currently at work.' I flipped my hair over my shoulder. 'Either sit down and buy a drink, or leave.'

Briggs narrowed his eyes, but Ellery spoke before he could.

'We're just here to talk.'

I raised an eyebrow. 'Talk,' I echoed.

'We've got a missing person. And you guys usually see all the comings and goings.'

My heart plunged into my stomach—then lurched into my throat and kicked up to a rapid pace. I swallowed hard, trying to subtly wipe my clammy palms on my apron. *No. Act normal. They don't necessarily mean Tam.*

'Missing person?' I croaked.

'Gabriel Tam.' Ellery wouldn't look at me, to my relief. His gaze drifted around the bar, with its scratched wooden furnishings and tarnished antique mirrors. 'I know he came in here occasionally.'

'Occasionally,' I repeated. I could feel Briggs's gaze on me, his eyes burning into the side of my face. *Look away, look away.*

But he didn't.

I gripped the edges of my apron, then smoothed it down. 'I last saw him about a week ago—I think?'

That was good. Casual. Casual was good.

I had last seen Tam just over a week ago. In fact, I was also the last person who had seen Tam, at least whilst he was alive. A little over a week ago, he'd tried to empty a gun into my head—because I had suspected that he was a traitor to the Iron Fists.

I'd tried to warn Ellery, but he hadn't believed me.

Turned out I was right.

Unfortunately—at least for Tam—he had underestimated me. I never went down without a fight.

It had been the last mistake he ever made.

Evander Hardwick, a figure of dubious allegiance, had helped me burn the body in a shallow pit in the wasteland. I hadn't wanted to help out with the task, but I sure wasn't going to let him take care of it without me. I didn't need to hand him opportunities to betray me.

Casual.

I reached for a bottle of the whiskey we usually used to serve the Iron Fists. 'Doesn't he travel a lot? Maybe he left town.'

Ellery shook his head in frustration. 'We would know if that were the case. You tried to talk to me about him a few weeks ago. Did anything ever... come of that for you?'

His voice was stilted. Our argument from a few weeks ago still lingered between us.

'If you're gonna act like a cheap whore...'

Ellery had refused to listen to my suspicions about Tam. He thought he knew better, because Tam was a loyal member of the Iron Fists and I was just some girl.

Well, if that was how he wanted to play it...

I took a steadying breath. 'You told me I was wrong, so I let it go,

Ellery. Don't you remember?'

Ellery grimaced. 'I'm just trying to explore every avenue.'

My confidence was growing as his diminished. 'That's not my problem anymore.' I held the bottle up. 'Are you drinking?'

'Can you at least ask around, see if anyone here has seen anything?' he pressed.

If Ellery thought I was going to make it that easy for him, he had another thing coming.

'I don't work for the Iron Fists. You, however, are welcome to ask any of my colleagues, or stay in the bar and watch, or whatever it is you want to do.' I waved the bottle pointedly. 'So long as you buy a drink.'

'Harley—' Ellery cut himself off with a groan of frustration. Briggs leant over the bar, pressing his hands into the splintery wood as he stared right into my eyes.

'It would be in your best interests to cooperate with us, *kitten.*'

'I am cooperating.' I wanted to back away, but I held my ground.

'Oh yeah? Seems to me like quite the opposite.'

The back door swung open, and Laura and Anna piled in, both giggling. 'Well, it's never like that here—' Anna cut herself off sharply. 'What's going on here?'

Laura hesitated uneasily in the doorway.

'Nothing,' I said, my voice coming out much calmer than I felt. 'Ellery and Briggs are looking for Tam, that's all. But I told them we haven't seen him.'

Anna's face fell. 'He's not here,' she said.

Ellery raised an eyebrow. 'What makes you say that?'

'I went by his flat. He's not there. His car is gone.'

His car?

I hadn't even thought about his car. *Crap!* Was it still at the bottling plant?

Briggs's gaze was on me again. I turned to Anna, struggling to hide my reaction.

'You had some kind of arrangement with him, didn't you?' Ellery asked. 'When last did you see him?'

'Last Thursday.' Anna said, winding the ties of her apron around her fingers. 'I wasn't feeling well, so I spent the day at his place. He dropped me home that night, then said he was going to work.'

'Work?' Ellery seemed surprised. 'Tam wasn't scheduled for patrols that night.'

He glanced at Briggs, who swept his gaze over the three of us: me barely suppressing my panic, Anna looking about to cry, and Laura, who was watching us all with a mixture of apprehension and confusion.

'I'd've thought Krani's would be more forthcoming, considering all we've done for them over the years,' Briggs drawled.

'We can't tell you what we don't know.' I had to force the words out, my throat was so tight.

'No, but you can ask around.' He shrugged. 'No matter. I'm sure we'll find someone more reciprocally minded.'

'I hope so,' I said neutrally.

Briggs nodded to Laura. 'Pretty new morsel you got there. She going to replace you now that you're coming back to the bunker, kitten?'

'Laura is helping out during the merchants' market,' I said tersely. 'I'm not coming back to the bunker. Sorry to disappoint.'

I couldn't have sounded less sorry if I tried.

'Such a shame.' Briggs shot a smirk in Laura's direction. 'If you're ever looking for better prospects… Harley can put you in touch.'

He turned and started towards the door, but Ellery lingered, staring at me with wide eyes.

'Run along,' I said. 'Wouldn't want to miss your lift back to the compound.'

'Harley, I…' But once again, his sentence went unfinished. He shook his head and shut his eyes briefly.

I bit my tongue. I felt too much towards Ellery, a dangerous mixture of lust and anger that flooded my veins and pushed all rational thought out of my mind. Even if I could find the right words, I didn't trust myself to say them.

'It would be better if you just go,' I said calmly. 'If I learn anything, I'll let you know.'

Ellery opened his eyes and nodded sharply. As he turned away, he shot a smile at Laura.

'Nice to meet you.'

Then he sauntered to the door, leaving me behind with my heart racing and a sick feeling in my belly.

The Iron Fists were looking for Tam.

Fuck.

FOUR

ON MONDAY MORNING, I dragged myself out of bed early to return to my usual schedule. I might have been working two jobs now, but I couldn't afford to let my training lapse.

Formerly, my morning routine had consisted of rigorous stretches to maintain flexibility and keep myself fit for dancing. I still did an abridged version of that, but now I also jogged over to The Arsonist, the pub behind my apartment block, to use their yard for self-defence training.

Bas was waiting for me when I arrived, a stoic silhouette against the greyish-brown skies. As per usual, he was wearing black cargo pants, a tight white T-shirt, and heavy boots. He could have passed for a soldier, if not for the fact that his T-shirt exposed the fist tattoo on his right biceps.

All gang members wore marks somewhere—a fist for the Iron Fists, a white hand on a black background for the Black Hands, and a playing card for the Aces. A long time ago, or so the story went, they had started out as marks to identify that the gang members were criminals. Now, gang members wore them with pride.

And the criminals were in control of our town.

I approached Bas with some caution. Saturday night had ended with him in a foul mood; if that was going to continue this morning, I didn't want to be the one to provoke him. I was already on his shit list.

Involuntarily, my gaze drifted over him. He cut an impressive profile, tall and strong. There was something immovable about him, from his squared shoulders to the visible strength of his muscular arms. *Every inch a fighter.*

My eyes settled on his hands. Long, slender fingers, resting lightly on the railing of the old fighting cage. His knuckles bore the marks of his fight the other night.

Less than forty-eight hours ago, those hands had been bathed in

Dean Hannover's blood. Not that I was sad about that part; Hannover deserved it.

But Bas had lost control.

And that unsettled me.

After, in the car, he had been his usual self: moody, volatile, at once totally apathetic, utterly hostile, and bizarrely caring. A walking contradiction.

I did not understand him.

But I liked him better as a contradiction than as whatever he'd been in the cage: feral, violent, uncontrolled.

This morning, his expression was blank and his shoulders were stiff. He watched me approach with a critical gaze. The only chink in his armour was the bruise on his cheek, which had faded to an ugly yellow.

'Hi,' I said awkwardly.

'Harley.' Bas nodded once. 'You missed yesterday.'

'Yeah, sorry. I was really tired.'

His expression didn't shift. 'Is that going to become a habit? If so, we can cancel lessons on Sunday mornings.'

He made it sound like I'd been lazy, not that I'd been up working until four AM.

'Yes,' I said flatly, irritated with him. 'It's going to *become a habit.*'

Bas gazed at me stonily. Not for the first time, I wondered why he kept showing up. If someone had hurt me the way I had hurt Bas, I would certainly have cut ties. I wouldn't have honoured some spurious promise to teach them to fight.

Finally, he jerked his head towards the cage. 'Start warming up, then.'

I clambered over the railing. I'd already warmed up at home, but Bas's idea of a warm-up was significantly more intense. Push-ups, crunches, squats… My muscles ached as much after training with him as they did after a night of dancing.

And I was already sore from Saturday.

Gravel crunched as Bas joined me, dropping to stand a few feet away. Out of the corner of my eye, I caught him flinching.

Is he hurt?

It was none of my business.

But when had he picked up the injury? I didn't think he'd been hurt during the fight with Hannover. Besides, surely I would have noticed in the car, afterwards?

'If you're finished warming up, we can get started,' Bas snapped. I realised I'd been staring at him instead of working out.

'Almost done,' I mumbled. 'Sorry.'

'Hmph.'

He was definitely in a worse mood than usual. Was it me? Or was something going on in his personal life?

I finished my exercises and stood up.

'We'll pick up where we left off,' Bas said. 'How to break holds.'

'Okay—' Before the word was even out of my mouth, Bas had grabbed my arm and twisted it behind me. I lost my footing and stumbled, trying to move with him so he didn't yank my arm out of the socket. 'Woah, fuck!'

Bas easily shifted his weight to balance both of us, even as he subdued my other arm. 'How do you break free?' he demanded.

'Uh…' It was difficult to think with his hands on me; I never seemed to be able to get used to it, no matter how much we trained together. I hadn't been expecting it when we first started. The gut-wrenching, chest-tightening panic had taken me by surprise. '…Um, stomp on your foot.'

'Try it.'

There was no point now. I'd warned him what I was going to do. But he expected me to try anyway. I lifted my foot and stomped on his as hard as I could—he barely flinched.

'Thick boots,' he said simply.

'Yeah, yeah.'

For several seconds, we just stood there, me trapped in his grip. I was hyper-alert to every sensation, every movement. The heat of his hands leaked through my shirt, and his breath tickled the back of my neck. My chest rose and fell frantically as I fought for calm.

I couldn't do this.

We'd started with fitness training, but last week Bas had introduced actual combat situations, and ever since then I felt like I went into free fall every time he touched me.

'Focus,' he snapped.

'I'm trying!'

I jerked my head back, trying to hit his chin with my skull. Bas kneed my lower back, and he wrenched my arms backwards.

'Argh!' I grunted.

'That won't work. You're not tall enough.'

You don't say.

I bit the inside of my cheek. Some days, I wasn't sure if he was trying to help me, or trying to remind me of all the ways he was superior to me.

Bas's grip tightened.

'You're not even trying.'

'I am trying! It's not that easy to get away from you. You're—' *Double my size. Big and strong. A man.* 'Okay, you know what? This is me trying.'

I tilted my head so I could see to aim, then jerked my leg backwards. The heel of my boot hit his knee, and he staggered, hissing in pain. His grip faltered.

I jerked free and twisted around, throwing a jab at his ear. Bas blocked the blow, caught my arm, and tried to twist it again.

I kicked his knee again.

His leg gave out, sending him crashing to the floor. He snarled under his breath. I took two quick steps back, my hands up in front of my face, then slowly lowered them as I realised he wasn't going to move.

'Are you okay?'

Bas lifted his head. The look in his green eyes was as sharp as razor wire.

'Why, are you going to report it to my brother?'

My mouth dropped open. *Ouch.*

'I didn't mean—That's not—' I stuttered.

Bas gripped the railing behind him. 'I don't care.'

'I'm just asking because you're hurt,' I said weakly.

'I'm not.' Even as he said it, Bas forced himself to his feet. His mouth was twisted in a grimace and his muscles were taut. 'It's none of your business.'

My stomach squirmed. 'I shouldn't have kicked you there.'

Bas brushed it off. 'You did what I told you to do. Let's move on.'

He took up a fighting stance again, but it was totally obvious that he was trying to keep his weight off his left leg.

'Maybe you should rest,' I said nervously. I didn't know a thing about treating injuries, but I was pretty sure it was bad. He hadn't been shot, had he? 'What happened anyway?'

'It's none of your business.'

'But—'

'We're not here to talk,' Bas said sternly. 'Get back to work.'

I ducked my head, my cheeks burning with shame.

The worst part wasn't that Bas hated me. It was how powerless I felt. This was on me. I had done something I knew was wrong—and I had no way to fix it.

He would never forgive me, and that was that.

Monday was my day off, so that afternoon I dragged myself down to my landlady's office to pay her my rent as usual.

Irina flicked through the banknotes with her thumb, a smug smile on her overly made-up face. 'Fifteen… sixteen… seventeen… Hmm. This one's damaged.'

My stomach, already tied in knots, seemed to twist even further in on itself.

'It was given to me like that, ma'am.'

'Even so.' She gave me a parody of a sympathetic smile. 'I can't accept it.'

I ground my teeth together, searching for the last vestiges of patience that remained in the depth of my soul.

I *really* hated my landlady.

Who else was there who could take such pleasure in the despair of others?

She was a parasite.

She raised an eyebrow expectantly. 'I take it you have another? If not—'

'I have another, ma'am,' I snapped.

She had the gall to look disappointed. 'Well, good.'

I fished through my coat pockets and found my purse, trying to hold it so Irina couldn't see inside. I didn't want her to know my net worth, for all it was only a small fraction of hers. Irina could raise my rent on a whim and kick me out for a laugh. I wasn't going to give her ammunition.

I peeled off a tenner and held it out. She pinched it between her fingers, adding it to her stack.

My heart leapt into my throat. 'And the other note, ma'am?'

'Surely you don't think that you can spend it anywhere else?'

'I can probably swap it.' I met her gaze, even though terror had turned my veins to ice.

Slowly, ever so slowly, she removed the damaged ten new pound note and held it out to me. I snatched it and shoved it in my pocket. My heart suddenly seemed to be beating in double time. I wiped my palms on my jeans.

'Well, that's it for this week,' she said in an overly cheerful tone. 'I'll see you next Monday.'

'Actually…' I cleared my throat. Our heating was on the fritz, and the wall in the bathroom was starting to rot from a leak in the pipes.

Irina raised an eyebrow. Her look wasn't enquiring, but more pointed. *Really,* it seemed to say, *are you sure?*

I swallowed. 'Nothing. I'll see you next week.'

'Have a good week, Harley.' She offered me a sharklike smile.

My hands shook as I left the office. I tucked them into my coat pockets to hide it.

All the gun-toting men in my town, and the person who scared me the most was my landlady. I felt like I was walking on a tightrope every time I entered her office, and below me was an abyss. One wrong move and I'd plunge to my death.

There was nothing I hated more than feeling powerless.

After a brief reprieve, the weather had turned awful again. The air was thick with reddish dust blown up from the crater to the east, and the sky was dark with clouds which would burst open every so often and shower us with icy rain that felt like knives driving into your skin. No one was out unless they had to be.

I really hoped the weather improved before the merchants' market. We needed a bit of good luck around here.

My building was diagonally across the road from Irina's, just a short walk away. I wrapped my scarf over my mouth and nose and ducked my head against the wind. I was drawing level with my building when someone caught my eye.

A man was standing in an alleyway across the street, neither hidden nor exposed, just sort of… there. And despite the gloomy brown light, he was perfectly recognisable: tall stature, proud posture, scowly expression.

Bas.

What, again? What the hell is he doing here?

I couldn't seem to escape the guy.

I ought to leave him alone, but this was too far south for the Iron Fists to be just hanging out. And even then, not Bas. We had regulars who looked after our area, like Anton Sorokin, Irina's son.

Making up my mind, I crossed the road. Bas's gaze jumped to me, his eyes narrowing as I came nearer.

'No,' he snapped. 'Get lost.'

I stopped in front of him and crossed my arms. 'Are you stalking me or something?'

Bas's expression creased in irritation. 'I'm on patrol. Why would I stalk you?'

I looked him over. He'd changed since earlier; now he was wearing a bulky black jacket and a buff which covered the bottom half of his face. He was also carrying a rifle.

Charming.

'The Iron Fists never patrol this far south.'

'The situation has changed.' The moment the words were out of his mouth, he made a face like he wished he could take them back. 'I didn't mean that.'

'Yes, you did.'

He muttered something that sounded very, very much like '*Fuck.*'

'Don't you have somewhere else to be?' he snapped.

'I live here.' I gestured around me. 'Where else would I be?'

'Work?'

'It's my day off.'

Bas tipped his head back, knocking his crown against the wall. 'For fuck's sake. Well, it's not *my* day off, so you can go bother someone else.'

'The other guys chat when they're on patrol.' At least, my friend Theo did. When he was here.

A fist clenched around my heart, and it suddenly felt difficult to breathe. It had been months since I'd last seen Theo, and I was starting to get worried. No, forget that. I wasn't worried; I was terrified.

Theo was a smuggler who made runs to the cities, but he'd never been gone this long before.

'I don't,' Bas said tersely. Why was I pushing him? He didn't want to talk. I ought to just leave.

I sighed. 'Fine, fine, I'll go.' I pulled my coat tighter around me. 'See you tomorrow, then?'

Bas nodded. I turned to leave.

'Harley.'

I glanced back. His expression was… strange.

'What were you doing in building four? That's not where you live.'

What…?

'Paying my rent. That's where Irina's office is.'

His expression cleared a little. 'Oh, okay.'

'Why? What did you think I was doing?'

Bas frowned. 'Nothing.'

Oh, that was not nothing. That was him hiding something. 'Uh-uh. Tell me.'

He winced. 'I thought… I thought… Irina is notorious for hiring young women for… *other services.*' He cleared his throat. 'Ellery said you were struggling with rent.'

My mouth dropped open. 'No!' I blurted. 'I wouldn't do that.'

I hugged my arms around myself, as though I could physically protect myself from the thought.

Bas looked away, obviously embarrassed. 'Just making sure.'

'Uh huh?' My skin itched all of a sudden, as though the thought itself could make me dirty. 'Why did you think I took on the extra shifts at the bunker?'

The expression on his face said that actually, he hadn't thought about it. Which… shouldn't have hurt me. Why would he be thinking about me?

Yet, somehow, it did.

'I'm a dancer, not a whore,' I snapped.

'I said I was making sure.'

'No, you were making assumptions.'

Bas's expression contorted. His buff had slipped down while he spoke, and I could see the way his mouth twisted. 'Don't blow it out of proportion.'

'*Blow it out of proportion?*' I clenched my fists. 'You can't go ten minutes without calling me a whore somehow!'

'That is *not* what I was doing!' Bas glowered down at me. 'Honestly, it's impossible to show concern for you without you jumping to conclusions—'

'Concern?' I echoed hysterically. ''Making sure' I'm not prostituting myself is not *showing concern!*'

Bas threw his hands up and the butt of his rifle scraped against the wall. 'You're impossible! Fine, you always have to be right. Go be right somewhere else.'

'I don't have to always be right,' I snarled. 'For someone who says they don't care about what's between my legs, you sure are fucking obsessed with the idea of me being a whore!'

Bas gritted his teeth so hard the veins in his neck showed. 'Fuck off.'

'Wow, polite.' I was being rude, but I was so angry I didn't care anymore. What was it about Bas that he just managed to drive me *crazy every fucking time?*

Bas shook his head. 'I'm tired of your attitude—'

'—I'm tired of you—'

'—Then leave! Why the fuck do you keep coming over?'

'Why can't you be nice?' I stepped closer to him. We were so close, I could feel the warmth coming off his body.

'You want me to be *nice?*' Bas stared at me as though I'd just grown a second head. 'You don't know anything about me.'

'I know plenty! You might think you're special, but you're the same as every other arsehole in this town!'

Bas laughed coldly. 'Oh right, I forgot Harley Benoit thinks she knows everything.'

'That's not true!'

'Isn't it? You think you know everything that goes on in this town, but you don't.'

His words stung. Recklessly, I hurled the first accusation I could think of at him.

'Oh, but you do? Then I'm sure you know all about why Hannover's been hanging around the old North Crater Charity Office on Blackwall Street.'

My heart leapt into my throat. Damnit, Bas was the last person I wanted to tell about that—after the way he and Ellery had treated me when I'd tried to tell them about Gabriel Tam. Typical me, being impulsive and blurting out the first thing that came into my head.

Bas frowned, shifting his weight back on his heels. His anger vanished in an instant. 'What? What's Hannover doing there?'

'Never mind,' I muttered.

'No, I do mind.' Bas took a step closer to me, eroding what little space had been between us to begin with. He loomed over me, and I had to resist the urge to back away. 'You're keeping secrets again.'

'*Again?*'

He glared.

'Contrary to what you think, my life doesn't revolve around informing you and Ellery of everything that goes on in this town.' I glowered up at him. 'In fact, I told you I was done with that.'

'You're done when we know everything.'

'Uh, I think not!' Now, I did back away, but it wasn't in fear. I could have strangled him, I was so angry. 'You have no right!'

'If you're talking about Hannover, yes I do.' Bas leered at me. 'You want to get mixed up with the Black Hands? You know what they do to their enemies. You'd make a pretty little slave—and don't even think that Hannover hasn't considered it.'

I shuddered. 'I'm not mixed up in anything, okay? I was visiting my friend who lives across the road from the NCC office, and I saw—I'm not even sure what it was, okay? And I tried to tell you and Ellery, but you didn't listen, of course, and you're not listening now, and I'm sure you won't believe me anyway—' I took a deep breath. My lungs ached. 'So just go and look yourself.'

Bas stared at me for a long moment, scrutinising my face. I hardly dared to breathe. Finally, the radio on his belt squelched, breaking the silence.

'Patrol four, report.'

Bas shot me a look. 'Off you go.'

Of course, fucking patronising arsehole. I was trying to help him out, and what did he do? Dismiss me like a child.

'Sure, whatever. Go chat to your cronies, then.'

I turned on my heel and stomped off.

FIVE

THE CONVERSATION WITH BAS bothered me for the rest of my day off, and well into Tuesday. I kept turning it over and over in my mind, unable to let go of it.

Why had I said that?

How had he provoked me so quickly?

What was going to happen now?

I should have been relieved. I'd tried to send Maddock to the North Crater Charity office, but nothing seemed to have come of that—at least from what I could tell. Maybe Bas would be able to get to the bottom of what was going on. Maybe the Iron Fists could put an end to Hannover's operation.

Maybe.

But I didn't feel relieved. I was wound up like a spring ready to release. I'd kept this secret for so long that I felt like it had eaten holes in me—and I couldn't help but think this was going to come back to haunt me somehow.

I struggled through my shift at the bar, my thoughts circling like vultures.

The bar was thrumming with activity that day. Anna was out, so I was on with Dana, which was good because she didn't know me that well, so she was the least likely to notice how distracted I was. I'd left her training Laura and taken refuge behind the bar.

Pouring drinks was monotonous work. We served plenty of different options, but most people ordered whiskey or ale. It made my job easy.

I'd just finished pouring another order and passed it off to Dana when Tom popped his head around the door. 'Harley, a quick word?'

I grimaced, butterflies starting up in my stomach. 'Sure, what's wrong?'

'Nothing, I just need to discuss stock with you.'

'Alright.' I untied my apron and followed him into the back hall. He led me to the office, a poky room filled to the brim with filing cabinets. There was just enough space for a desk against the back wall, and both it and the chair were covered in papers. Tom shut the door and moved to lean against the desk, clearing his throat.

'Sorry to pull you out, but it looked quiet.'

'Dana will manage for a few minutes,' I said.

He nodded.

'I wanted to ask you what you think of Laura.'

'Me?' I asked, stalling for time. I hated questions like that. Diplomacy was not my strong suit.

'You're the one who'll be working with her. I need people who can handle themselves on the bar.' He shot me a searching look. 'We all know it's not a walk in the park. She'll have to deal with the Cavanaughs and Rochesters, as well as the Fists, Aces, and the rest of that lot.'

'Sure.' I leant against the door, fiddling with the flaking paint. 'I guess she learnt the ropes quickly. She's a little quiet, but maybe that will improve after a few shifts.'

Tom hummed. 'What about you? I know you've had some… financial difficulties recently.'

'I'm still committed to my job!' I blurted hurriedly.

'Of course. I don't mean to imply that you're not.' He shuffled through a few papers before meeting my eyes again. 'I'll lay it to you straight. Brenda's decided to move on. We're down a person on the night shift. I need someone who's good at handling drunk customers. Keeping them in their place. Kayla suggested you.'

Damnit, Kayla.

'The night shift is only six hours,' I said.

'The pay is three NP extra per hour.'

I bit my lip. One third more than what I earned at the moment. *Appealing.* But working nights would mess with my entire schedule. I'd be going to work when Savannah got home. I'd be walking to and from work in the dark. I liked being out and about during the day—working nights was one of the things I had hated about the bunker.

'Can I think about it?'

'Of course.' Tom pushed off the desk. 'I'd appreciate it if you could give me your decision sooner rather than later, though.'

I nodded, my mind racing. I'd have to discuss the implications with Savannah. And there was something else…

'I already work Saturday nights. I wouldn't be available then.'

Tom frowned. 'I wasn't aware you had a second job.'

'It's a recent development.'

He nodded slowly. 'I'll take that into consideration.'

'Thanks.' I picked another flake of paint off the door. 'Where is Brenda going?'

'The auto garage, I believe,' Tom said. 'It's good for her. She has a good head for books. I'll have to find someone else to do ours.'

Not me. I hated maths.

'Maybe Laura knows how,' I suggested.

'Why don't you ask her?' Tom gestured to the door. I opened it and we stepped into the hall. 'Have a think then, and let me know,' he reiterated.

'I will. Thanks for the offer.'

Night shift. Damnit, where were these offers when I actually needed them? Now I seemed to be swimming in better prospects, and I was stuck.

I couldn't quit at the bunker.

Not without pissing off my fickle masters.

Damn it all to hell.

I wanted to go over to Brenda's and ask her about the new job straight away, but unfortunately, I was already fully booked for that evening. After cleaning the drip tray and wiping down the bar for the night shift, I tossed my apron in the laundry, donned my thick coat, and headed for the west side of town.

Bale Rocks was a small town, but for that, it did have several distinct areas. The lines on the map had been drawn by the gangs: north and east belonged to Sayle and the Iron Fists, west to Percival and the Aces, and south to the mayor. The centre was largely neutral territory, and Moriarty and the Black Hands had claimed the territory out of town to the south, meaning the mayor was hemmed in on all sides. The Black Hands were kept out of town because they worked with slavers— unfortunately, their territory overlapped with one of the two major roads from the south, so most deliveries had to come through them.

The rest came via the east road, from Crater's Edge, which was controlled by the Iron Fists.

In all things, the gangs held the power here. With enough digging, you could find their fingers in every construction project, every business, every casino, every brothel, every bar. What, and how much, they controlled determined how much power they had over the day-to-day decisions in Bale Rocks.

The Hawke and Tern was a pub on a side street in the southwest, bordering on both the mayor's and the Aces' territory. I felt as though all eyes were on me as I cut across the puddle-filled gravel lot and paused in front of the brown-painted front door.

A lone car rolled past me and vanished into the darkness. The pub's windows glowed with a warm, welcoming light.

Just go in.

Just get on with it.

My feet stayed rooted to the concrete.

A hundred bad decisions had landed me where I was today. In the grand scheme of things, this one didn't matter, but it still felt momentous. This was the moment when I would betray the Iron Fists.

Admittedly, it wasn't the Iron Fists I cared about, per se. But Ellery? Bas? I might not be on the best terms with them, but I still cared.

Bas would never forgive me for this.

Heavy-hearted, I let myself in the door. Music swelled out to meet me, an upbeat local tune played on an old—ailing—piano. The bar took up most of the back wall, the seating was haphazard, and the whole place had that sort of hazy golden glow that came from people smoking, a fire going in the hearth, and the warmth of having people around you.

It was nice. I wished it wasn't. It would only make this harder.

Hesitantly, I crossed the room towards the bar. The bartender was a ghostly pale man, his hair shaved on the sides and spiked into an impressive mohawk on top. He had bulging muscles, and his skin was covered in tattoos. He was talking to a lithe woman with a lip piercing, who wore an apron.

'You eating or drinking?' she called as I approached.

'Uh… drinking, I think.' I shuffled my feet. What was I doing? I was never this timid. 'I'm meeting someone.'

She jerked her head towards the bartender. 'Turner will take care of you.'

'Thanks.'

She left, her long blond hair flicking behind her as she walked. I turned to the bartender, who raised an eyebrow.

'What can I get you?'

In for a penny, in for a pound.

'Whiskey, please. Red label.'

'Coming right up.' Turner set a tumbler down and poured me two fingers. 'Rocks?'

I shook my head.

He slid the glass to me. 'Five NP.'

Peeling bills out of my purse reminded me of Irina. My stomach curdled. I never seemed to be able to escape; I bounced from one powerful master to the next.

'What's your name, then?' Turner leant on the bar, his T-shirt pulling taut over his thick arms.

I glanced around hopefully, sipping my drink. Hardwick didn't seem to be there yet. *Damn.* Guess I was making conversation.

'Um… Anna.'

'Anna, eh?' His expression was politely sceptical; he'd caught my moment of hesitation. *Oops.*

I schooled my expression, fighting the urge to fidget. 'You're Turner, right?'

'Yep.' He rolled his shoulders as though they were stiff. From fighting, maybe? 'You're new around here, aren't you?'

'I've never been here before.' I shrugged. 'My friend suggested it.'

'Yeah? Anyone I would know?'

'Maybe.' I turned away from him, feeling on edge. He was asking too many questions; his amber gaze was too sharp. Bar staff made excellent spies. They saw and heard everything. I was living proof.

I sipped my whiskey to steady my nerves. Behind me, the door finally swung open, letting in a blast of wind and a tall man clad in a bulky leather jacket.

Evander Hardwick strolled over to the bar, shucking his leather gloves as he approached. He was a weedy man with blond hair and icy blue eyes, not particularly prone to smiling.

Definitely not my favourite person in town.

When he saw me, he did smile. But it wasn't friendly.

'You're here. Good.' He nodded to Turner. 'The usual. We'll be in the back.'

'Got it.' Turner busied himself with Hardwick's drink. Hardwick turned to me. The light turned his blond hair to spun gold, but it couldn't melt the ice in his eyes.

'Glad to see you're punctual.'

'I would never miss such an important appointment.'

'Good to hear it.' Hardwick nodded coldly.

I swallowed and discretely rubbed my sweaty palms on my jeans. I was in way over my head.

For a long time, Hardwick's allegiances had been shrouded in mystery. I'd thought he worked for the Black Hands; Savannah had thought he worked for the mayor. In actual fact, he seemed to be working for everyone. I wasn't entirely sure whether his ultimate loyalty was to Percival and the Aces, but for now, that was the best I had to go on.

Whoever he did work for, I knew I couldn't trust him. He was the only person in this town who knew that I was the one who'd killed Gabriel Tam. He could ruin me with a single word to the wrong person.

And I was only as valuable as the intel I could provide him.

If it was just my life in the balance, I would run. I had, in fact, considered it. But to do that, I had to convince Savannah to go with me. If I left her behind, Hardwick would extract his pound of flesh from her, instead.

My stomach felt like a hard knot, but I was determined not to show any fear. I took another sip of my drink, staring defiantly up at Hardwick.

'So, how are we doing this?'

He accepted his drink and slid the cash onto the bar. 'This way.'

He led me through to another room, past mismatched chairs and tables, and then through a door marked 'staff only'. The pleasant atmosphere evaporated instantly. The air was cool back here, and the whitewashed walls lent the hall a sterile look. I preferred it that way.

We passed two women who gave us curious glances. Hardwick didn't acknowledge them, and I kept my head down. If I was recognised here, I was doomed.

'In here.' Hardwick opened a door to reveal some sort of office. A large wooden table dominated the room, covered in papers and half-empty glasses. There were three chairs squeezed around it, and in the corner was a drinks cabinet. He gestured me into a chair, then pulled out the chair beside me for himself.

'Let's begin.' Hardwick sipped his drink and set it down between the detritus on the table. 'You were at the bunker this weekend.'

I cleared my throat. 'Yes,' I said nervously.

'Taking a job there was not exactly the approach I had envisaged, but I supposed it's an adequate solution.'

I pressed my lips together. I knew exactly what he considered to be the *correct approach*.

'They aren't going to just trust me if I walk through their door, you know. I need a reason to be there.'

'As I said,' Hardwick steepled his fingers together, 'an adequate solution.'

'Uh-huh,' I muttered sourly.

'You are as formidable a dancer as your reputation implies.'

I lifted my head in surprise. 'You saw me?'

'Of course. Did you think I would miss your debut performance?'

I scowled. 'You know, if you can get in yourself, I don't see why you need me.'

A feral smile stretched Hardwick's lips. 'Because they don't trust me. But they trust you. Everyone falls for a pretty face.'

Great. And he wasn't going to let me forget it.

'That will take time,' I said.

'See that it doesn't.' He sipped his whiskey. 'I hope you have something for me tonight.'

His tone was deceptively mild. I ran over what I had learnt that night, most of it through dressing room gossip.

'There've been some financial difficulties.'

Hardwick waved his hand. 'You think that's news to me? Tam was well apprised of the Iron Fists' financial difficulties.'

I gritted my teeth and clenched my fingers around my glass. 'If he already told you everything—'

'That will not absolve you from the responsibility of doing your job.' Hardwick drummed his fingers against the table. 'Your job is to bring me new information.'

'It was my first night. I don't know what's new and what's old.'

'You're not trying hard enough.'

I could have snarled in his face. Not trying hard enough? I spent my entire fucking life trying hard enough. Screw him. 'If nothing I find out is going to be good enough for you, why did you bother in the first place? Just put a bullet in my head.'

Hardwick's placid expression didn't crack. 'I think you're more capable than you want to admit.'

Damn him.

'It's going to take me time to work my way in,' I pointed out.

Hardwick hummed mockingly. 'Time? No. Motivation? Yes.' He raised an eyebrow. 'How's your relationship with your sister these days?'

Ice slid down my spine. 'None of your business.'

'Maybe your position isn't clear to you yet. You work for me. If you don't want a bullet in your head—and your sister in my bed—then find a way to get the information I want,' Hardwick said.

'My sister would never sleep with you! She's too smart for that.'

He just smiled. 'I wouldn't bet on it.'

Ugh, fuck. I really, really needed to keep him away from Savannah.

'Bas and Jackson had a meeting in the back office after Bas's fight went wrong.'

Hardwick raised an eyebrow. 'Infighting isn't really the kind of thing I care about, either.'

It would help if he told me what he *did* want to know. I shook my head. 'Fine, then you won't care that there was someone else in the meeting, either.'

'Not unless it was someone important.'

'I don't know who it was—I didn't recognise the voice.' I paused for emphasis. 'But I don't think Bas knew he was there, either. It sounded like Jackson was conspiring with someone.'

At that, Hardwick did look intrigued for a second, before his expression went blank again. 'Something to consider. Is there anything else?'

I shook my head.

'Very well. That will do. On the whole, though, I hope next time you come better prepared.'

'If you told me what to look for, it would make my life easier,' I said.

'When you've earned that knowledge, it will be provided to you, and not before.' Hardwick looked me over from head to toe. 'Which seems unlikely to happen. We'll meet here again on Tuesday next week.'

'If I keep coming to the same place, people will get suspicious.'

He stood. 'That's your problem, not mine. Come on, I'll walk you out.'

Scowling, I downed my drink and stood to follow him.

Arsehole.

SIX

HARDWICK'S THREATS WEIGHED HEAVILY ON ME. I slept badly that night and was awake so early the next morning that I saw Savannah making breakfast.

'What are you doing up?' she asked in surprise as I stumbled out of the bedroom.

'Couldn't sleep.' I rubbed my eyes. 'What time is it?'

'Just gone six.' Savannah chewed her lip. 'Do you want something to eat?'

The thought of eating made my stomach churn. 'No thanks. I don't want to make you late for work.'

'Okay,' Savannah said in a small, disappointed voice.

Damnit.

'Actually, if you're offering… I could take something small.'

She smiled weakly. 'Alright, then. There's coffee on the stove if you want.'

I poured myself a cup and leant against the windowsill, trying to clear the morning grogginess. Work later was going to be a nightmare.

'If you don't want your sister in my bed…'

'Sav,' I said before I could stop myself, 'can I ask you something?'

'Mmhmm.'

'You know Evander Hardwick?'

Her shoulders stiffened.

'What about him?' she asked in a terse voice.

What about him indeed? I chewed over my words before saying in a carefully neutral tone, 'Have you seen him since… since that time we argued about him?'

Savannah didn't look up from the pan of scrambled eggs she was stirring. 'I don't spend my time hanging out with random men, Harley.'

'It's not an accusation,' I muttered, gripping the splintery windowsill to calm myself. 'I'm just curious.'

'Why?' she snapped.

What to tell her?

'I saw him a while back, with the mayor and a few other guys. At the bar.' Not a lie, actually. 'He asked about you.'

At that, Savannah did turn, her brow furrowing in surprise. 'Why would he do that?'

'I don't know.' I searched her gaze for any hint of deceit, but there didn't seem to be any. Hardwick had made it sound like he and Savannah had some kind of thing… but Savannah was dating Talbot. Savannah would never cheat—I believed in my sister fully on that point. If she said she hadn't seen Hardwick, I trusted her.

'Weird.' She turned back to the stove and took the pan off. 'He comes around the clinic every so often. You know how it is—the mayor likes to keep an active interest in it. Hardwick's usually the one poking his nose into things.'

'Does he talk to you?'

'Of course. He asks all sorts of questions.'

I cleared my throat, reaching over to pass her two plates from the counter. 'I mean, does he talk specifically to you? In a different way to the other doctors?'

'I… I don't know.' Savannah squared her shoulders, holding the pan in an oddly defensive posture. 'I don't pay attention to that stuff. Harley—you know I'm dating Greg.'

'I know.'

'Fine, then why all the questions?'

'No reason.' I put the plates down in front of her. 'I was just a bit worried about you, alright? I don't want to think that Hardwick is… perving on you, or something.'

'He's not.'

'Good, that's good.'

Savannah got back to plating the food, and we moved to the table. She tucked into her portion, but I picked at mine, thoughts still swirling around my head.

According to Savannah, there was no link between her and Hardwick outside of the clinic. Hardwick, however, had made it sound like there was one. I trusted Savannah—and I definitely didn't trust Hardwick. So, I needed to get to the bottom of what he thought he had on my sister which would get her to fall in line. Was he planning on just straight out threatening her? Did he know some awful secret? Or was he planning on trying to play us off against one another?

Whatever it was, I needed to get on top of this.

I swallowed a couple of bites. 'Would you ever go live in Crater's Edge?'

Savannah looked up from her plate. 'What? You're in a strange mood this morning.'

I shrugged. 'Just wondering. I know they offered you a job before. And Bale Rocks kind of sucks. Do you ever think about… just leaving?'

'But Bale Rocks is our home.' Savannah shifted uncomfortably. 'Besides… the clinic. I have a four-year contract with them. I can't just leave. They're short-staffed already.'

Of course, the clinic. Never mind my safety—never mind her own safety. All Savannah cared about was that stupid clinic.

'Yeah, don't worry. I guess it was just a stupid thought.'

'Do you want to leave?'

'Sometimes, yeah.'

'Where would you go?'

I shrugged. 'Dunno. Maybe Crater's Edge. One of the cities? There's got to be work somewhere.'

'You don't even have a plan!'

'I told you, it was just an idle thought.'

Savannah scowled. 'We can't just up and leave. We'd need money, we'd need to find somewhere to live… How would we even get to Crater's Edge? Surely you're not going to ask Ellery to drive us?'

'Alright, alright, I get it.' I was tired of the topic already; I wished I hadn't brought it up. 'I was just wondering. But you know, never mind. I'm going to go do my stretches.'

I was early to the training ground that morning, but even though I went through the motions of a dance warmup, I just didn't feel like actually dancing. I stretched my body out until it was loose and limber, then sat there doing the splits and staring at the grey sky.

It felt fucking pointless. Maybe I should just tell Savannah about the trouble I was in—she'd probably agree to leave if she knew we were in danger… But I couldn't bear the condescension I knew she'd hurl at me.

Reckless. Impulsive. You never think things through. If you'd just let me handle things, none of this would have happened.

Probably.

Sometimes I wondered if she was right. At least she had her life together. *Had* had her life together. Until she started hanging out with Talbot.

What did she see in him anyway?

There were plenty of men in this town. What made him special?

Then again, given the choice between him and Hardwick, I'd prefer Talbot. He was a pig, but he didn't have any weird plots up his sleeve. He might even protect Savannah from Hardwick if something happened to me.

I pushed that thought away. I didn't want to contemplate that possibility.

No, I'd be fine. Savannah would be fine. We'd get through this, just like we had everything else.

I heard footsteps and scrambled up to stand as Bas jogged over. He looked utterly focused, sweat dripping over his brow and making his T-shirt stick to him. Then he caught sight of me and a tremendous scowl crossed his face.

Great, someone had woken up on the wrong side of the bed this morning.

'Morning,' I said.

Bas grunted.

Oh, wow. He was in a really bad mood.

He jumped over the railing. 'Start warming up.'

'I've already finished.'

'Fine, let's get going.' He shifted into a fighting stance and threw a punch. I threw my hands up to block, my feet sliding on loose gravel.

'Woah, what the hell?'

'We're here to work.' Bas threw another punch, grunting with effort. I barely blocked it, my arm aching from the impact.

'What the hell is wrong with you?' I cried.

His next punch caught me in the breastbone. I yelled in pain, stumbling away from him. Bas pursued me across the cage.

'Time out! Holy, shit!' I rubbed my chest. *Fuck, that had hurt.* 'Is this a lesson or a beating?'

'Your enemies aren't going to give you timeouts,' Bas sneered.

'Yeah, fuck you too.' I shook my arms out and rubbed my chest again. 'I'm not Hannover, yeah? Lay off.'

A black cloud stole over Bas's expression. He was so furiously angry that it took my breath away.

'Get back to work,' he snapped.

'Alright, alright.' Clearly, there wasn't going to be any idle chitchat *today*.

As I stepped back into the middle of the cage, my lace caught under my boot and I felt it loosen. I sighed and crouched down.

'Damnit.'

'Get on with it, Harley,' Bas said impatiently.

'I just have to retie my boot.'

'I expect you to arrive ready.'

He said it so pointedly that I knew it was a direct attack. Okay, what was going on? He was angry with me—what the hell had I done now?

'What the fuck is your problem?'

Bas turned an absolutely lethal glare on me. 'What's my problem? I went to the NCC office yesterday.'

'You went?' I stood up hastily. Really? He'd gone? He hadn't mentioned it yesterday, and I'd thought maybe he wasn't going to go. Was he angry because he'd seen the slave pen? 'Did you see—'

'Do you think this is a joke?' Bas snapped.

My mouth dropped open. *What?*

He continued, hurling every word at me like a rock. 'I pushed you, so you gave me a fake tipoff? Does it amuse you to send me running all over town on a wild goose chase?'

'Fake?' I parroted. What the hell was going on?

'Hannover wasn't there, Harley. He's never been there.'

A chill ran down my spine. 'I didn't expect you to see him. You were meant to look inside. You did go inside, right? Did you see the slave pen?'

Bas crossed his arms. 'Of course I went inside. The charming lady from the NCC was quite happy to tell me all about their activities and who all works for them. Why would she have anything to hide?'

Oh, for fuck's sake. 'Because she's working for the Black Hands?'

'Don't be ridiculous,' Bas snapped. 'It's not funny anymore, Harley. If you keep messing me around, then this is the last lesson you'll be getting.'

I stared at him, disbelief and betrayal mixing in my chest. What the hell? I had never anticipated this result.

Telling Bas was meant to solve my problems.

What had gone wrong? Had Hannover moved the operation? Or had Bas just not looked properly?

Because he hadn't believed me. Because he'd rather believe the professional receptionist for the NCC over a washed-up waitress-slash-dancer.

Of course. Feeling cold all over, I said, 'Fine, don't teach me if you don't want to. Far be it for me to force you.'

Bas flicked his fingers. 'Off you go, then.'

'Yeah, I will.' I grabbed my coat and vaulted over the railing. 'You're an arsehole. You think you can talk to me however you like? I hope you get what's coming to you one day.'

If anything, Bas looked even angrier. 'If you want to talk consequences, I think you'll find that a very unpleasant conversation, Harley.'

His tone sent a shiver down my spine. Did he think I didn't know that?

Fuck him. I should have stayed away in the first place.

'Goodbye, Bas,' I said coldly, before turning and walking away.

My anger followed me for the remainder of the day, and by that evening I was resolved: if Bas refused to believe me, I would just have to find proof.

Find it and show it to him.

I was tired of the way he spoke to me, the way he treated me, the way he never believed me. I had seen Hannover and the slaves. I knew exactly what I'd seen. I also knew that Bas's anger issues had very little to do with me—and I was tired of him taking them out on me.

That evening after work, I headed over to Brenda's place. I'd been meaning to speak to her anyway, ever since Tom had dropped the bombshell on me about her leaving Krani's. Now was as good a time as any.

I made my way down to Blackwall Street. The darkness seemed to press in on me—winter was always darker, and it didn't help that today the wind was howling through the streets and battering every exposed surface like it wanted to upend trees, buildings, cars, and anything else it touched. When I got to Brenda's building her lights were still on, the yellow glow creeping around the curtains to illuminate the cracked paving beneath my feet. I rang the doorbell, and inside a metallic *dong-dong* sounded. As I waited, I flicked a glance over my shoulder at the building across the road. The lights were off.

Unease churned in my stomach.

The door swung open to reveal a stout woman with warm brown skin and voluminous dark brown curls piled on top of her head. She was dressed comfortably in baggy sweatpants, obviously not intending on going out again today.

Brenda squinted at me. 'Harley? What are you doing here at this time of night?'

I sucked in a breath. 'I… I wanted to say hi.'

'Hi?' she asked, confused. 'It's eleven o'clock!'

'I know… I…' I swallowed. 'I just wanted to talk to you. Tom said you found a new job.'

'Oh.' Brenda smiled sadly. 'Oh, love. Come in, then.'

She took my wrist and tugged me inside—and straight into a hug.

'It's been a while, hasn't it?' Brenda stroked the back of my head.

I breathed in the smell of Mum. It was hard to pinpoint exactly what the scent was, but all mothers seemed to have it, and it made me miss my own mother something fierce.

Tears pricked my eyes. 'Don't go. I'll miss you.'

'Nah. You won't even realise I'm gone.' She squeezed my shoulders and pulled back. 'You'll be fine without me. Besides, you can always come over and visit. You know that.'

'It won't be the same,' I mumbled.

'Yes, it will. Come down for a tea.'

I shouldn't. I was here for a reason. But I let her coax me down the stairs anyway.

'We have to be quiet. The boys are sleeping,' she whispered.

I nodded. 'Okay.'

Brenda's flat was mostly in darkness, but the main room was illuminated by a small lamp in the kitchen. Brenda made her way over and set the kettle on the stove.

'Have a seat.'

'Thanks.' I pulled myself onto a stool and leant against the countertop. Brenda bustled around the kitchen, and a few minutes later she served us both mugs of bitter tea and a plate of biscuits.

'Okay.' She heaved herself into her seat, sighing. 'Feels like I've been on my feet all day.'

'I'm sorry.' Maybe I shouldn't have come by so late. 'I can go.'

'No, no, don't worry.' She waved a hand carelessly. 'Tell me. What's eating you?'

'It's nothing, really.'

Brenda shot me an amused smile. 'Love, you're not fooling anyone. Is this about your new job? Or is it about your young man who you're not talking to anymore?'

I felt my cheeks heating up. Brenda had a way of cutting right to the heart of the matter.

'It's… it's complicated.' I sighed. 'I needed money for rent. But being back at the bunker is…'

'Complicated?' Brenda smiled kindly at me and picked up her tea to sip it. 'I think you're brave. I couldn't work in a place like that.'

'It's not that different from being in the bar, except the men are sweatier and the innuendos are cheaper.'

Brenda practically snorted her tea. 'Oh, *Harley.*' She shook her head, covering her mouth to muffle her laughs. 'Shhh, you'll make me wake the kids.'

'Sorry,' I said innocently.

We exchanged grins. I took a biscuit and nibbled on it.

'So is this about your man, then?' Brenda pried.

'It's… Maybe.' I dipped the edge of the biscuit in my tea and stuffed it in my mouth to stall for time. Brenda waited patiently whilst I chewed. Finally, I muttered, 'I told him about Hannover's activities across the road.'

Brenda frowned. 'Was that wise?

I shrugged helplessly. 'Have you told anyone?'

She grimaced. 'I don't want trouble. You know what happens to people who get involved with that sort of thing—and I have the boys to think of.'

'I know.'

'What did you tell him?'

I traced the ridges on the table with a finger. 'Just that Hannover had been here and I thought something was going on inside…' I trailed off.

'And?'

'He didn't find anything. He doesn't believe me.'

Brenda pursed her lips. 'Love…'

'He was so angry! He treated me like the entire thing was a waste of time, like I lied to him for a joke!' I took another biscuit and stabbed it angrily into my tea. 'He's such an arsehole. Would it kill him to be nice?'

'Are you angry because he didn't believe you, or are you angry because he didn't *believe you?*' Brenda asked.

'Because he didn't believe me!' I paused. 'What's the difference?'

'You know.' She helped herself to another biscuit. 'Is it because he's not going to do anything about it, or because of how he treated you?'

'I…' I stared at my hands, idly tracing the ridges in the tabletop. 'Does that matter?'

'You tell me.'

Fuck. As soon as she said it, I knew it did matter. What had really hurt was that Bas had acted like I'd been pranking him—he hadn't taken me seriously.

'He doesn't see me as an equal,' I grumbled. 'He thinks I'm a silly little girl.'

'You know people like that aren't worth the effort you put into them, love,' Brenda chided.

'I know.' I sighed. 'I know, but I can't seem to stay away, either. I don't know why.'

'Yes you do.'

I glanced at her. She raised an eyebrow. 'You're not that stupid, Harley.'

'I like him,' I admitted. 'And I don't know why. He's horrible.'

Brenda reached over the table and patted my hand. 'He's trying to survive in a shitty world, just like you are. Maybe he isn't coping quite as well. There must be something good about him, right? Or you wouldn't like him.'

It was on the tip of my tongue to tell her there was nothing good about him—but that would be a lie. There were plenty of good things about Bas: loyalty, steadfastness, inner strength, principles. 'He just doesn't show it to *me.*'

'Then the way I see it, you've got two choices,' Brenda said. 'Either forget about him or give him a reason to respect you.'

'Kind of hard to do that when he's constantly angry with me.' I scowled.

'Have you tried talking to him about that?'

'That just makes him angrier.'

Brenda smiled weakly. 'I'd give up on him. But what do I know? I married my childhood sweetheart—and look how he turned out.'

I grimaced. Brenda's husband was a drunk who frittered away money faster than she could bring it in.

'Maybe we should marry each other.'

Brenda laughed. 'The boys would love that. You can be their cool mum.' She winked. 'You should get home before it gets too late, love. You shouldn't be out on the streets at night.'

'I know.'

'And your bloke—if you can't have a calm discussion with him, and you can't show him you're worthy of respect, he's not the man for you. Don't kid yourself that he'll change, Harley. They never do.'

'I know.'

She patted my hand. 'Of course you do. Finish your tea.'

'Can I look upstairs before I go?'

Brenda's expression twisted. She sighed gustily. 'I'd love to tell you yes… but they came last week and boarded the windows up.'

'Damn.'

Brenda gave me a savvy look, like she had known all along that was the real reason I'd come over here. Oops.

'Come into the bar sometime and I'll buy you a drink,' I suggested. 'And thanks for the advice.'

'No thanks necessary.' Brenda finished her tea and shooed me up. 'Thank me by taking care of yourself.'

'I will.'

We headed to the door. Brenda pulled it open. The street was bathed in silvery moonlight, like an old-world black-and-white photograph. I paused, reluctant to leave.

'I'll miss you.'

'I'll still be right here, love. It's not as though we ever work together anyway.' Brenda ruffled my hair. 'You can visit any time. I love you. The boys love you. The dog—'

'—loves me. Even so. It won't be the same without you.' I shook my head and hugged her again quickly, before backing out the door. 'I'd better go, or I'll be here all night.'

'I don't mind.' Brenda smiled. 'But if you're going, go. You shouldn't be walking around after dark.'

I walked after dark every night—how else was I going to get home? Some of the other waitresses had ride-shares or took taxi-trucks, but I'd never been that fortunate.

I smiled weakly. 'Alright. Goodnight.'

'Goodnight, love.'

I could feel Brenda's gaze on my back as I exited and took the few steps down to street level. I turned to wave to her. She waved back and finally shut the door.

I turned back to the road, and my gaze settled uneasily on the building across the road. It was an apartment block, one of the more modern ones, its exterior painted a dirty white. Several of the units had been converted into businesses, with signs tacked up in the windows. There was a gun shop on the ground floor with burglar guards over its windows. And on the first floor was the main office of the North Crater Charity.

Or at least it had been.

A few weeks ago, Brenda and I had discovered that Moriarty and the Black Hands had taken over the office and were keeping slaves there. I didn't know how long they'd been doing it—not long enough that the rumours had started to spread around town.

But too long anyway.

Our town had always been safe. It was the benefit of living in a community; we could protect one another. Slavers picked off small villages, or people living on the outskirts of society. They went for the easy targets.

Not within the town.

There had always been someone to stop them.

The Iron Fists, the mayor, the other gangs. Someone.

Except now there didn't seem to be anyone doing it.

Even Bas hadn't found anything out—not that he'd tried.

So I was the only person left.

I glanced both ways and started across the road. My heart was racing in my chest. I had no idea what I was going to do, but I felt anxious and scared anyway, just being near the place.

'You'd make a pretty little slave and don't even think Hannover hasn't

considered it.'

Bas had been angry with me, for sure, but there was truth in his words anyway. Men like Hannover thought women only had one worthwhile quality.

I'd do anything to avoid becoming a slave.

And yet here I was, risking everything.

The lights were off on the first floor. The entire building was silent, in fact. Hopefully, that meant there was no one here. Hopefully, that meant I could take a look around without getting caught.

Hopefully.

The front door didn't lock. In older buildings, they almost never did. The handle depressed under my fingers, and I swung the door inwards. I felt like I'd swallowed a rock.

Just a peek.

I crept into the lobby and started up the stairs. The building was as dark and silent as a tomb; my footsteps sounded terribly loud on the stairs.

There were two doors on the second floor, each with a logo painted on the door: the NCC on one side, and a freight company on the other side. I approached the NCC's door.

North Crater Charitable Organisation

Head Office

Office hours: 9 am-5 pm, Mon-Fri

With any luck, that meant the office would be empty. With my heart in my mouth, I worked a bobby pin out of my hair and snapped it in half.

Picking locks was practically an inborn skill in our community. Years ago, in primary school, we had entertained ourselves by picking locks, hitting cans with slingshots, and drawing on our arms to imitate tattoos. As kids, those things had been cool.

Hopefully, I still remembered how.

I worked the bobby pin into the lock, gritting my teeth as I felt for the pins.

'Come on,' I whispered. 'Come on!'

Snap!

Damnit. I pulled the bobby pin out and shoved it in my pocket, then retrieved another from my hair. I only had a few of them—this had to work.

Breathing slowly to stay calm, I began to twist it. My fingers shook as I felt for the pins, gently wiggling them—

Thud, thud, thud. Click.

Something cold and hard touched my temple a moment before a man said softly, 'Wrong floor.'

My heart plunged to take up residence somewhere in the basement. The bobby pin fell from my suddenly nerveless fingers with a tiny clatter as my nose was assaulted by the scent of gun oil.

It was Hannover.

I didn't have to look—couldn't, in fact—because my entire body had frozen as still as a statue. I would have recognised that cruel, sing-song tone anywhere.

'You're right.' My voice trembled. 'I should have stopped at the gun shop on my way up.'

'Harley Benoit.' The gun barrel drifted down my cheek, before tucking under my chin and turning my head so I was facing Hannover. His face was a map of bruises and cuts. 'Fancy meeting you here.'

I swallowed. He was smiling, and I suddenly knew exactly how a fly must feel when caught in a spider's web. I was *fucked.*

'H-Hannover,' I whispered.

His smile grew. 'Away from the door, love.'

I backed away a step. Hannover moved with me, sliding between me and the door and keeping the gun firmly in place. He crunched the broken bobby pin beneath his boot before kicking it aside. 'What would a lovely lady like you be doing here?'

'N-nothing. I…' I had no excuse. My mind was as blank as a fresh sheet of paper. I stared at him, feeling terror rising in me like a river about to burst its banks.

'You…?' he prompted.

I shook my head.

'Shall I take a guess?' By the look in his eyes, it didn't matter what I said. Hannover's dark brown eyes were lit with feral excitement. He had me in his sights, and I was never getting free. Every one of Bas's warnings rattled through my brain at high-speed, too fast for me to grasp. 'I guess… you fancied yourself a bit of a hero, hmm?'

I shook my head again, though I wasn't sure what I was disagreeing with.

'Please… let me go.'

'Let you go?' Hannover chuckled. 'Love, you're in Moriarty's territory. I think you're begging for the wrong thing.'

'Bas will know. He'll come after me.' It was a desperate lie. I was clutching at straws.

Hannover clucked his tongue. 'Oh, I don't doubt he'll know. But will he really come after you? Are you sure?' He ran the pistol over my face again, before using it to flick my hair out from under my coat. 'I think we both know Bas is more scared of me than in love with you.'

In love with me? Hysterical laughter rose in my throat, and I had to tamp it down. Bas didn't even like me, let alone love me.

'No, Bas isn't coming to your rescue. Now Marco Ellery, he would have… but judging by recent events, you seem to have cut ties with that one. Really not a smart move.' He drew the gun back and aimed it at my face. My mouth went dry, and my heart lurched into overdrive. My mind was racing. There had to be a way out of this…

'Look, I won't tell anyone—'

Hannover shook his head in mock disappointment. 'What are you going to tell them? You bumped into me in the stairwell of an apartment block? Not exactly breaking news, love.'

'You think that's all I know?' Hannover's gaze narrowed. I plunged on, desperation making me reckless. 'I know you're keeping slaves in there. I've seen you entering and leaving. I know—I know that you schemed this up with the mayor, didn't you? Hardwick's your contact. The mayor is letting you take slaves in exchange for your support against the Iron Fists!'

I felt like a mad woman, and yet it all fit. All of the clues suddenly made sense: Hardwick's mysterious allegiances, the mayor's cryptic conversation with Rochester and Cavanaugh a few months back. *Oh. Oh, God.* My vision swam as horror overwhelmed me. Hannover jerked the gun back up.

'And how would you know about that?'

'I hear things.' My voice shook.

'You hear things?' He laughed, long and dark. 'Oh love, you aren't very clever, are you? What's to stop me from just shooting you right now?'

Panic clawed its way up my throat. 'I—I'm an informant for Percival!' I blurted out.

'Oh?' Hannover raised his eyebrows. 'And why should I care?'

'I have an in with Percival and with Sayle. I've been passing information—I could do the same for you. I—you know—everyone trusts a pretty face.'

Hannover chuckled again. 'Oh, so that's how it is? You are quite the little double-crosser, aren't you?'

Was it working? I could barely speak; there seemed to be an overwhelming pressure on my chest that made forming words quite impossible.

'Very well.' Hannover lowered the gun, flicking the safety back on. He tapped it carelessly against his palm. 'I think you're right. In fact, I know exactly who trusts a pretty face the most.'

He smiled ruthlessly. I skittered back a step, wishing I'd run, wishing I'd never come here in the first place. Was it too late to leave town? How far would I need to go before Hannover couldn't track me down? Was there a hole deep and dark enough to hide me from him?

'Sebastian really doesn't know what a little worm he's caught, does he?' Hannover shook his head. 'Fine, then. You can go.'

'I—I can?'

'But first...' He looked me up and down, his eyes invasive, as though he was looking beneath my skin. 'Kiss me.'

'What? No!'

'No? I really don't think you're in a position to say no right now.'

Bile rose in my throat. 'Why would I kiss you?'

'To seal the deal.'

I was going to puke all over his shoes. I swallowed hard, staring at him in horror. 'Why?'

Hannover shrugged. 'Maybe I want to see what the hype is about.'

I gagged. 'There's no *hype*.'

Smirking, he tapped his lips. 'Then I suppose you'd prefer a bullet in the head. The dead can't tell tales, can they, Harley Benoit.'

Stomach churning, I took one step forwards. Then another. I closed the gap between us and went up on tiptoes.

I couldn't do it.

Bas popped into my head.

I couldn't die, either. Not before making up with him. Not without making sure Savannah was safe.

Swallowing a mouthful of bile, I pressed my lips to Hannover's.

His lips were chapped and rough. His stubble was scratchy. He brought a hand up and gripped my hair, forcing me to stay in place for several seconds before he released me.

I stepped back. He was watching me, his eyes glinting wickedly.

'Off you go. I'll be in contact.'

My pulse thudded in my ears, and my breath came in short, sharp gasps. I turned and sprinted away.

What had I done?

SEVEN

A BOISTEROUS LAUGH SHATTERED the peace of the bar. The glass I was holding slipped out of my fingers, bounced off the edge of the counter, and hit the floor with a crash, shattering on impact. Glass went everywhere.

'Fuck!' I gasped.

'Harley?' Laura rounded the bar and headed over to me.

'Don't walk here—there's glass.'

She paused, hovering on the balls of her feet. 'Are you okay? What happened?'

'I'm okay.' I wasn't. My heart was racing, and my throat felt like I'd tried to swallow rocks. 'It just slipped. Didn't mean to cause a panic.'

I grabbed the dustpan and brush and hastily swept up the shards of glass, tipping them into the bin. When I straightened up, Kayla had reached the bar.

I'd arrived that afternoon to find Kayla on—where Anna was, I had no idea. If any of the rest of us missed as many shifts as she did, we'd be out on our arses. The privilege of being the owner's niece, I supposed.

'It's fine.' I stashed the dustpan under the counter and dusted my hands off on my apron. 'It was just a glass.'

Kayla squinted at me. 'Laura, can you handle the table by the window for a sec?'

'Oh, sure.' Laura shot a worried glance at me as she squeezed past Kayla. I pretended not to notice.

'Are you sure she's ready?' I asked Kayla in a low voice once Laura was out of hearing.

'I'm more worried about you right now. You're jumpy as fuck.'

'I'm not,' I denied.

'You are. You keep looking over your shoulder, and that's the third thing you've dropped.' Kayla's brown eyes swept over me. 'You're not on drugs, are you?'

'What? No!'

'Good, because I know what Sayle's lot feed their girls to keep 'em loyal.'

I winced. So Kayla knew I was dancing again too. Word spread fast around here.

'It's just a job. I needed the money.'

'Mm-hmm. I know how that goes. It's just a job for me, up at the casino, too. Nod, smile, serve drinks, don't tell no one what you saw or heard, right?'

I'd forgotten Kayla worked at one of the casinos—I didn't know which one, but it didn't matter much. Percival controlled all of them, eventually.

'I'm fine,' I repeated. I sounded like a broken record. 'It's just temporary.'

Kayla looked politely sceptical. She brushed her braids over one shoulder and pursed her lips. 'Let's swap. I'll man the bar for a bit.'

I'd asked to tend the bad so I had an excuse to hide from people—and so that I wouldn't have to pretend to be happy—but that wasn't working too well. Maybe being busy would be a better distraction.

'Alright.'

She waved me out of the way. I slipped out from behind the bar and grabbed the tray she'd discarded on the bar top.

'Start with table seven. They need a refill.'

I nodded and took off into the room.

My mind felt like it was scattered in a dozen different directions, and no matter what I did, I couldn't get myself to focus. Every time I tried, Dean Hannover would pop back into my head, and I'd start thinking of things I should have said, or done, or tried, or not done, or—

Damnit, Harley.

Why the fuck had I gone to the NCC office? Why couldn't I let sleeping dogs lie?

Why did I care so much what Bas thought of me?

On the surface, going had been the right decision: someone needed to know what the Black Hands were up to.

But I had been ill-equipped to be that someone, and like usual, I'd fucked it up.

If only I'd never found out about Hannover and the slaves in the first place.

Don't think like that.

Heavy footsteps rang out in the tiled lobby. *Hannover?* My hands shook, the tray tilting dangerously. I righted it with a grimace. Briggs appeared in the doorway.

Oh no.

I almost puked right then and there. Instead, I took a quick step back, dragging in deep breaths to keep myself from panicking.

Briggs's gaze settled on me, his smile pure malevolence.

Oh God, he knows.

That was stupid. He couldn't possibly know. Could he? Had Hannover told? But why would he do that? Still, I couldn't shake the feeling. The hairs on the back of my neck stood on end; my fingers and toes tingled with panic.

Briggs knew something.

'Good evening, kitten,' he drawled. 'Fine evening, isn't it?'

'Is it?' I squeaked.

'Oh, absolutely.' He nodded to a table. 'I'll just sit there, if that's alright?'

'Alright?' I gasped.

Briggs strolled over to the table. I followed him like a lost puppy.

Pull it together, Harley.

I couldn't let him get to me, after everything.

He sat, stretching his legs out.

'Wh-what can I get you?' I asked, turning his water glass over to give my hands something to do.

'A whiskey. Top shelf.' I glanced at him. He smirked. 'I'm celebrating.'

'Celebrating?' I echoed.

'Yes, you know. Good times, good people.' He leant back, radiating smugness.

I didn't know. What good times? Was it something I was supposed to know? I took a step back, then remembered my job.

'That'll be five NP.'

Briggs passed me a fiver, his eyes never leaving my face. My skin crawled.

What was going on?

I retreated to the bar, my hands shaking.

'Top shelf,' I mumbled, passing Kayla the cash.

She frowned. 'You look like you're about to pass out.'

'I'm fine. Briggs is just behaving weird.'

Kayla pursed her lips. 'Want me to handle him?'

If I asked her to do that, it would look like I was hiding.

'No thanks.' I shook my head.

'Alright, then.' She set a glass on the counter and poured two fingers of our top shelf whiskey. 'He's watching you.'

'Great.'

First Hannover, now Briggs.

I was so fucked.

By the end of my shift, I felt so wrung out I could have slept for a week. I let myself out the back door, scuffing my feet against the pockmarked asphalt as I rounded the side of the hotel. A freezing wind whipped leaves and rubbish up and blew under my coat and my knitted scarf. Winter was almost on us, and we'd barely had a month of autumn. The long, cold winters were the worst—you felt like it would never end, like it would never get any better.

My feet hit the cobblestones. The square looked gloomy and foreboding in the darkness. No streetlights tonight.

A car horn cut through the silence. I jumped and stumbled, my heart leaping into my throat. *Holy fuck.*

HONK! HONK!

I whipped around. The vehicle was parked outside the front steps of the hotel, in the puddle of light from the lobby. I was so tired, it took me several seconds to register what I was seeing.

Matte grey paint, covered in dents and scratches. A patched-up roll cage, and a neat shatter pattern in one of the rear windows.

It was Theo's truck.

I was moving before I'd even processed the thought, sprinting towards the truck. He popped open the cab, tumbled out, and pulled me into a hug.

'THEO! Oh my God, I've missed you!'

'I missed you too, Harley baby.' He scooped me off the ground, swinging me until my bum hit the seat and we were almost on eye level. Theo was really tall. He had curly brown hair, brown skin, and eyes so dark they were almost black, flecked with gold. His arms, neck, hands, and pretty much every scrap of exposed skin were covered in tattoos. And he was smiling from ear to ear.

'I have fucking missed you,' he declared, pressing his forehead to mine as he hugged me. 'How are you?'

The lump in my throat made it hard to speak. I'd dreamt of this day so much, but now it was here, I had no idea what to do.

'Great,' I whispered.

'Harley?' Theo pulled back, his gorgeous eyes boring into my own. 'What's wrong?'

I blinked, my eyes stinging suddenly. 'Nothing.' I didn't want to cry all over Theo the first time I saw him in months. What a shitty reunion that would be.

'Harley…'

I leant back a little, blinking furiously. 'I'm fine. I'm okay. I missed you so much.'

Theo bit his lip, studying my face, thoroughly unconvinced.

'I'm fine,' I insisted. 'Anyway, how are you? You've been gone months. You better not have gotten shot this time!'

Theo sighed and shoved his hands in the pockets of his skin-tight jeans. 'Alright. And no, I wasn't shot.'

'But?'

'No buts. I wasn't shot, I wasn't stabbed.' He grimaced. 'Maybe roughed up a tiny bit, once or twice, but that's par for the course—'

'*Theo.*'

'It wasn't bad! I've been trying to resolve a few issues with deliveries from Crater's Edge, seeing as we can't go through Moriarty at the moment, and TSE tried to give me trouble. Just the usual.'

I bit the inside of my cheek. 'The usual' could mean anything from a smooth drive through to Crater's Edge—which was around three hours on a good day—to being held at gunpoint whilst someone did a cavity search. Or running into slavers. Or someone shooting out the tyres of your car and having to walk through the wasteland. Or, or, or…

'Breathe, Harley baby.' Theo grinned and ran his knuckles over my arm. 'I'm here. I know it was ages. Hop in—I'll give you a lift home and we can catch up.'

'Alright,' I mumbled.

Rather than climb out, I swung my legs into the car and climbed over the centre console. Theo hopped in after me, folding his lanky body into the space. His truck was a bubble of warmth, noise, and comfortable disorder. The radio was playing Pre-Crash rock, the footwell was filled with an assortment of food wrappers, maps, binoculars, and the other junk that accumulated when Theo was off on a long run, and a bag had spilt clothes over the back seat. Theo lived out of his car for weeks on end, so it was no surprise.

I wriggled out of my coat as Theo gunned the engine.

'When did you get back?'

Theo turned the radio down to a more conversational level. 'Two hours ago. I pretty much unloaded and came straight to you.'

A warm feeling blossomed in my chest. 'Wow,' I croaked, 'I must be special.'

'The specialest.' He prodded my leg. 'But now tell me everything I missed. What's this I hear about you dancing in the bunker again?'

I squirmed. 'Who told you that?'

'Briggsy.'

The name sent a shudder through me. Briggs was the last person I wanted to think about right now. 'Let's not talk about that.'

'Harley…'

'Seriously. You know I hate Briggs.'

For a few seconds, Theo stayed focused on the road. His posture was stiff. Finally, he said in a dark voice, 'I don't want to hear my best friend's news second-hand from Briggs and Ellery.'

Irritation started to rise up in me like floodwater. 'It's hardly my fault that you spoke to them first.'

'I'm talking to you *now*.' Theo glanced at me, his eyes unreadable in the darkness. 'Come on, Har. You were doing well. Why'd you go back there?'

His gaze made me feel very small. Hunching my shoulders, I muttered, 'Irina put my rent up.'

'For fuck's sake,' Theo hissed.

The words hung between us. The atmosphere felt unpleasantly tense—this wasn't how I'd pictured my reunion with Theo going at all.

'Do you need any help?' he asked quietly.

'No. I'm taking care of it.'

'You shouldn't have to dance in the bunker, Har. It's exploitative. If I'd been here—'

'It is what it is,' I cut him off flatly. Even if he'd been here, I would not have taken his help. I looked after myself.

Besides, it wasn't as though he could have helped with Gabriel Tam and Evander Hardwick. That was my cross to bear.

Theo set his jaw and stared out the windscreen as we drove through the silent streets. Between the rain and the cold, our streets were in even worse shape than usual; the car bounced through potholes and over cracks. The only sound was the radio playing Pre-Crash rock. It felt like we were the only two people in the world.

The atmosphere grew heavier and heavier until I couldn't bear it anymore.

'How long are you here for?' I asked.

Theo relaxed a little. In a cheerier tone, he said, 'Sayle wants all hands on deck at the moment, so I think I'll be hanging around for at least the next month!'

'That's great!'

'Mm-hmm, so I'll be seeing all of your upcoming performances—'

'Yuck!'

'—and judging them.' He side-eyed me. 'Lots of judgement. No free passes for not pointing your toes.'

I had to smile. Theo and I had attended dance classes together as children; it was where we'd met and become friends. Thinking about it made me feel rather nostalgic for simpler times. Before he got kicked out by his dad and joined the gang. Before my dad died and I had to take over earning money.

'Just so long as I can judge your fights too.'

'Who says I'm going to be fighting? Maybe I've reformed since I hung out with all the goodie-goodies in Crater's Edge.'

I rolled my eyes. 'Uh, no you didn't.'

Theo hummed, pretending to think. 'Nah, you're right, I didn't.'

I giggled. Some of the tension ebbed out of the car. We'd reached my street, and Theo pulled up in front of my building.

'When's your next shift in the bunker?'

'Saturday night.'

'Want me to pick you up?'

A weight slid off my shoulders. This, at least, was an offer I was safe to accept.

'If you don't mind.' The taxi-trucks would only take me to the outskirts of town, and from there it was a long walk to the old station—long and dangerous.

'Course not.' Theo turned to look at me, his dark eyes glinting with sincerity. 'Look—I know I've been gone for ages, but if you need anything—anything at all—'

'I'm fine, Theo.'

'I know you keep saying that, but I also know you wouldn't be back at the bunker unless it was serious.' Theo shot me a searching look. 'You know you can tell me anything, Harley baby.'

I swallowed. His gaze was so sincere. Theo cared. He was maybe the only person left in this godforsaken town who actually cared about my well-being. I knew I could tell him anything.

Tam almost killed me. Hardwick and Hannover are blackmailing me. I'm in over my head and I'm scared.

The words were on the tip of my tongue… But I couldn't get them past my lips. Fear wrapped around my chest like a vice. I could barely breathe.

I swallowed again.

'If anything comes up, I promise I will.'

Theo stared at me for several long seconds. I'd hesitated too long, and now he didn't believe me. I could read it on his face, in his suddenly tense body language, in the way he was studying me as though he could see into my skull. My stomach seemed to twist in on itself, and nausea rose in my throat.

'Alright,' he said quietly.

A chasm seemed to open between us. I was stuck on the opposite side, and I had no idea how to cross it. *Help me,* I wanted to say—but it was too late.

'I'm going to head up,' I said instead. 'I'm exhausted.'

'Alright. I'll see you soon.'

'Yeah.' I leant over the console and hugged him hard. Theo squeezed my shoulders until his fingers dug in.

'Missed you.'

'I missed you too,' I mumbled into his neck.

I pulled away, fighting tears, and jumped out of the car. I could feel his gaze on my back as I hurried inside.

EIGHT

LAURA SAGGED AGAINST THE BAR beside me and dropped her tray on the counter. 'Is it always like this on Saturdays?'

'This?' Dana asked wryly, plopping her own tray down in front of Anna. 'This is tame. Four whiskeys for table seven.'

Anna grabbed a bottle and glasses and set to pouring.

'It gets worse?' Laura asked. She looked as tired as I felt.

'It's gonna be crazy once the merchants' market starts next week.' Dana fixed me with a glance. 'No rest for the wicked, eh, Harley?'

I rolled my eyes. 'Yeah, yeah.'

I grabbed a jug of water and rounded the bar. Dana fell into step with me.

'You're moping.'

'Uh, no.' I reached table nine and fixed a smile on my face. Dana watched primly as I refilled their glasses and took their orders. When I returned to the bar, she cornered me again.

'You are moping, and I bet there's a boy involved.'

'What boy?' Anna asked.

'There's no boy,' I said.

'Yes, there is,' Dana said. 'I spoke to Kayla yesterday, and even she agrees. And you know Kayla's a ball-buster.'

'Two ales for table nine,' I told Anna. I lifted the whiskeys she'd poured onto Dana's tray. 'Go do your job.'

'Tell me your boy's name.'

'There *isn't* a boy!'

'You're not married, are you?' Laura asked, leaning over the counter.

'No!' I yelped.

'It'd take a hell of a guy to keep Harley happy.' Dana smirked.

'I don't know, I think she's overdue some romance in her life.' Anna shot me a sly smile.

'I'm not,' I muttered. 'You're all awful.'

'Speaking of romance…' Anna nodded towards the door. I turned—and my heart sank. Ellery had just entered the bar.

'Oooh,' Dana cooed, twirling a strand of blonde hair around her finger.

'Isn't he a gang member?' Laura asked worriedly.

'Yep,' I muttered.

'Marco Ellery,' Dana said with relish. 'He's one of the good ones.'

'There are no good ones,' I disagreed.

'Oh, hush, you,' Dana said sassily. 'If you don't want him, well, more for the rest of us, right?' Winking, she sauntered off towards Ellery. He waved her off and approached the bar, pulling out a stool and sliding onto it.

I edged away, but Ellery didn't look at me.

'Hello,' Anna said brightly. 'What can I get you?'

'Whiskey, double,' Ellery muttered.

Anna shot me a wide-eyed look. I bit my lip.

Ellery looked rough. His hair was a mess and there were dark circles under his eyes.

'Coming right up. Just let me finish these off.' Anna slid two pint glasses under the tap and filled them before passing them over to me. 'That's for table nine.'

Ellery glanced my way. I wished he hadn't.

'Harley—'

'Sorry, I gotta run these to table nine.' I paused, feeling bad. 'Hey, this is Laura by the way. She's new.' I gestured to the redhead. 'Laura, this is Marco Ellery.'

'Nice to meet you.' Laura took my place as I stepped away, smiling brightly.

'Hey,' Ellery muttered.

I hurried to table nine. As I passed Dana, she mouthed, '*Smooth.*'

I rolled my eyes.

I dawdled extra long, making sure every table had full water glasses before Anna finally signalled to me that she wanted to take her break and I was forced back to the bar.

'An ale and a whiskey for six,' she said, 'and two whiskeys for twelve. I won't be long.'

'Enjoy your break,' I said.

Anna slipped out the back. I shoved a pint glass under the taps and poured, tilting it so it didn't foam as much. On the other side of the bar, Ellery downed the last of his whiskey.

'You want another?' I asked.

'Yes please.'

'Alright, I won't be a sec.'

I prepped the other orders and lined them up neatly for Dana, before pouring him a whiskey and sliding it over. 'Double.'

Ellery nodded his thanks.

'I'd have thought you'd be fighting tonight.' I wasn't exactly sure what I was doing trying to make conversation. Ellery and I had been avoiding each other just fine since my ill-considered trip to his flat two weeks ago. Why ruin a good arrangement?

Ellery shrugged. 'I'm not down for the night. Sayle wants us to lay low for a bit.'

''Us?'' I quoted.

'My team.' He sipped his whiskey morosely. 'I think Briggsy is on the roster for the night. Guess that'll be fun for you to watch.'

'I hate Briggsy.'

Ellery shot me an odd look. 'It's hard to keep up with who you do and don't hate these days,' he muttered.

Lovely. 'I think it's pretty simple,' I said flatly. 'If you're a misogynistic pig, you're on the shit list.'

Ellery winced. 'Look, Harley—'

'Unless it's an apology, I don't want to hear it.' I surprised myself at how angry I sounded. I'd thought I was coming to terms with the change in my and Ellery's relationship… but the moment he opened his mouth, all the hurt came rushing back.

'What if it is an apology?' Ellery asked.

I bit my lip. To be honest, I wasn't too keen on hearing him apologise. That meant I'd have to decide whether I was willing to forgive him.

'Are you ready to listen to what I have to say?' I asked.

Dana appeared at the bar. 'Is that the order for six?' she asked breathlessly.

I nodded.

'Great. And can I get a refill for table one? Boilermakers, shots on the side.'

I glanced at table one and suppressed a groan. We had a whole squad of soldiers in from the northern military outpost—they were always so relieved to be back amongst civilisation that they basically drank us out of house and home. Tonight's only saving grace was that I'd be going off shift before they started getting rowdy—hopefully.

'Coming up.'

Dana nodded and sashayed off, putting an extra swing into her hips for Ellery's benefit. He watched her for a few seconds before turning back to me. 'Am I getting in your way?'

'No.' I grabbed the pint glasses and started filling them. 'Let's hear it, then.'

Ellery scowled at his glass. 'I'm… sorry,' he said in a stilted voice. 'For… giving you the wrong impression.'

My stomach churned. I pretended to be extremely focused on filling pint glasses. 'Uh huh?'

'That's it? 'Uh huh?'' Ellery crossed his arms. 'Is that all you have to say?'

'What do you want me to say?' I kept my eyes on my work.

'I don't know. Something more than that, at least.'

I pressed my lips together. As far as things went, Ellery had a lot more to apologise for than just a romantic misunderstanding. 'I really don't know what to say.' I pulled out a stack of shot glasses. 'You hurt me in quite a few ways.'

'You think you didn't hurt me? You *used* me—'

'It's no more or less than you were doing to me,' I pointed out. Ellery was a user. He dressed his attentions up as flirting, but he had been using me for information and he'd cut me loose when I'd become difficult. 'I am sorry. I made a mistake trying to kiss you to get what I wanted. I admit that.' My voice was quiet.

'Do you really think it was a mistake?' Ellery asked hoarsely.

He was still stuck on the romantic aspect—but the truth was, I didn't see him that way anymore. Ellery had been a safe option for me, someone I could flirt with but never go any further. I had thought I liked him, but somewhere along the line, I had fallen out of love with him. I couldn't love someone I didn't trust.

'Yes,' I said clearly.

'I see.' Ellery was silent for a long moment, staring at the bartop with a strange look on his face. Then he picked up his glass and downed the contents. 'I'll go. I'm sorry I bothered you.'

He looked like he wanted me to stop him, but I couldn't even if I had wanted to. My throat was frozen; I had no words. Ellery left a twenty on the counter and walked away.

Dana skipped up. 'Marco Ellery? Really, Harley?'

'No,' I said.

She paused in the middle of shifting pint glasses onto her tray, examining my face. 'No,' she said. 'But then who is your boy?'

'There isn't one.'

Dana snorted and shook her head. 'That was what I said about Mack, and look where that got me.'

'You left Mack.'

'And good riddance too.' Dana flicked her hair over her shoulder. 'I'm going on break when Anna gets back, 'kay? I need a smoke.'

'Okay.'

I went back to pouring shots, half an ear on Dana's chatter. Most of my attention was on my inner turmoil.

Things should have felt clearer, but instead I felt like all Ellery and I had done was muddy the waters.

What I really wanted was to explain to him how he'd left me high and dry when I'd needed a friend. But doing that would mean explaining everything about Tam and Hardwick, and that was impossible. And until I could find a way to tell him the truth, I was stuck letting him think that our romantic attraction was the only problem we had.

It wasn't.

I rotated back to waitressing when Anna returned from her break, doing my best to smile and flirt. Even though I had two jobs now, I still couldn't get lax. In fact, I was saving every penny I could. Secretly, I still harboured the hope that Savannah and I could skip town. Maybe the next time Theo left? But where would we go? The Black Hands had a long reach—I didn't want to run to Crater's Edge or Brackfields, only to discover that Hannover could hunt me down there.

Hannover. My stomach squirmed. I dismissed the thought of him hastily. I didn't want to worry about him because if I did, I might just curl up and cry and never face the world again. It was a tempting option.

My shift wound down at ten, and at nine-thirty a welcome face entered the bar. Theo sauntered over, throwing an arm around me and almost knocking me over where I was clearing a table.

'Hey! Watch out!' I straightened up, grinning. 'What are you doing here?'

'Thought I'd come early and hang out.' He beamed at me. 'Miss me, baby?'

'It's only been a day.'

'A whole day without me.' He slapped a hand over his chest. 'How could you survive?'

I snorted. 'Come on, come say hi.'

Theo followed me to the bar and slouched into the stool Ellery had been sitting on earlier. I pushed the association away. Theo and Ellery were two totally different cases. No similarities at all.

For one, there was no romance between Theo and me. It'd be like snogging my own sibling.

Anna stood from where she'd been digging out a fresh bottle. 'What can I—Oh my God, Theo!'

'Theo?' Dana hurried over. 'It is Theo!'

'Hello, ladies.' Theo grinned. 'This is the kind of greeting a guy could get used to.'

'Greeting?' Dana asked. 'This is a chewing out. Where the fuck have you been?'

Theo laughed. 'Around. About. Crater's Edge, Brackfields, Langford.'

'You went all the way to Langford?' I demanded.

'For a bit. Relax.' Theo wrapped his arm around my waist, drawing me close. 'I always come back. You know that.'

But one day he might not. I swallowed against the lump of fear in the back of my throat. 'I'm not worried.'

'Good.' He squeezed my waist, before releasing me. 'How are you, Dana, Anna? And you're new, right?' He shot a glance at Laura.

'This is Laura,' I said. 'Laura, this is Theo—he's an old friend.'

'Hi.' Laura smiled shyly. 'I like your tattoos.'

'Thanks.' Theo glanced at his arms, which his tight T-shirt left bare. 'This is my favourite.' He gestured to one of a northern wildcat rearing up over his right forearm. I smiled to myself—I'd chosen that design.

'Very cool,' Dana said. 'Any new ones?'

'Not in places I want to show you.' Theo smirked at her. Dana laughed.

'Tease.'

'You bet.'

Dana grinned, glancing around the room. Table one hailed her and she sighed. 'Come on, Laura. Back to work.'

She and Laura went to take their order, and I started unloading my tray of empty glasses.

'What are you drinking?' Anna asked, leaning her elbows on the bar. Having Theo in the bar was an event for all of us. I didn't think he could go anywhere without instantly making friends with everyone—it was one of the reasons Sayle sent him on trips to other cities; he was the best diplomat in town.

'Not for me tonight.' Theo sighed gustily. 'Sorry.'

I flicked my fingers at Theo's wrist. 'No lurkers, only drinkers.'

He leant back out of my reach. 'I can't. I'm fighting tonight.'

'Really?'

'Yup.' He waggled his brows. 'Should be my lucky night, right? You'll be there.'

I felt my cheeks heating up. 'Don't mention that when I'm at work,' I hissed.

'Sorry,' Theo sang, not sounding at all apologetic.

Anna rolled her eyes at me. 'Get back to work. Table nine is looking for you.'

I sighed and patted Theo on the shoulder. 'I'll be done in a few, okay?'

'Sure thing. Miss Anna will keep me company 'til then, won't you darling.'

Anna giggled.

My shift drew to a close twenty minutes later. When I took my apron off, Theo slid off his stool and stretched. 'Time to rumble?'

'Where are you going?' Laura asked quizzically.

Theo tossed her a smirk. 'I,' he said dramatically, 'am going to get the shit beaten out of me by my homophobic ex-best friend, whilst Harley struts her stuff—'

'*Theodore!*' I hissed.

'—and shows off her ability to lick her own elbow.' Theo winked. 'Also there will be alcohol involved. You wanna come?'

'You have got to be joking,' I said. Turning to Laura, I added, 'I work two jobs. Theo is dropping me at the club because he has a fight tonight.'

'*You* fight?' Laura looked him up and down, her eyes wide.

Theo's grin grew even bigger. 'What, don't think I can handle myself? Baby, assuming that is the last mistake most men *ever* make.'

I leant over the bar and swatted him on the arm. 'Pipe down, you. Come on, let's get out of here before you ruin all my colleagues.'

'Aw, but they're so ripe to be ruined—'

'Inappropriate,' I snapped. Anna and Laura both giggled. I rolled my eyes at them. 'Don't encourage him.'

'*Do* encourage me,' Theo said. 'Someone needs to balance Harley out.'

'Shut up,' I mumbled.

'I hope you don't get beaten up,' Laura said anxiously. 'Aren't the fights dangerous?'

'Sure, for the other guy.' Theo winked. 'Don't worry, I'll be fine. I'll come in tomorrow and see you if you're worried.'

He blew her a kiss. Laura went scarlet. 'Uh—I—Um—I'm not really looking for—'

'Don't worry, I was joking. You're not my type.' Theo glanced her up and down. 'Wrong bits. Come on, Harley baby.'

'Ignore him,' I advised as I shrugged my coat on and rounded the bar. 'He loves to flirt.'

'Aww, are you jealous I'm not flirting with you?' Theo threw his arm around my shoulders and started to lead me to the door. 'Don't worry, baby, I'll always like you best.'

'Nutjob,' I muttered.

Theo laughed.

He had left his car outside on the square, in full view of every arsehole who might want to steal it—but then, I didn't doubt that half the town knew it was Theo's truck, and everyone loved Theo. We climbed in, and he floored it down a side street and onto Main, which would take us through to the industrial area out east.

I bundled my coat against the window and leant against it, watching as we hurtled through the eastern reaches of town. 'Who's on the roster tonight?'

Theo hummed. Leaning forward, he turned the radio on, Pre-Crash rock filling the car. 'Couple of the usual faces. The Aces have sent a few tonight. Briggsy for sure. And there's a new guy. Maddock?'

'Maddock will be there?' I perked up.

'Mm-hmm. You know him?'

'He arrived in summer. He lives in my building.'

'Re-ally,' Theo drawled.

I glanced at his face. His expression was obscured in the darkness. 'What? I can't control who lives in my building.'

'No, but we all know who does.'

Irina. And Irina had a deal with Sayle. Which meant the Iron Fists controlled who lived there.

'I know.' I scuffed my foot against the footwell. 'He's actually a good guy. Maddock.'

'No such thing as good guys, Harley baby. We all have a price.'

Don't I know it.

'Well, see what you make of him,' I suggested. 'But don't break him. Savannah likes him.'

'Must be a jackass then.'

'Oi!'

'What?' Theo laughed. 'Your sister has shit taste.'

'You're telling me.' I leant against the window again. 'You know who she's seeing lately? Guess.'

'Haven't the faintest,' Theo said. 'Some hoity-toity rich kid? Wait, please tell me it's not Brody Cavanaugh. He always had such a hard-on for you two.'

'What?' I gasped, choking on my own giggles. 'Theo, ew!'

Brody Cavanaugh was a rich prick. I hated him.

'Oh, good. You had me really worried there.' Theo spun the wheel, the tyres screeching as he pulled us onto a road north. I dropped my coat into my lap and sat up straight so I didn't bang my head. Theo always drove like he was in a car chase.

'Okay, but wait 'til you hear who it is.'

'Do tell.'

'Greg Talbot,' I drawled.

Theo jerked the wheel, and the car bounced straight through a pothole with a muffled bang.

'Harley! You are fucking joking.'

'I am not fucking joking. Believe me, I wish I was.'

'Holy shit.' Theo righted the car, shaking his head. 'Your sister is a fucking idiot.'

'I know.'

'She's going to get both of you killed.'

'Toss up whether I'm going to manage that first or she is.'

Theo glanced at me.

'Eyes on the road,' I warned.

'Why are you going to get her killed?' he asked.

Damn, should have kept that thought to myself. 'No reason. Just… things seem tense in town, don't they?'

'Do they? I've only been here a day.'

I shot him a look. Theo was not stupid. 'Don't pull that one.'

'Sorry.' He reached over and squeezed my hand. 'I'll look after you, baby. You know I will.'

'I can look after myself.'

'That doesn't mean I can't help. You can't stop me,' Theo said in a steely tone.

I sighed. 'Just look after yourself, as well. I'm not alone. I'll be fine.'

Theo hummed sceptically. I knew well enough what he was thinking. Theo and Savannah had never gotten along. She thought he was irresponsible; he thought she was a bitch.

'Don't let your sister drag you down,' he said finally. 'If she does anything stupid, we'll pack her in a car and drag her to Crater's Edge.'

'I actually tried to ask her to go.'

'Really?' Theo asked, obviously surprised. 'I thought you liked it here.'

'Not lately.' I shrugged as though it wasn't a big deal. 'But it doesn't matter. She said no.'

'Talbot has a temper. I bet she'll be falling over herself to get away from him soon enough.'

I smiled grimly. I didn't want that for Savannah, but I suspected it was true. 'She's got rose-tinted glasses on at the moment. Every time I bring him up, she shuts me down.'

'It'll change,' Theo said.

'I just hope she doesn't get hurt before it does,' I replied.

We bounced down the pockmarked asphalt roads, and then the scrappy dirt tracks, and eventually we reached the old station. Today, there were plenty of cars scattered around the lot. Theo parked off to one side, and we headed for the depot. When we passed Bas's car, I nodded to it.

'Do you know Bas?'

'Everyone knows Bas,' Theo said tightly.

'Really? Because I thought he was new in town since you were away.'

Theo glanced at me. 'He's been with the Iron Fists for longer than a few months. About two years. He just kept a low profile. Where do you know him from?'

Apart from the fact that he used to teach me self-defence, I betrayed him in the worst way, and now he hates me?

'Around. He first started coming in the bar over the summer.'

Theo paused to give me a hand over the tracks. 'Do you know who he *was?*'

'You mean do I know his real name, or that he was a slave?' I gripped Theo's shoulder to steady myself on the uneven stones.

'Both.'

'Yes. How'd you know?' Bas didn't seem the type to have heart-to-hearts with just anyone.

'His father and mine were friends.' Theo laughed, but there was no warmth in the sound. 'Probably still are. Arseholes love arseholes, right?'

'He has a brother,' I muttered.

'Rodney. I remember him.' Theo raised his torch a bit higher, illuminating the path to the depot. 'Why are you asking about Bas?'

'No reason. I was just curious.'

Theo frowned at me. 'Right.'

I was spared from having to respond as we reached the depot. The big space inside was stacked with crates and boxes. Theo led the way straight over to the manhole, where Alex Greene was standing guard.

'Halt,' he called, shining his torch in our faces. I squinted against it.

'Stop power-tripping, Greensy,' Theo called back.

'Theo?' Alex dropped the torch. 'No fucking way. When did you get back to town?'

'Yesterday.' Theo hurried over and clapped Alex on the shoulder. 'You're looking good. How's the wife?'

'Insatiable,' Alex said.

Theo snorted. 'Quit complaining.'

'Oh, I'm not complaining.' Alex waved his torch, blinding both of us. 'It's good to see you again. You fighting tonight?'

'Yep.'

'I pity the other guy.'

'Oh, you should.' Theo winked before glancing at me. 'Come on, Harley baby. Time to get to work.'

'Right.' I sauntered past Alex. 'See you later, Greene!'

'I'll come see you when I get off shift,' he called back.

'Go home to your wife, Greene!' Theo hollered.

Alex's laughter followed us down the ladder and into the tunnel.

Going through the weapons check with Theo was an ordeal. He hid all manner of knives, chains, piano wires, and all sorts of other things under his clothes. God only knew how—his clothes were tighter than mine—but he managed it somehow. Once he'd pulled them all out, the guard frisked him, scowling in irritation when he still found another stiletto in a secret pocket in Theo's jeans.

'Oops.' Theo shrugged innocently.

Once we were both cleared, we headed into the main hall, where a small crowd had already gathered.

'He missed one in my boot,' Theo whispered.

'You are unbelievable,' I groaned.

'Hey, you try going a day in the city without being armed to the teeth!'

He meant it as a joke, but comments like that didn't exactly reassure me, even though I knew Theo could handle himself. 'Come on,' I muttered. 'My shift will start soon.'

We cut through the throng and reached the inner circle. The bookie barred the entrance, keeping the common folk away from the fighters. When he saw us, he shifted aside.

'Money, Dunne.'

'Yeah, yeah.' Theo handed him a few notes—his buy-in fee for the fights—then caught my hand, and tugged me into the circle.

'Do you have time for a drink before you start dancing?'

'I thought you weren't drinking.' I glanced around, scanning the faces. I couldn't forget what my purpose here was.

'Look what the cat dragged in.'

I twisted around at the new voice. Theo groaned quietly.

It was Diego Bartholomew: tall, with brown skin, dark brown hair, and a perpetual cheeky grin, he was one of the rich boys who had haunted my secondary school career, and since then he'd never missed an opportunity to mock me for my fall from grace.

He shot Theo a sharklike smile. 'Thought you'd gone and snuffed it, you were gone so long.' His gaze drifted to me. 'And you brought a toy. How fun.'

Quick as a flash, he leant in and pinched my cheek. 'Maybe instead of getting my money, I'll take you as my prize when I win.'

I shoved him away hard. 'Hands off.'

'Bartholomew,' Theo drawled. 'Didn't know you were that keen to get your arse kicked.'

'Oh, I don't know about that. Seems to me the city has made you all soft around the edges.'

If anything, it had done the opposite: Theo always came back from the cities with hardened edges and an air of desperation, as though the city's aura was still clinging to him. His eyes narrowed. 'We'll see.'

Diego just smiled. He traced a hand casually, almost possessively, over Theo's chest, then leant in and whispered something in his ear. Theo's eyes went wide, and he shoved the other man back.

'Over my dead body.'

'That can always be arranged.' Diego's gaze drifted over me, openly undressing me with his eyes, then he turned away. 'See you in the cage, loverboy.'

Theo slid his arm around my back. 'Run along, Didi. Brody's waiting for you.'

Diego glared. Theo tugged me past.

'What'd he say?' I demanded.

'Nothing, baby.'

'*Theo.*'

Theo grimaced, throwing himself onto a sofa and waving one of the waitresses over. 'It was crude. Just leave it.'

'I want to know.'

'He called me a pretty cocksucker.' Theo scowled. 'As if I'd go anywhere near his cock. Who knows what diseases he's got?'

I snorted. 'Just ignore him. You know he likes provoking you.'

'I know.' Theo rolled his eyes. 'He'll get his, don't worry.'

'Are you fighting him?'

'Yep.'

'Oh boy.'

Theo laughed and cracked his knuckles. 'Don't worry about me. I'm going to break his pretty face.'

'Oh, I know.'

A waitress sashayed over, a tray of drinks held aloft in front of her. As she approached, I took a step back. 'I should go change.'

'Yeah, alright.' Theo tapped his cheek. 'Kiss for luck?'

I planted a deliberately sloppy kiss on his cheek. 'Kick his arse.'

'Your wish is my command.'

NINE

BY THE TIME MY BREAK rolled around, the main hall was chock full and I was drenched in sweat. Posy relieved me, passing me a bottle of water.

'Can't take our break together today. Sorry, babes.'

'How will I survive?' I asked mournfully.

'I know, right?' She rolled her eyes. 'Hey, did you see that Theo's back?'

'Yep.'

'Ugh, you knew, didn't you?' She made a face at me. 'Why am I always the last person to know?'

'Why are you blaming me?' I climbed off the stage. 'Blame your girlfriend; she should be the one giving you news about the Iron Fists.'

Posy laughed. 'Alright, piss off. I've gotta get dancing.'

She grabbed the pole and hoisted herself up. I took a sip of my water and scanned the crowd, looking for Theo.

There.

He was hanging out with a few other guys, including Alex Greene. I waved to him and he jumped up and started over to me.

I was weaving between the benches and overturned crates to reach him when suddenly, a voice beside me asked, 'Harley?'

I turned. Maddock and Kade were sitting on a bench to my right, both watching me. Maddock jumped up. His black hair hung in his eyes, and he was dressed in boxing shorts and a fitted vest. It took me aback; I'd somehow never imagined my soft-spoken neighbour looking ready to fight—even though I knew full well that he did participate in the fights.

I was the one who'd helped him get admitted to the bunker.

'What are you doing here?' he asked.

I raised an eyebrow, making a show of appraising him slowly. 'Dancing, obviously.'

'Dancing?' he parroted.

'Yeah, you know...' I did a little twirl. '...dancing. On the pole. For work.'

'I thought you worked at the Kranikovska.'

'I do work at the Kranikovska.' I rolled my eyes. 'Circumstances change. How you doing, Kade?'

Kade offered me a smile, smoothing a hand over his shaven head. His dark skin glistened under the lights. He, too, was dressed for the fights. 'Good, thank you, Miss Harley. Do you want a drink?'

I waved the water bottle at them. 'No alcohol whilst I'm on the clock.'

'Since when have you been dancing here? I thought you didn't come here anymore?' Maddock asked.

'Since last week,' I said flatly. Why was everyone so interested in my job lately? I didn't really want to discuss this, so I changed the subject. 'Are you fighting tonight?'

'Looks like it.' Maddock furrowed his brow. 'Does your sister know you're here?'

'Why all the questions?' I shot back, cocking my hip and glaring at him. Maddock's gaze flickered over my body, and his cheeks coloured pink.

'I don't, uh, I mean...' he sputtered. 'Uh... I didn't mean to pry.'

'No, I don't think you did,' I said ruthlessly. Kade muffled a laugh behind his hand.

Maddock ruffled his hair sheepishly. 'If you need anything...'

Oh, honestly.

'Don't be silly. I can take care of myself,' I said crossly.

At that moment, Theo sauntered over and slung an arm around my shoulders. 'Hey, baby.'

Maddock stumbled back in surprise. I shrugged Theo's arm off. 'Ew, you're sweaty.'

'Uh, pot? Kettle? Black?' Theo rolled his eyes. He'd lost his shirt somewhere along the way, the myriad of tattoos on his chest, almost too many to tell where one ended and the next one began. 'Gonna introduce me or are you too busy ogling me?'

'Eff off.' I swatted him on the arm.

Theo just grinned. 'Hey, Andy.' He waved cheekily.

Kade chuckled. 'Your saviour is here, Miss Harley.'

Maddock was eyeballing Theo as though he was an alien creature.

'Um, who are you?'

'The one and only Theodore Dunne, at your service.' Theo held out a hand. Maddock squinted at him before finally taking it to shake—and Theo lifted Maddock's hand to his lips, and kissed it exaggeratedly.

Maddock stared at him with wide eyes. 'Um…'

'What's your name?'

'James Maddock,' Maddock said blankly.

'James!' Beaming, Theo draped an arm around Maddock's shoulder. 'It's nice to meet you, James.'

'Uh…' Maddock squirmed away from him. 'Um…'

I stifled a giggle as Kade rolled his eyes. 'Don't scare him, Theo.'

'Aw, I'm just being my usual friendly self.' Theo dragged Maddock to the sofa and pushed him down before scooping an arm around my waist, sitting, and pulling me down onto his lap. 'So…' he began as I adjusted to being some sort of weird sandwich with my best friend and his new toy. 'Harley tells me you're new to town. What brings you up this way?'

Maddock looked like he wanted to melt into the floor. He kept glancing between me and Theo, as though trying to find a safe place to rest his gaze. Theo snapped his fingers in front of Maddock's face.

'You can stare at me, honey. Harley's off limits.'

'I wasn't staring,' Maddock spluttered.

'Don't mind him,' I said. 'He does this to intimidate people.'

'Oi!' Theo protested.

'I remember you doing more or less the same thing,' Maddock said.

Ouch. Before I could respond, Theo beat me to the punch.

'She learnt from the best, baby.' He trailed a finger up Maddock's arm. Maddock's gaze jumped to his hand. 'Where you from?'

'Brackfields.'

'Ooh, I was just there a couple of days ago. Nice place, if you ignore the smog.'

Maddock wet his lips. 'Um, you travel?'

'Yep,' Theo said, popping the 'P' with a wet sound. Theo could make almost anything sound sexual—and oh boy, was it working. Maddock could barely take his eyes off of him.

I could have laughed. Finally, I understood why Maddock had never responded to my flirtation. I'd never stood a chance!

'I… I didn't think too many people round here travelled,' Maddock croaked.

Theo leant away, wrapping his arm around me instead. 'I'm special. I do the city runs for Sayle.'

Maddock raised an eyebrow. The flush in his cheeks was visible even under the low light. 'City runs?'

'Oh, you know… bit of diplomacy, bit of negotiation, bit of reorganising the supply chains…'

Maddock snorted in understanding. 'You're a smuggler.'

'Such a nasty word for an essential service!' Theo protested. 'People have to eat!'

'You could rely on official supplies.'

'Tell that to the people starving on the streets because the Black Hands have blocked supplies coming from Brackfields again,' Theo pointed out.

Maddock rolled his eyes. 'Ah, yes, you're practically a guardian angel.'

'Precisely.' Theo smirked. 'Without me, what would Bale Rocks do?'

'Live lawfully?'

'Pfft,' Theo snorted. 'We don't do lawful, do we, Andy?'

'Don't bring me into this,' Kade said. 'I'm extremely lawful.'

'I'm the only lawful person in this group,' I declared. 'I'm the only person here with a proper job.'

'Hey!' Maddock cried. Theo shifted his hips and tipped me off his lap.

'Oof. Theo!' I grabbed his shoulder to catch my balance.

'That's what you get for being a bitch.' He prodded me on the nose. 'We aren't nasty to our friends, baby.'

'You can take it.' I prodded him back. Theo batted my hand away.

'Meanie.'

'Right back atcha.' Theo swiped playfully at me, but I stepped out of his reach. 'Neh-neh, can't catch me!'

'You two are such children,' Kade said.

'Excuse you, I'm the oldest here,' Theo disagreed, abandoning his attempt to catch me in favour of downing the rest of his whiskey.

'How do you know?' Maddock asked.

'How old are you?' I asked him curiously.

'Twenty-four.'

'Hah! I'm older. I'm twenty-five,' Theo crowed.

'Me too,' I reminded him.

'I'm still older than you.'

'You wouldn't believe it,' Kade stage-whispered to Maddock. Maddock laughed.

Theo elbowed them both. 'Mean, mean, you're all mean.' He shook his head.

I tapped his leg with my foot. 'When's your match?'

'I think I'm up next.' Theo twisted to look at the cage. 'Yeah, after these idiots.'

'Shouldn't you be warming up?' Maddock asked.

'Already done it. Besides, I can take Diego.'

'Don't get cocky,' I warned.

Theo shrugged and jumped up, rolling his shoulders. 'Kiss for luck?'

I leant over and pecked him on the cheek. 'Kick his arse.'

'Will do.' He sauntered off with a swagger.

Maddock glanced at me. 'Who… What…'

'Theo's been my best friend since forever,' I explained. 'We used to dance together.'

'Oh,' Maddock mumbled, his gaze drifting as though he was seeing something that I couldn't. 'He's quite something, huh?'

'You don't say.' I grinned.

'BENOIT!' And… I groaned. Turning, I saw Carlos hurrying over.

'Yes, Carlos?' I asked sweetly.

'If you're not warming laps, out of the circle.' He pointed at the back room. 'Scram.'

I sighed. 'Yeah, yeah.' Glancing at Maddock, I added, 'See you later.'

Maddock smiled. 'Bye.'

My shift wound down a few hours later. The crowd was still going strong when the lights came up and the music went off. Groans echoed around the room.

I slid off the pole and rolled my shoulders. I was going to be sore in the morning.

'Hey, babe, how much to take you home for the night?'

I twisted around to see a man leaning over the edge of the stage, waving a fistful of cash.

'I don't do house calls,' I said primly.

'Aww, come on, I'll make it good for ya.' He listed sideways and clung to the edge of the stage.

I suppressed a snort. Men always said that—as though hookers ought to be grateful their clients *made it good* for them. As though a sexy woman had no better prospects than a drunk arsehole with cash to spare.

'No thanks. I'm not for sale.' I turned to leave.

'You work in a club! Cut the attitude.'

I rolled my eyes. 'If you're such a gift in bed, then I'm sure you can show *yourself* a good time, arsehole.'

I climbed off the stage into the circle and headed for the back rooms.

Carlos was guarding the entrance to the back. 'Did I just see you sassing off a customer, Benoit?'

'Not my fault he doesn't know the difference between a dancer and whore.' I shrugged and held out a hand. Carlos raised an eyebrow.

'Tips first,' he said in a deadpan tone.

'You still owe me from last week!' I said indignantly.

'Absolutely not. Tough luck, Benoit. Hand 'em over or hand in your resignation.'

Scowling, I worked the crumpled notes out of my shorts and handed them to him. Carlos took great delight in smoothing each one out, before passing me back my cut. 'You'll get your salary next week.'

'Dick.'

'Call me that again and you'll be sucking it.'

'In your dreams.' I pushed past him, his braying laugh following me. *Asshat.*

I rounded the corner and almost ran into a group of men.

'…not sure, but I've passed it on to Jackson anyway.' That was Theo. He had his head together with Ellery and Briggs, all of them looking intent.

'Probably wise,' Ellery replied. 'Anyway—' He caught sight of me. 'Let's continue this some other time.'

Theo turned my way, and a smile broke out over his face. 'Hey, Harley baby. Good going tonight.'

'Yeah,' I replied coolly. I didn't want to hang out with Briggs and Ellery, not when Ellery was looking at me like a kicked puppy and

Briggs was leering at my chest. 'Thanks. I'm going to get changed.'

I pushed past them and marched towards the changing room. Hurried footsteps sounded behind me.

'Hey, wait up.' Theo dropped an arm around my shoulders. 'What's the hurry?'

'Nothing. I just don't feel like hanging around.' I glanced back; Briggs and Ellery were both watching.

'Alright. Let's grab your stuff and we can head home.'

'Fine.'

'Are you mad?'

'No.' I looked back again. 'I just don't want to be around those guys.'

'I thought you liked Ellery?' Theo frowned.

'Times have changed.'

'Really?'

'Yes, really.' I was starting to get annoyed with this conversation. 'What were you all talking about anyway?'

'Nothing,' Theo said quickly. Too quickly.

'Really? Cause you cut out pretty fast when I arrived.'

Theo squeezed my shoulders. 'It's nothing, really.'

'Uh-huh.' I shrugged his arm off. 'I'm not stupid, you know. You don't have to lie to me.'

Theo's lips twisted. 'I'm not lying. Look, it's gang business. It's not something I want you involved in.'

'Sure,' I muttered, speeding up my pace. 'Well if that's how it is, why don't you go finish your private conversation with them whilst you wait for me? I'll be a few minutes still.'

Theo stared at me, frowning. Finally, he said, 'Don't be mad, baby. I just don't want you involved in that stuff.'

I refused to look at him, turning the corner and hurrying towards my changing room. After a moment, Theo sighed.

'See you in a bit, then.'

He turned back. I rounded another corner, and someone grabbed my arm, yanking me through a doorway.

I gasped as I wrenched my arm away and lashed out with my other fist. I struck flesh, and someone grunted.

The light flicked on. I was in an unused storeroom... and facing me was Dean Hannover.

Fuck.

I took a quick step back. He hadn't closed the door, and I was halfway tempted to run, but before the plan could coalesce in my mind, he kicked the door shut.

'Hello, Harley.' Hannover smirked.

'You're not meant to be back here!' I steeled my shoulders, desperately trying to hide my fear. What did he want now?

'How could I miss an opportunity to talk to my favourite dancer?'

I crossed my arms over my chest. I felt horribly exposed in my bralette. 'I don't give private shows, so don't even think of asking.'

His smile sent chills down my spine. 'Oh, you'll give private shows whenever I ask.' He reached out and tucked a strand of hair behind my ear. I jerked backwards, my stomach churning. 'Remember our deal?'

'You want a lap dance in exchange for sparing my life?' I rolled my eyes. 'Didn't realise you were so fucking cheap.'

Hannover laughed. 'You're cute when you're pretending to be brave. No wonder the Iron Fists are tripping over each other to get in your pants.'

'There's no pretending about it,' I snapped. 'If you're not going to get to the point, then I'm going. My ride is waiting for me.'

'Oh yes, Theo Dunne, right? Fancy seeing him back in town.'

What the fuck? I stepped closer to him.

'What does that mean?' I demanded.

'Nothing that concerns you,' Hannover sang. He brushed his fingers over my cheek again, grinning when I shuddered. 'Actually, I think you have *much* more serious concerns right now.'

'Get off me,' I snapped.

Hannover laughed, a cold, brittle laugh. 'And you were so eager to be my friend last time. Dear, dear me. We'll have to work on that, or this is going to be a very short relationship.'

'We don't have a relationship. I owe you one favour. Tell me what you want, or get out before I call one of the Iron Fists to kick you out,' I snapped.

Hannover sobered abruptly. 'That would not be to your benefit, Harley Benoit.'

His sudden change in mood set me on edge. There was something unhinged about this guy. 'Just tell me what you want.'

His eyes bored into mine. 'Okay. Here's what I want. I want you to find out when the mayor and Percy are planning their strike against Sayle. I want you to make sure Percy is there when it goes down. And I want you to make sure he dies. You can do it yourself—or you can get one of your friends in the Iron Fists to do it. But whatever you do, it can't get pinned on the Black Hands, or I'll kill that sister of yours. Am I clear?'

I stared at him, mouth open in shock. 'You have got to be joking.'

'Not in the slightest, I assure you.'

Fuck. I had no idea how to respond to that. My chest closed up in panic, and for several moments speaking was beyond me.

He had to be joking.

He just had to be.

There was no way I could do that.

I was already indebted to Hardwick—and now this? How could I keep both of them happy? It wasn't possible.

I was going to die.

There was no way I'd escape this clusterfuck in one piece.

The future stretched out ahead of me, dark, gloomy, and terrifyingly short. How long did I have? Who could I turn to for help?

No.

I couldn't think like that.

If I was gone, who would take care of Savannah?

There had to be a way out of this. I was no delicate princess. I'd survived—when my parents had died, I survived. When Jackson had forced me to work for the Iron Fists at seventeen, I survived. When Gabriel Tam had tried to kill me, I survived.

I would survive this too.

I looked Hannover in the eye. 'And if I do, you'll leave me alone after that?'

His lips turned up in a grotesque smile. 'Oh, you'll be safe as the mayor in his fancy manor, baby.'

Reassuring.

'I want a promise.' I stared him down, unyielding. 'My safety, and my sister's, in exchange for doing this.'

Hannover laughed. 'I don't think this is a negotiation, darling.'

'We are negotiating. You let me walk away.' I stepped closer to him. He smirked, not moving an inch, so I was forced to invade his personal space. *Yuck.* 'I could have told a hundred people by now.'

'You haven't told anyone,' he whispered.

'You want to bet?'

For a single second, uncertainty flickered in Hannover's gaze. Then it was gone behind the empty façade he usually wore. Hannover's eyes gave me the shivers; they didn't seem human.

No person could have that little regard for the value of other humans. No human was that devoid of emotion. No way.

He was a monster.

He leant in, his warm breath caressing my cheek as he whispered, 'Why would they believe you? You're nothing but a cheap whore.'

I pulled away, shuddering. 'Even a whore can change the world if she says the right thing at the right time.'

Hannover's eyes narrowed. 'We'll see. Fine, I agree to your terms. You kill Percival, we leave you alone and consider the debt paid. Happy?'

I rolled my eyes. 'Ecstatic.'

'We'll see,' Hannover said. 'Killing a man in cold blood? I doubt you have it in you.'

'You have no idea what I'm capable of.'

Hannover laughed. 'No more and no less than every other whore in this town, darling. You think sucking dick makes you capable of playing in our world, but there's a reason why we're men and you're women.'

Misogynistic pig.

'Well, I can think of one difference.' I jerked my knee up, straight into his balls. We were standing so close he couldn't avoid it—he crumpled with an airless grunt. 'Men can't do that to women.'

I grabbed the door handle and wrenched it open. 'Better get out of here before I find someone to send your way.'

'You be careful, you little bitch,' Hannover wheezed. 'Bad things happen to women who forget their place.'

'I'd rather die than suck your dick.'

Brave words, and I knew they would almost certainly come back to haunt me, but right now I was beyond caring. I hurried into the hallway, darted around the corner, and almost immediately crashed into someone coming in the opposite direction.

It was like hitting a brick wall. Even as I stumbled backwards, I knew exactly who I'd collided with.

Bas caught my shoulders reflexively, frowning down at me. He looked better than the last time I'd seen him—the bruise was fading—but when he caught my eye, his face was immediately overtaken by irritation.

'Where are you hurrying to?'

'Nowhere.' I stepped out of his grip. Behind me, footsteps rang out. Bas's gaze jumped over my shoulder, and I didn't have to look to know Hannover had just followed me out. When I did turn, he was adjusting his trousers, his expression twisted with anger.

Bas's eyes narrowed.

'Hello there, Sebastian,' Hannover cooed mockingly. His tone made me shiver.

Bas's expression darkened like thunder clouds covering the sky. 'Hannover. You're not meant to be back here.'

I turned, trying to keep both of them in my field of view. The air felt charged with electricity, as though at any moment one of them might snap.

And I was stuck between them.

I edged backwards, and both their gazes jumped to me. Bas's eyebrows drew together in an unreadable look.

'Harley, get out of here.'

I locked my jaw and stopped moving. 'Don't order me about.'

Fury flickered across his face. 'Harley—'

'Ooh, a lover's tiff?' Hannover chuckled. The hairs on the back of my neck stood on end.

Bas turned back to Hannover. 'Get the fuck out of here before I shoot you.'

Hannover raised both hands, taking a step back. Smirking, he said, 'Don't mind me. I'd hate to intrude on the drama. I'll just…' He jerked a thumb over his shoulder to indicate the exit.

'Scram,' Bas snapped woodenly.

Hannover turned and sauntered off, utterly unconcerned about being shot in the back. Well, Bas would never do that—it'd be too hard for him to cover up one of Moriarty's lieutenants dying on the Iron Fists' territory.

But I'd bet he was tempted.

I started walking around Bas, heading for my changing room. His voice stopped me in my tracks.

'Where do you think you're going?'

I turned back. 'To change? Or did you think I wanted to walk home in the freezing cold in my underwear?'

Immediately, I could have kicked myself. What had happened to my resolution not to mouth off to Bas anymore?

But when he spoke to me in that tone… it was like I couldn't help myself.

Bas fixed me with a steely gaze. 'We need to talk.'

'I thought you were done talking to me?' I raised an eyebrow.

Bas scowled and crossed his arms. 'What were you doing with Hannover?'

Oh, for fuck's sake. Were we really doing this? Really? This guy just couldn't make up his mind whether he wanted to know my business or not.

Grinding my teeth together, I asked, 'What do you care?'

'He's dangerous.'

'So?' I shook my head. 'You cannot be serious. You don't get to pry into my business anymore, not after the way you spoke to me the other day.'

'The way I spoke to you?' Bas took a half step towards me, his body stiff with anger. 'You send me across town on a whim—'

'It wasn't a whim! Hannover was definitely keeping slaves in that office. I saw them!'

'Hannover's never even *been* in that office, Harley.'

He was so fucking sure—of course he had to trust anyone else except me. 'Oh yeah?' I snapped. 'And who told you that?'

'Sarah Stark, the receptionist,' Bas said with finality. 'Who I *highly doubt* is secretly in cahoots with the Black Hands.'

Great. Hurt engulfed my chest, making it hard to breathe. Who the fuck was Sarah Stark anyway? Why was her word better than mine?

Because he doesn't trust you.

Blinking hard to keep the tears at bay, I asked, 'Are you sure? Because I saw Hannover kissing the receptionist.'

Bas glowered at me. 'Now you're just making up stories.'

'I'm not!' I cried.

'I *lived* with Hannover, Harley. I know how he operates.'

I wiped the back of my hand over my eyes, hating myself for crying.

'Sure,' I hissed, 'you know everything. You're so fucking sure you're right, and that gives you the right to say whatever the fuck you want to me. You know what? You don't respect me, you don't treat me like an adult. I'm sick and tired of trying to earn your respect. Why'd you even bother talking to me? I thought you were done with me?'

Bas glared silently down at me.

For fuck's sake. I was so done with this guy, with his disrespect. How did we always end up here?

This couldn't only be my fault.

Pushing the tears away, I continued, 'You know what? Fine. I don't know why you followed me back here, but I know one thing: I'm done being disrespected. Until you can talk to me like a human being, you can fuck—'

'I came back here because I was worried,' Bas said suddenly.

My words died in my mouth.

Worried? What the fuck?

After all this? I might have believed that weeks ago—but if he was worried, why did he spend so much time being such an arsehole?

'Right,' I drawled sceptically, '*sure.* You're worried about me, the— what did you call me? *Glorified whore.*'

Bas flinched. 'Damnit, Harley—' He raked a hand through his hair, his expression twisted with frustration. 'What do you want me to say?'

I threw my hands up. 'You could try not being horrible for five minutes!'

'For fuck's sake.' Bas took a step towards me, his expression wild. 'I don't have the words you want me to say, Harley! I spent half my life sucking dicks just to stay alive. When the fuck was I supposed to learn to be kind?'

I jerked back, reeling. I didn't like the way he was talking, the way he looked at me. It was out of control—it reminded me of the way he'd fought last weekend, like a caged animal trying to savage its master.

No.

I wasn't going to let him do this to me. He had no right to talk to me this way, no matter what he'd been through.

'What, they hurt you so it's okay for you to hurt me?' I put my hands on my hips.

'No—damnit, you're infuriating. You take everything out of context.' Bas groaned. 'No! I... I don't want you to go through what I did. If it takes being nasty to you to get you away from Hannover then that's what I'll do! He's bad news.'

'I don't need you to protect me!' I shrieked.

'That's not the—God damnit. Stop. Taking. Everything. Out. Of. Context!' Bas stared at me, breathing so hard his shoulders shook.

'I don't know what the fuck the context is!' I snapped in exasperation. I didn't understand him, not at all. 'One minute you care, the next you don't. Now you're saying you do again. Make your fucking mind up!'

We stood, gazes locked together. I was inches from him, and I couldn't remember how we'd ended up like that—hadn't we been on opposite sides of the hall? Now I could practically feel his chest brushing mine when he breathed, could see the gears turning behind his eyes as he stared at me with an unreadable look. I felt all hollowed out, like I had no more words. All I could do was wait.

Wait for him to deliver my fate.

Wait for him to make his mind up.

Wait for—

Bas's eyes drifted down my face and settled on my lips. For long seconds he didn't move. I could hardly breathe. Then, abruptly, he shook his head, turned, and stalked off down the hallway.

What the fuck?

What the actual ever-loving fuck?

'Bas!' I yelled. 'You can't just leave like that!'

He turned the corner, his footsteps fading away. I stared at the spot where he'd just been standing, breathing hard as my heart raced frantically in my chest.

What had just happened?

There was nothing for it now—chasing after him would only end up making both of us angrier and… I was so tired. I'd worked two shifts, then Hannover had dropped the mother of all bombshells, and now this… I wanted to go to bed.

I turned on my heel and hurried to my changing room.

The other dancers were long since gone, the lights were off, and the whole place felt abandoned. I changed quickly under the dim glow of a single flickering fluorescent light, then threw my bag over my shoulder and practically sprinted through the halls. Theo would be waiting for me.

I found him at the weapons check, chatting with the guard. When I jogged over, they both looked at me in surprise. Theo held out my knife.

'Got this for you.'

'Thanks,' I panted, strapping the sheath to my belt. 'Shall we get out of here?'

Theo gave me a searching look, then nodded slowly.

'Night,' he called to the guard.

I started down the tunnel impatiently, ready to be shot of this place and all the idiots in it. Theo fell into step beside me.

'Where were you?' he asked.

I frowned. I didn't want Theo to know about Hannover, of course, but I wasn't keen to tell him about Bas, either. If I tried to explain the situation to Theo, I'd have to tell him about betraying Bas to Rodney, and I knew Theo would disapprove.

'Nowhere,' I muttered. 'I got held up changing.'

Predictably, Theo frowned at the weak lie. 'Come on. What's going on, Harley?'

A tired sort of irritation flared in me. Just for once, couldn't he leave me alone? Why did everyone in this town think they had a right to all of my secrets?

No, not every*one*. Every *man*.

Steeling my shoulders, I said darkly, 'Nothing I want you involved in.'

Theo shut his mouth with an audible click. *Message received and understood.*

We walked back to his car in silence.

TEN

SUNDAY WAS A STILL, clear day. The sun was a watery ball hanging low in the sky, too weak to burn off the clouds, let alone warm the earth. The wind had died, and the air was as still as a grave, with a cold snap to it that almost burnt.

It was the first day of winter. The weather was good. The bar hummed with contented chatter.

There were a thousand things I needed to think about, from Hardwick to Hannover to Theo, and everything in between, but instead, I scrubbed tables methodically and served drinks humourlessly. The day passed in a blur of exhaustion, whilst a singular image revolved in my mind over and over again, as ceaseless as the seasons.

That look Bas had given me.

The way his eyes had rested on my lips.

Was I crazy? Or had he been thinking about kissing me?

No, I was crazy.

Because Bas didn't like me.

Bas hated me.

A feeling which was entirely mutual.

Or… should have been entirely mutual.

I sighed and loaded a couple more glasses onto my tray before heading for the bar. I ought to hate Bas because Bas was horrible to me. And yet, I'd been honest with Brenda, and I had to be honest with myself: the reason why I kept going back, the reason why I couldn't resist rising to every challenge he set, was because some deep, dark part of me was attracted to him.

Bas and I had something in common—a dark, angry core that we struggled to hide. As much as I screamed at him, there was a part of me that wished I could soothe his hurt.

Insanity.

He was going to destroy me.

I groaned again. *Fucking hell.* I'd done that thing that no woman should do. I'd caught feelings.

'You know, people are going to start complaining about the breeze in here,' Laura said in a jokey tone.

I glanced over at her. She was training with Anna behind the bar today. 'Pardon?'

'All that sighing.'

'Oh.' I grimaced. 'Sorry.'

'It's alright. Is anything the matter?'

I shrugged. Nothing she could help with, even if I could tell her.

'I think Dana's right. She has boy troubles.' Anna smirked.

I shot her a dark look. 'Don't start with that again.'

'Alright, alright.' Anna grinned. 'You mind if I take my break while it's quiet?'

I nodded. 'Go ahead.'

Anna tossed her dishtowel under the counter and unwound her apron. 'I'll see you in a bit.'

'Yeah.'

She slipped out. I offloaded my stack of dirty glasses into one of the dishwashing trays.

'Harley?' Laura asked quietly.

'Mm-hmm?'

'I know we don't know each other very well, but… if you ever need to chat about anything, I'm happy to listen.'

I glanced at her in surprise. 'That's kind.'

Laura shrugged. 'I had friends who helped me out when I needed it… after my husband died. I know how much it sucks to go through things alone.'

I smiled weakly. 'I'm alright. But thanks.'

'You just seem quite… morose.' She quirked her lips in a tiny smile. 'I thought it might help to talk about it.'

'It's okay.' I shook my head. 'I'm the one who should be asking you if there's anything you want to talk about. How are you settling in?'

'Oh, fine, I think,' Laura said cheerfully. 'I'm staying with my brother and helping out with his kids. That's been alright. And I think I'm getting the hang of things around the bar. Right?'

'You're doing fine,' I assured her. 'Just don't let people push you around. And if there's any trouble, tell Anna to get Tom.'

'Yeah, that's what Dana said too. She also told me which guys to be careful around.'

'Yeah, we get a few nasties around here,' I said darkly. Curiosity gnawed at me. 'What's it like in Crater's Edge?'

Laura picked up a cloth and began wiping the counter down. One of the tables signalled to me for another round, so I grabbed a bottle of whiskey and set to pouring.

'What do you want to know?' Laura asked.

I focused on pouring as I thought the question over.

'Are there as many gangs? Is it safe?' I slid the glasses onto a tray and gestured to it. 'Bring that to table six. I'll think of more questions.'

'Alright.' Laura shuffled out from behind the bar. I busied myself bringing the tray of dirty glasses out to the kitchen, and when I got back, she was waiting for me.

'Two ales for table nine,' she said. 'And yes, Crater's Edge has gangs. But they're not as… prominent? Powerful? They keep to their areas anyway.' She shrugged.

'Their areas?'

'The outskirts of town, mostly. They will hassle people travelling into town, though. As for safety…' She toyed with the edge of her tray. 'The crime is quite high in certain areas. But the centre is safe.'

'Like here?' I asked.

'No, much safer,' Laura replied. I passed her the two ales and she set them on her tray. 'There's a strong police presence in the centre, at least.'

She reached for the tray, but at that moment the door burst open and Anna stumbled in, her hair a mess and a wild look in her eyes.

'Anna?' Laura asked sharply.

I took a step towards her. 'What happened?' I said urgently.

Anna scrubbed a hand over her eyes. 'Briggs—I—He—'

'Hey.' Laura put an arm around her. 'Shh. Take a deep breath.'

Anna pulled away, snatching a tissue from under the bar and blowing her nose noisily. 'No, I'm fine,' she said angrily. 'Fucking Iron Fists.'

I nodded my agreement. Laura made a sympathetic noise in the back of her throat. Abruptly, she stepped in and grabbed Anna's hand.

'You're hurt!'

Anna glanced at her hand. 'It's a little scratch. He pushed me and I tripped. I think my back is scraped too from when I hit the wall.'

'You need to clean that,' Laura insisted. 'It'll get infected.'

'Yes, Nurse Laura.'

I watched from a distance as they fussed over Anna's hand, picking gravel out of her palm. I was useless with injuries—I could deal with my own, but I had no idea how to play nurse. Laura was good at it, though. She cleaned the cut and wrapped a strip of gauze around Anna's hand.

When she straightened up, I passed Anna a tumbler with a finger of whiskey.

'Thanks.' Anna grimaced. Her eyes were red, but she wasn't crying anymore.

'What happened?' I asked quietly.

'Maybe we shouldn't discuss this,' Laura started. 'Anna doesn't need to be upset again.'

'She mentioned Briggs,' I pointed out. 'We don't do that here—if there's something going on, we all need to know—'

'There's a time and a place for that stuff!' Laura scowled at me. I stared at her in surprise; I hadn't been expecting her to put up a fight. 'Give her a chance to calm down.'

'She is calm.' If Briggs was lurking outside waiting to harass people, that was the sort of thing we needed to know. If the gang members were causing trouble for the staff at the Kranikovska, that was the sort of thing *Tom* needed to know. 'This is bigger than just Anna.'

'Have a bit of empathy—'

'It's okay,' Anna interrupted suddenly.

Laura glanced at her. 'Take a moment.'

'No, it's okay. Harley's right. He might try the same thing with the rest of you.' Anna brushed her hair out of her eyes. 'He was asking about Gabriel, the last time he was in the bar, what he said, where we all were on that day...' She shrugged. 'I told him what I knew, but I guess that wasn't enough for him, because he kept asking the same questions again and again, and then he pushed me.'

'He's a brute,' Laura said. 'I'm sorry you went through that.'

I nodded my agreement, but my stomach was churning with nausea. The Iron Fists weren't letting Tam's disappearance go. How long would it be before someone said the wrong thing and they linked it to me? What would happen then?

My chest hurt at the thought. I was dangling by a thread already.
What would be the blow that made it snap?

Hardwick's threats?

Hannover's demands?

Or would it be the Iron Fists? Who would they send after me?

Briggs would love to be the one to eliminate me, wouldn't he?

I turned away. Table four was watching me expectantly. As I met their gazes, one of the men waved pointedly.

'Let's get back to work,' I mumbled. 'The customers are waiting.'

'Yeah.' Anna grabbed her apron. 'Let's.'

My shift seemed to drag on forever that night. Finally, I handed the bar over to Kayla and slipped out the back. I was tense and jumpy, double-checking every shadow.

Would Briggs lie in wait for me?

Surely not?

I reached the square unhindered and started across it. For once, it felt safer to walk in the middle; there were fewer shadows a man could hide in.

A car hooted. I practically leapt out of my skin.

Heart racing, I glanced over to the hotel. Theo was parked up in front of the steps.

I jogged over. He opened the door.

'Were you trying to avoid me or something?'

'No.' I stopped, staring up at him. 'What are you doing here? I'm not going to the bunker tonight.'

'Giving you a lift.'

'I'm fine. I can walk home.'

Theo thumped his head against the headrest and groaned. 'Get in, Harley.'

Biting my cheek, I rounded the car and climbed in, flicking the radio and heater on. It was bloody cold.

'You're hopeless, you know that?' Theo said in a conversational tone.

'Because I don't want a lift home? You'll be gone again in a few weeks, and I'll have to walk anyway.'

Theo pressed his lips together. I crossed my arms. For a few seconds, we both stewed in our stubbornness.

'That's a stupid argument and you know it,' Theo said finally. 'Why deprive yourself now because you won't have something later? Why not enjoy the reprieve whilst you've got it?'

'Because.'

'Because…?'

I ground my teeth together. 'It's my life, Theo.'

'You're my best friend. I want to help you.'

I crossed my arms. What could I say to that? My reasons made sense to me—I had to be able to depend on myself. I couldn't stop, couldn't let anyone else look after me. That would be going against everything I'd vowed after my father had died.

It was me against the world. It always had been.

'It's not that I don't want your help,' I mumbled. 'It's just…'

'You can't accept it,' Theo said dully.

'It's not even that,' I said miserably. 'I have to be able to keep myself safe. There could come a time when you're not there—'

'We're going round in circles, Harley.'

'Because you're not listening to me.'

'I am listening to you!' Theo slapped his hand against the steering wheel. I flinched. 'I'm tired of you acting like I'm going to drop dead any second and leave you alone!'

'I don't think that!' I said. My chest felt tight—I couldn't breathe all of a sudden.

'You are. You know your problem? You don't trust anyone.'

'I do trust you!' I protested. My throat constricted. 'You're my best friend—'

'Yet I feel like I don't even know you anymore. You act weird every time you see me. You're not talking to me anymore.' Theo lowered his voice. 'You keep talking as though next time I leave we'll never see each other again.'

He'd noticed that? I was flummoxed. Scrambling, I muttered, 'You were gone ages—things change.'

'Is that what this is? I was gone too long?'

'No, I—'

A truck horn sliced through the tense atmosphere, sending my heart rate through the roof. A van hurtled past us, so close I heard metal scraping metal. Theo jerked the wheel to evade the other vehicle, and as it rocketed past us I caught a flash of a familiar logo. We swerved wildly until finally he got the car under control and slammed on the brakes, bringing us to a squealing halt.

'What the fuck?'

I jolted forwards and back again, my head slamming against the headrest. 'Oof!'

'Sorry.' For a second, we sat there in silence. Theo was gripping the steering wheel so hard that his knuckles glowed white. Finally, he asked, 'You alright?'

'Yeah,' I mumbled shakily. 'You?'

'Fine. Takes worse than that to throw me off.' He let go of the steering wheel, rolling his shoulders to release the tension. 'That was an NCC van, wasn't it? Wonder what got into them.'

I twisted around, squinting into the darkness behind us. 'Do you think someone was after them?'

'I don't see anyone.' Theo unlocked his fingers from around the steering wheel. 'I think they'd have passed us by now.'

'Yeah.'

Silence fell as we both panted in surprise. Gradually, my equilibrium came back.

'Why would they be racing through town like that?' I asked.

'Emergency delivery?' Theo rubbed his chest. 'They deliver supplies to the clinic and places like that, right?'

'They weren't heading to the clinic,' I pointed out.

'I don't know.' Theo shrugged. 'I'll call it in, see if anyone knows anything weird. We should get going, though.'

'I guess.'

I felt terribly exposed all of a sudden. My arms prickled with goosebumps under my coat. I rubbed them, trying to shake the feeling.

Theo straightened the car out and started towards my flat. I turned the radio up, and for the next few minutes we were both silent. Finally, he stopped outside my building.

'Look, I'm sorry I was gone so long. You know what my job is like.'

I glanced at Theo. He was looking at me, but in the darkness, I couldn't make out his expression.

'I know.' I picked at a loose thread on my coat sleeve.

'I'll always come back.'

'You can't promise that,' I mumbled.

'What do you want me to do, then? I can't just quit my job.' Theo sounded frustrated. Not that I blamed him. I frustrated myself most days.

'I'm not asking you to do that. But you also can't ask me to change everything about myself.'

'I'm not asking you to change anything.' Theo sighed. 'I just wish that we could make the most of it whilst I'm here. I don't want to argue with you.'

'You picked me up tonight *to* argue.' As soon as the words were out, I regretted them. That had been too sharp, too mean.

'I picked you up to *talk*. I'm worried about you.'

'I don't need you to worry about me.' I smoothed my hands down my legs and reached for the door handle. This was getting too uncomfortable.

'You can't stop me,' Theo said. 'Any more than I can force you to trust me.'

I groaned. 'I do trust you, Theo. What can I do to convince you of that?'

He stared at me, his eyes dark and shiny. 'I don't know anymore.'

I swallowed. 'Look, I have to go. It's late.'

Theo sat back in his seat. 'Alright, then.'

'Just like that?' I wavered, uneasily. Leaving felt like a mistake—he was upset, I was upset. I didn't want to leave things like this.

'What do you want me to say?' He reached for the ignition, fiddling with his keychain. 'I think you're hiding something. But you don't want to trust me, and that's fine. I guess I always knew this would happen—I'd keep leaving, and we'd grow apart.'

'We don't have to grow apart,' I said. Tears pricked at my eyes. 'I don't want to grow apart. Just because I want to rely on myself…'

'You're not relying on yourself, you're punishing yourself. And you can't keep doing that forever, Harley. You know you can't.'

A few tears escaped my eyes. I opened the door and threw my legs out. 'Let's… let's just talk another night, okay?'

I glanced back at Theo. He wasn't looking my way.

'Theo?'

'Yeah, alright. Goodnight, Harley.'

'Goodnight,' I whispered.

ELEVEN

TUESDAY NIGHT WAS A dark winter night—the air was still and cold, and the moon was hidden behind the clouds. It was so dark that in the areas with no streetlights I was forced to navigate by torchlight.

It was the kind of night where I wanted to be tucked up in bed, avoiding the world—but instead, I found myself walking to the Hawke and Tern to meet Hardwick.

Worries circled in my brain.

I had nothing new to report to him. Nothing but suspicions—and I knew it wasn't going to be enough.

Worse, Hannover's ultimatum hung over my head.

Kill Percival.

It was insanity. It was impossible. I didn't even know when or where the strike on the Iron Fists was going to be. I hadn't even known there was going to be one until Hannover had confirmed it.

And now I had to find out when it was and figure out how to make sure the Aces' leader got killed. Without Hardwick finding out what I was doing.

I was screwed.

Completely and utterly.

Maybe I should take Theo up on his offer. Maybe I should just tell him.

But…

Theo was a member of the Iron Fists.

I might have known him longer than he'd been in the gang, but that didn't change that he had to be loyal to them. There was a good chance that, forced to choose, he'd pick them. I couldn't guarantee that his loyalty to me would win out, especially when I had been such a bitch to him since he'd been back.

Fuck.

I was destroying the only friendship I really cared about.

This was such a fucking mess.

I groaned aloud.

How had my life turned into this?

Maybe I could convince Theo to drive Savannah and me to Crater's Edge. Could we force Savannah to go, between the two of us? But that meant I'd have to tell Theo the truth. How else could I persuade him to take us?

Ahead of me, a man turned onto my street. He was strolling in my direction, a dark silhouette under the paltry streetlights, and I could tell he was holding a rifle.

Fuck, that wasn't good.

Brazen it out or cross the road? Would that make it look like I was avoiding him? Would that provoke him?

He was probably a gang member, but which gang? We were still in the Iron Fists' territory—so hopefully that meant he wouldn't start something with me.

Hopefully.

My lungs ached. I had to force myself to breathe evenly as he drew nearer and nearer. All I had to do was keep walking. *Don't draw his attention. Just keep going.*

'Harley?'

My heart leapt into my throat. I knew that voice.

Bas.

No, no, no, damnit, of all the nights to run into him!

'What are you doing here?'

I dodged around him. 'Walking home.'

'We're nowhere near your flat.' Bas turned on his heel and fell into step with me. 'Why are you actually here?'

'Don't you have to stick to your route?'

'That's my business, Harley.'

'Yeah?' I glared at him. 'And where I'm going is my business.'

Bas's stride faltered as a frown flitted across his face. 'That's different.'

I stopped, turning to face him. 'Oh, really? How?'

'I'm not putting myself in danger.'

'Are you for real?' I spluttered indignantly. I crossed my arms. 'This is actually getting to the point of harassment. *Leave me alone!*'

'*You* crossed paths with *me*,' Bas responded.

'I didn't ask you to speak to me. I definitely didn't ask you to chew me out.' I took a deep breath, reaching for some kind of calm. 'Look, you don't like me, I don't like you. Let's try to be adults about it. We can just ignore each other, you know. That is a possibility.'

Bas pressed his lips together, looking distinctly unhappy. 'I'm not harassing you. I'm trying to keep you safe.'

'I'm a twenty-five-year-old woman, and you don't even like me. Why bother?'

Bas turned his head away. I honestly didn't think he was going to answer. Then he scraped a hand through his hair, messing it up, and muttered, 'It's my fault you got in this whole mess anyway.'

I couldn't help it; I laughed.

It was the most ridiculous thing I'd heard in *months*.

'Your fault? How the hell is anything that's happened in my life your fault?'

Bas squirmed. I couldn't believe my eyes. He was shuffling his weight like a five-year-old caught stealing cookies. 'If Rodney hadn't seen you and me together in the bar—'

Another laugh bubbled in my throat. 'You've got to be joking. Besides, Rodney was interested in me before that—he realised I recognised him the first time I saw him and your father meeting the mayor in the hotel.'

Bas grimaced, his gaze sliding over my shoulder. For a long moment, he said nothing at all. I was about ready to give up and leave. I was going to be late.

Fuck it, I'm going.

'Look, I actually have somewhere to be, so—'

'It's my fault we had you working in the hotel in the first place,' Bas blurted out.

The words evaporated right off my tongue. I stared at him in blank shock. *What the actual ever-loving fuck?*

'I've been working there for *two years*. You didn't even know me two years ago.'

Bas swallowed, his Adam's apple bobbing. 'I did. You probably don't remember, though. We met in the bunker when I first joined the Iron Fists.'

Two years ago, I'd been on my way out of the bunker. To be honest, my memories of the time were overshadowed by the sheer relief of escaping, followed by the weirdness of having a normal job. I hadn't spared much thought for any newcomers.

I shrugged. 'I don't know what that has to do with my job.'

'Ellery wanted to help you. I was the one who suggested he get you the job at the Kranikovska. I knew you liked Ellery, and if he suggested a deal, you'd take it.'

I gaped at him. 'Are you serious?'

Ellery had offered me the job in exchange for keeping an eye on the patrons of the bar. '*Just until you get back on your feet,*' he'd said. '*Consider it a transitional position.*'

Except, if Bas was right, they had never intended for me to move on from it. And it hadn't been nearly as innocent as Ellery had suggested.

'Why?' I demanded.

Bas's lips twisted. 'Harley…'

'No, tell me.' I glared at him. 'I want to know. Why me? Why there?'

'Fine.' He squared his shoulders. 'I had escaped the Black Hands recently. We needed to know if Moriarty and Hannover were going to do anything about it. Hannover had—has—a particular liking for women quite a bit younger than him, with particular features.'

'Like me,' I filled in.

'You fit the bill.' Bas shrugged. 'I didn't intend for you to actually get involved with him. He wouldn't have tried anything in neutral territory. But when he drinks, his lips get loose. If there was a chance, I had to take it.'

Un-fucking-believable.

'So for two years I thought I was doing one job, and really I was doing a whole different one?' A maelstrom of emotion was whipping up in my chest. Anger, hurt, and a bunch of others I wasn't sure I wanted to name.

'You provided Ellery with useful information,' Bas said defensively.

'I was acting under false pretences!'

'We did what we had to to keep you and ourselves safe.'

'You—' I shook my head angrily. 'You have got to be joking. Safe? It was never about keeping me safe. It was about controlling me—'

'It had nothing to do with you. You were incidental to the plan.'

That hurt worse. So any damage to my life was just collateral? 'Fuck you,' I sneered. 'You had no right.'

'If we had told you the truth—'

'If you had respected me, you would have told me the truth and let me make up my own mind!' I snarled. 'You're a jerk—and a hypocrite. And you had the nerve to be a dick to me after *I* betrayed *you?* Fuck you!'

Anger rushed through my veins. I wanted to hit him so hard he bled. I was absolutely furious. He'd played with my *life*—and he didn't even care about what danger I might have been in.

And he claimed he wanted to protect me from Hannover?

'If you think this absolves you—'

'Absolves me?' I echoed incredulously. 'I can't believe I ever considered protecting you from your brother. You and him deserve each other!'

'You're overreacting, Harley.' Bas's voice was infinitely calm. My anger exploded out of me.

'OVERREACTING?' I screamed. 'YOU PUT ME THERE TO REPORT ON HANNOVER TO YOU AND WHEN I ACTUALLY BROUGHT YOU INFORMATION ABOUT HIM, YOU TOLD ME I WAS LYING AND BEING RIDICULOUS. YOU ARE FUCKING JOKING!'

'*Stop shouting!*' Bas snarled.

I itched to punch him the way he'd taught me in self-defence classes—it'd bloody serve him right—but instead, I shoved my hands in my pockets. Anger was giving way to hurt, too fast for me to keep a good hold on it. Tears stung my eyes and my throat burnt with every breath I took.

'We're done,' I choked. A tear escaped down my face. 'I'm leaving. Goodnight, Bas.'

'For fuck's sake—'

'*Goodnight*, Bas.'

I spun around and fled down the road, my footsteps echoing off the buildings. I turned down the first side street I saw. The last thing I wanted was for Bas to follow me.

But he didn't.

Finally, I slowed to a walk. My heart was racing, and my face was a sticky mess from my tears. The cold air burnt my cheeks.

Unbelievable.

I felt used.

Two years—and they'd let me believe Bas was new, that I was only just meeting him… Ellery had let me believe he had my best interests at heart.

Meanwhile, they'd been directly and deliberately putting me in Hannover's path. Bait to lure him in.

Even if it hadn't worked, they had still messed with my life. Bas was right. They were directly responsible for the mess I was in. Granted, I had no idea where I would have ended up if Ellery hadn't got me the job… but that didn't excuse him from using me under the pretence of helping me.

And Bas… Well, he hadn't known me. I'd just been a convenient tool to him. I had come to care about him, and the whole time he'd been using me.

And now? Every time he'd been nice to me—the time he'd saved me from being raped—the self-defence lessons—was all that just because he felt he owed me? Was he just trying to repay a debt?

Was it all meaningless?

Since I was seventeen, every moment of my life had been manipulated and controlled by men. Leaving the bunker, I had thought I was freeing myself of that.

What a naïve idiot I had been.

I scuffed my boot against the ground. Well, now I knew. And it wouldn't happen again—I wasn't going to fall for their tricks ever again. Starting from now, I would cut Bas out of my heart. I'd tell Brenda the next time I saw her that I was done with him.

For good.

When I got to the Hawke and Tern, Hardwick was already waiting for me. As I entered the warm, smoky pub, he motioned for the bartender, Turner, to pour a glass of whiskey.

'I thought you weren't coming,' he said as I approached the bar.

'I was late going off shift,' I said dismissively.

'See that it doesn't happen again.'

If he thought I was going to be meek and compliant, he had another thing coming. 'Sure, I'll let Tom know that I have to get to my second job as a spy. I'm sure that'll go down well.'

Hardwick shot me a sharp look. 'What you do and don't have to do is your problem,' he said. 'Mine is ensuring the smooth transfer of knowledge. Let's go.'

He passed me my drink and began marching towards the back of the pub. I shot Turner a grimace and mouthed, '*Thanks.*'

He raised an eyebrow in question, but I didn't know what he was asking. I hurried after Hardwick and entered the back hallway. He led me to the same room as last time; it had been tidied, but in a hurry, and the papers were stacked in haphazard piles.

'Sit,' Hardwick said tersely.

I took a sip of whiskey and lowered myself slowly into one of the hardback chairs. He pulled his chair up opposite me. 'You had more success ingratiating yourself this week than last week.'

I gritted my teeth. I hadn't seen hide nor hair of Hardwick at the bunker on Saturday, and I'd been looking. 'Where are you watching me from?'

'You aren't my only spy.'

'Who else is there?'

Hardwick swirled his glass. 'That's for me to know.'

He was toying with me. He didn't even need me as a spy, and apparently he liked to remind me of that fact.

'Fine. What do you want me to tell you?'

'Who were you talking to on your break?'

I sipped my drink, stalling. Tell him about Theo, or not? No choice, really. 'James Maddock, Andrew Kade, and Theo Dunne.'

'Dunne?' He singled Theo out, just like I'd known he would. 'A relative of Alistair Dunne?'

'That's his father, yeah.'

'An interesting contact for a dancer,' Hardwick mused.

'Not really. Theo is an old school friend.'

'And a potential source of information.'

'I'm not—' I cut myself off. I knew better than to tell Hardwick I wouldn't use Theo; Hardwick had made it amply clear that he didn't care what lines he forced me to cross. But there was another line I could take to protect Theo. 'He won't know anything about his father's activities. They're not in contact anymore.'

'A clever spy could convince him to re-establish contact,' Hardwick mused pointedly.

'Unlikely. Dunne made it clear that he wouldn't speak to Theo again.'

Hardwick's lips twisted. 'That's a shame. I'd think you'd want to try a little harder.'

'I can't move mountains,' I snapped. 'Besides, you asked me to spy on the Iron Fists, not some snotty rich guy in his fancy house. Aren't you already in with the mayor and his lot?'

Hardwick raised an eyebrow. 'Mind your tone.'

Mind yours, I thought viciously, though I didn't dare say it. 'What else do you want to know?'

Hardwick tilted his head thoughtfully. 'Who is the other one? James Maddock?'

'He moved to town over the summer.' I shrugged. 'I don't know much about him, other than that he worked his way up in the fights.' I still hadn't seen him fight, either. I'd been dancing on the north stage, which had the worst visibility, during his fight on Saturday. I was still annoyed at Carlos for deciding to put me there.

'As usual, your information leaves much to be desired.'

Irritation surged through my veins, further eroding my already frayed temper. 'No one knows anything about him. He's from Brackfields. He's here working for a real estate construction supply company. He works with the Godfreys.'

Hardwick nodded along. 'Very well. I can look into that from my end. Would you say he's of any threat to the Iron Fists?'

How the hell did I answer that? Maddock's offer from months ago sprang into my head. He had somehow gotten it into his head that he could take down the gangs, but I had no idea if he could actually do it.

'I think he wants to be.' I shrugged again. 'No idea how, why, or if he can do it, though.' Thinking fast, I added, 'But he might seize an opportunity if one arose.'

Such as the sort that might arise if the Aces were planning on striking against the Iron Fists.

Hardwick, however, did not take my bait. 'Find out,' he said flatly.

I grimaced. 'Yes, sir.'

Hardwick glared at me. 'No cheek. What else have you got for me?'

We ran through a few questions on financials and gossip I'd heard from the other dancers before finally Hardwick's questions seemed to run dry. I still hadn't managed to glean anything about the upcoming strike. I didn't even know how to ask. How did you subtly sneak that into conversation?

Before I could try anything else, Hardwick slid a small device onto the table between us. It was perfectly round, made of black plastic, and about an inch in diameter and a quarter of an inch thick. On the top side were four tiny holes.

'What's that?' I asked, curious despite myself.

'Old-world tech, and that's all you need to know.' Hardwick turned it over. On the underside was a white square. 'Peel here.' He gestured to one corner. 'Then stick it to a flat surface, out of sight, and press the button.'

'And then what?' I asked suspiciously. That sounded way too simple—and weird—to be a standard request. 'Where am I sticking it?'

'I'm getting to that.' Hardwick placed a scrap of paper on the table beside the strange device. On it was written, *Reverie, room 04.*

'This is where you need to go. I trust you won't have trouble getting in there.'

I took the paper, frowning. 'I've never heard of the place.'

Hardwick raised an eyebrow. 'That disappoints me, seeing as you're well acquainted with the owner... or with his son, actually.'

I hadn't a clue who he was talking about. 'Who?'

'The parent company is RocCo. The same company that owns North Crater Security Company, Bale Rocks Transport Company, and a number of other auspicious enterprises in our cosy town.'

'RocCo...' I'd heard that name before, but where? I racked my memory, but nothing came to mind. 'Stop playing games, Hardwick. If you want me to help you, I need the whole story.'

He splayed his hands out on his knees, smirking. 'It's the company owned by Jonathon Rochester, father of Rodney and Sebastian.'

Abruptly, it hit me where I'd seen it before: on an office door at the industrial site where Rodney had taken me when he'd kidnapped me. I'd dismissed it at the time—I barely kept track of all of the big industrial companies around here. What did I care about them? They employed the bulk of the people in town and treated them little better than actual slaves.

'Wait, the Rochesters own a brothel?' I mimed gagging. Did Rodney Rochester know that? So much for his hoity-toity principles.

'It's more of a high-class establishment,' Hardwick said.

'High class or no, if people pay to fuck, it's a brothel.'

He laughed drily. 'Correct. In any case, it will also be used as the meeting point between a man named Malcolm Brady, and another whom I believe you know, Derek Jackson.'

Jackson was a lieutenant for the Iron Fists. I'd never heard of Brady. Was he a member of the Iron Fists? Or another gang?

'And you want me to listen in on the meeting?' That sounded dangerous.

'You? No.' Hardwick chuckled. 'I want you to plant this device somewhere in the room before the meeting next week Wednesday at nine PM, then leave. As simple as that.'

Simple? It sounded anything but. I picked up the device, studying it. It was utterly innocuous; no hint of danger, no clues as to its purpose. 'This isn't going to kill them, is it?'

'No.'

'Then what does it do?' I glanced up at Hardwick, but his face gave nothing away.

'You don't need to know that,' he said. 'You just need to follow instructions.'

I gritted my teeth. I hated not knowing—it felt like he was leading me into a trap. The less I knew, the less I wanted to be involved.

'What is the meeting about?' I pressed.

'That is for me to know.' Hardwick raised an eyebrow. 'You have one job. Plant the device.'

Fucking patronising dickhead.

But what else could I do? He'd already made his thoughts clear.

Besides that, whatever this meeting was, it was suspicious as hell. And even more strange was that Hardwick didn't want me overhearing…

Almost like he knew what they were going to discuss. Like it was something important.

Something it would benefit me to know.

'Fine.' I tucked the device in my pocket. 'Next Wednesday at nine PM.'

'Before then,' Hardwick stressed. 'The device has to be in place *before* the meeting starts.'

'I understand.'

'Good. Then we're done.'

He stood, and I followed suit a second later, downing the last of my whiskey. I took a moment to discretely observe my surroundings as I followed him down the hall. I was quite familiar with the back rooms of bars, thanks to working at Krani's, but the back rooms of the Hawke and Tern were strangely extensive. I'd have expected a kitchen, a storeroom, and an office, but we passed two separate staircases and at least three other doors. And the people back here didn't look like employees: two women on one of the staircases had dark, haunted eyes and wore oversized clothes.

What sort of operation were they running back here?

Almost certainly something illegal.

And I did not want to know. I had my hands full without getting involved in this.

I returned my whiskey glass to the bar. Turner scooped it up. 'Everything alright there?'

'Yes?' I murmured cautiously.

'Right.' He studied me with dark eyes. My skin crawled. Attracting attention was the last thing I wanted to do.

Apparently Hardwick agreed, because he barked, 'Off you go now.'

Turner's mouth immediately turned down. 'Problem, Hardwick?'

'Not at all,' Hardwick said smoothly.

'I don't recall inviting you to this discussion.' Turner raised an eyebrow. In one hand, he held my glass. The other gripped the edge of the bar, his knuckles white. A frisson of tension suffused the smoky air.

'I don't recall inviting you into my business,' Hardwick replied.

'Just remember, this is my bar.' Turner jerked his head between me and the door. 'You should go. Walk safely out there.'

'I will.' I took a step back, half-curious, half-wary. I'd assumed Turner and Hardwick were allies, but suddenly it didn't seem like it. They both watched each other with narrowed eyes, but neither of them spoke—and they wouldn't until I left. I wasn't allowed to observe this conflict.

I turned on my heel and escaped through the door, out into the cold winter night.

TWELVE

REVERIE WAS A BROTHEL on the west side of Bale Rocks. It was located just south of Hustle Highway, in the area where most of the brothels operated—but apart enough to feel exclusive. It was the sort of place that catered to the richer inhabitants of our town. It was as classy as brothels got around here anyway.

In short, I had no idea how I was going to get in.

I couldn't just pose as one of the prostitutes; I'd certainly be noticed. I didn't know anyone who worked there, nor did I know any of the regular clients. There were certainly people I knew who probably went there—Brody Cavanaugh came to mind—but I'd never ask them for help.

Maybe Posy knew someone who worked there? She was well-connected.

If not Posy, then maybe one of the other dancers at the bunker. I'd ask Posy first, though, because she was one of the only girls I trusted to actually keep a secret.

Otherwise, I had no idea.

Hardwick was way overestimating my abilities. Apparently he thought I could phase through walls or something.

Or he intended for me to pose as a hooker. But even if I did, I wasn't confident that was going to get me through the door. Places like that had vetting processes. I'd never pass muster.

I turned the problem over in my head a thousand times during the next few days. By Friday, I was no closer to a solution to any of my problems. I didn't know how I was going to get into Reverie, nor did I have any idea when the Aces were planning their strike on the Iron Fists.

I was running out of time. What happened if I missed the strike? Surely there would be some warning, though. Maybe Theo would know. But could I risk asking him?

I was driving myself crazy with this—forget Hannover doing me in, I was going to snap from the stress.

When I arrived at work, Kayla was there, wiping the counter down. The bar was quiet, which… was odd. We'd been expecting the caravans to arrive for the merchants' market towards the end of this week—they usually came a few days early so they had time to set up.

I strode over.

'No merchants?'

Kayla shook her head, a frown tugging at her lips. 'Not yet.'

'Weird. They usually arrive on Thursday.'

She shrugged, glancing out the window. 'Could be delays because of recent bad weather?'

'Hopefully.'

The alternatives were worse—the merchant's market came via Boughton, a town out to the west of Bale Rocks. The main road between Bale Rocks and Boughton had washed away a few years ago and never been rebuilt, so the only other option was to go south and then cut north again on the Brackfields—Bale Rocks Road… which ran straight through the slaver hunting grounds and Moriarty's territory. But there was no use catastrophising—it was out of my control.

'Maybe Tom's heard something?' I suggested.

'Not that I know of, but we can ask if he comes in.' Kayla nodded to one of the tables beneath the large antique mirror. 'Table eleven is probably due a refill.'

'Alright.'

I shoved my coat under the counter, tied my apron around my waist, and got to work. No use worrying about the merchant caravan— I had enough on my plate.

The afternoon continued to be unsettlingly quiet. Every time we heard vehicle out on the square, Kayla or I went to peek out, but there was no sign of the merchant caravans. By four, it was starting to get dark, and there was a palpable aura of worry amongst the hotel staff. Periodically, we would hear footsteps in the lobby as someone went to check at the front door.

But the caravans did not arrive.

'Tom's here,' Kayla reported when she came back from her break, the smell of cigarette smoke wafting off her clothes. 'I just saw him park at the back.'

'That's good, I guess,' I said.

'Or bad,' she replied.

'Or bad.' I dug my hands into my pockets, and my fingers found the little case Hardwick had given me. If there was no merchants' market, would that change the plans the Aces and the mayor had for our town?

Before I could make myself sick with stress again, Tom stepped through the back door into the bar.

'Hullo, Kayla, Harley.' He glanced around the room, which was still quiet. The after-work drinks rush would be starting soon, but for now it was peaceful.

'Hi,' I returned.

Tom sighed.

'Any news?' Kayla prodded.

'Not so far. The mayor sent a runner over; it looks like they're considering sending a security force down the road. Hopefully we'll know more soon.'

'Do they think something has happened?' Kayla asked.

'No news yet.' Tom shrugged and scrubbed a hand over her bald head. 'We'll see what happens. Be on standby for a sudden crowd, in any case.'

'Alright,' I said.

Tom disappeared through the door again, leaving Kayla and me to our thoughts. She shot me a grimace.

'So, trouble?'

'Looks like it,' I muttered.

'No use worrying. We'll check the stock room and make sure everything's up and running, then wait and see.'

'Yeah.' I ran my fingers over the little case in my pocket again and made a snap decision. Kayla's father owned a shop that salvaged old tech.

'Kayla, you're quite tech-y. Can I ask you a question?'

Kayla looked up from the inventory log she'd pulled out and propped her pen behind her ear. 'Depends what you want to know.'

I glanced around the mostly empty bar, then slid the device out of my pocket and onto the counter, keeping my hand around it so no one else could see. 'Ever seen one of these before?'

Kayla's brow creased in a frown. She reached out and picked up the device, holding it pinched between her thumb and forefinger. 'Where did you get this?'

'I can't tell you,' I said warily.

Kayla glanced at me, an eyebrow raised. There was a long, pregnant pause, in which I worried that she wouldn't let it drop. But Kayla's lack of curiosity won out. She had a strict rule about not asking questions or involving herself in anything potentially dangerous.

'Alright, I suppose I don't want to know.' She turned it over, the plastic casing catching the light. 'It's a bugging device. They're used to listen into conversations remotely.'

'It's not working now, is it?' I asked, panicking. Could Hardwick hear what we were saying?

Kayla shook her head, her long braids swaying. 'It's not active. This light flashes when it is. I've never seen one in person before, but my father has a book on them.'

'Could he use it?'

'Not without the other piece. It has to connect to something to transmit the sound. Like a radio—it needs a receiver.'

'Oh.' I stared at the little black dot. It didn't look like much. But it would help Hardwick hear what was said in that meeting.

I don't want you to hear the conversation at all.

He'd overhear, but I wouldn't. Meaning that, as usual, he'd hold all the chips. Did he know what they were going to discuss? Was there something important happening in that meeting that he didn't want me to know about?

Something that I could use?

No reason why I can't stick around and listen in too.

'Thanks.' I reached for the bugging device, but Kayla closed her fist around it.

'There's been a lot of old tech kicking around town lately,' she remarked casually.

'Has there?' I asked nervously. 'This is the first I've seen of it.'

'Hmm.' Kayla opened her fist and dropped the bugging device into my palm. 'Whatever you're involved in, don't go bringing it near the bar, yeah? We're all just trying to live our lives here.'

'I know.' I slid the device into the pocket of my jeans. 'I won't. But thanks for the info.'

'No problem.' Kayla gathered her braids into a ponytail. 'If you find anything else like that, though, you're welcome to bring it by the shop.

Daddy loves to take things apart.'

'I'll bear that in mind.'

On Saturday, the merchants still hadn't arrived. Tom, white-faced and stressed, was entertaining groups of serious-looking men in the upstairs rooms. He was serving them himself, though, leaving us girls to keep things feeling normal in the downstairs bar—no simple task.

We had the music on and were serving drinks by the dozen, but there was a pressure building in the air that couldn't be ignored. We all felt it, weighing on our shoulders. The stress of people starting to ask themselves: how am I going to provide for my family this winter?

Once again, Theo arrived at the end of my shift and sidled up to the bar, his expression sheepish. 'Hi, Harley.'

'Hey,' I muttered quietly, pretending to be incredibly busy refilling my water jug.

'Theo!' Anna called.

'Hey, honey.' Theo brightened, grinning at her. 'You're looking perky.'

'Thank you.' Anna preened. 'I'm turning over a new leaf. No more moping.'

'Moping?' Theo slapped a hand over his chest. 'What reason could such a lovely lady possibly have to mope?'

Anna's lips twisted. I focused intently on the water dispenser, wishing it would go slower.

'I was left behind.' Anna was obviously aiming for a cheerful tone, but she fell way short. 'It happens.'

'Left behind?' Theo asked.

'By Gabriel Tam... he skipped town without a word.' Out of the corner of my eye, I saw her shrug. 'It's just one of those things. I guess he didn't feel like he owed me an explanation.'

The jug was full, and I had no excuse to look away anymore. I heaved it onto my tray and glanced impatiently at Anna, who was filling a big order for table two.

'I heard about that,' Theo said thoughtfully. 'It's not like Tam to skip out, though. He usually reports to Jackson before he leaves.'

'It's one of those things,' Anna repeated forcefully. 'Anyway, let's talk about something else.'

An awkward silence fell between us. I shuffled my weight, and Theo glanced at me, frowning lightly. The back of my neck prickled with awareness.

Theo cleared his throat. 'No merchants?'

'Nope,' I said.

'Huh.' He tapped his fingers on the bar. 'They're always here by now.'

'They are,' Anna said gravely.

'No one knows anything?'

I shook my head.

'The mayor sent a security team,' Anna explained. 'They left first thing this morning.'

'And they're not back yet?'

We exchanged grim looks.

The other cities might feel like they were on the other side of the world, but the reality was that it was only half a day's drive from here to Boughton. We should have heard news by now.

Anna set the last pint glass on my tray. I picked it up, my shoulders straining.

'Let me run this to table two, then I can clock out for the night.'

Theo nodded, standing and stretching. 'I'll wait outside. I need to radio the compound.'

'Okay then.'

Was he radioing them about the mayor's security team going missing? Why? Because he thought the mayor might be vulnerable right now?

But the mayor would never make himself vulnerable; he'd be sure to keep a team around him at all times.

No—the realisation hit me suddenly. It was because the Iron Fists weren't up to date on the news. Maybe they hadn't even heard about the security team.

Had their network weakened so much?

The Iron Fists had always held the most power in town because they controlled the whiskey distillery. It wasn't just the most important business in Bale Rocks; it had a distribution network that they could use to receive and pass on information. If that was breaking down... then there was a good chance they might not hold the distillery for much longer.

Which the Aces and the Black Hands knew.

Which was why they were planning a strike.

On the *distillery*.

It had to be—I knew I was right. But how could I confirm it?

And more importantly, how could I warn the Iron Fists that it was coming?

Should I warn them?

I couldn't not. I might not support them, but that didn't mean I wanted them dead. At least, not Ellery, Theo, Bas... And I couldn't warn them without warning everyone, because they were all loyal to a fault.

Bloody idiot gang members.

Sometimes I wished they were less loyal. It would make my life easier. Theo and I could have run away together years ago...

Wishful thinking.

I delivered the drinks to Clem and his bridge buddies at table two, then pulled my apron off. As I was donning my coat, Brenda entered.

'Brenda!' I exclaimed. She held her arms out and I hugged her. 'Feels like it's been ages.'

'You should come visit me sometime.' She pulled away and hugged Anna as well. 'Dinner at my place on your next day off.'

'That'll be Monday,' I said.

'I can probably switch shifts,' Anna put in. 'At least, now that Laura's training is mostly done.'

'How's she doing?' Brenda asked.

'Great,' Anna said.

'She's shy,' I said. 'And stubborn.'

'But she's kind too,' Anna said. 'And she'll settle down.'

'Kind,' I muttered. What use was kindness for a waitress?

'Don't be such a cynic,' Brenda teased. 'Bring her along on Monday too. I'd like to meet her properly.'

'Alright,' Anna said. 'I'll speak to Tom and see if we can rearrange the shifts.'

'Excellent.' Brenda squeezed my arm. 'How are you doing after our conversation last week?'

I made a face. 'Walk me out and I'll tell you?'

Anna glanced between us curiously.

'Alright.' Brenda ushered me to the door. Once we were out in the hall, I pulled my coat around me.

'I found something out,' I confided in a low voice. 'Bas—that's his name, the guy—he was lying to me.'

'Oh, Harley,' Brenda said. 'What about?'

'It doesn't matter,' I mumbled. 'But he kept it up for a long time. Years. I don't think I can let it go.'

All of a sudden, I felt like crying. I hadn't cried since the night Bas had blurted out his awful confession, but now my eyes stung and I felt like a vice was wrapped around my chest.

It wasn't fair.

Why couldn't my life be simple?

Brenda put her arm around my shoulders. 'Hey, don't cry over him. Men like that don't deserve our tears.'

'I know.' I scrubbed at my eyes, but the tears escaped anyway—one, then another. *Damnit.*

Brenda rubbed my back for a few seconds whilst I breathed into her shoulder. She smelt mumsie. Familiar and wonderful.

Finally, I pulled away. 'I have to go. I have a shift at the bunker.'

'Oh, hon.' Brenda sighed. 'Alright then. Come around six-thirty on Monday?'

I nodded. 'As long as we can get people covering the bar for the merchants.'

'Hopefully they'll be here by then.'

'Yeah.' If they weren't, we would have a problem. Winters here were long and hard, and we depended on being able to stock up at the merchants' market. Without that, how would we manage?

I bade Brenda goodbye and headed outside. Theo was waiting in his car, his elbow propped against the window and his head in his hand, a pensive look on his face. When I opened the passenger door, he jerked upright.

'Hey, Harley.'

'Hi.' I clambered up and pulled the door shut. 'So… It's bloody cold.'

'Yeah.' Theo started the car and put the heating on. 'There you go.'

'Thanks.'

Awkwardness crackled between us. Without Anna's cheery mood to lighten the atmosphere, we didn't seem to be able to hold a conversation anymore.

I was losing my best friend.

The awkwardness persisted throughout our drive, only ebbing as the station came into view.

'Another day, another fight,' Theo sighed.

'Thought you enjoyed the fights.'

'Oh, I do. It's nice to have low-stakes violence.' He shot me a smirk. 'You'll watch, right?'

'If you time it better than last time.'

'I'll put in a special request just for you.' He fluttered his eyelashes at me. I giggled.

Feeling better, I let him help me over the train tracks and down the ladder. The bunker was already teeming with people when we arrived. After we checked our weapons, I went up on tiptoes and pressed a kiss to Theo's cheek. 'Enjoy your fight.'

'Dance like there's no tomorrow, baby.'

I grinned, pulling away. 'Always.'

We separated, and I headed through the metal corridors to my dressing room. Posy was there, making a face at the mirror as she tried to get her eye makeup symmetrical.

'I swear makeup techniques were invented to torture women.'

'You're telling me.' I dropped my bag on the table beside her. 'How bad will Carlos kill me if I go without?'

'Bad.'

'You're right. Damn.' I pulled out my makeup kit and twisted my hair up above my head in a loose bun. 'Hey, can I ask you something?'

'Sure.' Posy pouted at the mirror. 'Anything, you know that.'

'You heard of Reverie?'

She shot me a sideways glance. 'What do you want with a place like that?'

'Can you keep a secret?'

Posy raised her eyebrows. She looked over her shoulder at the door, then back at me and nodded solemnly.

'I need to get in there at a specific time on a specific day. I was wondering if you knew anyone who might be willing to trade favours.'

'Why would you need to do that?' Posy frowned.

'You probably don't want to know.'

Her forehead wrinkled. She lined up her makeup brushes on the dressing table absentmindedly, tapping the powder off each one.

'You're right. I probably don't. I might know one of the girls who works there.'

'Great.' I chewed my lip before spitting out the words I'd planned. 'I'm willing to make it worth her time.'

Posy shook her head. 'You know what, that's between you and them. I'll ask her—but that's all, alright? I don't want to be involved.'

'Of course not,' I promised.

'Good.'

'Thanks, though. I owe you one.'

'Anytime.' Posy shook her head and snorted. 'I don't know what you got yourself mixed up in this time, but you sure are a weird one.'

'Gee, thanks.'

Posy laughed. She recapped her mascara and pushed herself up. 'I'll come by the Kranikovska tomorrow. You're working, right? You can buy me a drink.'

'Alright, then.' I kicked my boots off.

'Now, to more important things,' Posy declared. She waved two outfits at me. 'Black leather or silver sparkles?'

THIRTEEN

MY SHIFT THAT NIGHT was uneventful—it was surprising how quickly I'd become used to the old routine. Or maybe it was that I felt a little more relaxed now that I'd spoken to Posy. She knew all sorts of people around town. If she could find someone to help me, she would.

After that, it would be up to me.

But that was okay. I'd find something to trade.

For now, I danced my heart out, and on my breaks, I watched the fights. Theo took down his opponents with his usual fluid grace, but the real surprise was Maddock. He looked so unassuming and vulnerable in the cage, yet he seemed to catch his opponents by surprise every time, winning with deft moves that knocked men double his size off balance and sent them crashing to the floor.

When the lights came up and I climbed off my stage, I was drenched in sweat and breathing hard. I cast about for Theo—he was deep in conversation with a few guys on the other side of the circle. I started to make my way over, but before I got too far, someone stepped in my way.

'Well, look who's here. Harley Benoit.'

Red hair, freckles, and a perpetual sneer. Greg Talbot. I stepped back, wrinkling my nose.

'Talbot.' I hadn't seen him in the bunker since I'd started coming here, and I was glad about that. He was dating my sister—the last thing I wanted to see was him carrying on with the sort of activities I knew she'd hate, or worse, carrying on with another woman. 'Shouldn't you be off with your girlfriend?'

Talbot snorted. 'Maybe I should bring her here.'

My hackles rose. 'Don't you *dare!*'

He tipped his head back, chortling. 'Oh, that's just great. You know she's a big girl, right?'

'Big girl or not, you're not bringing her here. She doesn't belong in this place.'

He offered me a patronising smirk. 'Your sister's sweet. I'd love to be the one who dirties her up a bit.'

'Harley?'

I turned. Theo had arrived. He was looking between Talbot and me uncertainly.

'Dunne,' Talbot sneered.

'Talbot.' Theo's expression closed off. 'What are you doing over here?'

'Oh, nothing.' Talbot threw his arm around my shoulders. I ducked away, fighting the urge to puke. 'Harley and I were just having a chat about her charming big sister.'

'Get away from me,' I hissed.

'Aw, don't be like that. For all you know, we could end up being in-laws.'

'You have got to be joking.' I suppressed a gag.

'Golly gosh, Savannah sure has lowered her standards,' Theo drawled. 'You sure there isn't something wrong with her eyes, Harley baby?'

'Could be,' I mused. 'Maybe I should check.'

'Oh go suck Diego's cock, Dunne,' Talbot snapped. 'You're just jealous that I managed to get my hands on one of the Benoit twins.'

'If I were thusly inclined, I could show Savannah a much better time than you.' Theo rolled his eyes. 'Seeing as I actually respect her. You're just hoping for a threesome—you may as well pay a hooker. I think there's a pair of twins who do that sort of gig over on Hustle Highway. They're much more your speed.'

Talbot balled his fist and swung it at Theo. His other arm flailed at me. I stepped hastily backwards.

Theo didn't bother moving—the blow struck him square in the chest. He caught Talbot's arm and twisted it rapidly, forcing Talbot around and down onto his knees.

'Next time I break your fingers, and then how will you keep Savannah happy?' he sneered in Talbot's ear.

Talbot spat on the ground. 'Fuck you.'

'Dunne!'

We all turned. Jackson was walking in our direction. Theo stepped back and raised his hands, an innocent expression on his face.

'What do you think you're doing?' Jackson demanded.

'He fuckin' went for me,' Talbot blurted.

'He fucking didn't,' I snapped.

Jackson waved dismissively at me. 'You, shut up.' I snapped my mouth shut, irritation rushing through me. 'Dunne, explain.'

'Just teaching Talbot a bit of respect.' Theo tucked his hands in the pockets of his gym shorts, shrugging artfully. 'Not sure the lesson stuck. Might have to repeat it.'

'Save it for the cage or you'll be suspended,' Jackson warned. His weathered face crinkled in a frown as he turned to Talbot. 'And you, get lost. We're closing.'

Talbot stood laboriously, rubbing his arm. 'Fine, I'm going. Fucking cunts.' The last part, he added quietly enough that we could conceivably have misheard.

But I was sure I hadn't.

This guy was all shades of jackass. I needed to get him away from my sister. But how? She never listened to me, and whatever I said, she'd dig in her heels. She actually seemed to like him.

Maybe he acted differently around her?

But I was pretty sure this was his true face.

He stomped past us. Jackson, Theo, and I watched him go. Finally, Theo turned to me. 'You want to go get changed? I'll drop you home.'

'Yeah.'

I started towards the back rooms, but Jackson held out an arm, barring Theo's path. 'Stay back a minute. I need to speak to you.'

I glanced at Theo, but he waved me on, mouthing, *'Be right there.'*

I shot him a thumbs up and took off, weaving between dancers and technical staff. I was rounding a group of men who were carrying a speaker between them when someone called out, 'Harley!'

I suppressed a groan as I turned. I could not seem to escape this place without getting waylaid at every turn.

It was Ellery. Tonight, he was out of his fatigues, wearing jeans and a T-shirt. Evidently, he hadn't been fighting—not that I'd been paying attention or anything.

'Can I help you?' I asked carefully, crossing my arms to cover my chest. My lacy red number didn't leave much to the imagination.

Ellery's gaze drifted from my head to my toes. I suppressed a shudder.

'Eyes up here,' I snapped, gesturing to my face before recrossing my arms. Ellery's eyes jumped to my face.

'Sorry,' he said awkwardly.

'Can I help you?' I repeated forcefully.

He shuffled his weight from foot to foot. 'Is it true? That the merchants are delayed? Theo said…'

Oh, really? He came over and ogled me, then thought I was going to go sharing information?

'How come the Iron Fists don't know? I thought you knew everything that happened in this town,' I retaliated, moving to walk around him. Ellery stepped deftly into my path again.

'Harley—'

I stopped dead, staring at him. The irritation I'd felt at Talbot was surging back; suddenly, I felt vengeful. 'Guess you're not so all-powerful anymore?'

Ellery flinched, a telling look on his face. Oh boy.

'Look—' he started, his gaze flicking to the ground. 'That's not—'

'I don't care,' I said brusquely. 'Yes, the merchants aren't here. No, I have no information. You want to find out what's going on? Ask someone else. I'm not your informant anymore.'

Ellery groaned and shook his head. 'For fuck's sake. Do you want me to apologise? Do you want me to beg? I don't know what you want anymore, Harley.'

'What I want?' I snorted. 'I don't want anything from you. You came over here.'

'Just tell me.'

Was that the tack he wanted to take? Well alright, then.

'Is it true what Bas said? About why you got me the job in the Kranikovska?' I asked.

Ellery's face fell. 'Bas shouldn't have told you that.'

'So it is true!'

'Just tell me what to say,' Ellery pleaded.

I stared at him for a long moment. I felt exhausted. Ancient. 'The truth,' I said finally. 'I want the truth. And nothing else.'

'The… truth.' Ellery opened his mouth and shut it again several times, as though the very concept baffled him.

'Yes, the truth. You know, the part where you stop lying to me and manipulating me and actually tell me what you want from me?' I pressed my lips together and glared at him.

'I want what I've always wanted, Harley. You.'

'Me,' I echoed.

'Yeah. I want what we used to have. When you first worked here.'

I bristled. As sincere as he sounded, I didn't like the sentiment. I didn't want that back. I'd been naïve and powerless then.

'You want me chasing after you like some lost puppy?' I asked scornfully.

'No!' He shook his head and raked his fingers through his hair, mussing up the golden strands. 'I want the relationship we used to have, when you used to trust me. But I want you—us—together.'

'If you wanted me to trust you, you shouldn't have used me.' I didn't even know what to do with the second part of his statement, but I was certainly not planning on trusting him any time soon.

'I know. That was a mistake. But still, I'd like to try.'

'I don't think so.' I took a step back, suddenly uneasy. He was looking at me with desperation in his eyes.

'Please. I've always wanted you.'

'Ellery, no.'

'I'll do anything. Just give me a chance.'

I shook my head. He was getting ridiculous now. I never believed a man when he said he'd do anything—it was either manipulation or desperation, and it was definitely an empty promise.

'If you wanted a chance, you should have taken it years ago. Now it's too late.' I was proud of how steady and strong my voice was.

'Don't say that,' he pleaded. 'I couldn't before. You know that.'

'And why not?' I asked coolly. I'd liked him, maybe even loved him. And instead of reciprocating, he'd used me. His words now rang empty.

Ellery dragged his fingers through his hair, groaning like a dying man. 'How could I tell you? How? You know, I still remember the day we met? You were so fucking terrified, you looked like you'd burst into tears any moment. We were the instrument of your demise. You should have been… I don't know… on stage in the city, with people coming from far and wide to see you, earning a fortune. Instead, we forced you to drop out of school and dance. I watched the hope drain out of you for five fucking years. I wouldn't have deserved you less if I'd been the one to shoot your father myself!'

He was offering up my history as though I hadn't lived it myself. I clenched my fists.

'That wasn't up to you to decide for me!'

'You'd never have gone for it. It wasn't the right time for us.'

Fury twisted in me, warring with hurt. I narrowed my eyes. 'Well, now we'll never know.'

Ellery hung his head in defeat. 'I miss you. Is there really no chance that…'

I took a deep breath. 'No, Ellery. I'm sorry. I think it's better if we stay apart from now on.'

I forced myself to walk past his despondent expression. After all of the mistakes Ellery and I had made, it would be better to have a clean break. We had never had a healthy friendship, and that would have been a poor foundation for a romantic attachment.

Never mind the fact that if I stuck around I was going to have to explain that I couldn't date him because I had complicated feelings for his best friend.

And that wasn't even digging into the layers of betrayal on both sides.

No, it was time to move on.

I changed quickly and headed out. Theo was waiting outside my changing room.

'Ready to go?'

'Hey.' I nodded. 'I thought you'd wait at the weapons check.'

'I didn't have anything better to do.' Theo shrugged.

We walked in silence, but for once it wasn't uncomfortable. Both of us were lost in our thoughts. I kept turning over Ellery's words in my head. Finally, I broke the silence.

'Ellery fessed up his feelings to me.'

'Did he?' Theo glanced my way. ''Bout fucking time. What'd you say?'

'That I think we need to stay away from each other. We're not good for each other.' The more I said it, the more resolved I felt about my decision.

Theo raised an eyebrow in surprise. 'Huh. I didn't see that coming. You're sure about that?'

'Yes.'

'Well… good,' he said decisively. 'I'm glad.'

'You are?' I asked. Despite how weird things had been between us recently, Theo's opinion was still important to me.

'Of course. I never really liked the way Ellery messed around with you. He never seemed to take you seriously.'

'Yeah,' I said. 'That's exactly it.'

We'd reached the ladder up to the depot. I paused and glanced at Theo. He pulled his torch off his belt and flicked it on, covering the light so it didn't shine in my eyes. 'You're happy, though?'

'About that, yes.'

'Just about that?' His eyes searched mine. I shuffled my weight uncomfortably. Theo sighed. 'Harley…'

'Just… just give me time to deal with some stuff,' I said. 'Then things will be alright.'

'I don't like it when you have stuff to deal with that you won't tell me about,' Theo said. 'You know I'd keep your secrets.'

'You have lots of stuff that you don't tell me.' Even saying it, I felt petulant. My silence had nothing to do with his secrets.

Theo scowled. 'You know that's not personal.'

'Neither are my secrets!'

'Well—' He shook his head abruptly, groaning loudly. 'I don't want to fight again. Let's get going.'

'Alright,' I mumbled.

Theo took the ladder first, his boots clanging with more force than usual. He was angry with me—again. Once he reached the top, I followed him up. Low voices drifted down, and when I stepped off the ladder my stomach curled in on itself.

Bas was on security.

That, in and of itself, was quite unusual; I'd been under the impression that he was senior enough to be exempt from guard duty. The stony expression on his face as he and Theo glared each other down sent a shiver of apprehension down my spine.

Then he turned to me.

'Harley,' he said lowly.

I'd reached my limit for stupid males today.

'Bas,' I replied coolly. 'Excuse me.' I stepped around him.

'I need to talk to you,' Bas said. He sounded like he was feeling sorry for himself—maybe doing door security was a punishment?

Well, too bad for him.

'It'll have to wait. I'm tired.'

Bas opened his mouth—but no words emerged. An odd silence engulfed the three of us, during which I thought with crystal clarity that I ought to leave.

And yet, somehow I was rooted to the spot, waiting to see if he'd respect my decision to stay away from him.

Finally, he nodded. 'Next time, then.' His gaze was dark.

'Thank you.' I turned around. 'Come on, Theo. Let's go.'

Theo strolled over, falling into step beside me.

'Anything I need to know? Or is that'—he jerked his chin towards Bas—'another secret?'

I chewed over that one. It wasn't that I didn't want to tell him, so much as that I didn't know where to start. In the end, I hesitated too long.

'Another secret, then,' Theo said bitterly.

'No—That's not—'

'Never mind, Harley. Forget I asked.' He sped up his stride, stalking ahead of me back to the car.

As promised, Posy came by the bar on Sunday.

'So I do know someone,' she said in a low voice. I slid a glass of whiskey in front of her.

'On the house.'

'You're too sweet.'

'Me? Sweet?' I raised an eyebrow.

Posy snorted. 'No, you're right. Your soul is as dark and bitter as coffee.'

'Gee, thanks.' I rolled my eyes. 'Now, spill.'

Posy glanced around warily, but at the moment there was no one near us. She'd seated herself beneath the window. The bar was filled with muted chatter and the tinkle of the radio, and only Anna and I were working this evening.

Nothing to worry about.

'My old roommate's sister,' Posy explained. 'Her name is Lettie. I checked and she still works there, but if you want to contact her, you'll have to do it without me. She hates me.'

Brilliant. I'd have to ingratiate myself. My speciality. 'Dare I ask why?'

'Relationship drama,' Posy said airily, waving a hand. 'Don't worry about it. It'll be fine so long as you don't mention my name.'

'Alright, so how am I supposed to find her?'

'Here.' Posy slid a scrap of paper onto the table. 'Her address. But if she asks…'

'You didn't give it to me. Got it.' I slipped the paper into my jeans. 'Don't worry, I won't involve you.'

This was my mess to sort out. I wasn't dragging anyone else into it.

'Alright.' Posy stretched out her legs and leant back in her chair. 'Now scram. I want to actually enjoy my free drink.'

'Love you too.'

'Always, babes.' She toasted me. Rolling my eyes, I retreated to the bar to pick up an order for table seven.

Posy lingered for a while, buying herself a second drink. I found her presence in the bar comforting. When I went by her table to refill her water, I commented, 'You should come here more often.'

'I would if I lived on this side of town.' Posy glanced around. 'It's a nice gig. I wouldn't pick the bunker over this.'

'You should come work here. We're short-staffed anyway.'

'Gianna would like that. She doesn't like the boys groping me at the bunker.'

'Gianna's got the right of it.' I picked up my tray again. 'Bring her around here sometime. I want to meet her.'

'Ooh, look who's getting bossy.'

I snorted. 'You'd think after all these years of knowing me, you'd want to introduce me to your partner.'

Posy tilted her head, pretending to consider it. 'I'll think about it.'

'Mean.'

She laughed. 'Maybe you'll get lucky at the bunker next weekend.'

'I'll be sure to remind you.' We exchanged grins before I caught sight of table three waving. I sighed, 'Duty calls.'

'Off you go, babes.'

There was still no sign of the merchants' caravan by the end of the day. The tension was approaching a breaking point: the market was supposed to begin tomorrow, and it was rapidly becoming obvious that the merchants wouldn't be here in time. At some point, someone was going to have to step up and take control of the situation—the mayor? If he didn't, who would? I couldn't remember a time when the merchants had been delayed by more than a day or so.

If there were no merchants, there was no trade. Our tradesman couldn't sell their wares, and our families couldn't buy food for winter. We had no textile factories this far north, which meant the merchants had to bring clothes and blankets. Would the supplies we had last the winter?

I needed to speak to Savannah about our own plans, sooner rather than later.

Fear hung over the hotel like a miasma as I headed out. It felt like our small town was falling apart at the seams.

I walked briskly towards home. Hopefully, Savannah would still be up and I could talk to her.

I was in luck. When I got home, the light was on in our kitchen window. I climbed the stairs and entered the flat to find Savannah slumped at the kitchen table.

'Sav?'

'Mmmmm?'

A frisson of alarm raised the hairs at the back of my neck. Dropping my coat on the sagging sofa, I strode over to her. Savannah looked up and scowled as I approached.

'Shouldn't you still be at work?'

'It's gone midnight,' I pointed out. I glanced her over with a frown; her eyes were a bit red, and her cheeks were flushed. Her hair was frizzing around her face. 'Were you sleeping?'

'No.' Savannah's eyes narrowed.

'Have you been drinking?' Savannah never usually drank—well, that was the way it had always been. Until Talbot. I honestly had no idea what her normal was anymore.

Her lips twisted. I wasn't sure if she was about to throw up or curse me out. Could have gone either way.

'I was jus' resting my eyes,' she mumbled. 'Long day at work.'

'Wasn't it your day off?' She usually had Sundays off.

'Pulled 'n extra shift.' Her words were running together, so little that I'd almost missed it, but they were. I leant closer, trying to smell her breath. Savannah jerked away. 'Fuck *off*, Harley!'

'Okay, okay.' I raised my hands, backing off. I was too tired to pick a fight with her tonight. 'I'm just concerned. I... I never see you anymore.'

'You're never here.'

Ouch.

I bit my cheek. 'Neither are you.'

'Maybe we should get separate places.'

I froze, gripping the fridge door harder than I needed to. The chilly air drifted over my face. 'Is... is that what you want?'

Silence. At length, I managed to get myself moving again. I pulled out leftovers and tipped them onto a plate. I didn't look at Savannah. I couldn't.

Live separately. That had never been an option before.

'I... I don't know,' she whispered. 'Greg wants me to move in with him.'

My heart skipped a beat. I spun around. Savannah had her head in her hands and was staring at the tabletop.

'It's too soon,' I protested.

'I'd be safe.'

'You're safe here!' I clutched my bowl, the ceramic digging into my palm. '*I* keep you safe.'

'Do you?' Dropping a hand, she idly traced lines on the table.

'Yes!' I felt sick, blindsided. This came out of nowhere.

I had done everything I could. And... maybe we'd had our differences, but... 'Don't you want to stay with me anymore?' My voice was small and weak to my ears. Vulnerable. 'I want to live with you.'

'You hate me, Harley.' Savannah sounded... downtrodden. I swallowed and stepped closer to her.

'I don't hate you.'

'Don't you? I'm boring. I lecture. Greg said—' She cut herself off.

'What did Greg say?' I asked sharply.

'No, nothing.'

It was something, alright. 'Savannah...'

'It's nothing,' she insisted. 'Just forget about it.'

I pressed my lips together. I couldn't just forget about it, but also, weariness layered on me like a thick blanket, deadening my senses. I had no energy left, between Bas and Theo, between Hannover and Hardwick. Lions, circling.

'I don't hate you,' I whispered. I held out a hand. 'Come on, let me help you to bed.'

Savannah stared at my hand for what felt like forever, before finally wrapping her clammy fingers around it. I helped her up; she swayed delicately.

'You have callouses.'

'Yeah, from dancing,' I muttered. I put my arm around her shoulders. 'Come on, bed. You're exhausted. We'll worry about where we're going to live after we've weathered the current crisis.'

'What crisis?' Savannah leant her head on my shoulder, yawning into my neck. She was drunk—I could smell her breath.

'Merchants' market,' I grunted. 'I'll explain in the morning.'

'Oh… I heard.'

'Yeah. So, I have extra cash frittered away. I'll pick up some stuff tomorrow. We'll make it through. I can pull a few extra shifts.'

'No need,' Savannah mumbled. 'I'll do it.'

'No, it's okay.' I pushed my way through the bedroom door and helped her sit on her bed. 'You rest. You're tired.'

'So are you.'

'You're tireder.' I smoothed her hair down and kissed her forehead. 'See you in the morning.'

'Yeah,' she mumbled. 'Sorry.'

She crawled under her covers and drifted off almost immediately. I tucked my hands in my pockets and watched her. What the fuck lies was Greg Talbot feeding her now?

And why did she want to move out?

Fuck.

The thought was like a vice closing around my chest. I pushed it away. One crisis at a time.

I didn't have the energy for more than that.

The next morning, I made my way over to Lettie's flat. It was in the northwest, a dingy building that seemed to hunch in on itself like an old man who'd seen too much of life. The front door didn't lock—didn't even close, in fact—so I let myself in and climbed to the second floor. The inside was dark, and my boots sank into a soggy, mouldy old carpet.

This place was gross. Was this really my ticket to getting into Reverie? I wouldn't put it past Posy to play some kind of elaborate prank.

Lettie lived in number five. I knocked on her door, and several seconds went by in absolute silence. This place was like a graveyard.

She probably wasn't at the brothel—did she work a second job? Or maybe she had gone out?

I knocked again, a little harder. The wood creaked in protest.

'YEAH, COMING, COMING!' someone hollered inside. A moment later, the door swung open. 'Fucking impatient, you dipshit, it's fucking early and you know I work late—Oh, you're not my landlord.'

Lettie was a diminutive woman with long black hair and tan skin. She peered at me with an unsettlingly aggressive gaze.

'Hi,' I said awkwardly. 'I'm Harley.'

'Har-*ley*,' she repeated, her voice dripping with scepticism. 'Not familiar. What do you want?'

'A friend of mine told me you might be able to help me out—'

'If you're looking for a job, you're fresh out of luck.'

'I'm not looking for a job.' Her rapid speech and aggressive posture were making me uncomfortable. 'I work at the Kranikovska. I need to get in somewhere and I'm willing—'

'Not interested.' She began to swing the door shut. I shoved my foot in the way.

'Wait!'

The door hit my foot.

'Fuck off,' Lettie said. 'I said I'm not interested.'

'I'm willing to trade favours, I just—'

'You got a magic wand?'

'No!' What was with this woman?

'Then fuck off. You ain't got anything I want, and I'm not doing anything for you. I have more important shit in my life right now.'

'This is important.' I wrapped my fingers around the edge of the door and pushed until I could see one of her angry grey eyes.

'It's not more important than my brother going missing, so take a fucking hint.' With a strength that belied her small frame, she threw herself at the door. I yanked my hands and foot away before she could crush me, and the door shut in my face.

Well, that had gone *excellently*.

What the hell was I going to do now?

There didn't seem to be much point in trying again; she hadn't even let me make my offer. Maybe Posy knew someone else?

Stomach roiling, I turned and headed out of the horrible block of flats.

So not only did I still have no plan for dealing with Hannover, but now Hardwick's request was looking more and more impossible.

I was fucked.

FOURTEEN

I OCCUPIED MONDAY WITH a litany of everyday—and not so everyday—chores.

I was stocking up.

I didn't have a choice. I'd been trying to sit on my tips from the bunker and save up, but we were going to need supplies to make it through the winter, and I could always pick up more shifts. It wasn't as though Carlos would turn me down, not when I was one of his best dancers.

The majority of my day off passed in the kitchen, pickling vegetables. It was a dull task—I'd never enjoyed cooking—but it had to be done. I also cleared out the space under my bed for storage and dedicated myself to mending some things I'd hoped to replace at the merchants' market.

There was still no news. Truth be told, we were all expecting the worst.

That evening, I walked over to Brenda's house as we'd planned. The windows of the NCC office glowed like eerie eyes, but I forced myself to ignore the feelings of unease as I waited for her to open the door. When she did, she ushered me straight in.

'Get out of the cold. Come on, come here.' She held her arms out for a hug.

I wrapped my arms around her shoulders. 'Thanks for having us.'

'Anytime.' Brenda smiled warmly. 'Anna and Laura are already here.'

'Great.' I followed her downstairs, into the low-ceilinged basement room, and found Anna in the kitchen stirring a pot on the stove, whilst Laura was sitting on the sofa with Brenda's sons, Ty and Cal.

'Hiya,' I called.

'Harley!' Cal jumped up, racing over to me and throwing his arms around my legs.

'Oof.' I pretended to stumble. 'Have you grown since I last saw you?'

'Of course! I'm almost as big as Ty now!'

I grinned, ruffling his hair. 'How are you? How's school?'

'Ugh, boring. Come see the dog.' He grabbed my hand, towing me over to the sofa. The dog was nestled between Ty and Laura.

'Hi,' Laura said brightly.

'Hey.' I leaned over and ruffled Ty's hair as well. 'Hey, Ty.'

'Don't do that,' he protested. 'I'm not little.'

'Course not. How's work?'

'Great.' Ty puffed his chest up. 'I'm learning tonnes of stuff. I drove a tractor!'

'That's great. You know more than me.' I elbowed him. '*I* can't drive.'

'Don't you wanna learn?' Cal asked. 'I want to.'

'Maybe one day,' Brenda said, wandering over. 'But not tonight. Boys, bedtime.'

'Ugh, no, Mum!' Cal whined.

'Yep. You have school tomorrow. Come on, come on.' She ushered them up and over to the bedroom door. 'The dog as well.'

Ty scooped the dog up, scowling as his mother steered him into the bedroom. 'I'll be back in a few minutes,' she said over her shoulder. 'Help yourself to a drink, Harley.'

'Thanks.'

I joined Anna in the kitchen to help with the dinner. Brenda reappeared about ten minutes later, brushing her unruly curls back into a ponytail.

'All down for bed?' Laura asked.

'Reluctantly.' Brenda laughed. 'They'll stay down, though. It's late for them. So,' she slipped into the kitchen and steered Anna out of the way so she could take over, 'tell me all the news. I feel like I'm missing out since I don't work at Krani's anymore.'

'That's what you get for abandoning us,' Anna teased. I glanced at her—she obviously already had a glass of ale in her, and her cheeks were flushed pink.

''Abandoning?'' Brenda clucked her tongue. 'I work just around the corner, I'll have you know.'

'How is it?' I asked.

'Fine. Surprisingly undramatic.' Brenda shot me a smile. 'Cars can't talk back.'

'Rocky can, though,' I pointed out. Rocky was her new boss and one of the Kranikovska's regulars.

'Oh, Rocky.' She laughed. 'He's harmless. Barely even comes into the office, most days.'

'The perfect boss,' Anna said.

'Oh, hush, you. You work for your uncle.'

Anna giggled. Brenda leant over me to grab a bowl, scraping a pile of dried herbs into the pot. 'Gossip?'

'There's not much,' I admitted.

'Tom's looking for more new employees,' Anna announced. 'Two of the cleaners quit. One's pregnant, the other is moving to Crater's Edge.'

'I wonder why everyone is leaving,' Brenda mused as she heaved the pot over to the table.

'Scared,' Anna predicted. We all took seats around the table and began serving ourselves the stew. 'People tend to retreat when they're scared, right?'

'You think it's because of the merchants' market?' Brenda asked.

'It's more than that.' Anna stared into her drink, swirling it slowly. 'There's a weird feeling about town lately, isn't there?'

'You think?' Laura asked.

'I've noticed it,' Brenda said. 'Harley too, right?'

I nodded gravely. Laura glanced at me, a questioning look on her face.

'This is such a depressing subject,' Anna declared. 'You know what else is new? Chef is getting married.'

'He finally proposed? That's fantastic!' Brenda beamed. 'I'll have to stop by and say congratulations.'

'He told us about a week ago,' Laura said. 'He was really excited.'

I hadn't known about that. I bit my lip, a pang of hurt shooting through me. Was I really that out of the loop?

'Oh!' Anna said suddenly. 'There's one other thing. Theo's back!'

'Theo?' Brenda exclaimed.

'Yep! Harley kept him all secret from us for ages.'

'He's really nice,' Laura put in.

'Don't be fooled,' Brenda warned. 'That one's a gang member too.'

'Theo's one of the good ones,' I protested. The words sounded idiotic the moment I spoke them. 'Genuinely. I've known him all my life.'

'Really?' Laura asked.

'We met in dance class when I was four.'

'Huh,' Anna said. 'I never realised you'd known him that long.'

'I didn't know you'd been dancing for that long,' Laura said, squinting at me. 'You must be really good.'

'Uh,' I mumbled, embarrassed, 'not bad. I guess.'

'She's very good,' Anna said loyally, although I wasn't sure if she had ever seen me dance properly before.

'I keep the boys entertained,' I said.

'But you didn't start dancing so you could end up in a club,' Laura said. 'Right?'

I squirmed. 'I… originally I wanted to join a dance troupe, but…' I shrugged.

'But?'

'It didn't work out.' I put my cutlery down and crossed my arms. 'My dad died, and I had to get a job instead. That's just life.'

'Sorry.' Laura looked away, fiddling with the edge of the table. 'I didn't mean to pry.'

Yes, you did, I thought uncharitably. I bit my tongue, though. It was an old hurt. And it wasn't Laura's fault.

'Sorry,' Laura repeated.

'It's okay.' I picked up my fork, swirling the sauce on my plate. My appetite had vanished. I *hated* talking about how I'd ended up dancing in the bunker—it had been a bitter lesson about childhood dreams and growing up, that was for sure.

'There is one other thing,' Anna said suddenly. 'Going back to the gossip.' Her voice was low and serious.

'What's that?' Brenda asked.

'I've been hearing things.'

Brenda raised an eyebrow. 'What sort of things?'

'People going missing. Mick Doleman—you know, the greengrocer? His niece disappeared one day on her way back from work. Left the house she'd been cleaning, never arrived home.'

'That's horrible!' Laura gasped.

'Did they find out what happened to her?' Brenda asked grimly.

'That's the thing,' Anna said. 'Doleman even paid people to look for her. He came and spoke to Tom about it too—that's how I know about it. But there hasn't been a trace of her. And she's not the only one. Two farmhands went missing from the Gibson farm, as well.'

'I heard about that,' Brenda said. 'Old Gibson thought they might have got into a fight over a girl and killed each other. But there was never any trace of them.'

'Exactly!' Anna said. 'People are disappearing all over town. No one knows where they're going.'

Disappearing? A cold feeling crept over me as I stared at my plate. I'd heard about a disappearance just this morning—Lettie's brother.

How many did that make? Four? Five?

Even though the curtains were shut tight, I suddenly felt like there were eyes in the NCC office across the road. Staring at me.

Hannover's eyes.

'Maybe they're leaving?' Laura asked.

'All of them, all at once?' Anna pointed out.

I glanced at Brenda. Her lips were pinched together, her expression uncharacteristically grave. She caught my eye with a pointed look, then tilted her head towards the window.

Towards the NCC office.

I nodded slightly, taking a sip of my drink to cover the movement. I wasn't surprised that people were starting to hear. In fact, I was surprised it had taken this long. It meant they'd been subtle enough in their endeavours that no one had really noticed people were going missing. But now? Now enough people had vanished that rumours were spreading.

It was only a matter of time before people started panicking.

And I was sitting on knowledge that could bring down this operation. But Bas hadn't believed me, and my options felt vanishingly thin.

What could I do without evidence?

The mention of the disappearances put a dampener on the conversation—and not only for me. Anna tried to cheer us up, but eventually we gave up.

'I guess we're all tired these days,' Brenda said as she walked us to the door.

'Always,' I muttered.

Brenda wrapped an arm around my shoulders and squeezed. 'See yourselves home safely, alright?'

I nodded.

'Come by the bar and see us again,' Anna said. 'We miss you.'

'I'm sure I will,' Brenda replied. 'Tom's asked me to stand by in case he needs me during the market.'

'If they ever get here,' I mumbled.

'They will,' Brenda said. 'I'm sure there's just a holdup in Boughton.'

She sounded chipper, but I couldn't seem to push off the fear that clung to me. Especially after my chat with Savannah the other night.

Was I going to end up alone?

No.

I said my goodbyes and headed out, dark thoughts swirling around my head. *Hannover. Hardwick. Bas. Theo.*

Just leave.

But Bale Rocks was my home. I understood life here, even if I didn't enjoy it. I had no idea what lurked beyond the boundaries of my town.

I was on my street, my building looming ahead, when a man pushed himself off his car, stepped into the path a few yards ahead of me, and turned to me.

I slowed my footsteps cautiously, reaching for my knife. It could be nothing, but the hairs rising on the back of my neck said it wasn't. He'd stepped purposefully into my way, and he was looking right at me.

'Can I help you?'

He shifted, and the meagre streetlight illuminated his face. It was Rodney Rochester.

'Hello, Harley.'

Damnit. He was the last person I wanted to see right now.

'You're too late,' I called, crossing my arms. 'Your brother doesn't want anything to do with me anymore.'

'I doubt that. I know you still see him.' Rochester shifted his weight. He was dressed differently than I remembered—no fancy suit this time. The jeans and knit jumper looked strange on him.

'I made myself clear before. We're done.' I shook my head. 'Whatever you think you saw, you're wrong. Bas doesn't want me around. And I told him about what I was doing for you, so he'll never trust me again.'

Rochester's gaze flickered with a myriad of emotions: frustration, exasperation, desperation.

'That doesn't matter,' he said. 'I want to make a new deal.'

'No.' I'd had enough trouble from this guy. I didn't need him in my life.

'Just hear me out. It'll interest you too.'

I started walking. 'I said *no.*'

'Miss Benoit—'

'I'm not passing you information. I have enough trouble in my life without adding you to the mess!' I sucked in a breath, trying to remain calm. I didn't want him to see how frustrated I was.

'The mayor has contracted with the military to drive the Iron Fists out of town.'

His words were barely audible over the whistle of the wind, but he may as well have slapped me. I stopped dead and slowly turned to face him.

'What did you say?'

'You heard me.' He pointed at his car. 'I know more, but I can't tell you here. Get in and we'll talk.'

Damn.

I swallowed hard, my insides twisting together even as I struggled to remain outwardly calm. 'What makes you think I don't already know?'

Rodney raised an eyebrow. 'I doubt you know everything I know. I want to trade the information I have for a meeting with my brother.'

Damnit. Fuck, shit, damn him to the darkest circle of hell. He *would* say that.

I turned to face him fully. 'I told you, that's not an option. I'm not trading information, meetings, or anything else.'

'If you care about this town, you will,' Rodney said. 'Your friends… your family. If the military gets involved, they could all be at risk.'

'Fuck you.' I ground my teeth together. 'You have no right to manipulate me like that.'

'I thought you had more compassion.'

'Compassion?' I echoed in disbelief. My chest felt tight, and my vision blurred as I struggled to breathe. I felt trapped in an impossible decision: betray Bas, get information. Don't betray Bas… fuck over half the town.

Easy decision.

Bas's gaze swum before my eyes: the anger, the betrayal. I wasn't sure he could take any more from me. If I betrayed him again, he might just decide to wipe me off the face of the Earth. I was hanging by a thread already.

'You have *no idea* what you're asking of me.'

I raked my fingers through my hair and turned my head away.

'I think it's quite a simple request. Arrange a meeting, get the information.' Rodney shrugged. He really thought it was that simple. Was he so disconnected from the real world?

'What makes you think I could even do anything with your information?' I pointed out.

'I'm sure you have the right contacts to make things happen. My brother, for example.' He raised an eyebrow pointedly.

I gritted my teeth. 'Don't *you* care about the town?'

'Of course I do. But that won't stop me from getting my money's worth.'

I stared down the street, battling to remain calm. This guy was ridiculous. I wanted to laugh almost as badly as I wanted to cry. This could not be happening.

A truck turned onto the street and blew by, sending up a flurry of leaves and dust.

'I'm not—' I paused as my mind caught up with what I'd just seen.

That was an NCC truck. The same type that had almost driven Theo and me off the road a week ago.

The NCC used bulky armoured vehicles to transport goods up and down the region, mostly to get them safely past the gangs in the wastelands. But it suddenly hit me that those trucks could be used for transporting other things.

Like people.

Slaves.

And if that was true, then this might be the break I was waiting for. Evidence for Bas. Something to get Hannover off my back. Anything.

I made a snap decision. I took two hurried steps closer to Rodney and darted my hand under his coat.

All men carried guns, and I was betting Rochester wasn't an exception, even if he was too posh to get his hands dirty. I pawed at his back, searching for the holster I was sure was hidden there.

Rodney all but shoved his back against his car to get away from me.

'What are you doing? Get *off* me!'

My fingers found metal. *Gotcha!* I yanked the gun out and turned it on him. 'I need you to follow that truck.'

'Are you insane?' Rodney demanded.

Yes, yes I am. 'Do it, or I'll shoot you and steal your car.'

He stared at me. Impatiently, I lifted the gun to point at his forehead. The colour had bleached out of his skin.

'Now!'

'Do you even know how to drive?'

'That doesn't matter. Get in the fucking car.' I marched to the back door and yanked it open. Overconfident bastard hadn't even locked it.

'You are crazy.'

'*You* are asking to get shot.' I jerked the gun at him. Rochester looked about to puke.

'Fine, fine. I'm doing it.'

He opened the driver's door and climbed in. I waited until he'd shut the door, then swung myself into the back and pressed the gun to the back of his head. 'Drive.'

'I can't drive with a gun to my head.'

The truck was vanishing into the distance. I lowered the gun a few inches. 'If you care about anyone in this town—really care—you'll start the fucking car and drive.'

'Fine.' He turned the key in the ignition, and the car came to life. A moment later, we roared into motion. As he floored it, he asked, 'What's so special about that truck anyway?'

'Keep following it and if you're lucky you'll find out.'

My voice was steady, but my heart was pounding in a frantic rhythm. I couldn't believe what I was doing. Had I gone insane? Clearly. And yet, I had to know. This was the only clue I had.

Rodney made an irritated noise in his throat as he put pedal to metal. We hurtled down the street, bouncing over the uneven, pockmarked asphalt. The truck hung a left.

'Faster,' I insisted.

'Do you want to get us both killed?' Rodney snapped.

'This is import—ugh!' My words were lost as Rodney jerked up the handbrake and sent us squealing around the corner so fast I thought the wheels were going to leave the ground. I fell sideways onto the seat, clutching the gun. Once we'd righted ourselves, I sat up and hurriedly put my seatbelt on.

'Where'd you learn to drive like this?'

'What?' Rodney asked drily. 'Did you think I had no useful skills?'

Pretty much, yep.

'Just don't stop,' I muttered.

'You aren't going to shoot me,' Rodney said confidently. 'I doubt you've ever fired a gun before.'

We were hurtling down one of the main north-south arterials, heading for the south side. Shops and businesses flashed by on both sides.

'I actually have, thanks.' Theo had taught me how to fire a gun. I'd hated it.

'If you shoot me when we're going at this speed, you'll die too,' Rodney said. He sounded remarkably calm, considering. 'Put the gun down and tell me why we're following the van.'

'I'm not giving it back to you or you'll stop driving,' I said petulantly.

Rodney sighed with the air of an exasperated parent dealing with a particularly wilful child. It was a sigh I was well acquainted with; in my family, *I'd* been the wilful child. 'You make everything much harder than it has to be, you know that?'

'It's a special skill,' I snapped.

Rodney snorted. I was forced back into my seat as he accelerated on the straight road. Ahead of us, the truck had reached the bridge which spanned the river. We were gaining on it, though. Rodney's car was much faster.

Take the risk or no?

'This is the second time I've seen an NCC truck driving like that,' I said. 'I'm investigating.'

'I didn't take you for such a good Samaritan.'

I wrinkled my nose. *Dick.* 'I'm not. I'm just trying to find a way to buy myself back into Bas's good graces.'

'An ambition we both seem to have in common,' Rodney said. 'Which brings me back to—'

He slammed on brakes suddenly as the truck swung right and vanished down a side street.

'I think we've been noticed.'

'Damnit,' I muttered. My mind raced. 'Wait, don't turn off. Just keep going straight.'

'Why?' Rodney asked, but he followed my instructions.

'Because if I'm right then I know where they're going.'

'And where are they going?'

To risk it or not? Damnit it all to hell. I was here now. 'The Black Hands' compound.'

Rodney hit the brakes, sending us squealing to a halt in the middle of the road. 'I beg your pardon.'

'Keep driving,' I snapped.

'Absolutely not. Explain yourself.'

'The NCC is working with the Black Hands, or the Black Hands have taken over, or something,' I said desperately. 'Look, do you want to speak with Bas or not? Get fucking driving.'

I could practically hear Rodney grinding his teeth together. 'You expect me to drive out into the wasteland in the middle of the night?'

'Basically, yes.'

I actually hadn't thought that far ahead. But I certainly wasn't backing out now.

Rodney snarled under his breath, but mercifully he started driving again. We set a steady pace down the arterial, through the rundown residential area immediately south of the river, and past the new developments that were springing up: the mayor's attempt to clean up the town. Those gave way to construction sites, their silhouettes like misshapen beasts under the moonlight. Rodney flicked the headlights off, plunging us into almost total darkness.

'What are you doing?' I whispered.

'They're less likely to see us without the headlights.'

'Oh.' Yes, that made sense. All of a sudden, I was uneasy. This had been a terrible idea.

But no one else is going to do anything about this.

I'd told Bas and he hadn't believed me. Who else could I turn to? There was only Theo, but I'd learnt my lesson from telling Bas. When I revealed this to my best friend, I'd be coming armed with proof.

We drove until we passed a fork in the road, the directions marked by the skeletons of ancient, rusted road signs. Rodney turned southwest, and a few hundred yards later he pulled off the road and stopped behind the remains of a concrete wall.

'Why have you stopped?' I clenched my fingers around the gun nervously. *He'd better not make trouble now…*

'If they're headed for the Black Hands' compound, they have to pass this way,' Rodney said evenly.

'Assuming they're behind us.'

'They will be. We took the direct route.'

'You'd better be right.'

Rodney turned to face me. 'Even if I'm not, this is as far as we can go. What is your grand plan to approach the compound? They'll shoot you on sight.'

'I need to see the van arriving.'

Rodney swore under his breath. 'You're going to get both of us killed.'

'If you help with this, I might be able to arrange that meeting with Bas.'

Rodney's expression was incredulous. 'After what I've done for you tonight, you will absolutely be arranging that meeting.'

'I told you, Bas hates me. We need this as a bargaining chip.' I met his gaze head-on, refusing to back down.

Rodney worked his jaw, obviously searching for the right phrase to drive home how mad I was. Well, he needn't bother. I knew, and tonight I was embracing it.

Before he could speak, light cut through the car, and we both turned back to the road. Rodney cut the engine abruptly, and darkness fell around us. A vehicle was approaching from down the road—from the compound. It stopped across the road, blocking the way. A person stepped out, little more than a shadow in the moonlight, but I could make out one thing: they were holding a rifle. The metal glistened under the moonlight.

Who was that? What were they doing?

We didn't have to wait long to find out. A few minutes later, the rumble of a large vehicle reached us, and a moment later the headlights of a truck came into view. I squinted, my eyes watering from the bright light. Was it the NCC truck? It had to be!

The truck slowed and finally trundled to a stop feet away from the stopped car. A moment later the cab door opened and shut again, and a second person rounded the front of the truck. The two figures stood together, obviously speaking. I reached for the door handle—we were deep in the wasteland, and the sound of their voices might well carry—but then I hesitated, remembering the night Bas and I had driven out to the distillery.

Opening the door triggered the interior lights. Which would warn them that we were here.

Better not.

I should have got out earlier, whilst we were still alone.

The two people strode around the truck. They were invisible, but their torch illuminated a patch of ground and the side of the truck in front of them—it was indeed the NCC truck. Then they stopped moving, and a moment later they opened the back doors and shone the torch in.

My breath caught in my throat.

I'd been right; they were transporting people. Four, by the looks of it, all of them slumped against the sides of the truck. They didn't react to the light on them—were they asleep? Or something more sinister?

A moment later, the truck doors slammed shut and the torch clicked off. The two drivers strode back to their respective vehicles, and we heard the car starting up. It made a tight circle and took off down the road, the truck following close behind.

Heading to the compound.

Rochester turned and looked at me. 'What's going on? Was that what I thought it was?'

'What?' My voice came out sharp with panic. 'I thought all of the mayor's cronies were in on his little plan.'

'The mayor? Mayor Darling would not be involved in something like this!'

'Wouldn't he?' I sneered. It wasn't Rochester I was angry at, but he was a convenient target. 'Because Hannover all but confirmed to me that he knew.'

'Who is Hannover?'

'My God, you really know nothing.' I wasn't sure whether to laugh or cry. 'I bet you think the sun shines out of their arses, right? The mayor would never do something to harm his town.'

'I'm well aware of the mayor's flaws, but I'm certain keeping slaves isn't one of them,' Rodney snapped.

'Looks like you don't know him as well as you thought you did.' I crossed my arms. 'I've got my proof. You can take me back now.'

'You are the rudest woman I have ever met.'

'Oh, sorry, did you expect me to beg?' I asked airily. 'We can always spend the night out here if you want.'

Rodney scowled but turned back to the front, starting up the car. 'You had better hold up your end of the bargain after this.'

I snorted. 'You'd better hope this information is good enough for Bas to look you in the face. What are you expecting anyway? He's not going to forgive you.'

'That is none of your concern.'

'You kind of made it my concern by asking me to arrange a meeting. Again.' I put my feet up on the seat, leaning against the door as we bounced over the uneven road.

'I'm not discussing my private business with you.' Rodney turned the radio on, pointedly raising the volume until it was too loud for conversation.

We drove back into town in silence. Rodney didn't switch the headlights on until we got under functioning streetlights, and then he sped up and made quick work of the last few miles to my flat. When he stopped, he turned to face me.

'I want my weapon back.'

I ran a finger over the gun. It was sleek and expensive, but it wasn't as though it was useful to me. I couldn't afford ammunition. Still, I wasn't ready to hand it over just yet.

'I also expect you to arrange that meeting with my brother. I will contact you later this week—let's say Thursday evening.'

'I can't make any guarantees.'

His eyes blazed into me. 'You will.'

Demanding arsehole. 'Fine, but you're going to need to make it worth my while.'

An idea had just occurred to me—potentially a very bad idea, but if it worked, it would make my life much easier.

Rodney shot me an absolutely exhausted look. 'What preposterous demand have you come up with now?'

'I need to get into one of the private rooms at Reverie.'

His mouth dropped open.

'And you can't ask any questions,' I added hastily. 'I know your family owns the place. You can get me in and out again without trouble.'

'You are impossible. How do you even—' Rodney shook his head in exasperation. 'Where do you come up with these insane ideas?'

I shrugged. 'I don't see what the big deal is. Just pretend you're trying to bang me without your daddy finding out.'

'I'm not having sex with you to cover for whatever insanity you're—'

'Mind out of the gutter, Rochester. I never said we actually had to have sex.' I scrunched my nose up and rolled my eyes at him.

'Pretending is hardly any better! It's my reputation on the line.'

I scowled. Oh, of course. Never mind *my* reputation—his was far more precious.

'I guess you don't really want to meet your brother, then,' I said casually.

He shot me a glare worthy of Bas. 'You are honestly unbelievable.'

I shrugged. 'Coming from someone who manipulates people for his own gain, that doesn't sting much.'

'I made you a very fair deal, which *you* backed out of,' he said tersely.

'Potato, potahto,' I said airily. 'I don't need money now. I don't need information. I need into Reverie. You want to see Bas? That's the price.'

'You'll arrange a meeting with my brother?' he asked suspiciously.

I was selling my soul again, for a deal that I was never ever going to be able to deliver on. But in the grand scheme of things, double-crossing Rodney was the smallest of my worries.

'Sure, but no promises on how it will go.'

He continued to eye me suspiciously for several seconds, before finally caving. 'I can get you into Reverie. Just tell me when.'

I smiled. *Perfect.*

FIFTEEN

THE FOLLOWING MORNING I DRAGGED myself out of bed early and headed down to the training yard behind The Arsonist.

Bas still went there. I knew that because I had watched him from my bedroom window several times since our big blow-up. He still went every day, training with the same fierce sense of discipline with which he approached every other aspect of his life.

So he would be there today.

He was going to be furious. Even if he'd made an overture to speak to me at the bunker, any goodwill he may have discovered in my absence was about to evaporate like water on a hot day.

I leant against the cage, shivering in the cold air. It was too cold to dance this morning, even if it would have calmed me. I didn't want to pick up an injury. Instead, I wound my scarf around my neck an extra time and huddled into my coat, my breath fogging the air in front of me.

A short while later, I heard footsteps. Bas appeared around the corner, jogging at a steady pace, but when he saw me he immediately slowed to a walk. Still he continued his approach.

'Harley,' he said gruffly as he stopped in front of me.

'Hi.'

He took me in from head to toe before asking slowly, 'What are you doing here?'

'Something you're going to be angry about.' I'd decided to be upfront, though now that Bas was standing three feet away from me, it was harder than I'd imagined it would be. 'Just hear me out before you chew me out, okay?'

Bas crossed his arms. 'What have you done now?'

I shifted my weight, gripping the railing to ground myself. 'I spoke to your brother, but—' He jerked his arms apart, his mouth opening on a protest. '—*but!* Hear me out.'

'For fuck's sake,' Bas growled. His expression had gone from cautious to furious in milliseconds.

'There was a good reason.'

Bas tipped his head back. 'I don't know what you're having so much difficulty understanding. I want *nothing* to do with Rodney Rochester.'

He sounded agonised. I flinched. 'I know,' I whispered.

'Then why the fuck are you here?'

'He ambushed me—but then we saw an NCC truck and I, uh, persuaded him to follow it—and I saw that they were bringing slaves to the Black Hands' compound. *I saw it,*' I insisted.

Bas clenched his fists, looking like he'd rather wrap them around my neck. 'You are unbelievable.'

'I saw it, and so did Rodney. You have to believe me!'

Bas shook his head. 'For fuck's sake.' He whirled around, marched several metres to the wall, and punched it with a dull thud. 'FUCK!'

I winced in sympathy. Punching a brick wall had to hurt.

Bas turned back.

'Look,' I started, 'I know this isn't ideal. I know you don't trust me. But Hannover is definitely taking slaves from the town. People are noticing their friends and family going missing. Something has to be done, and I can't solve this alone.'

Bas held his right hand cradled against his chest. I could see flecks of blood on the knuckles. 'I don't know what to say.'

Tears of desperation pricked at my eyes. 'Tell me you believe me.' *Please, please tell me you believe me.*

If he still didn't, I was going to scream.

'I can't do this, Harley.' Bas shook out his hands, his every movement jerky and abrupt, as though he was trying to shake the frustration out of his bones. 'I can't keep doing this. You're taking every limit I have and shattering it.'

I cringed. When he put it like that, it sounded every bit as awful as I imagined.

'Just say you believe me,' I said. 'Tell me who to tell. I can't… I don't know how to solve this myself.'

'I think you've done enough,' Bas said coolly.

Anger welled in my stomach, even as the first tears escaped my eyes. 'For fuck's sake!'

Bas jerked in surprise at how loudly I had spoken.

'You never believe me,' I snarled. 'Is it because I'm a dancer? Or because I'm a woman? You misogynistic prick! I can't believe I ever thought you were any different to the others.'

Bas opened his mouth. 'That's not—'

'That's *exactly* what it is!' I stalked closer to him, dashing my tears away with the back of my hand. 'It doesn't matter, does it? Doesn't matter what I sacrifice, doesn't matter that I have proof. You don't believe anything that comes out of my mouth. I'm just a girl—what do I know? You're just like the others. Ellery, Tam, Hardwick. Hannover. You're a patronising *git*, you—'

'I'm nothing like Hannover!' Bas snarled. 'You have no right—'

'Oh yeah? Cause he speaks to me the same way you do!'

'You fucking—' Bas clenched his fists, the skin on his knuckles splitting even further. Blood was trickling down his right hand. 'I am nothing like Hannover!'

He was breathing hard; we both were, actually. I could feel my heart in my throat.

'All I am to you is a glorified whore,' I said. 'I did think you were different, but clearly I was wrong. I hope when this all blows up in your face, you remember this conversation. Because I could tell you all sorts of things you'd just *love* to know—but it's your own damn fault that I won't.'

I turned on my heel. Internally, I was shaking like a leaf, seconds away from collapsing. Outwardly, I remained calm. I started walking, one foot in front of the other, each step carrying me away from him.

'HARLEY!' Bas screamed.

'Leave me the fuck alone!'

He snarled, a litany of curse words that bounced around in my head. I kept walking. I wanted nothing to do with him or his temper tantrum.

Bas still didn't believe me.

And I hated him for it.

I was still furious with Bas by the time I had to face his brother.

Two fucking peas in a pod. How ironic that Bas wanted to avoid Rodney. They fucking deserved each other.

I had to switch my shifts with Dana on Wednesday so that I could carry out Hardwick's mission—which he had spent Tuesday evening mockingly reminding me not to screw up. So I covered the afternoon shift, then went home to have a cursory dinner, changed into something that was both sexy and allowed for movement, and headed out to meet the other Rochester brother.

He was waiting on Hustle Highway, hidden behind the blacked-out windows of his sleek car. I climbed in, smoothing my hands over my slinky dress and tights.

Rodney looked less than pleased.

'Have you spoken to my brother?'

'The fuck do you think?' I muttered.

'I think if you didn't, then this is going to be a very short trip.'

I ground my teeth together. 'I haven't seen him since I spoke to you.'

'I don't think you're trying very hard,' he said flatly.

'Trying?' I was ready to tear my hair out. 'He doesn't live across the road from me. I can't just speak to him whenever I want. Besides, I'm not risking you throwing this because I couldn't persuade him on your timeline. You can deliver first, *then* I'll talk to Bas.'

Rodney pressed his lips together, jamming his foot on the accelerator. 'That was not our agreement.'

'Should have been more specific.'

'I'll remember that,' he said darkly.

'Feel free to.' I made my tone light and airy. It would piss him off for sure—it always did.

Rodney made a noise of frustration. He remained tense as we drove a few streets down and finally parked in a narrow lot behind a row of buildings that were fancy on the front but distinctly industrial and worn from the back.

This place was all about appearances.

'Behave,' Rodney said as I reached for the door handle. 'And let me do the talking.'

'That's what you're here for.' I flipped my hair over my shoulder, opened the door, and jumped out.

I could hear him muttering under his breath as he followed me. I waited at the corner of the building, tapping my foot impatiently until he reached me.

'So, what's the plan?'

Rodney was scowling again. 'The plan is exactly what you suggested. Pretend I've hired you. Cling onto me, act like I'm paying you. I'm sure you can come up with something.'

I rolled my eyes. Charming.

'Okay, then.' I grabbed his arm. He lurched away from me. 'You realise I'm actually going to have to touch you for this to work, right?'

Rodney glowered at the wall behind me. He took a deep breath. 'Fine.'

This time when I touched him, he didn't pull away. I draped one arm around him and slid the other hand under his shirt. His abdomen was tense beneath my fingers.

'Don't you dare steal my gun again.'

'Mm, someone's packing,' I teased. When he made to pull away, I said hastily, 'Don't worry, I won't touch it. Geez, you're jumpy.'

'Contrary to what you think of me, I do not typically engage in physical contact with other people.'

'Sounds lonely.' I teased my finger over his abs. Not as ripped as the boys in the bunker, but Rodney was hiding a decent body under his posh clothes.

'I'm perfectly content on my own, thanks.' He grabbed my wrist, forcing my hand to stop moving. 'I enjoy neither sex nor dating. And keep your fingers to yourself.'

Asexual, then. Fair enough; I'd gone far enough with the teasing. 'I might have to do some stuff to keep the charade going, but don't worry. Your virtue is safe with me.'

'I doubt it.'

'Hey. I don't force myself on people,' I snapped. I pulled him into movement.

'You're hardly a blushing virgin.'

'I've had sex *once*, not that it's any of your business.'

'With my brother?'

That little… I almost called the whole thing off then and there. Only Hardwick's threats kept me moving. 'No. And that is none of your business.'

Though it was quite possible Bas was asexual too. Or at least too traumatised to be interested in sex. Not that I'd blame him.

'Really?' Rodney said.

'Yes, it's really none of your business,' I snapped.

He laughed. I could have punched him.

'I wonder what he'd say if he could see you all over me.'

More of what he'd said before, no doubt.

'That is also none of your business,' I said tersely. 'Eyes on the prize, Rochester.'

We'd reached the front of the building. I checked myself, opening my coat a bit more so my dress was visible, then fixed an appropriately adoring look on my face.

Gross.

Reverie was unique in a row of very strange buildings. All of the buildings here were designed to exude wealth; the trouble was, no one could decide what looked wealthy. One building had an all-glass front, behind which women gyrated on poles, illuminated by red lights. Another building was painted pure white, with an archway providing access to an internal courtyard with a fountain. Reverie had a powder blue façade with gold curlicues and detailing. Combined with the name, the obnoxiousness set my teeth on edge.

This was not my world.

The front door opened into an equally ostentatious lobby. The walls and benches were covered in dark green velvet—the same as Bas and Rodney's eyes, I thought inappropriately. A huge gold-framed mirror hung opposite the door.

A woman appeared to greet us before we'd even got the door shut behind us. She was tall, wearing heels so high they made my thighs ache in sympathy, with her grey hair pulled into a strict bun.

'Master Rochester,' she said tersely. 'Welcome.'

Master? I suppressed the urge to roll my eyes.

'Thank you, Felicia.' Credit to Rodney, his tone was perfectly neutral. Only I could feel how tense he was. I leant my head lovingly against his arm and smiled fawningly at Felicia. She gave me a very prim look.

At least if she thought I was an idiot, she'd hopefully forget about me quickly.

She turned back to Rodney, her smile widening. 'What can we do for you, sir? We have a normal service...' She shifted, a little uncomfortable.

Confused at why Rodney was here?

Well, at least that meant he hadn't lied about his sexual

proclivities—or lack thereof.

'That won't be necessary,' Rodney said. 'I'd like a room, and for no one to bother me for a few hours.'

'Very good, sir. I'll have someone bring you upstairs.'

Rodney nodded tersely. Felicia vanished through the doorway, and a moment later a girl with porcelain skin and wavy black hair minced in, curtseying in a fashion that would have earned a prolonged scolding from my former dance teacher.

'Mister Rochester,' she said breathily. 'I'm Mina. Please follow me.'

Rodney practically dragged me after her. I giggled, clinging to his arm and pretending to stumble.

'Oopsie.'

The look he shot me was scathing.

'What?' I mouthed. *'Just doing my job.'*

I was doing more than that. Under the cover of stumbling, I'd managed to get a good look at the list of guests signed in at the desk. No Derek Jackson. Hopefully, that meant he wasn't here yet.

The inside of the brothel was dimly lit and decorated in reds, blacks, and golds. Everything was as opulent as possible. I kept looking for signs that it was fake, but if there were any, they were well hidden. Extravagant paintings hung on the walls, and furs covered the antique velvet sofas.

'Where does all this stuff come from?' I whispered.

'Stolen, no doubt.' Rodney's words were little more than an exhale against my cheek.

'Oh.' We reached the stairs. The bannister was painted gold, and beside the stairs hung a huge oil painting of brightly coloured flowers in a meadow. The paint was cracked and weathered.

'This way, sir,' Mina said, starting daintily up the stairs. I had to let go of Rodney to climb the stairs, so I took his hand. His palm was clammy.

Someone was not enjoying himself.

At the top of the stairs, the carpet became plush and brown. My feet sank into it. Mina opened a door, then turned to us and fluttered her eyelashes. 'This room is free. Is there anything I can get you?'

'No thanks.' Rodney's tone was terse. I squeezed his fingers in warning. 'We don't want to be disturbed.'

'Are you sure?' Mina's gaze flittered over me, taking in my tiny dress and high heels. She bit her lip coyly. 'I'm happy to share.'

'No!' Rodney spluttered.

'It's alright,' I purred, stroking a hand over his shoulder. He tensed beneath my touch. 'I'm *perfectly* capable of taking care of my man *on my own.*'

Mina's cheeks went pink. 'O-of course,' she mumbled. 'You can ring the bell if you need me.'

She curtseyed again and hurried past us. Rodney wrenched his arm away from me and practically sprinted through the door. I followed at a more leisurely pace, and shut it behind me.

'You know you're not subtle at all?' I asked, surveying the room. It was as sumptuous as the rest of the building, with an enormous bed occupying the space, covered in black silk. 'You're meant to want to be here.'

'This was your idea, not mine,' Rodney spat.

'It was five minutes of acting.' I picked up a bottle of whiskey on the shelf and poured two tumblers. 'If you blow this, I won't speak to Bas for you.'

'There's nothing left to blow. I'm staying here for half an hour, then leaving,' Rodney said.

'Excuse you?'

'This is as far as I go.' Rodney snatched the tumbler of whiskey I was holding out and took a generous sip before leaning against the wall. 'From here, you're on your own.'

I frowned. 'What?'

'You heard me.'

I clenched my fingers around my glass. 'How am I meant to get out without you?'

Rodney raised an eyebrow. 'That is not my problem. I only agreed to get you in.'

For fuck's sake. Should have seen that coming.

'Won't people be suspicious if you leave without me?'

'I would assume so, but again,' he sipped his drink with a smug tilt of his head, 'that is not my problem.'

'You're such a fucking prat.'

'That is what you get for not fulfilling your end of the deal, Miss Benoit.'

I ground my teeth together. *God damned smug prick.*

'Fine, but don't expect me to share what I find out with you.'

'What are you finding out?'

'Oh, didn't you realise why I'm here? Guess Daddy doesn't tell you what people get up to in his brothel.'

Rodney narrowed his eyes. Then he tilted his head up imperiously. 'I don't care what you get up to in here. I certainly don't need you holding any more information over my head.'

Damn him.

'Fine, stay.' I threw my hair over my shoulder with a flounce. 'I don't need you tagging along anyway. You have all the subtlety of an armoured truck.'

I took a sip of my drink, watching as Rodney's expression twisted into a scowl.

'I have more than upheld my end of the bargain.'

'You were supposed to get me *in and out again*.'

'That was not what we agreed.'

I gnashed my teeth. This was going nowhere fast, and I was on a deadline. If he couldn't be manipulated, then I'd have to make do. 'Fine, but you do still have to get me to the right room.'

Rodney downed his drink. 'Which room do you need?'

'Four.'

'There's going to be someone watching from the hallway to see when we leave. Fortunately for you,' he set his glass aside and strode to the cupboard, 'there are other ways in and out.'

He opened the cupboard, shoving aside a hotch-potch assortment of lingerie and props. Once the wooden back of the cupboard was exposed, he laid both hands against it and pushed. There was an audible click, and when he took his hands away the whole thing swung inwards, revealing a narrow passageway into the wall.

'Are you serious?' I demanded, staring into the dark gap. 'There are *secret passages?*'

'These are used for cleaning purposes.' Rodney steered me in. 'Good luck, Miss Benoit.' Then he shut the door behind me, plunging me into darkness.

'Fuck!' I cursed. *Sodding prick!*

I fumbled under my coat until I found my torch tucked into the inside pocket. Pulling it out, I flicked it on and shone it ahead of me. I was standing in a long, narrow hallway with plain whitewashed walls.

It was cramped—if I turned forwards, my arms brushed the wall on both sides.

I wasn't claustrophobic, but I sure wouldn't want to spend too much time in here.

'What now?' I whispered. I twisted around. The corridor ended a little ways down behind me. In the other direction, I could see a corner ahead of me. Was I going to have to try every door? I shone my torch at the door I'd just come through. Painted in black in the middle was a seven.

Oh, phew. The rooms were numbered.

I crept down the hallway, past six, then five, before stopping outside of four. This was it: my target.

All I had to do was place the listening device.

That was it.

Then I could leave, get out of here, pretend this had never happened.

Or… I could stick around and listen in.

Jackson would never catch me in here—I doubted he even knew there was a secret passage. I could eavesdrop on their conversation and find out what was going on in town.

Or I could just leave and forget all about this.

There was a handle on this side of the door, but it took me several seconds of muffled twisting and pushing and pulling to figure out that I had to yank it up and towards me. There was a click, and the door swung away from me, revealing a dark space. I waded in and got a faceful of fabric.

Of course—I was in the cupboard.

I felt my way to the door and cautiously pushed it open. Beyond was a dimly lit room, rather like the one I'd left, except there was no bed. A black leather sofa was flanked by two deep armchairs. There was a drinks cabinet against one wall and a chest of drawers beside it. The room was empty.

Perfect.

Holding my breath, I crept out of the cupboard. I crouched down beside a little coffee table between the sofa and one of the armchairs and pulled the listening device out of my pocket. The sticker had already begun to peel away. I pulled it off the rest of the way and stuck the device underneath the tabletop, then pressed the button. The light sparked to life.

There, done.

Was that really it?

Nerves tightened around my throat like a vice. It felt too easy.

Would Hardwick really send me to do something this easy?

What if the device didn't work?

Would he blame me?

How would I know if it was working?

I peered under the table: the device looked totally innocuous. The light glowed steadily.

It doesn't matter. You've done your job. The rest is Hardwick's problem.

True, but I couldn't help worrying. Hardwick would use any excuse to punish me; I was already on thin ice. I didn't want to give him a reason to go after Savannah.

Soft voices approached in the hallway, and my heart leapt into my mouth. *Oh crap. Was that—*

They were coming closer.

I jumped up and sprinted to the cupboard. I made it just in time— I'd barely closed it behind me when I heard the door opening and voices in the room.

Shiiiiit. I had to get back into the secret passage. I crouched down to get beneath the clothes and crawled to the back of the cupboard. Everything I did seemed to make a noise: scratches, squeaks, bumps. My heart was thumping so loudly against my ribcage, I worried they'd hear that as well. Then my hands felt the cold concrete floor of the secret passage. I scrambled into it, stood, and pulled the secret door most of the way shut, leaving a gap to hear through.

'If there's anything I can do for you gentlemen...' A female voice drifted back to me.

'A little privacy, if you don't mind.' That voice was clipped and brusque. I didn't recognise it. Malcolm Brady, most likely.

'Yes, sir.'

A door opened and closed. My pulse was thundering in my throat. I clenched my fingers around the hem of my dress.

'Thank you for meeting me.' My heart skipped a beat. I knew that voice: a bit rough, a lot blunt. Croaky and hoarse from smoking. It was Jackson.

'Ah, not at all. It seems apropos to iron out the details.' There was a pause, then: 'A drink?'

'Why not?' Jackson asked.

The voices gave way to shuffling, and then someone sighed luxuriously. 'Alright.' That was the presumptive Brady. 'Have the arrangements been made?'

'As discussed,' Jackson said. 'The forces will be split according to our original discussion.'

'Good. And Sayle?'

'He will not leave the compound.' Jackson paused for a long moment. I held my breath, afraid to miss anything. 'Concessions will have to be made in order to convince him.'

'I will relay the message. And the security at the distillery?'

'Workers and a few loyal men. Nothing more. So long as it doesn't happen on a night when there's a delivery or pick-up—'

'If you could provide the schedule—'

'I told you,' frustration had crept into Jackson's voice, 'there's no schedule. The trucks arrive when they arrive. We don't—'

'—control supply. Your one job, you continue to fail at.'

'It depends on the road to Crater's Edge, you know that,' Jackson snapped. 'We're in negotiations with Tango Sierra Echo, but—'

'My people don't care about that.'

'If your people spent a bit more time caring and a bit less time being arrogant shits, none of this would be a problem.'

A cloying silence followed Jackson's angry words.

'Mind your manners,' Brady said tersely. 'You can be written out of this deal.'

'You need me,' Jackson said. Was it my imagination, or was there a thread of fear in his voice? 'You'll never pull it off without me.'

'You think you're the only dog in town who'll betray his master for a sack of coin and a minor ego boost? Don't be ridiculous.'

A gasp wrenched out of my throat. I stuffed my hand over my mouth to muffle it.

Jackson was a traitor?

Several tiny clues clicked into place suddenly. The mysterious voice I'd heard after Jackson had chewed Bas out in his office. The fact that the Iron Fists were hunting so desperately for Tam.

Jackson was a traitor.

But if that was the case, who was he working with? It couldn't be the Aces, or Hardwick wouldn't have needed me to listen in on the meeting.

Tam? I still didn't know what side Tam had been on—except that he was passing information to Hardwick.

If only I knew who Brady worked for. Maybe he was with Hannover and the Black Hands. Or was there someone else?

Or was Jackson on his own side?

'No one else could have told you what I have,' Jackson said angrily. 'You think I can't cut you out? Watch yourself, or the mayor will find our dogs at *his* door.'

Crack!

One of them had slammed his hand against the table. I jumped— and froze. *Shit.* They hadn't heard that, right?

'Do not think the mayor will tolerate threats,' Brady said tersely.

'We had an agreement.'

Silence. I rubbed my chest, trying to breathe shallowly and quietly. What the hell was going on?

'So long as everything is in place, the strike will go ahead *as planned,*' Brady said. 'Assuming no one from your side messes anything up.'

'I've done my part.' Jackson sounded like he was struggling to contain his fury. 'If you could give me a more precise idea of the timing—'

'I've told you everything I can.'

'I can't give the final order without it.'

'You'll know. The signal will be unmissable.'

'If I can't miss it, then neither will my men. They'll be suspicious. I have to separate our forces before then. I've explained this before.'

A long silence ensued. Someone put his glass down on the table with a quiet *thunk.* 'Two weeks,' Brady said. 'Maybe three.'

'That's too long.'

'The timeline is not negotiable,' Brady said. 'There are too many parties—'

'The situation is precarious,' Jackson said. 'There have been developments—'

'You choose now to reveal that? We've asked dozens of times—'

'It's a new development.' They were talking so fast, interrupting each other so frequently, I could barely keep track of who was talking. 'I don't have proof yet.'

'I don't have time for hearsay and rumours,' Brady snapped. 'The mayor needs—'

'Hearsay?' Jackson scoffed. 'You think I'd act on rumours? The Rochester boy is a threat. He has a source that I don't know about.'

Rochester? Did he mean Bas? What had Bas done now?

'Impossible. He's not in contact with his family. Jonathan and his son have assured me—'

'Well, either one of them is lying to you, or he's getting his information from somewhere else. He's poking his nose where it doesn't belong.'

'So stop him!'

'It's not that easy. Sayle trusts him.'

'Then get rid of him,' Brady dismissed. 'His family won't miss him.'

No! I bit my lip. If they were talking about Bas, I needed to warn him—

'What you're asking for is impossible. He's too close to Sayle.'

'It's your job to curtail any threats to our operation.' I heard the shuffling of feet against carpet. Someone was pacing, maybe.

'I can't do it without proof. Sayle likes the boy. He trusts him. Move the timeline forwards or you'll risk this whole plan being exposed.'

'We can't—the merchants' market—'

Brady cut himself off suddenly. I could have cursed. What about the merchants' market? Did he know something about what had happened to it?

'So that's it,' Jackson said smugly. 'You're waiting for them? No, of course, Moriarty interfered to keep them out of town—to weaken our position. Yes. That must have been the plan all along.'

'We're done here,' Brady said angrily.

'I don't think so. Your plan is about to go up in flames, Brady. You're going to need all the help you can get.'

'From you? Not a chance. Play your part or get killed with the rest of Sayle's men.'

Whoosh! Slam! The door opened and shut, and silence fell. All of a sudden, I could hear my pulse in my ears, a dull roar of elation.

This clue was vital. But what did it mean?

How would delaying the merchants' market weaken the Iron Fists anyway? The distillery didn't depend on the merchants' market for supplies. They bought grain from the local farmers and shipped it to the rest of the region via Crater's Edge. So it had to be something else.

I'd have to think about it.

I heard someone shuffling around, and then the door opened and shut again. They were both gone. I waited in tense silence for uncountable minutes, until I was sure they were gone.

Time to get out of here.

Silent as a mouse, I shut the door to room four and returned down the corridor. Five—six—seven. I had the knack for it now, and the door opened easily. I plunged into the cupboard, threw the door open, and emerged into the room.

'Rodney—'

I froze.

Rodney was gone. In his place were two men on the bed. Two naked men.

Very, very naked.

With hands in places I didn't want to see.

Oh God.

I stumbled back.

'Sorry, I—'

The two men pulled apart. One of them scrambled off the bed, yanking the covers with him to conceal his junk. '*What the fuck?*' He stopped dead, his mouth hanging open. 'The fuck are you doing in here, Benoit?'

Brown skin, curly brown hair, amber eyes. It was Diego Bartholomew.

You could have fried an egg on my cheeks. Burning with embarrassment, I choked out, 'Diego! What the fuck are you doing here?'

'Having sex in private like a reasonable person. Get the fuck out of my room!'

'Alright!' I practically sprinted for the door, grabbed hold of the door handle, and—

'Hold up. What the fuck are you doing here?'

'Nothing.' I turned, reluctantly. Diego was pulling his pants on. 'Don't let me interrupt you or anything. I'll just be going.'

'No, you won't.' His expression was twisted in anger. 'You just climbed out of the fucking cupboard! I'm calling security.'

'Don't you dare!' I hissed, panic making my head swim. If he called security, I was screwed. 'Look, me being here has nothing to do with you. Just let me leave.'

'And tell everyone what you saw? I don't think so.'

He stormed towards me. The other man shifted off the bed, trying to cover his privates whilst simultaneously working his pants on.

A bad idea occurred to me.

Oh, that was just fucking perfect. Diego had spent years being nasty to Theo because he was gay. Now here he was, in bed with a guy. Guess mister homophobe had some internalised prejudices going on.

'Does Theo know you shack up with men in your free time? Because I think it would interest him a great deal.'

Fury flickered across Diego's handsome face.

'Don't you fucking dare blackmail me, Benoit.'

'Who ever mentioned anything about blackmail? This is a mutually beneficial arrangement.' I shot him a fierce look. 'You keep my secret and I'll keep yours.'

He glared at me, crossing his arms over his chest. 'That is not how this is going to work. You don't belong here.'

'Uh, I think you'll find I walked through the front door like a normal person.'

'Sure, and hid in the cupboard to spy on me!'

'Spy on you?' I laughed. 'Don't be ridiculous. There's a passage back there for the cleaners. Why the fuck would I care about you?'

His mouth dropped open. He looked so ridiculously surprised that I realised he had, indeed, thought I cared about him. I snorted. *Perish the thought.*

I grabbed the door handle. 'I'm going now. Enjoy your… liaison, or whatever this is.'

'Wait!' Desperation threaded through Diego's voice. I raised an eyebrow at him. He avoided my gaze. 'Don't tell anyone.'

'I told you. You keep my secret, I keep yours. Mutually beneficial.' I shot him a mocking smile. 'Goodnight, Diego.'

I let myself out, shutting the door behind me. A hysterical laugh exploded out of my throat. *Shit.* This was crazy.

Alright, act confident.

I propped my hands in my pockets, holding my coat open enough that my short dress was in full view, and sauntered down the stairs. Mina was lurking in the hallway — she watched me suspiciously. I shot her a smile, then headed for the exit and stumbled out onto the street.

Phew.

Holy shit.

What a crazy adventure.

Next time, I'd bloody well stick with Rodney—if there was a next time. Which there wouldn't be. I wasn't cut out for this subterfuge crap.

The merchant's market. The signal.

I'd have to figure out what it all meant—preferably before Hardwick figured out what it all meant—but it could well be that I finally had the clues I needed to escape Hannover.

It was a short walk home. I was still riding my high as I climbed the stairs and entered my flat. I shut the door behind me and turned to lock it.

'Hello, Harley.'

I whipped around, a gasp wrenching from my lips. Theo was sprawled on my sofa, tapping his fingers pointedly against his legs.

SIXTEEN

I STARED BLANKLY AT my oldest, dearest friend.

'You've been gone a while,' he added, as though we were having a normal conversation. 'I was worried.'

'What—' My throat had closed up, and every word had to be forced past the blockage. 'What are you doing here?'

'Waiting for you.'

Clearly. I shook myself, drawing in a few deep breaths. With feigned calm, I hung up my coat and pulled my boots off. 'This is my flat.'

'Yep.'

'You broke in.'

'I went by the bar to see you. Imagine my surprise when you weren't there and Dana told me you switched shifts.'

Oh my God. My heart was in my throat, its beat a frenetic thudding like a bird trying to escape a cage. 'I'm entitled to do that on occasion.'

'You never switch shifts. The tips are better on the dinner shift.'

'I had things to do.'

'That you couldn't have done in the morning?'

I set my boots neatly aside and turned to Theo, mustering my courage. 'How did you get into my flat?'

'I let myself in,' Theo said.

'You let yourself in,' I echoed. 'To my flat.'

Was this a fucking joke?

'It's not very hard to break into your flat,' Theo said. 'I thought Savannah would be here, but I guess she's out late too.' He levelled his gaze on me. 'Where were you?'

'I'm not okay with you breaking into my flat!'

'And I'm not okay with you lying to me, Harley.'

I crossed my arms. 'I'm not lying to you.'

'Aren't you? Why weren't you at work today?'

I dug my fingers into my sides, taking a deep breath. 'It's none of your business? How *dare* you break into my flat?'

For several seconds, we just stared at each other, the air crackling with tension. Finally, Theo broke.

'Harley, I want to help you,' he said gently, frown lines appearing around his eyes as his lips turned down. 'I'm worried about you. You've not been yourself lately. If Bas and Ellery did something...'

'No!' I blurted out. I sucked in a breath, then repeated in a quieter voice, 'No. They haven't done anything.'

'Then what is it?'

'I...' What did I tell him? What *could* I tell him? I'd intended to explain what I'd discovered about Hannover and the slaves to him, but now that it was happening, I couldn't find the words.

'For fuck's sake, Harley.' Theo groaned, tipping his head back to stare at the ceiling. 'Did you think I wouldn't figure it out? I've known you since you were four.'

'You have no idea what's happening in my life anymore,' I snapped, clenching and unclenching my fingers.

'I still know *you*. Whatever's going on, you can tell me. I won't judge you.'

'There's nothing going on!'

'Damnit, Harley!' Theo stood abruptly. 'Why do you always do this? You lie, you push me away. We're supposed to be friends!'

'We are friends!' I cried in a panic. I couldn't lose Theo. Not him.

'I'm not sure about that anymore. I don't feel like I know you. Just tell me what the hell—'

'I killed Gabriel Tam.'

My words fell between us like bombs. Theo's mouth dropped open, and the silence stretched between us.

I hadn't meant to say that. I'd never meant to tell him that at all, but I also didn't like him pushing and pushing.

'That's it,' I said angrily. 'You wanted the truth? That's the truth.'

'You... what?' Theo croaked.

'You heard me.' I glared at him. 'Ellery and Briggs are trying to find out what happened to him. But he's not missing—he's dead. His body got dumped in the wasteland weeks ago.'

Theo was staring at me like I'd grown a second head. He sagged back onto the sofa as though he had no strength left in his body. 'Holy shit.'

Seconds passed, though they felt more like hours. Theo studied the ragged carpet. I looked anywhere but at him. Finally, he said, 'How did it happen?'

'It's a long story.'

'I mean,' he glanced around, huffing an odd little laugh, 'it's not as though I have anywhere else to be.'

Savannah could come back at any moment, though she probably wouldn't. Lately, it seemed like she often spent the night with Talbot. Or maybe like she was avoiding me. I sighed. 'Fine.'

'I'll make tea,' Theo suggested.

'I don't know if we have any.' Like Theo, I preferred herbal teas over coffee, but Savannah only drank coffee, and I couldn't justify paying for both.

He made a face and hauled himself off the sofa to check. A few minutes later, he emerged with a half bottle of whiskey instead. 'This'll do.'

'That's not mine,' I muttered.

'I'm sure Savannah will survive.' Theo poured us each a generous glass. I trailed him over to the sofa, trying to arrange my thoughts into a semblance of organisation. I had no idea where to start, and my brain felt like grated cheese.

Theo sat opposite me and passed me my drink before taking a sip of his own. 'So.'

'I don't know where to start.'

'The beginning is usually the best place.'

'Ha-ha.' I rolled my eyes. Where the fuck was the beginning? 'Okay. Um... Okay. About two months ago, Brenda told me that the Black Hands were hanging around the charity across the road from her. We investigated and it looked like they were holding people captive in the office.'

'What?' Theo demanded.

'In slave pens.'

'Holy shit. Please tell me you told Ellery.'

I shook my head.

'Harley—'

'Just hear me out,' I warned. I stared into my glass for a few seconds, then put it to my lips and downed the contents. It was like paint-stripper. I gagged.

'Shit, what is Savannah drinking?'

'Maybe she keeps it for medicinal purposes?' Theo asked.

I wiped at my eyes, grimacing, and set my glass aside. 'Ew. Okay. I went to the drop point to leave a note, but Tam was there talking to a guy named Evander Hardwick.'

'I know him,' Theo said. 'Works with the mayor. He's a shite.'

'He works with the Aces too,' I said. 'And I've seen him rubbing shoulders with Hannover.'

Theo frowned. 'How do you know he works for the mayor?'

'I'm getting there. Tam saw me and when I ran away, he chased me. I got to the compound, but—'

'How'd you get away? Did he know it was you?'

'Not at first I don't think.' I thought back over it. 'I don't think so. And Hardwick dragged me into his car and dropped me there.'

'That makes no sense.'

'I've given up trying to understand Hardwick,' I muttered. I wished I hadn't finished the whiskey—I could have gone for a bit more, even if it was the most disgusting alcohol I'd ever tasted. 'I tried to get in to speak to Ellery, but they wouldn't let me.'

'But you're on the list of informants.'

'Well, apparently not everyone got the memo,' I snapped. I barely had to think of that day and the anger came flooding back. 'I saw Briggs instead, and he said he'd let me in if I did… *something*… for him in exchange, but of course, he fucking lied, so I got nothing and then he lied to Ellery too—' I had to break off because my tears were clogging up my throat. I turned away so Theo wouldn't see.

'What did he want?' Theo asked quietly.

'It doesn't matter.'

'Harley—'

'It doesn't matter,' I said more forcefully. 'What matters is that he didn't tell Ellery until days later, and then Ellery confronted me at work and almost got me fired, so I couldn't tell him anything and I couldn't figure out what to do. Then, before I managed, Tam overheard me trying to warn Anna off him, and he lured me to the old bottling plant to kill me, but—'

The tears overwhelmed me again. I covered my face, struggling to breathe. I hated crying; it was the action of the powerless, and I hated feeling powerless. But it was so easy to feel that way, thinking of these things. They weren't even that far past, but they felt like a lifetime ago.

'Harley…' Theo touched my shoulder. I shrugged him off.

'Don't.' My voice was a harsh whisper. 'You haven't heard the rest.'

'It can't get worse than this.'

I laughed grimly. 'Hardwick knows. He was going to help Tam, I guess, to dispose of my body. But I survived, so he helped me instead. And then he made me repay him by taking Tam's place.'

'Fuck.'

'Yeah.' I shuddered. 'I've been spying. That's why I started dancing again. I couldn't think of anything else—well, I know what *Hardwick* wanted, but he's a psychopath. Anyway, I don't think I've actually told him anything important, but he makes me do other stuff, and he's threatening Savannah as well—'

'Harley, breathe,' Theo said.

I sucked in a huge breath, too fast, and coughed loudly. 'So then—'

'Have you told anyone else about Hardwick?' Theo asked.

'Of course not!'

'And the slaves?'

'I'm getting to that. Bas knows.'

'Bas?' Theo groaned. 'You barely even talk to him.'

'Yeah, because I told him and he didn't fucking believe me!'

'And that surprises you? Bas is never going to do anything that jeopardises his position in the Iron Fists. Not when Sayle promised him revenge on Moriarty.'

The realisation hit me right in the gut. *Oh.* That made so much sense. Bas's reluctance to take action, his need for evidence. He wasn't going to risk taking the information to Sayle unless he was sure beyond all shadow of doubt.

Not that it made his arseholery forgivable, but it did explain it.

'Well, who else was I supposed to tell? It's not as though I'm swimming in allies, here.'

Theo frowned. 'You could have told me.'

'You weren't there,' I pointed out.

'I've been here for two weeks, Harley. That's not an excuse. You said you'd known for months.'

I bit my cheek, squirming uncomfortably. Theo raised an eyebrow.

'I didn't think you'd believe me, alright?' I blurted. 'Ellery didn't, Bas didn't. I'm just a stupid little girl to you lot. No one believes anything I say.'

'That's not true!' Theo said fiercely. 'I've always taken your side.'

'Never over anything like this. And I didn't know, okay? You're one of the Iron Fists. How could I be sure that you wouldn't decide to turn me in?'

'You should have trusted me!'

'Well, I can't.'

'I haven't done anything to you.'

'I just can't, okay Theo? I'm not one of you, I never will be. I don't have that automatic bond. The Iron Fists aren't my friends, they're the people who took advantage of me when I was seventeen and—'

'And I tried to help you then!'

'But you couldn't! You didn't have that power then, and you don't now!'

'So you chose to trust Bas instead?' Theo's tone was hurt. 'He's one of us too.'

'I made a mistake with him. I'm not making that mistake again.'

'A mistake,' Theo echoed hollowly. 'Your mistake was not trusting me in the first place. You think you're so good at taking care of yourself? You've made a fucking mess.'

'You think I don't know that?' Anger twisted up my insides. 'Get out.'

Theo jerked his head up. 'What?'

'You're not coming in here and telling me what I should have done and who I should have trusted when you weren't stuck here, living through all of it.' Tears were flowing freely down my face again. 'If that's all you're going to do, you can go.'

Theo stared at me, open-mouthed. 'I'm not telling you what to do!'

'You're preaching. Maybe I should have told you. But when you arrived I had just told Bas, and he didn't believe me. What was I supposed to think? And Hannover's breathing down my neck too, and I didn't want anyone else involved in—'

'Hannover?' Theo asked sharply.

'He caught me when I was trying to get proof—'

'Harley!' Theo groaned loudly. 'You have got to be joking.'

'Actually, I'm not,' I said flatly. I'd about had it with this conversation.

'How have you made such a fucking mess in such a short time?'

'Short?' I hissed. 'You were gone for five months. That's not fucking short, okay? You want me to trust you, rely on you, but you're gone for most of the year. I'm the one who has to stay here and look after myself, day by day, with no one to confide in. So don't dare preach to me, Theodore Dunne. I'm sick of it.'

Theo stared at me for several seconds, then turned away abruptly. He scraped a hand through his messy brown hair. 'Damnit, Harley—' He cleared his throat. 'I'm sorry, alright. I'm trying, I—I've been—'

He cut himself off, and there was a long, pregnant pause. I had no idea what he was going to say, so all I could do was wait.

'I thought...' Theo started finally. 'Look, I wanted better... for both of us. I thought if I could... pay off my ten years' service to the Iron Fists early, save up money, then I could leave and persuade you to come with me. I thought... I don't know. I didn't realise... I should have told you.' He shook his head. 'Somehow I never realised that I was so busy planning, I hadn't bothered to share the plan with you.'

He turned to me, his brown eyes beseeching. I swallowed hard. I couldn't—the way he was looking at me, with such sincerity—his words—I felt my heart breaking.

'Theo, I...'

'I'm sorry,' he muttered. 'I've been so stupid, haven't I?'

'Both of us have,' I mumbled.

'Maybe... I probably shouldn't judge you.' He shook his head. 'I do horrible shit to survive. I guess I just hoped that meant you wouldn't have to do the same.'

I laughed bitterly. A couple more tears trickled down my face. 'Hannover. He almost killed me, but he spared me. Now he wants me to do something really horrible. And I don't know if I can.'

'What is it?' Theo asked.

'Kill Percival.'

'Holy hell.'

'Yep.'

For a beat, neither of us found words. Theo fiddled with his glass and I pulled at a loose thread on the sofa.

'You're never going to... Percival locks himself up tight behind layers of security. Those casinos are more secure than our compound. You won't get close.'

'He wants it done during the strike on the distillery,' I said.

'Sayle's pretty confident they're going to back out of that. The mayor hasn't got the guts.'

I shook my head. 'He's got the Aces and the Black Hands on side. I think he's going to give it a shot. I just don't know *when*.'

Theo stared at his hands. He had long, elegant fingers. I'd always admired Theo's hands—they were very capable in every sense of the word. As capable of producing art as they were of taking life.

'Damnit, this is terrible timing, you know that?'

'Sorry I couldn't time my life imploding for when it was convenient,' I snapped, rolling my eyes.

'No—that's not what I mean.' He shook his head. 'It's just… I came here to tell you I was leaving again.'

My heart sank. 'Already?' I whispered.

'It should just be a short trip this time. They need someone to look into what's holding up the merchants' market. And I'm the best man for the job.'

Damn. Of course he was. Theo knew the wastelands like the back of his hand—he could sneak past the Black Hands and get to Boughton and back, find out what was going on, and report back to Sayle. He could probably do it in a day, as well, unless something went wrong.

'When do you leave?'

'First light,' he said. 'I have to travel by day. I'm not taking the roads.'

'Right.' I scuffed my toes against the ragged carpet. 'So… I'm on my own.'

'No.' Theo's voice was resolved. 'I need time to think about this. Can you… try and hold off on making any big decisions before I get back? I'll make a plan.' He met my gaze. 'We're going to get you out of this.'

'Okay,' I mumbled. I didn't believe him for a second. He was sincere—but I felt like I was in a tunnel. It had caved in behind me, and there was no light ahead.

No escape.

'I promise.' Theo grabbed my hand, wrapping his tattooed fingers around it. 'Just give me a few days. Okay?'

'Okay.' I squeezed his fingers, smiling bleakly. He pulled me into a hug, the whiskey and mint on his breath washing over me.

'You're going to be okay. If it comes to the worst, we can load up my car, kidnap Savannah, and drive until we leave all of this behind.'

'Yeah.' I laughed wanly. 'Savannah will hate that. I already tried to convince her to leave.'

'Let me worry about that.' Theo ruffled my hair. 'You worry about keeping yourself safe until I get back.'

'Alright.' I hugged him tighter. 'Thanks, Theo.'

'Any time, Harley baby.'

Theo leaving wrenched a hole in my chest. No sooner had we made up, then he was gone again. Just like every time.

And like every time, I was afraid. Would this be the last time I saw him?

I spent Thursday fearful and angry. Even the antics of our more harmless regulars couldn't cheer me up, and when Maddock came in, I felt like chucking a towel at his face.

'Evening, Harley, Anna,' he greeted brightly.

'James!' Anna called. 'Long time no see!'

'Yeah,' I said sourly. 'He's been too busy beating people up in the bunker to come visit his old friends.'

Maddock cut me a sharp look. Even Anna looked surprised.

'Ignore her,' she said, setting a glass upright on the bar counter. 'She's been moody all day. What can I get you? Your usual?'

I couldn't deny the accusation, even if it made me grind my teeth together.

'Whiskey, hold the ice,' Maddock said, before turning to me. 'Are you alright?'

'Fine.'

'You sure? You seem on edge.'

I shrugged. Grabbing a water glass, I filled it and put it in front of him. 'Same old. What's new with you?'

Maddock frowned. 'I don't know. I got some bad news recently, and I thought I could maybe talk it out with my friendly neighbourhood bartenders.'

'Bad news?' I asked in surprise. 'What sort of bad news?'

'We're happy to help.' Anna passed him his whiskey.

'Thanks.' Maddock slid a tenner to her.

'So... what's the problem?' I asked.

'I might have to go back to Brackfields. My company is cancelling the contract here.'

'Really?' I could barely contain my surprise. After everything… I hadn't really believed Maddock was here with a company at all, or that they had the power to call him back. Wasn't he with some kind of secret organisation or something like that?

Not that I really understood much of what he'd told me. Maybe I should have taken him up on his invitation to help out, just to find out more.

'That sucks,' Anna cried. 'You should tell them you want to stay.'

'I'm considering it,' Maddock said. 'Strangely, this town has grown on me.'

'Oh, it does that,' Anna said sagely.

'Yeah.' I snorted. 'Like mould.'

Maddock laughed. 'Considering how mouldy my flat is, that hit me right here.' He patted his chest. 'Seriously, though. It's not a bad town.'

'I'd miss you,' Anna said. 'So would Harley, right?'

'Of course,' I said, offering him a careful smile.

'Thanks, ladies.' Maddock grinned. 'Anyway, I have to decide whether to stay or go. I feel like this town needs me, you know? But on the other hand, I have a stable job back in Brackfields.'

'And it would be stupid to let that go,' Anna filled in.

'Exactly.'

I didn't buy it, and I was struggling to pinpoint why. Was it the tilt of his head? The way he wouldn't quite meet my eyes? His finger tapping on the side of his glass? Something about him seemed… not deceitful, necessarily, but not entirely honest. There was more to his story.

I flicked a glance around the room to check on my tables. Laura was leaning up against table two, chatting with a group of men and women, arrivals from the north who were here to attend the merchants' market… which still hadn't arrived.

I turned back to Maddock. 'But why are they cancelling?'

'I guess they decided the contract wasn't as lucrative as they originally thought.'

'No one wants to invest in our town,' Anna said glumly.

'I don't know if it's that,' Maddock said slowly. 'Let's say I had a… business proposal. Initially, they agreed to support it, but now they've changed their minds.'

'So they don't trust *you?*' I asked.

'Harley!' Anna hissed, elbowing me in the side.

'Ouch!' I pulled away from her.

'That was mean.'

'It's alright,' Maddock said, playing with his glass. 'I'm not sure it's that, either. The company wants to make money, and the money is in the cities. Maybe I'll be sent to Providence next. Who knows?'

'Theo says the cities are awful,' I said.

'They're not great,' Maddock agreed. 'They have their pros though. There are a lot more opportunities than here.'

'If it were me, I'd leave,' Anna said. 'But then, I want you to stay. Sorry.'

Maddock laughed. 'Glad to hear it.'

'Let us know what you decide, alright?'

'I will.' He shot us a grin. 'I have a few weeks to decide—I have to close up business here for the company. But you'll be the first on my list to tell if I'm leaving.'

'Seems a shame they didn't stick it out,' I said.

'I agree. I hate leaving things unfinished.' He shook his head. 'But that's the way it is. The corporations are gods, pushing us mere mortals around.'

'And they're not the only gods around here,' Anna said sourly.

Maddock lingered for a little while longer, mostly chatting with Anna. As I closed out my shift that evening, I kept replaying his story in my mind.

Maddock had wanted to change things here. But now he might be leaving. What did it mean? He had mentioned all sorts of goals to me: saving the townspeople. Protecting them from the mayor and the gangs. Some kind of connection to the military. Was all of that just going to be forgotten? Or had it all been lies to get me to trust him?

I had no idea.

If only Theo were here so I could bounce ideas off of him—but I didn't even know when he'd be getting back. As usual.

I was alone.

I never thought I'd miss the arrangement I had when I was passing information to Ellery, but I wished I could go back to that. It had been easy—to just pass the responsibility on to others. And now I was stuck figuring things out by myself.

As it turned out, the grass wasn't greener on the other side.

Not that we had much in the way of grass out here.

Heading home that evening, I continued contemplating the matter. If Theo got back soon, I would be sure to tell him what was going on—in the meantime, maybe I could arrange another dinner with Savannah and Maddock. Do a bit more prying. Not that I didn't have enough on my plate at the moment.

Maybe I should just let it play out?

Or maybe I should just pass it on to the Iron Fists anyway and let them worry about it. They had decided Maddock was a problem. Let them solve it.

But how?

I shrugged my coat on and stepped out the back entrance, into the little courtyard where we kept the bins. It stank of rubbish and cigarette smoke, the usual combination. Wrinkling my nose, I ducked my head and made for the exit.

Someone stepped in my way.

'Hello, Harley.'

I ground to a halt, my heart slamming against my ribcage. I darted a glance over my shoulder at the door—could I make it back through there? Why, oh why, had I taken the back exit?

And how was he here?

'This is private property,' I croaked.

'So it is,' Briggs sneered, his face a rictus grimace cast in silver under the moonlight. 'And in case you'd forgotten, it's also our territory.'

'The hotel is neutral territory.' My breath was short, my heart thumping so fast I feared it would explode.

'We're not *in* the hotel.'

'This is the hotel's property.' I backed up a step, looking at the door again. It was about ten feet away. Barely anything. But he could grab me in that time, and the door was heavy—I might not get it open in time.

'Go on then.' Briggs stepped towards me. 'Call for help.'

I opened my mouth, but my throat seemed to have closed up. Who could I call? None of the other waitresses could help—Briggs would steamroll right over them. Tom might have been able to boss him around, but he wasn't in tonight. Chef could handle a knife, but he'd gone home at ten.

'Ju-just leave me alone. I don't want any trouble.'

'Funny, considering what a knack you have for finding it.' Briggs took another big step, bringing him so close I could taste his breath. I shuddered but stayed where I was, standing my ground.

'What do you want?'

'Just a little chat.' His smile sent a shiver down my spine. Oh, this was bad. Was he going to pull the same thing on me that he had on Anna? Was this about Tam? This was the last thing I needed right now.

I have to get out of here.

I tried to sidestep. 'I really need to get home. It's late.'

'Actually, I think you're right where you need to be.'

'I'm definitely not.' My vision tunnelled. I tried to dive around him, but he stuck an arm out and I collided with him. 'Ah! Get out of my way!'

'I don't think so.' Briggs laughed, an angry, wicked sound. 'In fact, I think you'll want to hear what I have to say.' He licked his teeth. My stomach rolled, and I had to turn my head away.

'Fuck off. I want nothing to do with you.'

'Really?' he jeered. 'That's funny. You seem to be interested in all sorts of other people these days.'

'Wh-what?' What was he talking about?

He smirked. 'I saw you—chatting with Hannover at the bunker the other night? Yeah, I saw that. You two looked awfully friendly. Almost like two little traitors talking shop together. Two murderers, maybe?'

Oh, fuck. Had he seen that? How? We'd been alone!

'I don't know what you're implying—'

He leant in close, close enough that I could smell his breath— whiskey, garlic, and cigarette smoke. 'I think you know, kitten.'

'No!' I put my hands on his chest and shoved him away. I couldn't bear to have him in my personal space. 'Get away from me!'

Briggs hauled his arm back and slapped me.

'ARGH!' A sharp sting washed over my cheek. I stumbled, my back hitting the wall. 'What the fuck?'

'You're a right little bitch, you know that?' He grabbed the collar of my coat with two meaty hands, leaning in so his face was all I could see. 'I reckon it's time you got a whole hell of a lot nicer. Unless you want me to tell people you're getting friendly with the Aces and the

Black Hands…'

He shot me a leering look, his eyes drifting pointedly over my chest. 'Real friendly, in fact, from what I've seen.'

I shuddered. 'I don't know what you're talking about. I need to *go*.'

'Go? No.' Briggs laughed. 'I don't think you do. How about a little generosity, *kitten?*'

He stroked a hand down my neck. My stomach turned.

'Get off me!'

Briggs forced his leg between mine. Panic closed my throat up, and black dots began to dance on the edges of my vision. 'Oh, you don't want that. After all, what would happen to you if I told Jackson—or maybe Sayle—that you were the last person seen with Gabriel Tam?'

Cold permeated my limbs, electrifying my nerve endings. The panic threw everything into hyperfocus.

He could not possibly know that.

'You're insane,' I hissed.

'Am I?' Briggs cupped my cheek, stroking my hair. I gasped in several breaths, but no air reached my lungs. 'You're not nearly as good at keeping secrets as you think you are.'

'GET OFF ME!' My hoarse shriek bounced off the walls around us. I writhed, trying to get in a position to knee him in the balls, or something—

Briggs grabbed my neck and shoved me against the wall. My head scraped the brick, my hair snagging, and my eyes watered from the pain.

'You know, I thought you'd be more willing, but clearly I overestimated you.' Briggs snorted and began pushing my coat off my shoulders. 'It would have been such a nice arrangement. You come by my room occasionally, scratch my back and I'll tickle yours. But if that's not how you want to play it, we can go a round or two here, first.'

His grip on my throat eased. 'Fuck you,' I hissed.

'That's the plan, kitten.'

My stomach turned. I had to get away from him—but how?

Think, Harley, think.

My mind was swimming; I couldn't focus on anything except my need to get away.

Use your environment.

Bas! Unwittingly, his face swam before my eyes. Maybe it was the lack of oxygen. But Bas had saved me before, and much as he hated me, I didn't think he'd want this to happen to me either.

Use your environment.

But when I'd escaped Bas, I'd been able to use his injury against him. Briggs wasn't injured.

But my hands were free.

He leaned in, forcing his lips against mine. My stomach turned, but I pushed the nausea away and focused. I put my hands on his shoulders and ran them down his back, his sides. He groaned and broke the kiss.

'That's spirit, baby. I knew you'd see it my way.'

'Kiss me again,' I whispered.

He smacked his lips back on mine, his tongue wriggling wetly against my face. I was going to puke. Just when I thought I couldn't take it anymore, I found his knife.

Gotcha.

I had to wriggle it out of the sheath very carefully. I didn't want him to figure out what I was doing.

I managed to get my hand around the hilt—

Briggs broke the kiss, pulled back, and smacked me around the face.

Slap!

I gasped, my head knocking the bricks, my ears ringing. Somehow, he was holding the knife.

'You little bitch,' he snarled. 'You think you're clever?'

Shit!

Without missing a beat, I launched myself towards the alleyway. Briggs grabbed my arm. I twisted, kicking out at his ankle. He stumbled, his grip loosening.

'You stupid slut!'

'NO!' I screamed.

I had to get out of here—he didn't seem to have any evidence. There was still a chance I could prevent him from telling anyone. Theo knew—he'd help me. I just had to stay safe long enough to speak to him.

Briggs grabbed my shoulder and stabbed the knife upwards. He was—

Bas had taught me this in my first lesson. I threw my arm out, knocking his arm away. He stabbed again—again I knocked him away—

A burn of agony split my side—he'd cut me—but I was still standing. He thrust the knife again—

'NO!'

His arm hit mine again—I lashed out with my foot wildly. It struck something, and Briggs stumbled.

I turned and sprinted.

'YOU LITTLE BITCH!'

I could hear him behind me, but I didn't stop. I sprinted around the hotel and onto the square. Up the stairs. Into the lobby. Benny, our weapons check guy, lurched to his feet as I stumbled to a stop in front of him.

'What the hell, Harley?'

'Briggs,' I panted. 'I—He—'

'Woah.' Benny put his hands up. 'Breathe.' He stalked to the door, peeked out, and slammed it. 'He's on the square.'

'Waiting for me.' I clutched my neck, trying to shake the panic.

'You want a lift home? I get off shift in ten.'

I sagged against the counter and smiled weakly at Lou, the receptionist. She stared back with wide eyes.

'Want me to call Tom?' she asked, pushing herself up.

'No, no, it's okay. He's—' I sucked in a huge breath. My lungs were screaming. 'I think he's only after me. He won't give anyone else trouble.'

'My car is out back,' Benny said, shuffling his feet. 'I still owe you from… you know.'

'Yeah.' I coughed. 'Yeah, okay. A lift would be good.'

Home. Home was what I needed. First aid, a shower, bed. Put it out of my mind. I'd survived before, and I would survive now.

'Sure.'

Benny dropped me back at my place. I spent most of the drive trying to keep my breathing even. Every movement aggravated the cut on my stomach. It wasn't deep enough to be dangerous, but it was definitely bleeding. I sincerely hoped it wouldn't need stitches.

That would be a challenge.

After thanking him profusely, I let myself into my building and crept up the stairs. My flat was dark—maybe Savannah wasn't there? But my luck was out. The bedroom door was shut, and we only ever shut it when one of us was sleeping.

Damn.

By torchlight, I crept into the bathroom. We were equipped with a first aid kit, courtesy of my sister. I just had to find it, and then… figure something out. We'd probably have antiseptic. I crouched down in front of the cabinet—and swore under my breath as pain wrenched through my abdomen.

Fuck!

I put my torch between my teeth and pressed my hand to my stomach. My jumper was wet with blood. Grimacing, I managed to open the cabinet and peer inside.

Where was it? *There!* I grabbed the metal tin and pulled it out. It was heavier than I thought it would be. It slipped clean out of my fingers and hit the floor with a sonorous *clang!*

Fuck.

The lid had opened. I shoved a few loose things back in and struggled to gather the box up one-handed. At least it didn't seem dented—any more than it already had been.

There was no room to work in our tiny bathroom, so I returned to the main room and set the box and torch on the table.

Clang!

The torch slipped out of my grip and bounced on the table.

Damnit, why couldn't I do anything quietly? I glanced over my shoulder at the bedroom door, but it remained shut. *Please don't wake up.*

For several tense seconds, I stood still. There was no sound of movement. Finally, I turned back to the first aid kit and started thumbing through it. Bandages, antiseptic, something? I had no idea how to stop the bleeding.

'Harley?'

I jumped away from the table, swearing. 'Savannah! You scared me.'

'I scared you?' She marched over. 'It's the middle of the night. Couldn't you get through the flat quietly?'

'I had a bit of trouble,' I muttered through gritted teeth.

'Have trouble at a reasonable time! What the hell were you doing?'

'Nothing, I just—'

'Is that my first aid kit?' She turned to me, her eyes wide in the torchlight. 'What's going on? Are you injured?'

I grimaced.

Savannah marched over to me. 'Show me!'

'It's not a big deal—'

'I'll decide that. Show me.'

I backed up against the counter so she was out of my personal space. 'Alright, alright!'

I pulled my coat off and dropped it on the floor, then eased my jumper up. It was torn on the left side, and the blood had soaked into it, making it sticky. I winced as it came free. 'Look, it's really not a big deal...'

The colour had bleached out of Savannah's face. 'Harley, you— This—Is this a knife wound?' she stuttered.

'Um, maybe?'

'Who stabbed you?!' she screeched.

'No one. It's just a cut. Look, it was an accident—'

'An accident?' I winced as her voice pierced my ears. 'How did you get cut by accident?'

'I didn't, I just—'

Savannah shook her head. 'I—I—' She staggered back a step, grabbing the edge of the table. 'Okay. Stitches. You need stitches. Alcohol. Cupboard. Right.'

She bustled past me, her movements becoming more and more efficient. A few moments later, she had an array of tools assembled, all of them varying degrees of terrifying. She pulled a chair out.

'Sit.'

I sat.

'This is going to hurt.'

'I've had stitches before, remember?'

Theo and I had gone playing around in an abandoned building near the school when we were eleven or twelve. I'd tripped and scraped open my leg on a jagged piece of rebar.

'I know, I know.' Savannah shoved a glass of whiskey into my hand. 'Drink.'

That, I wasn't going to say no to. I welcomed the burn of her disgusting paint-stripper whiskey.

Then she wet a cloth with it and wiped my stomach down.

'Ouch! Fuck!' I yelped.

'Sit still. If you let me work, it'll be over quicker.'

'Yeah, yeah.' I grabbed the edge of the table, clenching my fingers against the urge to push her away. 'I'm not made of steel, you know.'

'You can't run around with an open wound.' Savannah grabbed a needle and held it in front of her to thread it. Her hands were shaking so badly she missed. 'Damnit, go in!'

She missed again and almost dropped the needle.

'Fuck!'

'Hey!' I grabbed her hands. 'Sav, relax.'

'I can't relax! You got knifed!'

'I'm fine. It's not deep. It was Briggs being an arsehole. Benny drove me home, and now you're gonna stitch me up. It's fine. I'm fine.'

'You're not fine.' Tears welled in her eyes. I watched in alarm as they began flooding down her face.

'I am!'

'Shit.' Savannah turned away, burying her face in her elbow. 'Sorry. I'm just gonna—I—'

She set the needle and thread aside and grabbed the whiskey instead, taking a liberal sip. I watched her warily.

'Sure that's a good idea, Doctor Benoit?'

'It's fine. I don't get drunk that easily.' Savannah took a few deep breaths, then picked up the needle and thread. 'Okay. Alcohol. I need to sterilise this.'

She put a new pair of gloves on, snipped the end of the thread off, and wiped the needle with alcohol. It seemed like following procedure soothed her, because by the end of it she wasn't shaking anymore, and this time she managed to thread the needle on the first try. She knelt in front of me and cleaned the wound again, re-examining it.

'Okay. Okay.' She sighed gustily. 'It's not that deep. Just… just the top layer. I'll put a few stitches in so it doesn't tear any further, alright?'

The idea *filled* me with enthusiasm. I gripped the edge of the table. 'Just get it over with.'

The next few minutes were nothing short of agony. Savannah applied a topical painkiller, and I had thought I had a high pain tolerance from dance, but even then I had to drink another glass of whiskey to get me through. Finally, she tied off the thread and snipped the ends.

'There you go. I'll take them out for you in ten days.'

'Thanks.' I stood, rolling my shoulders. 'Can I shower?'

'Try and keep it covered when you do.'

'Alright.' I grabbed my jumper. Savannah started packing her stuff up.

'Are you going to tell anyone?'

I paused by the door, bending down to unlace my boots. 'No.'

'You really should,' Savannah insisted. 'He shouldn't get away with this!'

'What am I going to tell them?' I straightened up, glancing down at the cut as I did. Savannah sewed much more neatly than I did—I should get her to do the mending. 'No one would take my side.'

'If more people reported the gangs for stuff like this—'

'—then more people would get harassed by them, Sav. Really? Who am I going to tell anyway?'

'Another member of the Iron Fists.' She turned to me, the first aid kit clutched to her chest, and her eyes blazing. 'If we can't get rid of them, then they need to keep their own people in line.'

I snorted. 'Why would they bother? Anyway, none of them are going to take the word of a waitress over a guy like Briggs.'

Savannah scowled. 'See, it's that attitude that gets you in trouble in the first place.'

'Wow, sympathetic.' I wadded up my ruined jumper and threw it in the sink—I'd see in the morning if it could be rescued. 'I'm going to wash up and go to bed.'

'You're being irresponsible. You could help other people by speaking up and—'

'And what would the consequences be for me?' I shook my head, heading for the bedroom. 'That's not me. I have enough trouble right now, without taking on Briggs as well.'

'So what are you going to tell them on Saturday when you can't dance for them?'

I paused. 'I am going to dance on Saturday.'

'You can't dance,' Savannah said. 'You'll pop your stitches.'

'I can't *not* dance,' I replied.

'I'm not redoing your stitches for you if you do.'

If I didn't go to the bunker, Hardwick would take it as a sign of disloyalty, and what then? If I aroused suspicion now, it wouldn't be a question of if I got killed, only who would be wielding the gun. Hannover, Hardwick, or Briggs?

If Briggs even knew.

Damnit, Theo, I need you.

So much for being an independent woman.

'Then don't. I'll find someone who actually cares,' I snapped.

'I wish you wouldn't go back to that place,' Savannah said. 'It's bad for you.'

'Says the woman who's dating Talbot.'

'Greg isn't a club full of priggish men.'

'No, he's one priggish man who's in your bed. None of the men at the bunker are in mine.'

'Are you sure about that?'

'Yes!' Out of nowhere, tears stung my eyes. 'You know what? Thanks for patching me up, but I'm tired. I'm going to bed.'

'Wow, so mature.'

'Get fucked.' I turned and marched to the bedroom. 'Talbot's volunteering.'

Savannah cursed under her breath, but I ignored her. If she wanted to always think the worst of me, she could do it alone. I wasn't going to stick around to entertain her prejudices.

SEVENTEEN

HIDING THE CUT ON MY stomach was more of a challenge than I'd initially expected. If I were only working at the bar it would have been fine. But pole dancing by nature required at least a degree of nudity.

When I came out onto the floor wearing a sparkly leotard, Carlos frowned. 'What do you call that, Benoit?'

'What do I call what?'

'That dishrag.' He gestured at my middle.

'Sexy?' I asked, raising an eyebrow.

'Looks like lower tips to me,' he sneered.

Posy came to my rescue. She sauntered over and wrapped herself around Carlos's arm. 'What's going on here?'

'I thought we had a dress code. You know we have a dress code, right?'

'I think Harley looks hot. I'd bang her.' Posy waggled her brows. 'Besides, have you ever tried any of the moves Harley does? The Ayesha…' She trailed a hand down Carlos's arm, sucking in a breath. 'The friction burn is unreal, man. I don't blame her for covering up for special routines.'

Carlos watched Posy's fingers for a second, before stepping away. 'It better be a fucking *special* routine, you got that, Benoit?'

'Sir,' I muttered.

Carlos stomped off. Posy turned to me, winking. 'Ignore him. He's sour 'cause you have nicer abs than him.'

I snorted, then winced as it pulled my stitches. Doctor Savannah would not be pleased if I popped them. 'Thanks for the assist.'

'No problem.' Posy brushed her hair out of her face. She'd cut it again, in a sharp bob right beneath her ears. Her makeup was exaggerated. She looked like a queen. 'Did you manage to get in contact with Lettie?'

'Who? Oh, yeah.' I made a face. The woman who had slammed a

door in my face. 'Yeah, she didn't feel like helping out. But I found someone else.'

Not that I wanted to think too much about *that* right now.

Posy snorted. 'That does not surprise me.'

I shrugged—and cringed as it pulled at my cut. 'Thanks anyway.'

'Hey, don't thank me. I got a free drink out of it.'

I laughed—and regretted it. *Ouch.*

Everything went downhill from there. The moment I got on the pole, I knew my shift was going to be a disaster. I could do approximately two percent of the moves I usually pulled: none that involved contact between my stomach and the pole, and none stretched my abdomen. Even with those limitations, about halfway through my set, I felt the tell-tale snap of the thread breaking.

Fuck.

The rest of that half was murder. I was pretty sure I was bleeding, and I was afraid to put any more pressure on the wound. Carlos glared at me periodically, and I was afraid the closest of the guests would notice a dark patch on my leotard.

During my break, I went back to the changing room to put a new bandage on. I was right: I had popped my stitches.

Savannah was going to kill me.

I doubled up the bandages, thanking the foresight which had led me to choose a black leotard. At least it wouldn't show through.

For the rest of the night, I danced conservatively. Carlos was visibly pissed off, but my tips didn't suffer significantly. Most people cared more about the shape of my arse than the fancy moves I pulled anyway. He still gave me a disdainful look as he counted my tips out, but he didn't skim extra off of my share, at least.

I could feel that my leotard was glued to my skin with blood, so I lingered in the hallways until the other girls left my dressing room.

'There you are,' Posy said as she and Jana passed. 'What held you up?'

'I was chatting. I'm heading out now.' I forced a smile. 'See you next week.'

'Bye, babes.' Posy hugged me, but Jana passed by, wrinkling her nose. She didn't seem to like me much.

Once they were gone, I headed for the dressing room. Fortunately, it was empty. Grimacing, I stood in front of the mirror and stripped my leotard off slowly.

It had glued itself to me pretty well. When I peeled it down, I found the bandage was soaked, and so was the skin around it.

'Fuck,' I mumbled. I tossed my leotard aside and scooped my towel out of my bag. Unwrapping the bandage hurt like a bitch, and beneath it was a horror scene. I was pretty sure I'd made the cut worse. It was leaking blood slowly but steadily.

'Harley, you're an idiot,' I groaned. Hardwick was so not worth this. I was going to have to tell him I couldn't dance next week. He'd have to come up with something else for me to do—and not whoring, because sex was off the table too.

I pressed the towel to my stomach, breathing through the pain.

Knock-knock.

Oh, fuck. That was bad timing. I glanced around in a panic. 'H-hold on!'

I threw the towel and bloody bandages in my bag and snatched my top and jeans out, yanking them on and wincing in pain all the while. *Ouch, ouch, ouch.*

'Hello?' a voice called out.

'JUST A MINUTE!' I buttoned my jeans and pulled my top down, then zipped my bag up. 'Alright, I'm decent.'

The door opened.

It was Bas.

He was dressed in uniform, a strange, unreadable expression on his face as he surveyed the dressing room before finally zeroing in on me.

'Harley.'

I crossed my arms. 'What are you doing here?'

Bas shuffled his weight. 'We… we need to talk.'

My mouth fell open. I couldn't hide my surprise. 'Are you serious? Because I really don't think we need to rehash this again.'

'Harley—'

'I thought I had made myself clear—'

'*Harley*,' Bas repeated, 'I'm sorry.'

Silence engulfed the room. I stared at him; he stared back at me. He looked extremely uncomfortable, like he wanted to turn around and flee the room. Yet he stayed, gripping the doorframe as though it was the only thing keeping him up.

'I…' I trailed off. What did I say to that? *Thank you? Too little, too late? I forgive you?*

'I'm sorry,' Bas repeated. 'For going off at you on the training ground. And... and for not believing you.'

I stared at him in shock—I had no idea what to say. Out of everything I could possibly imagine him saying, this would have been my last guess.

I'm sorry.

'I...' I gripped my dressing table, letting the metal edges cut into my palm and ground me.

'Can I come in?' Bas asked.

I nodded silently.

He pulled the door shut and approached me with long strides. The room felt like it halved in size in an instant, like he'd sucked all the air out of it.

Bas stopped halfway to me, gripping the edge of Jana's dressing table. 'I went to Moriarty's compound.'

There was definitely no air left in the room. I drew in a breath, but although my lungs went through the motions, no oxygen entered my body. My head swam. 'R...really? You... what?'

'There's a secret way in.' Bas shrugged, as though he was talking about the weather, not *sneaking into an enemy stronghold.* 'You were right. I saw them. And her—Sarah Stark, the NCC receptionist. She must be a plant because I saw her in the compound.'

'That... that's great,' I said weakly. I was struggling to process where to go from here. I'd spent so long at odds with Bas that him suddenly believing me seemed more like a product of some weird fever dream than reality.

What the hell was going on?

Why had he gone back to check?

If he had always intended on checking, why tell me he didn't believe me in the first place?

'So...' Bas paused awkwardly.

'So?' I echoed. I needed him gone now. Why wasn't he leaving?

He squinted at me. 'Are you okay?'

'Fine.' I shook my head, forcing myself to focus. 'Great. Well, now you know. What do you want me to do about it?'

He blinked, his brow furrowing in surprise. At length, he said uncertainly, 'Forgive me?'

I laughed. It burst out of my chest like water out of a hose that had been blocked, accompanied by a jolt of pain. *Ow.* 'Are you joking?'

Bas's expression shifted to a frown. 'I don't usually joke.'

'Forgive you? After everything you said to me?' I pointed to the door, wiping the tears of laughter of out my eyes. 'Fuck off. I'm glad you know. It's your problem now, not mine.'

Bas stayed stationary. 'That's it? After everything you went through to convince me—'

'Yeah, *everything I went through.*' I took a step closer to him, anger wiping out my pain. 'That's exactly the point. I'm done, Bas. I'm not interested in having to fight for the slightest scrap of respect from you. I *don't* accept your apology. You don't deserve my forgiveness.'

Bas gaped at me as though I'd told him I planned on quitting my job to take up freshwater fishing. *Really?* I smothered another snort. He hadn't seen that coming?

Of course not. The arrogant dick believed he could do no wrong.

'I…' he said. 'But…'

'Leave,' I said forcefully. 'I want to change. I'm not doing it with you here.'

'But…' He wavered, his gaze flitting around the room as though searching for something. 'But I…'

'Seriously? Fuck *off*, Bas.'

I was done. I turned to my dressing table, crouching laboriously to pick up my bag. There was a cloth in the front pocket to wipe my makeup off.

'I still need to talk to you,' Bas insisted.

I turned back to him. 'You're really taking the cake right now.'

'Please.'

'All those times I needed to talk to you? You mocked me and belittled me. Have a taste of your own medicine.' I waved my hand at the door.

'No.'

'Yes,' I snapped. 'I'm not your friend. You can't push me around.'

Bas opened his mouth, a defiant expression on his face. But then his eyes dropped to my shirt. 'What's wrong with you?'

Shit. Was he looking at… *No.* No way were we doing this. 'Nothing. The fuck are you on?'

'That's not nothing.' Bas gestured to my stomach. 'You're bleeding.'

'N-no I'm not.' There was no hiding the tremor in my voice. I took a step back. Bas moved with me.

'You are,' he said in a low voice. 'Show me.'

'No.'

'*Harley,*' he snapped.

'Just leave it alone! It's none of your business.'

'I'm making it my business. You're hurt.'

Bas took another step forwards. I covered my stomach protectively, hunching over, but all that did was aggravate the cut. 'Ouch,' I hissed.

'You're being ridiculous,' he warned. 'Show me.'

'Fine!' I straightened up and yanked my shirt up. 'There. Are you happy now?'

Bas glanced around, then abruptly shed his jacket and pulled his T-shirt off. He wadded the shirt up and pressed it against my stomach.

I froze. We were literally inches apart *and he was half-naked.*

'G-get—get b-back,' I mumbled. My teeth were chattering.

'You need to clean this up. Stay here, I'll go get water.'

He backed out of my personal space, and suddenly I could breathe again—and did so, overtime. My lungs flooded with so much oxygen that I felt dizzy. I collapsed onto the chair at my dressing table.

'Harley?' Bas asked in alarm.

'I'm fine,' I croaked.

'You're losing blood.'

'It's not that deep.' He came closer and I waved my arm wildly, accidentally swatting him on the biceps. 'Get *away!* I can't breathe when you're near me.'

Bas stopped dead mid-step, staring at me awkwardly. His hands opened and closed helplessly. 'I...' He scrubbed a hand through his hair. 'What...'

I tugged my bag towards me and pulled the towel out, pressing it against my stomach.

'Let me get water,' he muttered.

'There's a jug on the table.' I pointed vaguely. 'Can you... put a top on? Please?'

Somehow it was so much worse when he was shirtless than if he was just close to me fully dressed. I seemed to have lost all control over my eyes; they kept trying to trace the lines between his abs, the trail of hair above his trouser line, the dusty pink of his nipples.

Get it together, Harley.

Clearly I was delirious with blood loss, or something, because I literally could not think of a worse time to be checking him out.

Fortunately, Bas seemed oblivious to my see-sawing mental state. He found the water without too much trouble, then brought it over and set it on my dressing table before pulling his jacket back on and zipping it up. Then he wet the edge of his T-shirt and crouched down in front of me to daub the blood away.

I sat back, fighting not to hyperventilate.

'Who did this?' he asked without looking up.

'No one.'

Bas glanced up, one eyebrow raised. 'Try again. This is a knife wound.'

'I was practising and cut myself.'

'You're not that careless. And you wouldn't risk your ability to dance with foolish knifeplay.' His tone was totally deadpan; there wasn't an ounce of uncertainty in it.

Damnit.

He continued wiping the blood away, before folding the T-shirt and pressing the clean side against my skin. 'Keep pressure on that. I'm going to get a first aid kit. Do *not* try and sneak out, or I'll tell Theo Dunne about this when he gets back.'

I jerked my head up indignantly. 'Don't you dare!'

Bas shot me an even look. 'Then stay.'

'I'm not a dog!'

His expression softened. 'I can stitch it up again, but I need a first aid kit.'

A tempting offer, because it would mean not having to beg Savannah to help me. I nodded meekly. Bas handed me the T-shirt and headed for the door.

I ought to have left.

But I didn't. I dressed properly, except for my top. I contemplated bra choices, and why I hadn't chosen a sexy one to wear tonight, and why that was a totally idiotic thought to be having *because I shouldn't want Bas to see me in my bra.*

I donned my boots and considered making an escape and damn the consequences.

The door opened. Bas entered, a plastic box and a half-empty bottle of whiskey in hand.

'Do you have a lift back to town?'

I shook my head.

'I'll drive you home once we're done here.'

'You don't have to do that,' I muttered. The last thing I wanted right now was to be stuck in a car with Bas.

Bas shrugged. He dropped the box on the table beside where I was sitting and handed me the whiskey. 'Drink, but only a little.'

I knew the ropes. I uncapped the bottle and took a decent sip, relishing the burn down my throat. At least it was better than the crap Savannah kept in our flat. Bas fished a needle out of the first aid kit and sterilised it with a match.

'This is going to hurt,' he warned.

'I am aware,' I muttered. 'My sister had to stitch me up a few days ago.'

Bas frowned in concentration as he threaded the needle. 'You were an idiot to dance on it.'

'You make it sound like I had a choice.'

He glanced at my face, studying me with an uncomfortably intense look. 'Didn't you?'

I looked away. 'Just get on with it. Waiting doesn't make it easier, you know.'

Bas made a noise of frustration under his breath, but he did hurry up. When he crouched down in front of me, I tensed.

'I am going to have to touch you,' he warned.

'I know.'

Bas stared up at me. With him crouching, I was taller than him. It was strange to be at a similar height for once, rather than having him looking scornfully down at me. It felt more balanced.

I grabbed the whiskey and took another deep sip. When I set it aside, I met his forest-green eyes. 'Go on.'

He touched his fingers gently to my stomach, then started to work.

I had to look away. Somehow, this had been much easier when Savannah was doing it. But now the pain competed with completely loopy and inappropriate observations about Bas. He bit his bottom lip when he was concentrating. He had callouses on his fingers. There was a tattoo just below his collarbone, on his chest, that I'd never noticed before. I could see it now because, without his shirt, his jacket exposed the tip of it.

It looked like a feather. Maybe the wing of a bird? It was stylised and geometric, and figuring it out kept my brain distracted from the pain of the needle stabbing me.

Once he was done, Bas swabbed my stomach with alcohol. I swallowed as the burn made bile rise in my throat.

'Thanks,' I croaked once Bas had moved out of my personal space.

'You're welcome,' he grunted. He used the remaining water in the jug to wash his hands, then cleared away the remaining medical supplies. I put my top on properly and instantly felt better now that my bra wasn't on display.

'So,' Bas said.

'Yeah.' I stood. 'Thanks for the help, but—'

'I'm driving you back, remember?'

Crap. I'd agreed to that, hadn't I? So much for making a speedy escape.

'Well then, what are we waiting for?'

Bas leant against the next dressing table. 'Tell me how you got injured.'

'No.'

'Seriously? I just stitched you up.'

'And I'm very grateful,' I said levelly, busying myself with putting my things back in my bag. 'But I'm not telling you.'

'*Harley…*' he said in a low voice.

'No.'

'I'm not going to judge you.'

'It's none of your business,' I shot back.

'What are you afraid of?'

I pressed my lips together. Pulling a cloth out of my bag, I wiped the worst of my makeup off. I'd shower the rest away when I got home.

'Harley,' Bas repeated.

'What do you want me to say?'

'The truth.' He paused, and I could feel his eyes on the side of my face. 'You're afraid I won't believe you.'

Got it in one.

'Can you blame me? After everything?'

'Won't you give me a chance?'

'A chance to what? Laugh at me?' I threw the cloth back in my bag and zipped it up. 'Pass.'

'To believe you.'

'Pass.'

I snatched my bag and headed for the door, but Bas stepped in my way. 'Harley.'

I stopped before I could collide with him. 'Bas.' I backed up a step. 'Don't do this.'

'Just tell me.'

'I want to go home.'

'Me too.' He shrugged. 'But I also want to know who's knifing women in Bale Rocks.'

'No one,' I said.

Bas's eyes narrowed. 'So it was a targeted attack?'

Damnit. He was smarter than me. I didn't know what to say to him—so I went for the jugular.

'Seeing as I've got your attention,' I said in an airy tone, 'can you please speak to your brother?'

Bas's gaze darkened like a storm blowing in. 'You're not going to distract me.'

Wanna bet?

'It's just, if it wasn't for him, I wouldn't have seen the slave being taken to the Black Hands' compound—so you wouldn't know the truth. Which means you owe him. So can you please just bloody well speak to him and tell him to leave me the fuck alone? And find out what he knows about the strike on the distillery whilst you're at it. He was hinting at it, but he wouldn't tell me until I arranged a meeting.'

'We're not playing this game,' Bas said.

I crossed my arms. 'It's not a game.'

'Really?' Bas raised an eyebrow. 'So even if I agree to tell Rodney to leave you alone, you won't tell me who hurt you?'

Tempting as that deal was, I knew a trap when I saw one. If I said yes, he could accuse me of manipulating him.

'Nope. I'm just upholding my end of my deal with Rodney. Now you know, and I never have to speak to him again.'

Bas scowled. He glanced around for inspiration. 'Do you want to resume self-defence classes? After you're healed?'

'Not particularly.' All things going well, Theo and I would be leaving town.

'*Harley.*'

'You know, I'm starting to think you just like the sound of my name.' Bas flinched, his eyes going wide in surprise. I added, 'Which is rich, considering what you said about it in the beginning.'

Bas groaned. 'Do you want me to apologise for every single wrong thing I've said to you? Is that what it would take to get you to trust me?'

'We could be here a while,' I said.

He rubbed his temples, then looked away, obviously thinking *very deeply*. I edged around him, heading for the door, but he pinched the sleeve of my coat.

'Hey!'

'You don't want to tell me because you think I won't believe you,' he said quietly. 'Which means it's someone I know, probably a gang member. You had no trouble grassing on Hannover, so it's not him. Besides, his weapon of choice is a pistol. And you would probably have told on most members of the other gangs, in any case. So it's one of the Iron Fists.'

I dug my fingers into my palms. *Fuck, fuck, fuck.*

'Don't do this,' I begged.

'I'm right,' Bas said with certainty. 'Who was it?'

'Bas…' I pulled away, turning to face him properly. I didn't like it when he was behind me. 'Look…'

'Ellery?'

'What? No! Ellery wouldn't,' I spluttered.

'You're right.' Bas nodded. 'Not Ellery; not Kade. He's too nice. It was Briggs.'

My stomach lurched. I tried to think of a protest, but my mind had gone blank.

'Briggs.' Bas's expression shifted—anger, annoyance, resolve. *Uh oh.* 'Why?'

'It wasn't Briggs,' I said quickly.

'Don't do that,' Bas snapped. 'You can hate me all you want, but don't lie to me. It was him. Why?'

I opened my mouth, but I had no answers to give. For a moment, we just stared at each other, the seconds trickling by. Finally, I muttered, 'He wanted to fuck me. I said no.'

'So he pulled a knife on you?' Bas asked incredulously.

I flinched. There it was.

'I knew you weren't going to—'

'It's not that I don't believe you!' Bas snapped. 'Not everything I say means I don't believe you!'

'Really? You're going to take my side over Briggs's?'

He scrubbed a hand over his face. 'I get it. You have a complicated history with Briggs. Do you want me to speak to him?'

'No!' I gasped in horror. If Bas did that, Briggs would know I'd told him. And that would give Briggs an opening to—to—

'No, don't you dare.'

'I can tell him to stay away from you,' Bas said. 'Or I can ask Sayle to reassign him somewhere where you won't keep crossing paths.'

I shook my head. 'I don't want you to get involved. Please.'

'Then what do you want?'

'Nothing!' I insisted. 'Nothing except to just bloody well go home now.'

Bas stared at me, his eyes jumping from my face to my stomach, and back again. He seemed to be searching for something, but whether he found it or not, he finally started to the door. 'Fine, let's go.'

We made the drive back to my place in silence. For my part, I was drowning in my own worry. Bas knew about Briggs. I could ask him not to deal with it, but I couldn't force him. It was out of my control.

Not that I'd ever had any control over Bas to begin with.

Whatever he was thinking about, he didn't tell me. But he did keep looking at me. It started once we got under the flickering streetlights of the centre of town and continued periodically until he parked in front of my building.

I immediately reached for the door handle. 'Thanks for the lift.'

'You're welcome.' Bas cut the engine. 'Harley...'

Something in his voice made me turn and look. He was watching me with shadowy eyes.

'Listen. I know you don't want anything to do with me, and that's fine...' He cleared his throat. 'But I would appreciate it if you would consider telling me what you know. So I can make a plan.'

'You don't need to concern yourself. Theo is dealing with it.'

'I don't know if you've missed the latest, but Dunne isn't here. He was sent out on Thursday.'

I scowled. 'I'm well aware, but he won't be gone forever, and—'

'And I'm here *now,* and offering to help you *now,* Harley. You can hate me all you want, but at least let me do the right thing.'

'I'm not really concerned about you doing the right thing,' I snapped. 'You're good at that. I'm concerned about how I'm going to feel when you're done doing the right thing for *everyone except me.*'

Bas winced. 'I have helped you in the past.'

'Maybe,' I said. 'But you've also mocked me, belittled me, called me a whore—which isn't even true, and you know how it bothers me. You've put me in really difficult positions, then criticised me when I tried to do my best. You're entitled to have high standards, but God, your standards are just fucking impossible.'

He looked away. For several seconds, he studied the dashboard, and I studied the side of his head. His hair looked soft. He had a tiny scar along his hairline, near his left ear.

'What would it take for you to be willing to work with me?' he asked in a stilted voice.

I pressed my lips together, considering the question. *A lot.*

'Depends how serious you are about that,' I said.

'Deadly.' Still, he kept his eyes averted.

'Fine.' I turned my words over in my mind for a second. 'Fine, then here's what I want.'

Bas turned back to me, his expression apprehensive.

'You have to share everything you find out with me,' I started. 'No matter how small or big, if it pertains to Hannover and the slaves, you have to tell me.'

Bas pressed his lips together.

'And,' I continued before he could object, 'you have to let me come along if you're working on this. And lastly, you're not allowed to insult me in any way, call me a whore, imply I'm having sex with anyone for money, or generally make comments about my sex life. And you can't treat me as though I'm incapable. We're partners or we're nothing, you got that?'

He frowned. 'I'm not taking you along with me.'

'I want to be involved.' I crossed my arms, unwilling to budge an inch. If he wanted my forgiveness, it would be my way or the highway.

'It could be dangerous,' Bas said.

'You wouldn't know about any of this without me. I'm already in danger every day, and I hate not knowing when it's going to get worse.'

Bas stared at me for a long, long time. My skin prickled with awareness.

'Fine,' he said. 'But I'm not taking you to the Black Hands' compound. That's where I draw the line.'

'If you go—'

'That's where I draw the line, Harley,' Bas repeated quietly. 'It's not negotiable.'

I frowned. 'I don't get to have things that are *not negotiable*.'

Bas hesitated, his Adam's apple bobbing as he swallowed. 'If it's important to you, I'll honour it. But I'm not taking you into Moriarty's compound, nor anywhere near it. It's too dangerous.'

This was the best I was going to get. It chafed because it left a loophole open for him to exploit later—but I could accept it for now. I had to.

'Okay.' And then, because there was no way I was leaving his resolution untested, I added, 'But you have to let me deal with Briggs on my own. That's non-negotiable for me. I won't have you fighting my battles.'

Bas scowled. 'There wouldn't be a battle if you let me deal with it.'

'This falls under treating me as though I'm incapable. It's my problem, and I want to solve it.'

Bas turned away, a troubled look on his face. His hair fell into his eyes, and my fingers itched to brush it away. Would it be soft? Was I going crazy? Why was I suddenly obsessed with his hair?

'Alright,' he said finally, resolve in his tone. 'I agree to your terms if you agree to mine. I won't take you to the Black Hands' compound, and… and I need you to be patient with me.' He caught my eye, a haunted look in his gaze. 'I'm not perfect, Harley. Not even close. You want to talk standards? Because yours are quite high too. I haven't learnt the things you have. Whilst you were making friends and learning social skills, I was just trying to survive.'

Ouch. High standards?

I swallowed. 'I know that, but—' I took a steadying breath. '—but I can't stand by and let you insult me.'

'I know.' His gaze turned distant again. 'I won't insult you again. Just… just cut me a little slack. It's easier to be cruel than to be kind.'

Truer words.

When we'd first met, what felt like a million years ago, I had felt some kind of connection to Bas, a sort of mutual understanding born through suffering. Somewhere along the line, I'd forgotten. We had erased the connection with our harsh words. But that was enough to remind me.

It's easier to be cruel than to be kind.

It was easier for me too. Easier to shout at him and push him away than to trust him and risk being hurt again.

'As long as you try, I will too,' I said.

Bas nodded. 'I can accept that.'

EIGHTEEN

I SPENT SUNDAY IN A state of disbelief, so much so that I regularly had to pinch myself to remind myself I wasn't dreaming.

Bas believed me.

He *believed* me.

And, granted, it wasn't as though everything was going to be instantly okay now. In fact, nothing was really okay—Bas was closer than ever to discovering some really dangerous secrets about me.

Yet I couldn't help but feel a pervasive, all-encompassing sense of relief. It was light and heady. I floated on air the entire day.

Bas *believed* me.

I wanted to shout it to the heavens.

I controlled myself, however.

He was picking me up on Monday afternoon, so on Monday morning I performed the one chore I couldn't postpone: I headed down to Irina's office to pay her my rent. It was a struggle to hide my good mood; she kept giving me suspicious glances. Irina preferred her tenants with a generous helping of misery.

We had to remember our place, after all.

I could barely focus on my chores for the rest of the morning. It was only the threat of not having anything to wear for the coming week that prompted me to drag my things to the laundromat—and Savannah's insistent note on the counter that forced me to the shops for coffee.

At two-thirty, I donned my coat and boots and headed downstairs to lurk on the street. It was a windy day, and to the east, the sky was the colour of rust: dust blown up from the crater where a meteorite had struck Earth hundreds of years ago.

I shuddered; I was glad I hadn't lived then. We might struggle to survive now, but in those days—according to what records we had— the skies had burned, people had died in droves, and those who were left had battled with terrifying weapons for control of the remaining resources. The harshness of my day-to-day existence seemed tolerable by comparison.

Bas pulled up not two minutes later, rolling to a stop on the side of the road. I opened the passenger door and climbed into the by-now-familiar four-by-four. Also familiar was the pain that greeted me when I stretched to get in. *Fucking Briggs.*

'Hi,' I murmured, feeling oddly shy.

'Hello.'

When I dared to look at Bas, I found him watching me. There was a strange look on his face: not quite a frown—it was too gentle. Was it concern? Worry?

Other than that, he looked normal: same neatly combed brown hair, same black uniform, same upright posture. Still, there was something different about him—something I couldn't quite put my finger on.

I focused on my seatbelt instead. 'So, where are we headed?'

'To start with, RocCo Industries.'

My head jerked up in shock. 'Your father's company?'

Bas was staring straight forwards; he'd tensed up again. 'You said Rodney wanted to meet with me, so we may as well get that out of the way.'

My jaw felt like it was on the floor. I cleared my throat. 'Are... are you sure?'

Bas was silent for several seconds. 'You mentioned he knows something about the attack on the distillery, so I need to know what that is. And I need to take care of an issue that I should have resolved a while back, really.'

What issue was that? He probably wouldn't tell me. It was outside of our terms—he only had to tell me things pertaining to the Black Hands and the slaves. Loosely, that included the attack too, but it definitely didn't include private business with his brother.

'He said that the mayor has contracted with the military for the strike,' I said. I was curious to see Rodney and Bas interact, but that didn't mean I wouldn't at least try and save him the indignity.

'Even more so, then,' Bas said. 'I need to know what he knows and where he heard it from.'

Interesting. But also not what I was here for. And truth be told, I was feeling a bit impatient; I hadn't fully made up my mind whether I was going to forgive Bas or not—trust him, or not—and the issue with the slaves was much more important. If he took care of that, I'd be free of Hannover.

I hoped.

'Are you going to free the slaves?' I asked.

'I can't at the moment.' Bas's voice was stilted. 'I want to, but it's not a matter of just walking in. There'll need to be a distraction, and I'll need support.'

'I can help.'

'Not at the compound,' Bas insisted.

'But—'

'We discussed this, Harley,' he said tersely. A moment later, he said in a softer tone, 'You are helping. For now, I need you to tell me everything you know.'

'I have already told you a lot,' I said sulkily. 'The least you could do is tell me your plan.'

'I'm working on it,' Bas said. 'There isn't a plan yet. I thought we were going to pool information.'

Typical. 'If you're just using me to get information on the distillery…' I trailed off. No good threat came to mind.

Bas sighed. 'Please trust me, Harley. I want to work with you.'

'Until I tell you something else unbelievable.'

Bas tapped the wheel agitatedly. 'Check the cubby,' he said suddenly.

What the hell now? I opened it, the lid flopping against my hand. The hinges were broken. There were two metal tins inside, and on top of them was a handgun—old, but functional.

'That's for you,' Bas said. 'On loan, until we've dealt with the Black Hands.'

A chill of awareness ran down my spine. 'The gun?' I croaked, half in hope, half in terror. My hands were shaking.

'Of course.'

I took it in trembling fingers. I had never owned a gun before, not even on loan. Guns were currency in our town; if you had one, you were automatically set apart from the rest of the rabble.

It seemed like an impossible amount of power to hold between my hands.

'I have a spare harness. We can resize it for you. I'll show you how to use it,' Bas said—rambled, more like. He didn't seem to know what to say.

'Uh, I do know how to shoot.'

'Brushing up on your skills can't hurt.'

'Yeah, um, yeah.' I swallowed. I couldn't believe he was giving me this. It was too much for my mind to wrap around. 'Thank you.'

'You're welcome.' Bas cleared his throat. When he spoke again, his tone was all business. 'When did you first find out about the slaves?'

I put the gun back in the cubby for now and straightened my coat. 'It was a month, maybe a month and a half ago, now. Brenda tipped me off that the Black Hands had been hanging around the NCC office, so we went upstairs to look in—'

'Brenda?' Bas asked.

'She's a colleague of mine. About ten years older than me.' I paused. 'You've probably never met her.'

'I don't know any of your colleagues except the blonde bartender.'

'Anna,' I muttered.

'Yes, her.'

'Brenda used to work the night shift.'

We'd passed the square by now. Bas steered us onto the main arterial heading east, out into the industrial area.

'So what happened when you checked?' he asked.

'From the second floor of her building, we could see down into the first floor of the building opposite. In one of the rooms, they'd set up a kind of... pen where they were keeping the slaves.' The horror of it hadn't faded in the slightest. It came back now, a kind of spine-tingling dread.

'How many?'

'Six, I think.'

'And why didn't you tell us?'

'I did try, but then Briggs—' The words stuck in my throat. '—the thing with Briggs happened, and Tam, and then you and Ellery were, well...' I shook my head. 'I didn't know what to do. Should I have told the police?'

Bas was silent, but his knuckles were white where he was gripping the steering wheel.

'Who else knows?' he asked.

'Theo—I told him right before he left town. And Maddock. At least, I tried to tell him, but I'm not sure he ever followed up on it—or cared.'

Bas tapped his fingers against the wheel. I wished I knew what he was thinking, but his face was inscrutable.

'Will your colleague let us into her building?' he asked.

'Maybe, but she won't be there now. She's switched jobs. She'll be at work.'

Bas hummed. 'Fine. What else have you learnt?'

'I overheard the mayor talking with your father and a few other people, remember?' By Bas's expression, he remembered all too well. 'I don't know for sure, but he strongly implied that he was allowing the Black Hands to kidnap the slaves from within the town limits in exchange for their support against the Iron Fists.'

'Makes sense,' Bas said. 'Moriarty is quite lazy—he'd like a deal that allowed him easy pickings.'

'I think…' I chewed my lip. I was still afraid Bas would turn around and laugh at me. *Sorry, I was only joking. I don't believe you after all.* I forced myself to talk past the fear. 'I think the Black Hands' side of the deal was to blockade the merchants from entering town. I just don't know why.'

Bas glanced at me in surprise. 'Where did you hear that?'

'From a guy named Malcolm Brady. He was talking to Jackson.'

'Our Jackson?'

I nodded.

'Who's this Brady guy?'

'I don't know, but I think he works for the mayor.'

Bas's eyes narrowed. 'Why was Jackson in contact with someone from the mayor's office?'

'I only know what I heard,' I hedged cautiously.

'*Harley,*' Bas muttered. 'Spit it out.'

'It sounded like Jackson was plotting against the Iron Fists,' I said.

Bas jerked the wheel. 'You have got to be joking.'

'I only know what I heard.'

Bas groaned.

'You promised you would take me seriously!' I cried.

'That's going to be difficult if you see traitors on every street corner, Harley.' Bas shook his head. 'Do you have evidence, or is this just a crazy theory?'

'It's not a crazy theory! Just because you're so determined not to trust anything I say! Jackson had a meeting with Malcolm Brady, which I overheard recently, and it sounded like he was plotting against the

Iron Fists,' I repeated stubbornly.

'I have no idea who that is,' Bas said.

Neither did I.

'I know what I heard. Look, do you remember after your fight with Hannover, you had a meeting with Jackson?'

Bas's expression darkened. 'Yes. How do you know that?'

'I listened in. Never mind that—'

'I do mind, actually. What the fuck? Where were you?'

'In the ceiling. It's not important right now. How many people were in the room?'

'Two.' Bas glared. 'How were you in the ceiling?'

'There's a crawlspace. After you left, Jackson spoke to someone else who was in the room with you.'

'There was no one else in the room, Harley.'

'There was. I heard him.'

'Maybe you heard something else.'

'I heard Jackson speaking to another man, asking if he was happy with how things had gone.'

Bas frowned. 'This is farfetched. And what were you doing crawling around in the ceiling? Are you honestly insane?'

I crossed my arms. 'You're doing it again—you never believe me. I don't know why I thought that would change.'

Bas huffed. For several hundred yards, the only sound was the tyres on the asphalt. Finally, he spoke.

'Let's say I did believe you.'

'Which you obviously don't,' I snapped. Did he think I was stupid?

Bas made a noise in his throat. '*Harley.* I'm not saying I don't. I'm saying that it will be my word against his. And I don't have that kind of clout.'

'See, you say that, but I know you don't believe me.' I glared out the window. The tall walls surrounding the factories and plants rushed by. 'And I've been right every time.'

Bas sighed. He slowed the car abruptly. 'I'll look into it, but I'm not making any promises. You, however, need to stop crawling around in the walls.'

'I'll stop crawling around in the walls when people stop giving me reasons to.'

We were pulling into an industrial complex—a familiar one. The last time I'd driven in here, I'd been trapped in the boot of a car. But I remembered walking out all too well. It was the RocCo offices.

There were several buildings scattered around, most of them made of breezeblocks, with corrugated metal roofs. Several had boarded-up windows. Beyond them, I could see the silhouette of some kind of industrial plant.

A security guard jumped out of a hut and approached us, but Bas sailed straight past him and double-parked in front of one of the buildings. 'Stay here.'

He climbed out of the car and marched to the door, throwing it open. I watched in a mix of horror and amusement.

Shit. What had I unleashed?

Not a minute later, Bas reappeared, dragging Rodney with him. He threw his brother towards the back door, then rounded the car and climbed into the driver's seat. 'Get in.'

Rodney stared uneasily at the car. I opened my door and glanced out at him. 'Isn't this what you wanted?'

'Harley?' he asked, his eyes wide with shock.

'In the flesh.' I put my feet up on the dash. 'And here you thought I couldn't make good on our deal.'

'Get your boots off my dashboard,' Bas snapped.

I dropped them down again, and had to bite my lip to hold in a snicker. Rodney opened the back door and jumped up, flinching when Bas started driving before he'd even shut the door.

'Where are we going?' he asked, an edge to his voice.

'That's for me to know.' Bas steered us to the exit, every movement jerky with barely contained violence. 'You keep your fucking mouth shut.'

'So polite,' Rodney muttered.

'Keep running your mouth and there'll be no conversation. I'll leave you here to walk back,' Bas said.

Rodney finally took the hint and shut up. We drove along the wide road and past several lots before Bas turned us sharply into the wasteland, and we bounced along a dirt track that wound between hunks of concrete and finally ended in a gravel- and weed-covered lot amidst four broken-down buildings. He cut the engine.

'Stay here.'

'Don't order me about,' Rodney snapped.

'Unless you want to run across the sort of riffraff that lives in a place like this, you'll stay in the car.' Bas shot him a glare. Rodney cowered into his seat. 'Got it?'

Rodney nodded.

'Good.' Bas jumped out, pulling his gun, and went to the first building to check it. In short order, he'd checked all four. He returned to the car and opened Rodney's door. 'Out.'

Rodney immediately hopped out of the car. 'I just want to t—'

Bas grabbed the collar of his shirt and hurled him against the wall. Rodney hit it with a helpless 'oof!' Bas followed him with two quick steps and shoved his head against the bricks, leaning his whole weight onto Rodney's back.

I jumped out of the car and sprinted over to them.

'Let me make two things clear to you,' Bas snarled.

Rodney moaned in pain.

'Shut up.' Bas elbowed him in the spine. Rodney grunted. 'One. There is no possibility of any reconciliation between us, ever. Do you understand?'

'I just want to—'

'Do. You. Understand?' Bas snarled, shaking Rodney with every word.

'Yes!' Rodney gasped. 'Yes, I understand. Let me go!'

'Two,' Bas continued mercilessly. 'Leave Harley *the fuck* alone. Understood? I am sick and tired of you sticking your interfering nose into my business. You will not speak to her again. You will not ask her to advocate for you again, nor will you try to make deals with her. You will not even look at her ever again. Do I make myself clear?'

'It's a free world,' Rodney said stupidly.

'Yes.' Bas's words were twisted with fury. 'I am free to put a bullet in your head right now. If you don't want me to, you will agree to my terms.'

I couldn't see what Bas was doing, but Rodney suddenly whined in pain. 'I agree! I agree!'

'Good.' Bas stepped back, wiping his hands on his trousers. 'Tell me what you know.'

Rodney turned to face us.

'That's not what I...' Rodney trailed off as Bas's hand dropped to his gun. He shuffled his weight and cleared his throat. 'I was hoping we might trade.'

'I make the terms,' Bas said coldly. 'Information first.'

Rodney frowned. After a moment, he pushed off the wall, dusting off his suit. He looked at me.

Bas clicked his fingers. 'Eyes over here.'

'I didn't realise you felt so strongly about her.'

'Harley is not an allowed topic of discussion,' Bas said shortly.

Rodney crossed his arms. 'This is going to be a very short conversation if you won't allow me to discuss anything.'

'This isn't a conversation. It's an exchange. You told Harley you had information. I'm here. You can deliver it directly to me.' Every pore of Bas's body exuded his fury: I'd seen him angry before, but never like this. This was a whole new level of anger and betrayal.

Rodney twisted the hem of his jacket between his fingers. 'Fine. Fine. As I told Harley, the mayor intends to attack the distillery.'

'That's not news to me,' Bas snapped.

'He's spent the last six months cultivating allies,' Rodney said. 'All of the wealthier families in town have contributed. The Aces and the Black Hands are on board.'

'Do you really think I don't know any of this?' Bas studied his fingernails. 'Your information is old.'

'Is it? Then I suppose you've noticed the greater number of military recruits in the town as of late?'

Bas didn't say anything, but his body language shifted: suddenly, he was alert.

'They've been coming here under the guise of spending their downtime in town,' Rodney continued. 'But the truth is that they're bringing weapons. There's a team stationed to the northwest. When the strike goes down, the plan is that they'll occupy the centre of town, keep the civilians safe, and—'

'Keep the mayor safe, you mean,' Bas sneered. 'I doubt he cares about the civilians.'

'Like your side cares?' Rodney asked. 'They extort the townspeople, rape the women. The violence is at an all-time high.'

'Where there are people, there's violence,' Bas said. 'Which doesn't change that the mayor's goals have nothing to do with the town.'

'The mayor—'

'The mayor wants to line his pockets,' I said. 'And I was there when he admitted it. So don't bother pulling that. Your father and the others—they're all the same.'

Rodney pressed his lips together. 'Driving the gangs out would be good for our town. You, of all people, should understand that.'

Did he think I was going to take his side?

'Driving the gangs out would make no difference to me. It doesn't matter whether I'm ruled by one side or the other—they're all the same.' I crossed my arms. 'Besides, he's collaborating with the Black Hands to drive the Iron Fists out. He hardly has the moral high ground here.'

'It's a stepping stone on the way to his end goal,' Rodney said.

'Which is?' But even as I said it, I realised. 'First the Iron Fists, then the Black Hands. Then he'll use the military power he's been stockpiling to get the Aces out as well.'

'The Aces have agreed to step back when the time comes.'

'No one agrees to give up power,' Bas said.

'You'd be surprised.'

Interesting, but not important right now. What was important was the upcoming strike. And the fact that I knew neither the Black Hands nor the Iron Fists planned on rolling over and accepting their fate. The mayor wouldn't have nearly as easy a time getting rid of them as he thought, and if what Rodney said about the military was true, then the civilians were definitely in danger too.

'How many men?' I asked.

'Pardon?'

'How many men is the military sending?'

'Roughly fifty, at a guess,' Rodney said. 'There's room for more, though.'

'If they're well trained, it'll be enough to blockade the centre,' Bas said. 'Especially if they have greater firepower.'

'People are going to get slaughtered,' I said.

'The mayor has a plan for that,' Rodney said.

'Let's all agree that the mayor is full of hot air,' Bas said loftily. 'The Aces and the Black Hands have plans. They're cooperating with the mayor so long as his plans align. If you think it will stay that way, you're more naïve than I ever realised.'

'I wouldn't underestimate the mayor—'

'Did you really come here to argue his case?' Bas asked. 'Not how I would have wasted my reunion.'

Rodney snapped his mouth shut.

'When is the strike going to happen?' I asked.

'Ask your boyfriend.'

'He's not my boyfriend.' My cheeks burnt with embarrassment, but I ignored it. 'Everyone thinks something different. I'm asking you.'

'I don't know.' He shifted his weight. I could practically smell his deceit.

'Not good enough,' Bas said. 'Try harder.'

'Do you want me to make something up?'

Bas slid his gun out of his harness. 'Maybe you need motivation. You don't need both legs, do you?'

Rodney stiffened. 'No—I—Soon! It's soon!'

'How soon? A week? A month?'

Rodney wiped his palms on his trousers. 'N-not a week—they won't be ready. There'll be a signal! They have a signal—it has something to do with the merchants' market—'

The merchants' market. Again.

'When is the market arriving?' Bas asked.

'I don't know.'

'Funny all the things you don't know.' He aimed the gun at Rodney's kneecap. 'You never know anything, do you? It must be so convenient, having other people to take care of you all the time.'

'Wait!' Rodney gasped. 'Look—you're angry, I get it. I'm sorry.'

'I don't care.' Bas's tone was utterly unyielding. 'I'm here for information only.'

'You said you were here to talk!'

'This is our talk.' Bas shoved the gun back into its holster. 'And now we're done. Let's go, Harley. He doesn't know anything we can't find out for ourselves.'

He turned back to the car and crossed the distance in two long strides. I hurried after him.

'There's another faction!' Rodney called. 'The mayor doesn't know, but the Godfreys have been making arrangements!'

'I don't care about your infighting.' Bas threw open his car door and climbed up. 'Let's go, Harley.'

He might not care, but I did.

'Who?' I asked.

'I've only heard whispers—'

'Harley!' Bas called.

'Who?' I repeated urgently.

'They're out-of-towners—'

The car engine roared. *Damnit, Bas.* I turned and jogged to the car, and scrambled up into the passenger seat. The second I shut the door, Bas pulled off, swinging the car in a wide circle.

'You couldn't have waited for him to finish?'

'He doesn't know anything. He's just grasping at straws.'

I leant back in my seat, groaning. 'You know, it wouldn't kill you to do things my way for a change. Without being so bloody forceful.'

'When we're interrogating your family, we can do things your way.'

'My family isn't involved in any potentially life-threatening plots.' We bounced through a hole in the track, and I grabbed the handle above the door. 'Can you slow down?'

'Sorry.' Bas slowed the car to a more manageable pace.

'S'alright. I don't think Rodney can chase us down on foot anyway.'

'You never know,' Bas muttered. 'He's a bloody snake.'

I laughed. Inappropriate though it may be, it was funny. When I looked at Bas, a tiny smile was playing at the edges of his lips.

I'd never seen him smile before.

'I can't believe you did that,' I said. 'Threatened him like that.'

Bas shrugged. 'He deserved it.'

'What did…' My courage deserted me. 'Never mind.'

'What happened between us?' Bas interpreted.

'You don't have to answer that if you don't want to,' I muttered.

Bas stared straight ahead, studying the road intently. Several minutes passed, we merged with the main road, and I started to relax. Okay, he wasn't going to answer. Okay. That was fine. It was his right to keep his past private. And hopefully, he wasn't going to get mad at me for prying, either.

'My mother worked as a maid in Jonathan Rochester's home.'

My stomach swooped as though I'd just missed a step going down the stairs. 'Bas…' I started uncertainly.

Bas kept speaking over me. 'He slept with her. Multiple times.'

I swallowed. I could see where this story was going. 'I'm sorry,' I whispered.

'She quit the job when she realised she was pregnant.' Bas's voice was steady and detached, as though he was telling someone else's story. Maybe that was the only way he could cope with it; I wished I'd never asked. This was too horrible to bear.

'How... how did he...'

'The same way you figured out Rodney and I were related: we look too similar.' Bas cleared his throat and added darkly, 'It was his way of hiding his indiscretion. He couldn't risk his wife finding out he had another child. So he sold us both.'

A fist seemed to have wrapped around my heart. My chest ached. 'Your mother?'

'Dead.' Bas shook his shoulders as though he could rid himself of the memories that way. 'Now you know.'

'I'm sorry.' I had no idea what else to say.

'Don't be. It happened. It can't be changed. It's history.'

'I shouldn't have asked.' I picked at a thread on my jeans; a hole was starting to form—another thing to mend.

'It's better this way,' Bas said.

Was it? Or was he just trying to deflect from how nosy I had been? I studied Bas's profile as he steered us through the outskirts of town. His expression was set: not angry, not sad. More... determined. Bas carried himself with absolute discipline at all times, and I was starting to understand why. Being in control was important to him.

I'd threatened that control time and again, and yet here we were. Apparently, Bas had a much greater capacity for forgiveness than I did.

'Thank you for telling me,' I said quietly.

'You told me about Briggs.'

'I didn't expect you to repay me for that,' I muttered.

'I'm not.'

We drove in silence until we reached a large crossroads which marked the edge of the town centre. Bas turned us south towards the river.

'Can I ask a question?' I asked. Hastily, I added, 'You don't have to answer if you don't want.'

Bas snorted. 'Ask.'

He was laughing! At me! I wasn't sure whether to be offended or surprised. I couldn't remember seeing Bas laugh ever before.

'Uh, the fight. Against Hannover...'

Bas scowled. 'I thought I could handle it,' he said sharply.

'What did he say to you?'

Bas glanced at me. 'You saw that?' he asked in a surprised tone.

'I was watching from the tech room.'

'You have an unimaginable capacity for sneaking around, don't you?'

'Sneaking around?' I repeated indignantly. 'There's a whole room full of people up there doing lights and music every night. I wasn't sneaking!'

'What room?' he asked.

'You really don't know? Do you know anything about the bunker?'

Bas shrugged. 'It's just a big underground building.'

'Theo told me it's left over from before the Crash. Governments used it as a safe place in case of a war.'

'It didn't do them much good,' Bas said.

'Well, there's no way of knowing now. They're long dead.' I fiddled with my loose thread again. 'What did Hannover say to you?'

"Roll over, boy." He said it without inflection or emotion. 'It was meant to remind me of that time.'

'I'm sorry.'

'Don't be.'

What could I say to that? I stared out the window at the passing buildings. 'My mum… never really spoke about the years she spent as a slave. I mean, I guess she told my dad, but she never told me.'

'How did she escape?' Bas asked.

'I'm not sure. She said she jumped off a truck and walked to the nearest town. But she also told me the story when I was little, so it might be… a sanitised version?'

How many times had I obsessed over every little thing Mum had said when I was growing up? After she'd died, her every word had taken on extra importance. I'd asked Dad thousands of questions.

Questions which he had refused to answer.

'It's plausible,' Bas said. 'The slavers move people in big, open trucks. If a rope came loose, it would be possible for someone small to slip between the bars.'

'She was small. Smaller than me.'

He glanced at me critically, as though assessing how small I was.

'Much smaller than me,' I said.

Bas smirked. He looked back at the road. 'You could get through the bars. If you were appropriately starved. Which is a side effect of slavery.'

I wrinkled my nose.

'She was always pretty sickly,' I said.

'What happened to her?'

'She died when I was nine. Lung disease.'

'I'm sorry.'

I shrugged. 'Don't be.'

Bas grimaced. 'Fair play. We'll park here and walk over.'

He turned us down a side street, and a moment later he pulled into the yard of Dougal & Phelp's Gas & Tyres. Kurt Dougal came waddling out, his beer belly wobbling. Bas jumped out of the car and handed him a folded ten-NP note.

'We'll be back in half an hour, tops. Can you clean up whilst I'm gone?'

'Sure.' Kurt squinted in my direction. 'Who's the lass?'

'No one important.' Bas shifted so he was blocking Kurt's view. 'Check the oil as well.'

'Tyres?'

'Yeah, you can check those.' Bas beckoned me imperiously. I climbed out of the car, following him as he stalked towards the road.

'Did you have to do that?'

'What have I done now?' Bas asked, exasperated.

'I don't like it when you do this thing.' I stuck my chin in the air and beckoned. 'That thing. Do I look like a dog?'

'Do you want Kurt Dougal telling the entire town you were in my car?'

'I can take care of myself.'

'Why make it hard on yourself?'

I glanced at him. He didn't seem angry; in fact, he looked genuinely curious. So I answered.

'Because it's all these little things. You acting like I can't tell him off myself. It makes him think I can't take care of myself. That's how I become a target.'

Bas frowned. 'You're a target anyway.'

'I'm trying to become less of one.'

'And not being a target and accepting help are mutually exclusive?' Bas asked.

That was a hard question. No… but yes. 'I guess it comes down to where you draw the line.'

Bas raised an eyebrow. 'And you draw the line…'

'It's easier to not receive help.' I shrugged weakly. 'I mean, if you help me today… are you going to help me tomorrow, or next week, or whenever Dougal decides I'm an easy target?'

'There's nothing stopping me.' He shrugged.

'It doesn't work like that,' I said. 'I can't just call you for help. And if I did, the next thing you know, I'd be calling you for help every time. And then I wouldn't be able to rely on my own skills anymore.'

'I think you might be underestimating yourself,' Bas said drily.

'Maybe, but it's better not to risk it.'

Bas frowned, but we'd reached Brenda's building, so I was spared his opinion. I pressed the doorbell for the basement flat.

Ding-ding.

We didn't have to wait long. A few moments later, heavy footsteps sounded from within.

'…right, alright, I'm coming!'

The door swung open, and a red-eyed, red-faced Manny stared down at us. For all I loved Brenda, I didn't like Manny at all. Many a time he'd come into the bar, groping at the girls, acting like a dog. I smelt the alcohol on his breath even before he opened his mouth.

'You're that chick from the bar,' he slurred. 'What're you doing here?'

I steeled my shoulders. 'I need to speak to Brenda. Is she in?'

'She never said she was expecting people.'

'She doesn't know I'm coming.' I met his gaze head-on. 'It's important.'

Manny's eyes flickered between Bas and me. 'Whatever.' He turned around and hollered, 'BREEEEENDAAA!'

I winced at the sudden volume. Manny jabbed a finger in my direction.

'Wait here.'

He slouched off, vanishing down the stairs. I glanced at Bas.

'Charming,' he said drily.

I shrugged. 'I've seen worse.'

'What, in a pigsty?'

I fought a smile. 'Tom wouldn't like you describing his bar that way.'

For a second so fleeting I might well have imagined it, Bas actually smiled. His eyes lit up, and his cheeks dimpled, and it was so breathtakingly beautiful that I felt like he belonged in a Pre-Crash portrait. Then it was gone, and he sobered again, nodding inside a moment before Brenda appeared up the stairs.

'What—oh, Harley.' She hurried over, catching my hand and tugging me over the stoop. 'I'm so sorry,' she whispered. 'He just got up. Was out all night again last night. You know how it is.'

'It's okay.' I squeezed Brenda's hand. 'I need a really big favour.'

'What?'

I glanced at Bas. Brenda followed my gaze, tensing. 'That is a really big favour, Harley.'

'We just want to see if we can look into the charity office. We'll be real quick.'

'I told you, it's been boarded over.'

'Just let us up. We'll be gone before you know it. You don't have to be involved.' I squeezed her hand reassuringly.

Brenda looked distinctly unhappy, but she nodded. 'Be quick. I'd invite you down, but Manny—'

'BRENDA!' Manny brayed from down below.

'I know. See you later.'

Brenda nodded and vanished below. I caught Bas's eyes and nodded to the stairs. 'Quietly.'

When he wanted to, Bas could move absolutely silently. He crept up the stairs with me, until we reached the second floor and paused at the windows. As Brenda had said, they'd boarded the windows up with black-painted plywood. Without skipping a beat, Bas took a knife from his belt, slotted it between the plyboard and the window, and used it to lever one of the sheets of plywood away. Once he could get his fingers under it, he pried it off and tossed it to the ground.

'That's one way of doing it,' I muttered, stepping closer to the window.

'Stay to the side,' Bas said. 'I don't want anyone to see you.'

'I'm pretty sure they know I'm involved with you.'

He shot me an odd look, and a sudden shiver jolted down my spine.

'That doesn't mean I'm going to offer you up on a silver platter,' Bas said. 'You don't know if they're still watching this office.'

'They're not going to be watching here.' But I stayed back. I didn't need to give Hannover another excuse to extort me.

Braced on either side of the window, we both peered down into the building opposite. In the late afternoon light, it was hard to see through the windows. But from what I could make out, there was no evidence of a slave pen. Only rooms full of filing cabinets.

'They've moved out,' I said.

'Looks like it.'

'That's my fault,' I muttered glumly.

'It could be mine,' Bas said. 'No doubt Sarah Stark told Hannover I paid her a visit. It doesn't matter anyway. What's done is done.'

I was pretty sure I was the one who had let the cat out of the bag when I'd tried to break into the office. I chewed my lip.

'Harley.' Bas's voice was low and strangely intimate, considering we were standing in a dirty stairwell. I glanced at him—his eyes were shadowed.

'Yeah?'

'It's not your fault. You did the best you could have.'

I swallowed, tears pricking at my eyes. How many days had I longed for those words? And yet, now that I heard them, I didn't believe them. 'You don't know that.'

'I do.' Bas's voice radiated confidence. 'That's what it means to trust each other.'

I felt sick to my stomach. If only I could take those words at face value—but Bas didn't know the full story yet. He didn't know that I had killed Tam. He didn't know that I was spying for Hardwick. And he didn't know that I owed Hannover my life.

I still had so many secrets—I didn't deserve his trust.

'Can you do one thing for me?' Bas asked.

'Sure,' I said meekly. 'Anything.'

His lips quirked up in a wry smile. 'Keep your ear to the ground. See if you can find out where they're keeping their captives now. If they're taking them from within the town, they need a base close by to hide them.'

I nodded. That made sense. They couldn't run people out to the Black Hands' compound individually or they'd attract too much attention. And they needed somewhere that Hannover and his lot could come and go freely at all hours of the day.

'I'll keep an eye out,' I promised.

'Don't do anything that would put you in danger.'

'Sure.' But that was a lie. I had no intention of keeping that promise. How could I, when my entire life hinged on Hannover's mercy?

NINETEEN

IN ALL THE EXCITEMENT, I had forgotten about Hardwick. It was only on Tuesday as I was walking to work that I remembered I had to see him that evening.

Crap!

What the *hell* was I going to tell him?

So much had happened—I didn't want to accidentally let something slip that I shouldn't. But I couldn't tell him nothing, especially when I needed him on my side so he didn't make me dance this coming weekend.

Speaking of which, I was going to need to get a message to Carlos.

Ugh.

That would be easier, though; I could go by Posy's flat tomorrow morning and ask her to pass along the message.

In between working that day, I spent my time organising my thoughts. I'd spoken to so many different people about so many different things, I was struggling to keep track of who knew what. And I couldn't afford to make a mistake.

Theo knew the whole story—except for the conversation between Brady and Jackson, which I'd forgotten to tell him. I'd have to update him when he got back.

Hopefully soon.

I pushed those thoughts away. If I started worrying about Theo, I'd spiral into despair. He was so reckless, I lived in fear of waking up one day and realising he was never coming home.

Bas knew about the slaves and the upcoming attack of the distillery—and I'd told him about Jackson, whatever he chose to believe about that—but not Hannover and Hardwick. And I wanted to keep it that way. Our tentative peace would explode if I layered another betrayal on it.

Besides, I wasn't ready to trust him with every aspect of my life.

He'd demonstrated more than once that he would turn on me at a moment's notice.

That left Hardwick and Briggs. I had no idea how Briggs had found out about Tam, or what, exactly, he knew. He'd never outright said, and in the cold light of day I really hoped that meant he wasn't sure.

The thought made my stomach twist in on itself. With all of the secrets I was balancing, I must have gotten careless. I just didn't know *when*.

Hardwick had no idea I had made a deal with Hannover, and I didn't want him to know I was in contact with Bas or Theo, either. Nor could I let slip that I'd overheard the conversation in the brothel.

Another day, another balancing act.

After work, I made my way over to the Hawke and Tern. Hardwick wasn't there yet when I entered; the place was almost empty except for the bartender, who was methodically wiping down glasses.

'You again,' he said.

'Hello.' I approached the bar. 'Turner, right?'

'That's me.' He looked up, his shaven head catching the dim overhead light. 'You're Anna, right?'

'Uh—' Just in time, I caught myself. I'd almost forgotten I had told him that was my name. 'Yeah, that's right.'

He raised an eyebrow, a smile playing on his lips. 'Right. What can I get you?'

'Whiskey, please.'

He served me up a glass, sliding it across the warped countertop. 'You're not the sort I'd have thought would get mixed up with Hardwick.'

'Didn't know Hardwick had a type.' I avoided his gaze, picking my glass up and swirling it. *Play it cool, play it cool.*

Bartenders were perfect spies. Get them on your side, and you could learn all sorts of things.

'Not a type, per se.' Turner went back to his cleaning.

'Do you work with him?' I asked, leaning casually against the bar.

Turner raised an eyebrow. 'I'm just a bartender.'

Doubtful.

'Uh-huh? I didn't know bars usually let customers in the back rooms.' I twirled a strand of hair around my finger, smiling.

Turner laughed. 'True. I suppose you could say he's an old friend.

We go… quite far back.'

What was that supposed to mean? I sipped my whiskey to buy myself time to come up with a response.

'Must be nice to know someone will have your back,' I said neutrally.

Turner paused in his wiping. 'Actually, now that you mention it…' He hummed thoughtfully. 'I hope you have friends like that. It seems a young lady like you would need them.'

Okay, this was getting weird. 'I…' I thought of Theo. 'I think I'm covered, thanks.'

Turner drummed his fingers on the bar. 'You know, I've helped a few people out of tight spots. And I know Evander. He wants the best, but he does tend to get people in trouble. You ever need help, just let me know.'

What the hell?

'Wants the best' was not how I would have described Evander Hardwick. More like… snaky, slimy, slippery. Treacherous. A dickhead. Who had landed me in trouble multiple times. He certainly didn't want the best for me—or my friends.

Was Turner for real?

If he was friends with Hardwick, why offer to help me?

He was watching me as though he expected a response.

'Uh… thanks,' I muttered and hid my face behind my glass.

Behind me, the door swung open, letting in a blast of cold air that displaced the smoky warmth of the pub. With it came the one person I really didn't want to see. Hardwick strode up to the bar, shedding a pair of black leather gloves as he went.

'Good, you're here.' He flicked his hand towards Turner. 'The usual.'

'Mind your manners,' Turner said in a surprisingly terse tone. For friends, they sure didn't act too friendly.

Turner dispensed two fingers of whiskey into a glass and slammed it on the bar. He looked unhappy, his brow wrinkled and his shoulders tense—was it because of Hardwick's attitude? Or something deeper.

Hardwick picked the glass up and turned to me. 'Let's go.'

Scowling, I turned to follow him. As I did, Turner met my eye and gave me a significant look.

I strode after Hardwick without acknowledging him. Whatever the drama those two had going on, I wasn't getting in between them.

We headed into the back, and Hardwick led me once again to the poky little office.

'How come you're allowed in the back rooms?' I asked as I sat.

'That's not for you to know,' Hardwick said haughtily. 'Let's get started.'

'I can't dance for a few weeks,' I said immediately. I'd decided on the way over to get it out there as soon as possible. 'I'm injured.'

'That's not my problem.' Hardwick raised his eyebrows.

'Well, it's going to be,' I said forcefully. I was not letting Hardwick weasel out of this one. 'Briggs cut me up, and he's found something out about Tam. *I* didn't tell him, so…'

'I trust my men,' Hardwick snapped.

'Someone has to have given the game away,' I pointed out. 'And if he takes his suspicions to Sayle, you won't have a spy anymore.'

'You're not much of a spy.'

'Really?' I crossed my arms. 'I got into Reverie no problem. Could you have done that?'

Hardwick pressed his lips together.

I leant forwards. 'Your friend out there—Turner?—he was quite happy to tell me I could come to him if you *got me in trouble.*'

Hardwick's expression contorted. 'Fine. I'll take care of Duncan Briggs. You mind *yourself.*'

'I will.' I bit the inside of my cheek to conceal my triumph. *Gotcha!*

'If you can't dance, you need to find an alternative—'

'No sex. It'll pop my stitches—'

'How you get the job done is up to you,' Hardwick said flatly. 'So long as you deliver. I need to know what the Iron Fists are doing about the merchants. They've stopped sending their teams out to patrol.'

Had they? I hadn't noticed. Though now that I thought about it, I had seen fewer gang members in the bar lately.

'They're getting information from somewhere,' Hardwick continued, 'but they're not asking questions.'

Interesting. What was more interesting, however, was the poorly concealed desperation in his eyes. The way he clenched his glass a little too tightly. The way he rolled his shoulders as though he'd been working long hours and was feeling stiff.

He was short on answers.

And I had them—at least a few of them.

I could use this.

'I know they sent someone to investigate what happened to the merchants,' I said lightly.

Hardwick leant in. 'Who?'

'Theo. My friend.'

His eyes narrowed. 'One person?'

'Theo's worth ten people!' I snapped. I bit my lip. *Don't reveal too much.* 'What if the same person who tipped off Briggs is passing info to the Iron Fists?'

Which, if I thought about it, was an alarming possibility. Who else, apart from Hardwick and Percival, knew that I was spying for the Aces? What if they told Briggs? What if they told someone else, who was more motivated by loyalty and less by his dick?

I swallowed, trying to surreptitiously wipe my palms down on my jeans.

'I'll mind my team, you play your role,' Hardwick said curtly. 'What else is there?'

What else, indeed? I took a sip of my whiskey as I turned over all of the information I was sitting on. What to tell him?

'Rodney Rochester mentioned the mayor working with the military.' That didn't seem harmful, or at least, not to my friends.

Hardwick frowned. 'Where did he hear that?'

'He didn't say—but he told Bas. So the Iron Fists know too.'

I held my breath, hoping he wouldn't press the topic. I didn't want to reveal anything else. No matter how things had gone down, several of the Iron Fists were still my friends. I didn't want to be the cause of anything bad happening to them.

No, better to drip-feed Hardwick the information. If he wanted anything else, he'd have to ask. I was telling him enough to save my skin and not a drop more.

Hardwick tapped his index finger against his knee. 'Are the Rochester brothers in contact, then?'

I shrugged. 'I don't know.'

'It's your job to know.'

'I didn't realise you wanted to know menial details about relationships.' I rolled my eyes. 'I'll find out for next time.'

'See that you do.'

His tone annoyed me. Hardwick annoyed me. He seemed to view me like a puppet he could manipulate.

Well, he'd see the error of his ways.

Narrowing my eyes, I asked, 'When is the strike anyway?'

Hardwick picked his glass up and took a smooth sip. 'You don't need to concern yourself with that.'

I stared at him. He tilted his head, his expression neutral. I got nothing from him, but something about him felt deceitful.

I trusted my gut.

'You don't know, do you?'

'We're done here.' Hardwick stood abruptly.

'You don't!' I crowed.

He glowered at me, lifting his chin. 'I expect you to have more to report next time. If you find out anything about the Iron Fists' movements before next Tuesday, contact me.'

No way that was happening.

'Sure.' I stood as well, downing the last of my drink. 'So long as you deal with Briggs.' I turned to the door. 'See you around.'

I sashayed out, making sure to put an extra swing in my stride. Maybe it was a bad idea to piss off Hardwick… but then again, I hadn't tipped Briggs off. So he needed to deal with it. As long as I was passing him information, he bloody well better ensure my safety.

I headed home to discover that we had no electricity.

Again.

Coming home to a dark flat was getting pretty old.

Would there be a better electricity supply in the cities? If I left? When I left?

I was midway through eating when the door slid slowly open, the hinges creaking slightly. Savannah squeezed through the gap and tiptoed into the room. I swallowed. Apart from when she'd stitched me up, I had hardly seen my sister recently. There hadn't been a chance to talk about what she'd said when she was drunk.

'Maybe we should get separate places.'

Savannah and I had stuck together since Dad died. We couldn't give up on that now.

Could we?

'You're back late.'

She gasped, twisting to face me and almost falling over. 'Harley!

What are you — Why are you —'

'Why am I?' I prompted sardonically. *Why am I here? Apart from, you know, it's my flat?*

'I thought you'd be in bed! It's so late!'

'Yeah, so it is.' I swirled my fork through the food on my plate. 'Pretty late for you to be running around too.'

'Don't be a hypocrite.' Savannah kicked her boots off and dropped her coat on the sofa. 'You stay out just as late as I do.'

'For work!' I took a deep breath, trying to tamp down on my annoyance. There was no point in getting into an argument with my sister in the middle of the night. 'Look — I'm just worried.'

'Well, don't be! I can take care of myself.' Savannah shoved her messy hair out of her eyes. 'And I was out for work too. I went out with my colleagues to celebrate the fact that the NCC finally opened a new storage facility for us.'

'Did they?' I perked up — could this have anything to do with them moving the slaves?

'Of course.' Savannah swung into the kitchen, pulled a bottle of beer out of the fridge, and cracked it open on the counter. 'They've been promising it for a while. The gangs keep robbing us — it's sickening.'

She took a sip of her beer and made a face. 'Ugh, this is warm.'

'Electricity's off.'

'Evidently.' She rolled her eyes. 'I didn't think you were sitting in the dark for fun.'

'Whatever.' I turned back to my food. 'Hey, have you noticed anything funny going on with the NCC lately?'

'Funny? I don't work with them, Harley. I just send them paperwork,' she said exasperatedly.

'I'm just asking!'

'You see funny things everywhere.' Savannah rounded the table, plopping down opposite me. 'They're a charity. What would be funny?'

'If they were in cahoots with the Black Hands, who were trading slaves out of their office.'

Savannah gaped at me. 'Are you insane? That would never happen.'

'It did, actually. I saw them. They're transferring people in their armoured trucks.'

'You've cracked.' Savannah shook her head. 'The NCC helps people. The clinic wouldn't exist without them.'

'I'm not the only person who knows.' I leant back in my chair and crossed my arms. 'And I'm not cracked, thanks.'

'They're a *charity*.'

'So? Charities can't do bad things?'

'Of course not!' Savannah stood abruptly. 'I can't believe you'd even say that!'

I stared at her, regretting saying anything. So much for warning her.

'Just be careful, alright? I don't want anything to happen to you.'

Savannah shot me a glare. 'Nothing's going to happen to me, because you're making up stories again—just like you always do. This is real life, not some childish fantasy, alright? We're not wasteland pirates trying to defeat slavers.'

I glared at her. 'It's not a fantasy. You know, I'd expect you of all people to listen to me, but I guess I have too much faith in my own sister.'

'Clearly you did.' Savannah spun on her heel and stomped towards the bedroom. 'I'm going to bed. You can hang out with your fantasies alone.'

She slammed the door behind her.

Another day, same old drama. I drifted around the bar on Wednesday, aimlessly touching things up on the off chance that today was the day the merchants finally arrived. In between taking orders, I worried about Theo.

Where was he now?

What was he doing?

In the dead hours of the afternoon, I slid behind the bar and poured myself a glass of water.

'Can I talk to you?' Laura asked quietly.

'Sure.' I let my eyes rove over the bar; it was mostly empty. 'Let me just check on the tables and then we can talk in the back?'

Laura nodded.

Only two tables were occupied, and neither of them needed anything. I slipped through the back door and found Laura leaning against the door to the stock room. Her red hair was piled on top of her head in a bun, and she was wearing a men's shirt tied off around her waist.

'Hey. What's up?'

Laura smiled—an odd, sad little smile. 'Not much. And you?'

'Uh, yeah.' I brushed back a strand of hair that had stuck to my face. 'Same old, same old, right?'

If you ignored the fact that my life had gone to hell in a handbasket.

'Your friend hasn't been by recently. Theo, right?' Laura tilted her head.

'He's out of town. Should be back soon.' I glanced back at the door. We couldn't linger out here too long. 'Was there… something you needed?'

'Uh…' Laura scuffed her foot against the ground. 'Okay. I'll just spit it out. Anna mentioned that your father was… killed… by one of the gangs.'

Oof. I felt like I'd been punched in the gut. Even after so many years, mentions of my father's death never failed to catch me off guard.

'Uh.' I swallowed. 'Why… Look, no offence, but I'm not really that happy with you guys gossiping about that.'

Her eyes widened. 'God, no, I didn't mean it like that!'

'Right.' I crossed my arms. 'Then I'm not sure how it's any of your business.'

'Sorry,' Laura said. 'It's just… it made me think about my husband. He was also killed by the gangs. And then… well, I wasn't going to say anything, but then I couldn't help but see the similarities…'

I frowned. 'I don't think there are as many similarities as you think—my father was killed here, not in Crater's Edge, by the gangs here.'

'I know, but you know what it's like.' Laura stared at her feet. 'I wanted to look into my husband's death, but it was all covered up, and, well…'

Well what? She seemed to be getting at something. Maybe I was just tired, but my brain didn't want to make the connection.

'So?' I asked bluntly.

Laura flinched. 'I was wondering if you wanted to look into it together, maybe.'

I ground my teeth together. Was this a joke?

'I'm not sure that's a good idea,' I said flatly. 'I don't want to rile up the gangs. And I doubt there's a connection between my father's death and your husband's. Besides, even if I wanted to help you, my father died eight years ago. I doubt there's anything left to find.'

'Right.' Laura turned away. 'Sorry to bring it up then.'

I swallowed. 'I'm sorry.'

'It's fine. I thought we might be able to help each other, but clearly not.'

I was the wrong person to ask for help. 'Look, if you want my advice, don't rock the boat. Especially right now. There's too much going on, and the men here are way too trigger-happy.'

Laura's expression contorted. A light appeared in her eyes that raised the hairs on my arms. Anger? No, not quite.

'I didn't realise you were such a coward.'

I gaped at her. *What the fuck?* Frustration surged through my blood. Who the hell was she calling a coward?

'Coward? If that's what you call looking out for myself and my sister, then sure. I'll be a coward.'

I turned and marched back through the swing door. Anna looked up in surprise.

'You alright?'

'Yeah,' I said sharply. I sucked in a deep breath and said in a calmer tone, 'Look, please don't tell people about my dad. I... It's...'

'I'm so sorry,' Anna said, her face a picture of innocence. 'I didn't mean to upset you.'

'It's fine! I'm not upset.' I clenched and unclenched my fists. My palms felt sweaty, and my heart was beating too fast. 'I just...'

'Okay, okay.' Anna raised her hands. 'Do you want to go on break?'

'No.' I grabbed my tray. 'I'm going to... do my job.'

I pasted a smile onto my face and escaped around the bar. Anna's gaze seared into the back of my neck, but I refused to turn around. It was just human decency, right? They shouldn't have been talking about it, and Laura shouldn't have surprised me with it. I wasn't overreacting.

This was normal.

I was *normal.*

I was *not* a coward. She had no right to call me that.

Shakily, I wiped down one table and refilled the water at the next. I brought an order to Anna—Laura was watching me from behind the bar with a hurt look on her face, so I left them to it and went back to wiping down tables.

I was bent over table six, working on a stubborn stain, when heavy boots thudded through the lobby. I turned to the door, just as Theo appeared in the doorway. He caught my eye and rushed over to me.

'Theo!' I dropped my cloth on the table and threw my arms around him, squeezing him as hard as I could—and covering my wince. I'd forgotten about my stitches again. 'You're back!'

'You'd think I'd been gone months.'

'Shut up.' I rapped my knuckles against the back of his head. 'I hate when you leave. I hate that you had to leave again—'

'I know, I know. I'm only teasing.' He raked his fingers through my hair, tugging my head back gently so he could kiss my forehead. 'I missed you too.'

'Did you find anything out?' I glanced around warily and lowered my voice. 'Is the merchants' market—'

'On their way,' he said. 'I escorted them to the edge of town, then drove ahead. You can warn Tom if you'd like.'

I looked at the bar and jerked my head to tell Anna to come over. As she wove between the tables, I turned back to Theo.

'That's great news!'

'It is.' His voice was low, his eyes dark. 'Listen—I need to speak to you in private, urgently, but I don't know exactly when we'll have a chance. Things are crazy on our side. We might have to sneak away, or—'

'Just tell me when,' I interrupted. 'I'll make it happen.'

Theo nodded. 'I'll be in touch. Soon.' He pulled away, his hands lingering on my arms. 'Love you, Harley baby.'

'Love you too.'

Theo headed for the door. I turned to Anna, who approached with wide eyes. 'What's happening?'

'Theo said the merchants are here. He left them just outside of town.'

'That's fantastic!'

I nodded. 'We should warn Tom—he'll want to make preparations.'

'I'll go,' Anna said. 'Can you watch the bar?'

'Sure.'

'And get Laura—she just went on break.'

'Okay. Go!'

I sent Benny to look for Laura, then did a quick stock-take to make sure we had everything we'd need for a crowd on hand. The merchants arrived before Anna got back—I heard the first vehicles pulling up on the square and immediately ran to the window to see the trucks parking up.

'Is it true?' I turned to see Laura hurrying in from the back room. 'The merchants are here? Benny said—'

'It's true—look!' I waved her over. 'They just started arriving.'

'That's great news!' We shared looks fuelled by pure relief. With the market here, we'd be able to stock up for winter and trade our surplus for the supplies that would keep us fed and warm during the hardest months.

The tips would enable me to pay our growing heat and electricity bills over the winter.

This changed everything.

Within the hour, we were swamped. The merchants were an assortment of craftspeople, cattle farmers, and hardened traders who made a living reaching remote settlements in the wastes. They wandered in and out, between the hotel where they were staying and the hall on the north bank of the river, where the market would be held. Their security force was enormous, a combination of their men and the mayor's additional security teams who'd been sent to escort them. The bar rapidly filled up with people wanting a hot meal and a hard drink, along with curious townsfolk who had come to see if the rumours were true.

Gossip was flying between locals and the newcomers.

'They blockaded the road,' one young man from the security team explained to Anna as he lounged at the bar. He had buzzcut hair and a very rough-and-ready look, though, like the rest of his team, he'd thrown his jacket off and put his boots up when he came in. 'Trapped us in—we couldn't go back or forward.'

'Were they trying to steal your wares?' Anna asked, aghast.

'Nope,' another man chimed in. 'Didn't do a thing. Just kept us there.'

'How weird!' Anna said.

It wasn't, though. In fact, it tallied exactly with what I'd overheard in Reverie a few days ago. The Black Hands had blocked the merchants from entering the town.

The pieces were starting to fit together. The mayor had brought the Black Hands on board for that. The question was—why? What had he achieved by keeping them out of town? And what would happen now? It seemed like we were hurtling towards something, but I wasn't sure of the next steps.

Two or three weeks, Brady had said.

It didn't feel like we had that long.

By the end of the day, I was exhausted. I'd covered at least four times my usual workload and spent my break running extra stock in because everyone was drinking so much. I passed the baton to Kayla and Dana with no small sense of relief.

Still, I'd hoped Theo would find me on the way home—because we urgently needed to speak—but he didn't. Instead, I came home to an empty flat and crawled straight into bed, too exhausted to even worry about Savannah.

As she had said, she was a big girl. She could live her own life.

Even if she was being a stupid idiot about it.

The next morning, I woke up early and decided to head down to the north bank where the large steel-roofed market hall was located. It was a huge square structure, draughty in winter and stuffy in summer. The market would officially be opening at midday—or at least, that was what I'd heard from the merchants yesterday—but they'd probably be setting up already.

As it turned out, I wasn't the only person who'd had that idea. There was a healthy crowd of people milling about. One of the doors was already open, and several of the stalls seemed to be selling already. I headed in, studying the wares that had already been set up: all different kinds of cheese, fruit and vegetables, dried meats, even fish. We never got fish this far north; there were no lakes, and the river was too polluted. Not that Savannah and I would have been able to afford it, even if it was available.

I was browsing a table full of scarves and hats when a playful voice said, 'I'd go with the darker blue.'

I jumped, my heart lurching into my throat. Turning, I saw Theo.

'Theo! You surprised me! What are you doing here?'

'I told you I'd find you.'

'Yeah, but now?' I glanced up at the market clock, hanging beneath the high ceiling above the entrance door. 'I have to be at work in half an hour.'

'Time enough.' Theo fished his wallet out of his pocket. 'I'll buy us a snack and we can talk in the car.'

Five minutes later, he'd purchased a paper bag full of apples. I bit into one as he pulled his car out of the parking spot on the side of the road, the fresh, tart flavour exploding over my tongue.

'Fuck, that's good.'

'I know. Our fruit season is so short. I really miss that when I'm here.' Theo groped at the bag, his eyes still on the road. I passed him an apple. 'Thanks.'

'So.'

'Yeah.' He took a bite of his apple, chewed, and swallowed. 'I have a plan, but it's a bit rough around the edges.'

'I think the strike is going to be soon—something to do with the merchants' market—'

'I know,' Theo said. 'There's no other reason to blockade the merchants. Everyone knows the trade is good for the town. Sayle knows it too—he has us out in force to make sure nothing goes wrong during the market.'

My stomach squirmed. I remembered, suddenly, Jackson's comment about splitting the forces. 'If he spreads you guys too thin…'

'I'll worry about that,' Theo said. 'Let's figure you out. The Black Hands have a lot of their forces in town at the moment too. We can't help that.'

'Do you think Hannover will be watching me?' I asked nervously. I licked a trickle of juice off my fingers.

'I think we're going to watch Hannover,' Theo said mysteriously. 'Very closely.'

'Would he interfere?' I frowned. 'He said he wanted me to make sure Percival's death couldn't be pinned on the Black Hands.'

'It won't be.'

'Oh.' I glanced at Theo, but he was focused on the road. 'So, what's the plan?'

'We're going to kill Hannover.'

TWENTY

MY JAW DROPPED. He had *not* just said what I thought he'd said.

'We're going to *what?*'

'I thought about it a lot,' Theo said. 'Percival almost never goes anywhere without security. And even if he did, he won't now. He's afraid of pre-emptive strikes from the Iron Fists. Getting at him—we'd need a trained sniper, and even then it's touch and go. Unless you want to get a job at the casino and work your way up.'

'There isn't time,' I protested. The thought of being a triple agent made my head swim.

'Exactly,' Theo said. He slowed us down, turned onto a quiet side street, and parked on the side of the road. 'But Hannover is notoriously reckless. He runs around on his own, makes enemies left and right, and provokes people whenever he can. The tricky part is knowing where he'll be—he's too unpredictable.'

My mind raced through all the possibilities. Why had I never thought of that? If Hannover was dead, he couldn't kill me or hurt Savannah. It would be a huge problem solved.

'I guess we could follow him,' I said.

'Neither of us has the time,' Theo said. 'We'd need to get someone else to help out. But there might be another solution.'

My mind jumped—as it seemed to be doing lately—to Bas. Bas would help. Bas hated Hannover.

'There's an old technology that I've seen before,' Theo said. 'I encountered it in Boughton a few years back. One of the gangs put some sort of device on slaver vehicles which showed them its location at all times, followed them back to their HQ, and blew it sky high. Sent a great message. It's kept the slavers out of Boughton for years.'

'We could use that,' I muttered.

'Exactly. I was hoping to pick one up, but I never made it to Boughton. So we need to see if we can scrounge up anything here. I know Sayle is sitting on a hoard of old tech they pulled from the bunker, so—'

'Kayla,' I said suddenly.

'Pardon?'

'Kayla—my colleague! Her dad runs a shop that fixes up old tech. We can ask her. She said I could speak to her dad if I ever needed anything.'

Theo glanced at me, a grin breaking out on his face. 'Harley, that's genius.'

'I have my moments.' I swatted his arm. 'We probably have time to get over there now.'

'Do you know where it is?'

'Uhhh, the far end of Busker Street, I think.'

Theo tossed his apple core in a bag in the back, then gunned the engine. 'To Busker Street, then.'

He set a hair-raising pace through the streets, but for once I didn't mind. My brain was racing ahead, forming plans, analysing them, discarding them.

'Hannover's going to be really hard to kill,' I said. 'He's so clever.'

'He's arrogant, though. I doubt he even really thinks you'll kill Percival. He's probably just planning on using your attempt as a distraction. Or he thinks you'll jump town and not be his problem anymore.'

'Tempting,' I muttered.

'We'll get to that,' Theo said. 'That's the next step. As soon as this is done, we're leaving. I have money—'

'Me too.'

'Good.' He turned sharply into a side street. 'And as for your sister, she either comes along or she stays without you.'

'No!'

'Yes,' Theo said darkly. 'You can't keep doing this, Harley. She's holding you back. And she's not your child. If she wants to fuck up her life, let her.'

'I can't just leave my sister!' I cried shrilly.

Theo hit the brakes, and we hurtled around a corner. 'For fuck's sake, Harley!'

'You'd understand if you had siblings—'

'No, I wouldn't.'

'What if it was me?' I demanded.

Theo scowled. 'That's different.'

'It's not. I wouldn't leave you behind.'

Theo groaned. 'Damnit, Har. Fine. Fine! You get one chance to explain everything and convince her. But if she refuses, I'm taking you and leaving her. I'll have to. The backlash if we succeed is going to be huge.'

I dug my nails into my knees. 'She's my sister.'

'And Moriarty will kill you and stick your head on a pike as a reminder of what happens to his enemies.' Theo glanced at me. 'I'd die for *you*, but I definitely won't for your sister.'

Theo had never liked Savannah, not since the first day they'd met.

'She's not that bad a person, you know,' I muttered.

'She's bad for you,' Theo said. 'You're worth so much more, but you've given everything up for *her*. I'm going to fix that, even if I have to kidnap you to do it.'

What to say to that? I had no answers. I bit my tongue, gripping my knees as Theo squealed to a halt on Busker Street.

'That the place?' He nodded to a storefront. Metal bars crisscrossed the windows, and a weathered old sign proclaimed: *NO GUNS – NO GANGS.*

'Yep,' I said.

'Damn.' Theo eyed it. 'Knew there was a reason I'd never been here.'

'Do you think he enforces it?' I asked warily. I'd never had to worry about places with a no-guns rule before.

'If he has the sign, he enforces it.' Theo sighed. 'Better not piss him off if we want his help.'

'I guess.' Nervously, I trailed Theo to the front door. A bell dinged as we entered. Inside was a maze of tables and shelves, all filled to the brim with strange devices. Big black boxes with cables protruding, thin, shiny metal rectangles covered in buttons with letters, car parts, piles of cables, and boxes of scrap.

'Got a weapons check?' Theo called out.

'Coming!'

Kayla appeared from the back. She looked different from what I was used to in the bar. Instead of tight-fitting clothes, she wore a pair of sturdy overalls, and her braids were piled on top of her head. 'Harley?' she asked in surprise.

'Hi,' I said. 'How are you?'

'Good.' Kayla flicked her eyes to Theo. 'I'll let you in because it's you, but I don't want any trouble, yeah?'

Theo unbuckled his harness and worked it out from under his jacket. 'Don't worry, I come in peace.'

'Ta.' Kayla hung the harness in a battered metal locker. I passed her mine, as well, and both Theo and Kayla eyed me in surprise.

'Since when do you have a gun?' Theo demanded.

'It's on loan.'

'From…'

'Bas.'

'Fucking hell.' Theo shook his head. 'What'd you trade for that?'

'Nothing,' I said flatly.

'I leave town for a few days and you're making nice with that arsehole.' Theo groaned. 'I think I preferred it when you had a crush on Ellery.'

'Shut up!' I could feel my cheeks heating up. 'I never—'

'Oh, you so did.' Theo caught Kayla's eye and smirked at her. 'Didn't she?'

'I'm not getting involved in this,' Kayla said airily.

'You'd better not.' I rubbed my cheeks. 'Come on. We need to hurry or I'll be late for work.'

'Alright, alright.' Theo nodded to Kayla. 'Your father in?'

'He's in his workshop.' She strode back to the counter and poked her head through a door behind it. 'Daddy!'

'Comin'!'

A tall black man with a bald head and a neat, greying beard stepped out, dusting his hands off on his overalls. 'Hullo,' he said, his gaze flicking between Theo and me. 'What can I help you with?'

Theo glanced at me. I smiled nervously. 'Hi… Kayla said you buy and sell old tech.'

'That's right.' He gestured expansively around the shop, which was filled to the brim with its dusty old contraptions. I didn't know what any of them did. 'Computers, radios, TVs, lights—you name it, we got it.'

'What if I wanted to track someone?'

His eyebrows crept up his forehead. 'Track someone? That's trickier.'

'But it can be done, right?' Theo pressed. 'I heard about a guy in Boughton—'

'Boughton has more of a market for old tech. Stuff travels up and down the gauntlet from the junkyards around the cities,' Kayla's father said. 'Up here, we only have what we can scrounge for.'

'So you can't do it?' I asked, disappointment welling in my chest. There went that idea.

'I didn't say I can't do it,' he said. 'Just that it's difficult.'

'So you can?' I asked hopefully.

'I can. But it'll cost ya.'

'Money's no object,' Theo said.

'That so?' He studied Theo for several long seconds before jerking his head towards the door. 'You'd better come in back then.'

The back was even more haphazard than the front. We picked our way between piles of junk to an open space around a sturdy workbench. Kayla's father wiped his hands down again, then leant against the table. 'I'm Declan. Names?'

'I'm Theo and this is Harley,' Theo said.

'You're one of Kayla's colleagues.' Declan nodded to me.

'That's right.'

'And you—no wait, I can guess from the outfit.' He eyed Theo. 'I got good reasons to not deal with the gangs. But then, my daughter let you in, and I trust her judge of character.'

'I won't make any trouble,' Theo said. 'This is personal business.'

Declan nodded, though he was still frowning. 'Fine. We'll leave it at that. The thing you want is a geo-tracker. I assume neither of you have any experience with old tech.'

'I can repair radios,' Theo said. 'And I keep my car running.'

'A car's a very different beastie to what you're looking for,' Declan said. 'We're on a whole different level of complexity. Books have been written about this stuff.'

'I don't have time for books,' Theo said.

'Oh, I know. No one has time for books anymore these days.' Declan pushed off the table and strode over to a battered old dresser that would have looked more at home in an old-world lady's bedroom. He opened the top drawer and rifled through it, before coming back over and setting a small plastic disk on the table. It looked remarkably like the listening device I'd used in Reverie.

'That's it?' I asked incredulously.

Declan snorted. 'Girlie, this is more complicated than anything else you'll ever encounter in your life. This little thing can pick up a signal from a satellite in space and send it to a receiver, so you'll know where it is at all times.'

Whoosh. I couldn't even pretend to understand a word he'd said.

Declan could tell. He smirked. 'I won't bore you with the details.' He tapped the little disk. 'This is the beacon. It goes on the person or vehicle you want to track. You switch it on, and it will send out a signal to this.' He fetched another piece of tech, this one a boxy thing about the size of my palm. 'This will show where the tracker is on the map.'

'Sounds simple enough,' Theo said.

'Simple, no. Useable, yes.' Declan slid the box-thing to Theo. 'Let's talk price.'

We returned to the car with our pockets significantly lighter. Declan was a fierce negotiator—though at least he'd agreed that we'd get some of the money back if we returned the receiver.

Even so, it didn't sit well to pay him more than what I earned in a month.

'You should have let me chip in,' I grouched.

'Harley, leave it.' Theo started the car up, before pausing to readjust his gun harness. 'I have the money. We need this.'

'I know, but—'

'No buts. We're a team. You have to start trusting me.'

'That doesn't mean you have to pay for me!'

Theo steered the car onto the road. 'Am I dropping you at work?'

'Yes,' I muttered, seething inwardly.

We looped around and started back toward the square.

'I think we can run this thing for a few days,' Theo said. 'Get a read on Hannover's movements, then set up an ambush.'

'Okay. How are we going to get it on his car, though?'

Theo chewed his lip. 'Let me take care of that.'

'What? No!'

'Yes.' Theo's voice was unyielding. 'You're going to have to trust me on this one.'

'But—'

'I can do it without him noticing, Har. I'm good at stuff like that.'

'Fine,' I muttered. It didn't sit well with me at all, but Theo obviously wasn't going to budge—and he was the one holding onto the geo-tracker thingy. So I was shit out of luck. 'Will you do it today?'

'I'll go right now, but then I have to get back to the compound. I've been assigned to security during the merchants' market.'

'Sayle's expecting trouble,' I said. 'Do you think they'll make the strike on the distillery whilst the merchants are here—oh!'

'What?' Theo asked sharply.

'I just remembered. I spoke to Rodney Rochester. He said that the mayor is working with the military. They have men on standby to take over the town when the strike goes down.'

'Damn,' Theo muttered. He glanced behind us, then frowned and sped up the car. 'Okay, I need to drop you and get that news back to Sayle.'

'Bas knows.'

'Has he passed the message on?'

'How would I know?'

Theo glanced at me. I scowled.

'Okay,' he said. 'I need to anyway. Anything else you found out whilst I was gone?'

Was there? I had to think for a moment; I was struggling to keep up with who knew what.

'Um, there might be another faction, something to do with the Godfreys. Rochester didn't know much about it, though. And Jackson is conspiring with a guy named Brady who works for the mayor, I think.'

'Shit,' Theo said. 'Okay, that's bad. I'll look into it.'

He hung a quick left and pulled up in a side street. The square was at the far end, thrumming with people. 'Can I leave you here?'

'Sure.' I grabbed the door handle. 'Brady told Jackson to split the troops. And I warned Bas, but he didn't believe me.'

Theo groaned. 'Bas is a dick. If I see him, I'm going to put my fist through his face.'

'Please don't. He'll be pissed.'

Theo laughed. 'Let me worry about that. Do me a favour?'

'Sure,' I said.

'Keep that gun where you can reach it. I don't approve of him giving it to you, but I have a feeling you're going to need it.'

'I will.' I bit my lip.

Theo smiled weakly. 'Okay, I'll see you tonight—at the party, alright?'

'Right. I'll find you.' I leant over the centre console to hug him. 'Stay safe.'

'You too, Harley baby.' I pulled away and opened the door. Theo was still watching me. 'And Harley?'

'Yeah?'

'Just trust me. We're gonna work everything out.'

'Alright,' I replied.

TWENTY-ONE

THE HOTEL BAR WAS closed that evening. Instead, we'd set up a booth on the square in front of the hotel, where the celebration was being held. It was easier than making all the guests traipse through the lobby to get to us. Several other bars and pubs had sent their staffs over to run booths as well, and there were games, food stalls, and other attractions.

We so rarely had an excuse for a party; everyone was making the most of it.

There were several fire drums scattered around the square, and people were gathered around them roasting skewers and warming their hands. A ragtag group of travelling musicians who'd arrived with the merchants were playing a slow Pre-Crash song on a stage near the fountain.

By ten PM, the party was still going strong. I'd been on shift all day, and my feet were killing me. When the evening shift arrived, I was ready to drop. Still, I managed to summon a healthy dose of surprise when Brenda arrived with Dana and Kayla.

'Brenda! What are you doing here?'

'Tom asked me to cover a shift or two, just whilst the market is on. Don't want you lot run ragged.'

'It's so good to see you.' Anna hugged her.

'And you, both of you.' She shot me a smile over Anna's shoulder. 'I'm relieving you, right? Off you go—you youngins should be enjoying the party.'

I laughed. 'I'm not really one for partying, but alright. I'll see if I can find some snacks for us if you want?'

Brenda nodded. I untied my apron and ran it into the hotel for washing, then let the crowds on the square engulf me.

Everyone was really enjoying themselves.

There were kids everywhere, despite how late it was. The townsfolk were out in force, drawing comfort from the safety of a large crowd.

The weather was even playing along—the wind had died down, and it was a balmy, almost pleasant night. I meandered between the crowds, keeping an eye out for anyone I knew. Savannah was probably here somewhere—though she was still avoiding me. But I'd seen her from a distance earlier, along with Talbot.

I was really hoping to find Theo sooner than later and make sure he'd managed to get the tracker onto Hannover—and find out how— so I browsed the stands I knew he'd visit: one selling fried apple rings, and another that was peddling mulled cider for eight NP a mug. I had to admit, it was tempting. I'd tried it once, and it was the most delicious thing I'd ever tasted.

But if Theo and I were leaving town soon—and Savannah; I hadn't given up on her yet—then I needed to save my money. There'd be time to drink all the mulled cider I wanted in the future.

I was making my way to a cart selling roasted chestnuts when I caught sight of a familiar face.

'Maddock!'

He turned, a grin breaking over his face when he saw me, and hurried over.

'Harley, hi. I was wondering if I'd see you here.'

'I was working.' I waved to the hotel. 'We've been swamped.'

'But you're off now?'

'Yeah, my shift ended.' I stifled a yawn behind my hand. 'I thought I'd look around for a bit before I head home. What about you?'

'I was looking for someone, but I don't think he's here.' Maddock rubbed the back of his head sheepishly. 'So I've just been browsing the stalls for a bit before I take off.'

'Who?' I asked. 'I might have seen him.'

'Nah, it doesn't matter. A friend I wanted to catch up with before I leave.'

A cold feeling blossomed in my chest. 'So you are leaving?'

'Looks like it, yeah.' Maddock glanced away, studying the nearby chestnut cart. 'It's a shame, but I guess that's how it is.'

'Oh.' I bit my lip. 'What happened to… what you asked me about before?'

'What?' Maddock frowned. 'Oh, you mean… Look, don't worry about it, okay? I came on too strong, I get that.'

'No…' I stepped out of the way as a group of teenagers squeezed past us. 'I mean, what's happening with that? I thought you were... involved in the politics here.'

Maddock's face closed off. 'Like I said, the people I work with have pulled funding. I really can't tell you more than that.' He glanced around furtively. 'Unless you've changed your mind?'

'I... No,' I muttered. I didn't need even more complications in my life. 'I was just curious. But I guess it's for the best, right? I mean, this isn't your town. We should solve our own problems.'

A pensive expression crept over Maddock's face. He tipped his head forwards so that his hair fell over his eyes, and for a moment he looked quite strange... almost inhuman. Then he shrugged, and the weird moment was broken.

'I guess. That's up to you guys. We would have been happy to help, though.'

As long as there were financial benefits in it for you, I thought sardonically.

'Anyway, I should be getting off. Do you want anything?' Maddock jerked his thumb towards the chestnut cart. 'I saw you eyeing it earlier.'

'Oh no, that's alright.' I glanced around. 'I was looking for one of my friends. See you around? We could have dinner together before you leave. As a farewell.'

'Oh, yeah.' Maddock grinned. 'Sure. Let me know when?'

'Will do.'

'Right, goodnight!' Maddock turned and dissolved into the crowd. I stared after him, even though I lost sight of him almost immediately. That had been... weird. It still felt like he was lying to me. His story didn't make a lick of sense.

What's he planning?

Could he have made up a reason to leave town to make a quick escape? Did that mean he was going to do something here before he left?

But it's not your problem anymore. Worry about Hannover. Nothing else matters right now.

I tucked my hands in my pockets, feeling through the lining of my coat for the comforting shapes of my knife and gun. I'd been doing that more and more the last few days, as though the weapons provided me with some kind of reassurance.

They didn't. I'd rather not have to use them.

But at least I knew if it came down to it, I wouldn't be helpless.

I meandered through the crowd for a few minutes, keeping an idle lookout for Theo's familiar tall frame and mop of curls. He'd said he would be here—but maybe he was running late?

What if something had gone wrong and Hannover had caught him trying to plant the tracker on him?

What if—

Hannover was standing in front of me.

He was half-turned, talking to someone beside him—someone quite a bit shorter than him, whom I couldn't see over the crowd. But Hannover himself was unmistakable: choppy shoulder-length hair, broad shoulders, compact stature. His shape was imprinted into my brain; my instincts were primed to go on high alert whenever I saw him.

What was he doing here?

Of course, Theo had said the Black Hands were all over town at the moment. Why wouldn't he be here?

He started walking. I hurried after him. Maybe I could get him on his own, and—

And?

The thought of cold-blooded murder made me feel sick.

But then, it was him or me.

So—

The crowd shifted, and suddenly he was gone. I stopped, standing up on my tiptoes. Where the hell had he gone? People didn't just disappear! But, ugh, there were so many people there tonight, it was just impossible to keep an eye on anyone.

Damnit.

He was gone.

I dropped back on my heels, sighing. I'd go grab some chestnuts and head back to the booth. I could wait there for Theo—chances were, we'd never find each other in this crowd.

I turned, weaving around a group of teenagers who probably ought to have been in bed. Their conversation reached me in snippets.

'—heard the mayor sent a team to break them out!'

'No way! The mayor's useless. I heard it was the Iron Fists.'

'Why would they do that? The Iron Fists would never go head-to-head with the Black Hands.'

'Of course they would! Remember when…'

They drifted out of hearing. I slipped my hand onto the handle of my knife again. Word was spreading that the Iron Fists and Black Hands had been involved in the delay of the merchants' market, and it made me strangely uneasy. Everyone else seemed to be celebrating, but I couldn't completely get myself in the mood. Theo's crazy idea hung over my head, keeping company with Hannover's threats and my fears of what would happen if—when—the distillery was attacked.

Bas knew.

The Iron Fists had a plan.

Even so, not knowing was killing me.

A hand touched my shoulder. I jumped and spun around, already pulling my knife—and came face-to-face with Bas.

'Bas!' I shoved the knife back into my belt. 'You scared me!'

'I called your name.' Bas rolled his shoulders. He was dressed in uniform and had a radio clipped to his belt. 'What are you doing here?'

'It's a party?' I raised my eyebrows. 'I was working and then I stayed on after my shift. Or is that not allowed?'

Bas frowned. 'Of course it's allowed. Why wouldn't it be?'

'Then what's with the weird question?'

He stared at me. 'I didn't mean it like that.'

'Then why—'

Bas's lips twisted. 'Give me a break, Harley.'

I swallowed. Damnit, I'd promised I'd cut him some slack—and here I went again. 'Sorry. I guess I'm just on edge.'

Bas jerked his shoulders in a half-shrug. 'Whatever.'

'Really.' I glanced around at the people, drinking, dancing, and making merry. 'It feels weird—to be partying after everything. I guess. Sorry, I shouldn't have taken it out on you.'

I looked back at him. The creases eased out of Bas's forehead. 'I know,' he muttered.

'Are you working?'

Bas nodded. 'You should be careful—the Black Hands are out in force tonight.'

I glanced over my shoulder uneasily. 'I know. I saw Hannover—'

'Stay away from him,' Bas said firmly.

I bit the inside of my cheek. He meant well, but I didn't like his tone. *Give me a break, Harley.*

I took a breath and changed the subject. 'Have you made any progress? On what we discussed?'

Bas surveyed the crowd again. He seemed on edge. 'Not yet. I spoke to a few people. I've posted someone to watch the compound and find out where the slaves are being taken.'

'Who?'

'An old friend.'

He was being evasive again. I scowled.

'Just remember our deal,' I warned.

'I'm not taking you to the compound,' Bas said, shooting me an unyielding look.

'I got that,' I hissed heatedly, 'but—'

'I don't want you to get hurt again!' Bas said suddenly. 'So just… let me… let me take care of this, alright?'

My chest felt strange and fluttery all of a sudden. How was I supposed to feel about that? What did he even mean by it?

'I… I can take care of myself,' I muttered.

To my surprise, Bas smiled. 'I know. I heard you the first four hundred times.'

'Hey!' I swatted him on the arm—and froze.

We didn't do casual touching. Bas hated casual touching. I'd forgotten that far too easily.

Bas rubbed his arm.

'Sometimes it helps to share the burden.'

'Uh huh?' I said sceptically, flexing my fingers subtly. Wasn't he going to chew me out for touching him? 'Is that what you did?'

Bas raised an eyebrow. 'Maybe. Has Rodney spoken to you again?'

Someone tried to push past me. I stepped a bit closer to Bas. 'No. Was he meant to?'

'No,' Bas said. 'I don't want him near you.'

'I think the message finally got through.' I certainly wasn't going to forget Bas and Rodney's reunion any time soon.'

Bas smirked. 'He always was a bit slow on the uptake.'

I gaped at him. Was he joking? Actually cracking a joke? He was! I'd never seen Bas like this—mellow, relaxed. It suited him—and I wasn't the only one who'd noticed. A group of teens a few feet away were watching none-too-discretely, and the lady at the cider booth was staring at us.

I felt scrutinised.

'Do you, uh, do you want to get something to eat?' I blurted.

Bas grimaced. 'I can't… I have to work. Actually, I should get going.' He unclipped the radio from his belt. 'Ellery will be looking for me.'

Damn.

'Okay, I guess.'

Bas shot me a sidelong glance that I couldn't read before hitting the call button on the radio. 'Ellery, come in.'

The radio spat out a few garbled noises, then went silent.

Bas's forehead crinkled as he frowned. He hit the button again. 'Ellery, come in. Ellery, come in.'

More garbled noise. Like the response had been scrambled up somehow…

Bas looked up, meeting my eye.

'Maybe Ellery's radio isn't working?' I asked. 'Or the crowd—'

'No.' Bas shook his head. 'He wouldn't turn it off. This is something else.' His eyes widened in realisation. He leaned forward and said urgently, 'Harley, go home. Go and hide.'

'Is it the strike on the distillery?' I gasped. Not now—it couldn't be! 'It's too soon!'

'They must have moved it forward to try and catch us off guard.' Bas frowned. 'You have to go. Promise me—go and hide, Harley.'

'No.' I stepped back hurriedly. 'I have to find Theo.'

'He'll be busy.'

'It's urgent.' I spun around already scanning the crowd.

'Harley, where are you going?' Bas demanded.

'There's something I have to do! Don't wait for me!' I ground to a halt, realising something. Bas was about to go running into the midst of danger to save the Iron Fists. It was a fool's errand.

Quite possibly a deadly one.

This might be the last time I saw him.

'Actually, wait up just a second.' I spun back around, striding towards him. 'Don't you dare get yourself killed.'

I grabbed his shoulders, went up on tiptoes, and hugged him. 'Come back to me,' I whispered.

As I pulled away, Bas put his arms around me. I froze. His touch was so tentative, no matter everything could implode any second now,

I didn't dare move in case I broke him. He splayed one hand out against my back and pressed me into his chest. 'Harley, I—'

Whatever he was thinking, the words never made it past his lips. Several seconds passed, seconds that I couldn't afford, before Bas shifted and pulled away.

'We'll talk later, okay? Hide. Somewhere they won't find you if the worst happens.' He seemed to chew on his next words before spitting them out. 'If you need to get out of town, or get a message to me, go to the old factory where we spoke to Rodney, okay? They won't know to look for you there.'

'O-okay,' I whispered. My heart was pounding like a drum, each beat heralding the oncoming doom. This was real. Our town was going to war.

Bas stared at me for another few seconds. Then he turned and jogged into the crowd.

TWENTY-TWO

THE ONLY PLACE I COULD think of to wait for Theo was the Kranikovska's booth, so I hurried back through the crowd towards the hotel.

'Coming through—oof—Sorry!' I ducked and wove between merry-makers. No one seemed to realise that anything was wrong; I was the only person showing any kind of urgency.

Finally, the booth came into view. Brenda and Dana were manning it, both of them pouring drinks like there was no tomorrow. I ducked around it and climbed the stairs, squinting out over the crowd. Where was Theo? There were hundreds of people here—I'd never find him unless he came to our booth.

Please, please let him come here.

My throat felt so tight I could barely breathe. We weren't ready—we'd barely hatched our plan. What were we going to do? We'd never find Hannover—Theo wouldn't have had a chance to get the tracker on him yet!

Should I look for Hannover instead? He'd been here—

'HARLEY!'

I jerked around to see Theo sprinting up from the north side of the square.

'Theo!' I jogged down the stairs and hurried over to him. 'You're here—thank God!' I threw my arms around him. He squeezed me briefly, then pulled away.

'You know—right? Wait, how?'

'Bas—I was with Bas—the radios stopped working.'

Theo nodded grimly. 'They've cut off communications. Sayle anticipated this, though. It'll be fine. But we need to move quickly. The Black Hands are a step ahead of us.'

I bit my lip. 'I saw Hannover here, but I lost him—'

'It's fine.' Theo waved the boxy device Declan had given us. 'His car is moving; it started heading south a minute ago.'

'So he knows.'

Theo and I exchanged grim glances. 'Makes sense,' Theo said. 'We'd better hurry—if he gets inside the compound…'

I nodded. 'Let's go.'

I took a step, then paused and turned back to the booth.

'Harley,' Theo warned.

'I have to warn them.'

'You'll start a panic. The mayor isn't going to open fire on the square.'

I knew that, and yet, I couldn't leave without saying something. I jogged back to the booth, squeezing in between a few men. 'Brenda!'

'Harley?' Brenda hurried over. 'What can I get you?'

'Nothing. Listen—' I grasped her wrist. 'There's something going down with the gangs tonight. You should get inside, you and the other girls.'

'I can't leave.'

'Speak to Tom. Tell him there's an attack going down tonight. Please!'

I must have looked pretty worried, because Brenda said soothingly, 'Alright, I'll do that. Don't worry about us, though. Theo is waiting for you.'

I glanced back at him. He curled his lip, jerking his head impatiently.

'Alright.' I gave her wrist one last squeeze. 'See you soon.'

'You too.' Brenda smiled.

I pulled away and hurried over to Theo. He grabbed my arm and towed me into the crowd. 'We can't waste time,' he hissed.

'Saving people is not a waste of time!'

'It is if we don't get to Hannover—you'll have saved them at the cost of your own life.'

I scowled. We burst out of the crowd a few moments later, and Theo set a brisk pace down a side street; I considered myself pretty fit, but I was panting trying to follow him.

His car was hidden in an even smaller street, parked so it could only be seen if you were standing at the entrance to that road. Theo squeezed into the driver's seat and drove out so I could climb into the passenger seat.

'Right.' He handed me the boxy thing. 'You need to tell me where Hannover is going.'

I stared at it. It was covered in all sorts of green squiggly lines. I had no clue what they meant. 'I can't read this.'

'The map is Pre-Crash. Just ignore it and use the compass,' Theo said urgently as he navigated the narrow street.

'Where—' I found the compass in the bottom corner and compared it to the flashing dot in the middle. 'South, he's moving south. No, wait. He's stopped.'

'Heading for the compound,' Theo said grimly. 'We'll have to hurry.'

He hit the gas and sent us wheeling around the corner onto the main street. As we straightened out, a wave of horror washed over me.

The road ahead was blocked. Two sturdy cars were parked nose to nose, with metal fences on either side of them, and men dressed in brown camouflage milling around.

'Theo—'

'Fuck!' Theo snarled. 'The military—of course, half of the Iron Fists are on the square. They want to keep us there—hold on!'

I grabbed the door as Theo accelerated.

'You're going to hit—argh!'

We crashed headfirst into the barrier. I was jerked forwards then backwards, and then we were accelerating again. We'd gone right through the flimsy metal fence, and I could hear bits of it scraping against the road as we drove on.

'Holy shit!' I gasped.

'You alright?' Theo asked.

'Yeah—I just can't believe you did that!'

Theo snorted. 'No one blockades me in, Harley.'

'You don't say.' I loosened my death grip on the door, rubbing my chest to soothe my pounding heart. 'At least you didn't hit one of the cars.'

'I'd have done that slower,' Theo said.

'Har-har.'

'Not joking, actually.'

'Great.' I let my head thump against the headrest. 'I think there are bits of your job I'm happier not knowing.'

Theo reached over the centre console and squeezed my knee. 'You'll live, baby. Now, let's find Hannover.'

'Right.' I lifted the tracker console. 'He's still not moving.'

'Is he north or south of the river?'

'Um…' I was guessing the river was the wide green snake. 'South.'

Clumsily, I managed to navigate. Why hadn't I paid more attention in school? After a few minutes, I had somewhat mapped the main features on the console to what I knew of our town.

'I think he's on the main arterial.'

'Still heading south?'

'No, he hasn't moved in a while.'

'Weird.' We reached Main Street, and Theo pushed his car faster and faster. I squinted at the map, trying to figure out how far down Main Street Hannover was. The dot was getting closer and closer. We had almost reached him—and then Theo abruptly hit the brakes, sending us skidding down the centre of the road. The console tumbled out of my hands.

'Theo!' I gasped. I dived after it and retrieved it from the footwell.

'We don't need that anymore,' Theo said. 'Look.'

I followed where he was pointing. There was a car abandoned by the side of the road, one of the wheels blown out.

'Oh fuck,' I said. 'The tracker was on his car?'

'It was,' Theo confirmed.

'Shit.'

The tracker was on his car… but Hannover was on foot.

TWENTY-THREE

'SOMETHING ISN'T RIGHT,' Theo murmured. He cut the engine abruptly and pulled his gun out from under his jacket.

'What do you mean?' I asked in a shaky voice.

'Why would Hannover just leave his car here and bail? That doesn't make sense.' Theo glanced at me, frowning. 'Maybe someone else was driving?'

'Maybe he thought he'd come back for the car?' I asked.

'I would stop and change the tyre if I could,' Theo said. 'An abandoned car is begging to be stolen. Unless he couldn't.'

I looked back at the car. The back left tyre was completely flat. 'Couldn't?'

'If he was under attack, for example.' Theo pursed his lips, looking around. I stared at the car. There were scrapes and scratches and holes all over it. Impossible to say which ones were old and which were new.

Something shifted in the back seat.

I froze.

'There's someone in the car,' I muttered.

'What?'

We both stared intently at Hannover's car. Nothing moved. Then—

There. A head peeped out of the back window: pale skin and hair like red ink in the darkness. I gasped.

'There's a child—Theo, there's a child!'

'What?'

'In the back seat!'

Theo leant forward. The head ducked down again, but it was too late. I'd definitely seen it.

'There's a kid in the car. Is that Hannover's kid?' I couldn't imagine anyone less suited to parenthood than that man.

'No way. Hannover doesn't have a kid,' Theo declared. 'Did you see if it was a girl or a boy?'

'I think it was a girl.'

'Are you sure?' Theo hissed.

'No! But she had long hair!'

'Fuck,' he snarled. 'Fuck!'

I started in alarm. 'What? What is it?'

'Did she have red hair?'

'I think so.'

'It's Rionach.' Theo cursed. 'It has to be. God damnit!'

'Rionach?' He'd totally lost me.

'Hannover's still here.' Theo reached for his gun, then abruptly seemed to change his mind and put his hand back on the wheel.

'How do you know?'

'He'd never leave Rionach alone—she's Moriarty's daughter.'

'Moriarty has a *daughter?*' I hissed. *What the fuck?* How had I never known this? How long had *Theo* known?

Theo was looking around the car, scanning the street. For the moment, nothing moved. Where was Hannover?

'Damn, we've blown our cover,' Theo muttered. 'We'll have to call off.'

'We can't!'

'We can't take him out whilst he's protecting Rionach. Hannover will kill us, Harley.' Theo shook his head. 'We'll find Savannah and leave town.'

'But—'

A spray of bullets cut me off. The car jerked. I threw myself into the footwell as Theo flattened himself over our seats. From an inch away, I saw his lips form the words '*Oh fuck.*'

The gunfire stopped.

'Fuck,' Theo mumbled. 'Fuck. This is a shitty situation, Harley. Let's just go.'

He threw himself back into the driver's seat and twisted the ignition. The car made a sick-sounding noise which cut out suddenly. My heart sank to take up residence somewhere around my feet.

'What's wrong?' I whispered.

Theo's eyes were so wide I could see the whites all around his irises. 'They must have hit something important. Damn. Fuck.'

I crept up into my seat, squinting out into the darkness, poised to drop out of sight again if the shooting restarted. The whole street was silent and empty. Where were they?

A shadow moved in the doorway of a boarded-up shop.

'There!' I hissed, jerking my head. 'By the newsagent.'

'I see him,' Theo said grimly. He pulled his gun and reached for the door handle. 'Stay here.'

'What? No!'

'Stay, Harley. Wait for my signal, then run for cover.' He swung the door open and threw himself out, ducking behind the door as a hail of bullets sprayed over the road.

'Theo!' I screamed.

'Stay!'

Someone else started shooting. My ears rang from the noise, but for a second we weren't under fire. Theo sprinted for the side of the road, leaving me alone in the car.

I reached over and slammed his door. My heart was thudding in my chest, almost as loud as the gunfire. We were both dead.

This had been such a mistake.

How had things gone so wrong?

Theo darted out of his doorway, firing twice. The shadow by the newsagent jerked back—Theo was firing at him. But who was he? Was that Hannover? I couldn't tell.

He turned his gun towards me. I dropped down, and the car jerked as it was hit. The glass shattered, raining down over me.

Fuck! Could the car blow up? I had to get out of here.

I lifted my head, staring out at the street. Abruptly, Theo blew his cover and sprinted down the road.

I barely had a second to decide.

I opened my door and dropped to the asphalt, running for the closest side of the road—away from the gunfire. Towards Hannover's car.

The kid! I should help her!

I threw myself around the car and hauled the door open. A tiny face with wide eyes stared at me.

'Come on!' I hissed. 'Let's get out of here!'

'Dean told me to stay put,' she said haughtily. 'You can fuck off, lady.'

My mouth dropped open. Holy shit. 'They're shooting! Are you crazy?'

As if to punctuate my words, several shots rang out.

'So what?' Rionach demanded. 'I can shoot too.' She raised a gun—I hadn't even noticed it before, and it looked comically large in her hands. 'I'll shoot *them* if they come for me.'

I took a step back, the hairs on the back of my neck standing on end. The girl lowered the gun, and at the same time I heard footsteps. A shiver of awareness slid over me. I spun around.

And looked straight at Hannover.

His gun was levelled at my head.

Fuck.

'I...I...' My mind was blank. Hannover grabbed my arm and dragged me away from the car and around to the driver's side. I could see Theo across the road, watching us.

'It's over, Rochester,' Hannover called out.

Bas? Bas was here? My stomach lurched.

'I'll shoot your girl if you don't let me go.'

Hannover's words echoed off the buildings around us. A moment later I heard soft footsteps, and Bas emerged from a side street.

'Gun on the floor,' Hannover said.

Bas set his gun down on the road without taking his eyes off of us for a single second.

'And you, Dunne.'

Theo stepped up beside Bas, lowering his gun as well. I felt sick.

I'd ruined everything.

'Very good,' Hannover sang. I heard him opening his door, though I had my back to his car. I couldn't take my eyes off Bas. Hannover's gun dropped away from my head, then touched it again.

'You're lucky Rionach's here or I'd shoot you.' His voice was a savage whisper. 'But I'll remember this, darling. Trust me.'

He shoved me. I tumbled to the ground, my hands scraping the asphalt. Before I could right myself, the car door slammed and Hannover squealed away, the blown-out tyre thwacking the ground. I stumbled to my feet, staring after him.

Thud!

I whipped back around. Ellery had appeared from his hiding place. He strode into the road, an expression of absolute fury on his face. 'What the fuck, Harley?'

'I—I could ask you the same question,' I stuttered. My heart beat unevenly against my ribcage. Could this get any worse?

Bas picked up his gun and shoved it back in his belt. 'You were supposed to hide,' he said flatly.

'And you were supposed to tell me the truth!' I cried.

'I think it's time we all had a little heart-to-heart,' Ellery said grimly.

TWENTY-FOUR

WHEN THE DOOR OPENED, I lurched to my feet.

I'd been waiting in Ellery's flat for four hours, each one more tense than the previous. I wanted to check on Savannah. I wanted to run away and hide. I wanted to get out of town. Instead, I was stuck here. The compound was on lockdown, and a very polite and apologetic Andrew Kade—Ellery and Bas's teammate—was my jailor.

Now, I stood facing the door as Ellery and Bas filed in. My heart sank. I didn't want to have this discussion in front of Bas, not after everything.

'I think we can take it from here,' Ellery told Kade quietly.

Kade glanced hesitantly between Ellery and me a few times before nodding.

'I'll see you around, Miss Harley.'

'A-alright.' My voice broke. I cleared my throat. 'Could… could you do me a favour?'

Kade tilted his head askance.

'Can you check on my sister, please? Just… make sure she's alright.'

He glanced at Ellery, who was staring at me, his eyes narrowed. After a moment that felt like an hour, he nodded. 'That's fine.'

'Alright, then.' Kade turned to the door. 'See you later.'

He slipped out, shutting the door behind him. A deafening silence engulfed the flat. I wanted to melt into the floor.

Bas shrugged his jacket off, unbuckled his weapons harness, and laid both on the sofa. Ellery snapped out of his stupor and marched to the kitchenette. 'Drink?' he grunted.

'Yes, please,' I said.

He returned with a bottle and three glasses, set them in front of me, then backed away to shed his jacket. I poured us each a generous helping and retook the spot on the sofa where I'd been vegetating for the last four hours. The scene felt almost painfully familiar. We'd been here before, Ellery and I, with a glass of whiskey and dangerous truths, and I had the feeling that this time was going to be much worse.

Ellery sank down beside me and picked up a glass. Heaving a sigh, he looked my way. 'What the fuck, Harley?'

It was impossible to meet his gaze. I felt like my insides had curled themselves into knots. I'd done a lot of thinking in the last four hours—there hadn't been anything else to do—but I still had no idea what to tell them.

Turning my head away, I muttered, 'If Bas had told me the plan—'

'Don't put this on me.' Bas reached down and grabbed his glass. When I looked at him, he was glaring. I looked away hastily. 'You lied to me.'

'I didn't!'

'Really? We spent the entirety of Monday going over what you knew, and you just *forgot* to mention that you planned on going after Hannover?'

'I hadn't planned it yet then!' I took a deep breath. 'And you were supposed to tell me *your* plan. It was a stipulation of us working together.'

'A stipulation of an agreement which you apparently had no intention of following,' Bas sneered. 'Typical. You hold everyone to such high standards—except yourself.'

I gritted my teeth. 'It's not like that!'

'Then what is it like? Enlighten me.'

I sat forwards, anger coursing through my body. 'Hannover was threatening to kill me! I had to—'

'You should have told me that earlier!'

'I was going to—I just never had a chance. We weren't expecting to have to plan everything that quickly!'

'There should never have been a plan,' Bas said. 'You were supposed to be trusting me to deal with things!'

'It's your fault I was in this mess in the first place!'

'My fault?' Bas rolled his eyes. 'You have some nerve!'

'Yes!' Tears sprang into my eyes. I dashed them away angrily. 'If you'd just believed me—'

'Your ability to transfer blame is without limit,' Bas snapped. 'If you had told me from the beginning about the slaves, none of this would have happened and you know it.'

'I tried!'

'Did you? I don't remember that.'

I pressed my lips together. He was such an arsehole, and I wanted to shatter his calm. I wanted to hurt him the way he had hurt me.

'Well, you and Ellery were a bit busy calling me a whore and accusing me of being hysterical and a liar. I'm not surprised you don't remember.'

Bas glared. I met his gaze head-on. I was tired of the blame being pushed on me. I had done the best with the information I had—every time. Even when I had no information. Wasn't it Bas who had said I'd done my best?

Clearly, he hadn't meant it.

Not that I was surprised he hadn't. He'd been manipulating me for information all along. He had never intended to involve me.

Git.

'When was that?' he asked.

'You mean, on which occasion when you were insulting me and calling me a liar? Gosh, there are so many. I don't remember.' I threw each word at him like a knife. He flinched, turning away slightly.

'Harley,' Ellery warned. 'You're in more trouble than you realise. We were instructed to kill Hannover on Sayle's orders. You interfered with that. We can't help you unless you help us.'

Right. All of this was about *helping me. Sure.*

I believed that.

I crossed my arms. 'I don't owe you anything.'

'If you'd like to try your luck with Sayle, you're welcome to,' Bas said. 'Or you could save yourself the trouble and shoot yourself now. It'll be quicker.'

I flinched back, gaping at his harsh words. 'I—That's—' My throat closed up. Would Bas really prefer it if I was dead?

'No one's dying here today,' Ellery said. 'Harley, just start from the beginning, alright? I know we've had a shit time of it—but whatever you think of me, I want to help. Just tell the truth. The whole truth.'

The whole truth. I swallowed and rubbed my eyes. 'You'll be furious.'

'More furious than we already are?' Bas asked sarcastically. 'Seems unlikely.'

I glared at him.

'When did you first find out about the slaves?' Ellery prompted. 'And, for that matter, the strike on the distillery. You knew an awful lot about that too.'

I inhaled slowly. Exhaled. Again. Again. I was going through the motions, but it wasn't helping. My fingers tingled and I felt faint. There was no escape.

I was going to have to tell him.

Unless I wanted to face Sayle.

What was worse? Ellery meting out my fate, or Sayle? Who was I more afraid of?

I leant forward and grabbed the bottle of whiskey to refill my glass. 'Okay,' I said, and my voice was surprisingly steady. I recapped the bottle. 'I found out about the slaves the same night I tried to speak to you about T-Tam.' My voice broke. I sucked in a breath. 'But I found out about the distillery attack before that. The mayor—the mayor and his friends had a private meeting in the hotel.'

'You never told me about that,' Ellery said.

'I tried to—but you never contacted me.'

Ellery frowned. 'I don't remember that.'

'I left a note,' I insisted. So much had happened, but I remembered that. 'I told you to speak to me. But you never came.'

'And you didn't check?'

'I assumed you were dealing with it yourself! You hardly reply to any of my notes.'

Ellery shook his head. 'How could I deal with it when I didn't know? I never got that note.'

'I *definitely* sent you a note.'

He shook his head. 'About the mayor? No.'

'I told you I needed to speak to you.'

'The last note I got from you was about Maddock.'

'But...' My mind was running a mile a minute. 'I definitely sent it to you. I even told Bas I had! Could someone else have intercepted it?'

'Only my team uses that drop point.'

'But...' I trailed off, his words turning over in my head. *Only my team. Only my team...*

I'd told Bas... And Bas was a member of Ellery's team. I turned to him. His expression was blank, a closed book. I got nothing from him.

'You removed the note,' I hissed.

'I told Ellery to go speak to you.'

'You removed the note.' I was so angry, I could have punched him. 'You have got to be kidding me! How can you blame me for any of this?'

'What?' Ellery asked. 'Bas, is that true?'

Bas's lips thinned. 'The note mentioned Rochester. I told you to speak to Harley. Multiple times.'

'Unbelievable!' I shot to my feet, whiskey splashing over my hand. 'You fucking *arsehole*.'

I couldn't sit still. I climbed over Ellery's legs and marched into the kitchenette.

'Where are you going?' Ellery demanded.

'Away.' Hot tears trickled down my face. 'From him. I don't believe it. I just don't.'

All of this could have been avoided, all of it! If I had just never made one stupid mistake.

If I had never trusted Bas.

'Fuck!' I snarled. I put my glass to my lips and downed it in one go. *Shit. Fuck.* God, I could kill him with my bare hands. Forget Hannover; I hated Bas ten times as much.

Everything, *everything* that had happened could have been avoided.

I turned back to them. 'I hate you.'

'What makes you think I care?' Bas sneered.

'Oh, you will.' I marched back over and grabbed the back of the sofa. 'Just you wait.'

'Harley—' I cut Ellery off with a glare. He leaned back, almost like he was intimidated by my anger.

'You,' I snarled at Bas. I shook my head. 'In that meeting, they discussed attacking the distillery. You know what else they discussed? The mayor all but admitted he was allowing the Black Hands to take slaves inside the town in exchange for their support. I didn't realise it then, but—'

'Harley,' Ellery repeated quietly.

'*But* a couple of days later Brenda told me the Black Hands were hanging about the NCC office, and when we looked, we saw the slaves. I went straight to the drop point to tell you! Straight there—but Tam was there instead—he saw me.'

'What does Tam have to do with any of this?' Bas asked.

'Everything!' I cried. I lifted my hands, twisting my fingers into my hair. I was so angry, I was hyperventilating. I spat every word. 'Tam saw me and chased me. Hardwick brought me to the compound. I wanted to tell you everything, but instead, I get Briggs, and his stupid deal—give me a handjob and I'll let you in? What a fucking joke. *You are all a fucking joke!*'

I inhaled deeply, my throat rasping and the cut on my abdomen burning from the effort.

'Briggs, of course, didn't pass on the message until *days* later—and then you didn't believe me.'

'You never mentioned the slaves!' Ellery cut in.

'Because you didn't believe me! You called me a liar! You patronised me. So I tried to deal with it on my own. What the hell was I supposed to do?'

'Set your personal feelings aside for the good of the community,' Bas snapped. 'Like the rest of us do.'

'Oh, like you did with your brother?' I mocked. 'Or is that only a rule for me?'

Bas narrowed his eyes.

'I did the best I could with the means I had—which was nothing. You left me with nothing. The only power I had was passing information to *you*.' I glowered at each of them. 'A position *you* had put me in in the first place. And then you took it away. How powerful you must have felt.' I laughed bitterly. 'You left me *alone!*'

'Harley—' I cut Ellery off with a glare.

'No, I'm talking now. You can shut the fuck up. I tried to tell Bas about the slaves—because even though you guys had been arseholes to me a thousand times over, you were *still* the only chance I had at fixing things.'

I had to pause for breath. Neither of them spoke. Bas was staring at me, his gaze dark.

'And, of course, he didn't believe me,' I continued. 'Story of my life, right? So I tried to get proof. I tried to break into the NCC office myself.'

Bas tipped his head against the wall, staring at the ceiling.

'And I got caught by Hannover.'

Ellery swore under his breath.

'He agreed to let me live if I made sure Percival died in the attack on the distillery. I was never going to be able to do that. Going after

Hannover was Theo's idea—he's been helping me for the last couple of days. But seeing as that failed, I guess maybe I will take my chances with Sayle.' I smiled darkly. 'I suppose he'll kill me faster than Hannover, right?'

I met Bas's gaze head-on, daring him to challenge me. He tapped his fingers against the wall. The silence was becoming cloying.

'Why the hell didn't you tell us?' Ellery demanded.

'When was I supposed to tell you?'

'Any time! It's been months—'

'Yeah, months of you ignoring me and insulting me and degrading me.' My fury was a living thing. After everything, I couldn't believe Ellery wanted to push this back on me.

'It wasn't like that. I tried to apologise!'

'Oh, yeah, so you did. And I was supposed to forgive you after one half-hearted apology?' I glared at him. 'Don't make me laugh.'

'It's not fucking funny.' Ellery stood abruptly, his expression wild as he faced me. 'Don't you see? All of this could have been avoided—'

'Yeah, if you pulled your heads out of your arses!'

'You put your ego ahead of telling us the truth, Harley!'

I swallowed hard. 'That—that's not true.'

'Isn't it?' Ellery shook his head angrily. 'If you had tried just a little bit harder to tell us—'

'Excuse me for not wanting to fight through the insults!' I cried. My eyes were prickling traitorously. *Fuck.* I couldn't cry, not now.

'This isn't just about you,' Ellery snapped. 'It affects the whole town!'

'Well, maybe you should have tried harder too!' I screamed. 'And Bas! Why the fuck is this on me? I spent weeks trying to convince him.'

'And then undermined him when he did take action!'

'THIS IS NOT ON ME!' The words erupted from my chest, scratching my throat. Ellery flinched back. 'All you ever do is blame me! Look in the fucking mirror for a change!'

Ellery stared at me, his face set. 'Maybe you need to look in the fucking mirror, Harley.'

Knock-knock.

We all froze, suddenly brought back down to Earth by the knock on the door. I was breathing hard, my insides in turmoil.

Ellery's brow creased in a frown. 'Don't move,' he told me.

'Where the fuck am I going to go?'

Ellery scowled and turned away, marching to the door. He opened it.

'Briggs?' He sounded confused.

'Ellery.' Briggs's voice was low and smug. 'I've found out something interesting. I think you might want to hear it.'

A chill ran down my spine.

Briggs was the last person I wanted to see right now.

'Now's not really the time,' Ellery said.

Briggs glanced past him, his piggy eyes settling on me. 'Actually, I think now's the perfect time.' He pushed his way past Ellery, who grunted in protest. 'I think you'll thank me for this.'

'This is my fucking flat.' Ellery slammed the door, following Briggs over. 'Fine, spit it out then get lost. I'm busy.'

'Don't worry.' Briggs smirked at me. 'It's highly relevant.'

Oh fuck. I pushed off the sofa. 'Briggs—'

'You see,' he continued as though I hadn't spoken, 'I recently discovered something very interesting about your girl here.'

No. This had to be a joke. *Not now!*

Ellery leant against the wall next to Bas, crossing his arms. 'Get on with it.'

'She's the one who killed Gabriel.'

I gripped the edge of the sofa as dizziness overwhelmed me.

They were going to kill me.

Oh God.

I'd never meant for them to find out.

Oh God.

Fuck.

Please, please be a dream.

Please, let there be some escape from this nightmare situation.

Please.

'What the hell?' Ellery demanded.

'Didn't you know?' Briggs crooned. 'Oh yeah, she's a regular little murderer.'

'No…' My voice was barely a whisper. Ellery turned a burning gaze on me.

'Is that true?'

I shook my head desperately.

Briggs laughed. 'Oh, it's true alright. Your girl's a traitor.'

'I'm not—'

My throat was closing up. The world had gone into a tailspin. I couldn't tell if I was even still standing, didn't know where to look. I squeezed my eyes shut. 'Stop!'

'You should have taken my deal when you had the chance,' Briggs crowed.

My stomach churned. 'I'd never—You don't even—You can't know—'

Briggs smirked. 'It wasn't hard to put it together. A few drinks and Talbot was quite happy to spill the beans about how Tam had been taken down by some girl, how they'd had to dump his body in the wasteland. And then there you were, acting all suspicious, and your little friend said you argued with her about him the day he disappeared. Yeah, it didn't take much at all. Fancied yourself a hero, didn't you? Thought you'd protect your friend and get rid of her man? Well, joke's on you, *kitten*. You've been busted.'

I stared at him, open-mouthed.

What could I say?

What magical words would save me from this?

I glanced nervously at Bas and Ellery. Ellery looked shocked; his face was pale.

Bas looked me straight in the eyes. 'Is it true?'

'I...' I had no words. I clenched my fingers around the sofa cushions. 'I don't...'

Bas's lips pulled down in a frown. He shifted his gaze to Briggs.

'Who else knows about this?' Bas asked.

'Apart from us, no one.'

'Good.' In one swift motion, Bas picked up his gun, flicked the safety off, and fired a shot straight into Briggs's head.

TO BE CONTINUED

WHAT'S NEXT?

Dear reader,

Thanks for giving *Revolution* a chance! I hope you enjoyed reading about Harley's adventures as much as I enjoyed writing them.

I'd love it if you could take the time to leave a review on my Amazon and Goodreads pages. Reviews are the best reward an author can receive.

If you want more from this world, please join my mailing list. You will receive a free short story, as well as updates about my writing, sneak peeks at new projects, and freebies from other series.

And if you want to explore my other books, check out my website.

You can also follow me on my socials to learn more about me.

See you in the next book!

REDEMPTION
THE IRON FISTS #3

Harley and Bas's adventures continue in REDEMPTION.

Hunters are supposed to hate vampires—but everyone will betray their people for a price. Nathan is about to discover his.

Nathan is a vampire hunter on the cusp of graduation. He's been training for this his entire life: the moment he qualifies and joins the rest of his family in their noble calling.

If only it were that simple.

His grades are a mess, his social life is a disaster, and what's worse, his best friend is a witch! Add to that, his vampire uncle is back in town and his crush might just be supernatural too, and you have one big melting pot of potential parental disapproval. Nathan doesn't think he can take much more, and then the dark mages come to town.

As bodies begin piling up in the streets, Nathan finds himself pulled deeper into political intrigue and a deadly plot that will pit him against his own family. When the girl he likes comes under threat, Nathan races against time to solve the mystery... well aware that with every step he takes, he comes closer to his father exposing all his secrets.

ACKNOWLEDGEMENTS

It's that time again! I swear it comes around so quickly. Didn't I just write the acknowledgements for the last book?

REVOLUTION was an adventure, and like all adventures, it took the support of a team to make it work. My sincerest thanks go out to:

MiblArt, who designed the gorgeous covers for books one and two.

Josh, the incredibly talented artist who turned my scrappy sketch into a phenomenal map.

My editor, Cameron, who excavated all of my plot holes and illuminated all of my grammar failings (you think you know English until you work with an editor…).

My Discord group, in particular Bone and Chuck (you know who you are), for their invaluable advice during the writing process. I'm late to the writing group party, but I couldn't have done it without them.

My dad, for his unceasing support of my dreams.

And of course, my mum, jack (and master) of all trades, for supporting me and helping me turn my late-night scribblings into real books (and letting me cry on her shoulder when the characters aren't behaving). I couldn't do it without you!

Margot de Klerk is a British author who writes fantasy and science fiction for teens and adults, with a bit of comedy, a dash of romance, and a whole lot of plot. She is most often found in her favourite coffee shop typing furiously on her computer with an iced latte at hand. When not writing, she enjoys photography, travelling, sewing, and various sports.

Follow her on social media, subscribe to her mailing list, and get information on new books: